Cooper Morgan, Headmaster

Cooper Morgan, Headmaster

A novel by

Donn Wright

iUniverse, Inc.
Bloomington

Cooper Morgan, Headmaster

iUniverse books may be ordered through booksellers or by contacting:

iUniverse
1663 Liberty Drive
Bloomington, IN 47403
www.iuniverse.com
1-800-Authors (1-800-288-4677)

ISBN: 978-1-4620-5132-8 (sc)
ISBN: 978-1-4620-5133-5 (hc)
ISBN: 978-1-4620-5134-2 (ebk)

Library of Congress Control Number: 2011915964

Printed in the United States of America

iUniverse rev. date: 10/14/2011

For Barbara Wright
&
Elizabeth Rouse

I send warm regards to buddies: Andrea, Jefferson and Jason, for their assistance in this book; also to Joe Barrett, Nancy Spencer and Dick Jacker, for their guidance. Mimi Dwight and Ruthie Metcalf, thanks for your encouragement. Essex Academy and St. Burges School are fictitious. Some of the people in the story are real: Bill Coffin, Mike Bois, Frank Boyden, John Verdery, Bruce McClellan and Jim Howard. All the others are products of the author's imagination. Any similarity with real people is a coincidence.

Book One

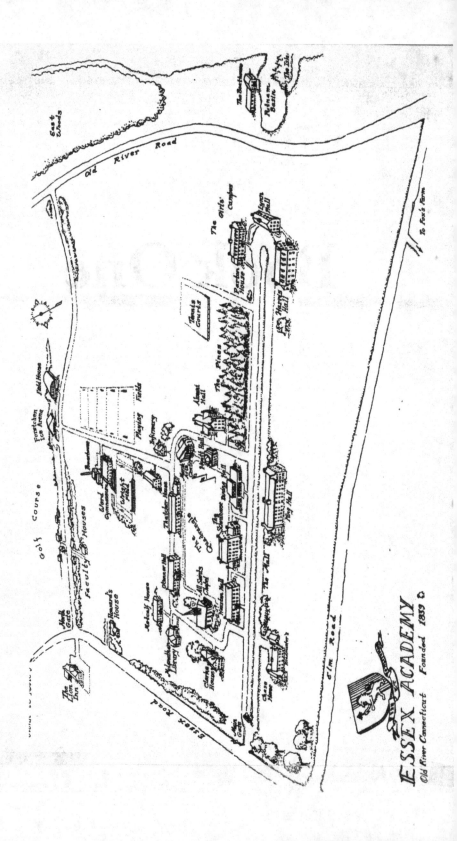

ESSEX ACADEMY
Old River Connecticut   Founded 1839

CHAPTER 1

1966

Sherri said, "Gee Mr. Morgan, I hope you don't mind, I washed out my panties and hung them up to dry on the bathroom towel rack."

He looked surprised, then concerned.

Before he could speak she said, "Well, I sort of wet them." She giggled. "I was in a hurry, I couldn't stop. You know, to go to the bathroom. And I was excited. I always do that when I'm excited. Well not sexy excited," she laughed. "The other kind of excited. You know what I mean."

He said, "Yes, I do."

"They'll dry out. The panties, I mean." She looked at him intently. "I don't ever dry out."

"Do you want to borrow something?"

"No, it feels good without anything on. Sort of cool and nice. I don't have a bra on either."

"I know." He looked as if he was going to say something, but he was silent.

"I didn't know you ever looked at me that closely. You know, checked me out. I'm a big girl."

"Yes" he said, "I have looked. I know." He stammered, "That is, I know you're a big girl." He stared at her, frowning. "I think we are venturing into a subject area that I would prefer not to pursue."

"I think you're annoyed with me," she said. "You expected Julie to come and babysit for you, and you got Sherri, and Sherri flirts with you. You don't like that do you, Mr. Morgan? You're always so cool and in charge. You like people to think you have everything all worked out. Am I right?

His face broke into an amused smile. "I think you're right, Sherri, and I think you know too much." His voice was deep and warm. His dark eyes were clear and intent. "How can you be so smart?" He started to move away, detach himself. "Don't answer that. I'm just trying to defend myself by putting you on the defensive. You're all right, Sherri, and I am not annoyed at you. I've just got problems of my own. I'm a little down." He paused and started to pat his pockets to see that he had his wallet and keys and pen. He looked restless. "And I had better get out of here or I'll be late to the English Department meeting."

Sherri swung her graceful, voluptuous body away from the door with a swish of her full skirt and a toss of her blonde wavy hair. She squinted her eyes and gave him a slow knowing smile. "And I was hoping we were going to talk some more about my not having on any bra or panties."

"You are a devil and I'm going to get the hell out of here," he said it decisively, his voice a deep rumble. Sherri jumped for the door and opened it for him.

The April evening was chilly and she hugged herself against the cold. She watched his tall lean figure stride purposefully down the walk of his faculty apartment, which was attached to a large, stone, ivy-covered dormitory. She wondered how tall he was—two, maybe three inches over six feet. She had imagined him so many times as her lover. She wondered for the hundredth time what he looked like with his clothes off.

Oh, you poor Baby, she thought. I know what has you down. It's your bitch of a wife running around on you. How long has she been gone this time, a week, maybe two? If you were mine, I would never run around Baby. And I'd keep you in bed where you belong. I'd wrap my legs around you and never let go. Her small voice said, "Shit!" as she slammed the door. Her mind conjured up an image of her amused girlfriends laughing at Sherri Huff, the school's leading cockteaser, who could have any boy in the student body just by curling her littler finger. Who couldn't have the one male on the campus she really wanted.

Cooper Morgan felt less self-assured than he hoped he looked. Sherri had spotted it. He smiled to himself. What am I going to do about that girl? How am I going to be able to keep my hands off of her? She's just eighteen, ten years my junior. Yet no one has ever excited such pure raw lust in me. At least, I don't think they have. But I can't touch her. It would get out. Those things always do. I have my career to think about. What career? Am I really going anywhere? Plus, there is Sherri herself. I must not do what is wrong for her. Damn it, why can't she see that? Do I have to pretend I'm unaffected? Yes. I just have to act dumb. Damn it!

Cooper greeted his colleagues in the English Department at Essex Academy, a prestigious New England boarding school. They met in the classroom of Smoke Johansen, the department chairman. Smoke was given his name by students of a past generation, some of whose children were now at Essex. Smoke probably went through two or three packs of cigarettes a day. Cooper had noted early on, however, that he did not inhale. Smoke's fingers and moustache were stained with cigarette tar but his lungs were probably as pink as they ought to be. Well, perhaps not. It was hard to imagine that anything about Smoke Johansen was pink. He was all tweeds and leather patches, and his wrinkled skin was as tan-brown as the leather on the elbows of his jackets. His hair was grisly and wiry stiff. Smoke was a character, and he liked being one. Smoke did not think creatively. He was not particularly logical. Sometimes he did not make any sense at all. However, he believed sincerely in all the old prep school virtues. He believed in grammar, and he could teach it unfailingly to any boy or girl lucky enough to fall within his grasp.

The meeting proceeded evenly. The men and women of the department drank coffee, made clever small talk, and arrived at small decisions. Changes in a required summer reading list for the students in each form were discussed. Students at Essex were not grouped in grades and seldom, if ever, did one refer to seniors or juniors or freshmen. The classes were divided into forms. The form about to graduate and go to college was the sixth form. Ninth graders were third formers. First and second formers constituted the lower school. Third through sixth formers made up the upper school. Each form had its own list of books to read during the summer. There was a test in the English Department in the first week of the fall term. Few students did well on it because few students ever did their summer reading. Most, however, bought the books, and read them at some point in their adult lives. The chairman asked Cooper what he thought about the summer reading list and Cooper said he thought it would help if they emphasized the fact that the students would be tested on their summer reading when they returned in the fall and that the test would affect their grade for the term.

Cooper had been at Essex for three years. He was a comparative newcomer in a very stable faculty of ninety men and women. There was only one member of the English Department newer and younger than he.

Yet Smoke, and the other teachers, often deferred to Cooper. He accepted their deference because things had always been that way for him. He had been a leader in every group he had ever been in. He assumed it was because he was tall and his voice was deep. His voice had been deep ever since he started to talk as an infant. Cooper knew that Smoke admired him because he had attended school at Lawrenceville, where Smoke had gone when he was a boy. Smoke believed that private boarding schools were the source of all things good and right, and the best of all these schools in his view, even superior to Essex, was Lawrenceville.

Perhaps the real reason that colleagues sought advice and assurance from Cooper was that he seldom spoke before thinking, he was a good listener, and he possessed that wonderful and elusive quality known as good judgment. Faced with that assessment, Cooper might have thought for a moment, smiled, and ventured the opinion that good judgment avoided him in affairs of the heart. Events that evening were to bear that out.

A wiser man might have invited a friend home for a nightcap, relieved Sherri of her babysitting duties, and sent her to her dormitory for the night. But even if Cooper had thought of that, he probably would not have done it. He thought he could handle the temptation, and he saw no harm in enjoying being teased.

After arriving home and letting himself in, Cooper stepped into the downstairs lavatory. Her panties were still on the towel rack. They were pale blue bikinis.

They are so tiny, they must fit tight, he thought. He felt the silky material and found they were still wet. A shiver went through him as his fingers touched them.

He found Sherri in his study, hunched over a math book. The curve of her breasts inside her soft-looking white sweater unnerved him. Sherri grinned, "Hi. Lisa, is asleep, and she's been good, and I just love her." Her soft voice warmed him.

Sherri really is a sweet girl, he thought.

"Do you know anything about calculus, Mr. Morgan?"

"Not much, Sherri, but I'll try," he said.

She jumped up from the chair with her finger pointing to a place in the textbook. "Look at this," she said.

He sat down at the desk, conscious that the seat was warm from her. He tried to concentrate. "What's the trouble?" She moved close to him.

He realized that her breast was pressing against his shoulder. He felt the warm glow of her, smelled the clean sweet aroma from her hair. He felt curls of it against his cheek. He turned his head and her clear blue eyes were staring intently into his. He pulled her to him and pressed his face between her neck and shoulder.

In the middle of the night, Cooper Morgan woke up disoriented. He was in the double bed in their guest room. He started to think, why am I here? Then he remembered. He reached out his arm for her, but the bed was empty. Cold. Then he came wide-awake.

He thought, Oh my God! What a mess I'm in.

He snapped on the light. The room was in disarray, his clothes scattered on the floor. Sherri's clothes were not there.

He thought of her. Did I dream it? No. Oh, wow. She's wonderful. Do I love her? No, stupid. That was just sex. Wonderful sex. The best I've ever . . . I won't complete that thought. I hope she's all right. Oh, you fool. Of course she's all right. She got what she wanted. She's probably told all her buddies. Tomorrow, everyone will know. Could she? Oh, damnit, I don't know. I hope she's safe. She might have been caught going back to her dorm. No, clear your head. Stop acting stupid. Relax. You'll just have to find out how things stand in the morning. Maybe I'll have to leave. Nancy will laugh. Oh God. Calm down. Go to sleep. Not likely.

But he did go to sleep. He woke up with the early light of dawn. He was calm, thoughtful.

Damnit, he thought. Come what may, I feel great.

CHAPTER 2

Cooper Morgan was twenty-eight years old in April of 1966. It was two and one half years since John Fitzgerald Kennedy had died from a killer's bullet. The nation had slipped into an unpopular war in Vietnam. The new idea of burning draft cards was just coming into vogue. Black people had rioted in a place called Watts in California. Skirts were getting shorter. Bridget Bardot was touring America. *Doctor Zhivago* and *Thunderball* were playing at the movies. *Batman* and *Get Smart* were new shows on television. The Supreme Court had just decided that *Fanny Hill* was not obscene.

Cooper and Nancy had married right after he graduated from Harvard. They got married because they wanted to. They got married fast because they had to. Lisa was born six months later. The unexpected pregnancy changed Cooper's plan to go to England and study for a year at Oxford. He had won a Rhodes scholarship. Instead, he accepted another scholarship that paid full tuition, plus generous living expenses, including extra for married students, in order to earn a Bachelor of Divinity degree at a theological school. The scholarship was highly competitive and had been designed by an imaginative foundation to induce a few exceptionally talented college graduates to enter the ranks of the clergy, instead of other, more lucrative professions. To qualify, a candidate had to be an "outstanding scholar and also be unsure of his desire to become a clergyman." There was no requirement that a recipient follow through with ordination. The qualifications fitted Cooper. He went to General Theological Seminary in New York City, as his father had before him. He graduated at the head of his class. He chose not to become ordained in his church.

At the same early hour that Cooper Morgan woke up and contemplated the events of the night before, his wife, Nancy, lay awake in bed in New York City. She was in the beautiful master bedroom of a brownstone on

Manhattan's aristocratic Upper East Side. It belonged to her parents who were seldom there. She stretched and enjoyed the feel of rumpled sheets against her bare skin. She, too, abstractedly contemplated her guilt. Not because of the man taking a shower in the adjoining bathroom. She hoped he would rejoin her in bed. Rather, her pang of guilt concerned, as usual, her daughter, Lisa, whom she was neglecting.

Cooper always seemed so self-possessed, so adequate unto himself, that it never occurred to her that he needed her. It also never occurred to her that her husband would succumb to the charms of a budding young coed. Or, for that matter, that one would have the nerve to, or know how to, seduce a man like Cooper. There were others, she was sure, who might try it. Some faculty wives would like to get him in bed. And certainly a number of the bachelor lady teachers would jump at the chance. It would have to be their initiative, she thought. Cooper would never set out to do something wrong. Nancy sort of hoped some faceless woman had succeeded. Then, perhaps he would not feel so betrayed when he found out about her.

Fat chance, she thought, as she looked at the magnificent, muscular, naked male who now stood in the bathroom doorway looking at her.

She pulled down the sheets, twisting her white body. Her knees were drawn up and apart.

"Come back to bed you beautiful bull," she said. "I'll show you something new."

"Nancy, you are too much! I'm late now."

She squirmed and arched her back, pointing her exposed bottom straight at him. "But it's early, Love," she whispered.

"I'd like to Doll. I love being with you. But I have to catch an early shuttle to Washington. I'm going to testify for my red brothers and sisters." He smiled. "Cover yourself, you shameless lady, before I smack your fanny."

"Do it," she giggled. She stretched out and rolled over facedown. "Do it. Do it!" she shouted.

George RedThunder smiled at her, but went to a thick black attaché case and fished out a clean, white, button-down, oxford-cloth shirt, black knee socks and red jockey shorts. He put them on quickly and retrieved a black knitted tie from the back of a chair. Before he put on his plain gray suit (he never wore anything but plain gray suits, black ties and white shirts) he quickly took out a small case, opened it, produced a disposable hypodermic needle, filled it with insulin and injected it into his very muscular thigh. Watching him, Nancy pretended to pout, but her eyes were mischievous. "Who in Washington would trust the testimony of a blue-eyed diabetic Indian?" she asked.

"Ah, my dear, I'm famous in Washington. They remember my touchdowns and the Harvard Crimson winning mighty victories."

"I know, I know," she said. "You fucking football hero. You're famous everywhere."

"Perhaps, but those adoring female admirers seem to have forgotten me already."

"Don't worry, my love, you can get all the pussy you want, right here."

"Yes, I know," he said quietly. "I love it, and I hate myself for it."

"Don't get maudlin on me, Love. Call me and I'll meet you here when you want."

"OK," he whispered, kissing her quickly on the forehead. He swept out of the room, attaché case in hand.

Nancy O'Brian Morgan smiled to herself. She pulled up the sheet and covers. She stretched and twisted her supple body. She felt aglow, but she also felt unfulfilled. She sensed a yearning, a wanting.

Why is it, she thought, I am always wanting? What is it I want? It isn't George because I can't have him, really have him. I don't want Cooper because I do have him. Is that true? Don't I want Cooper? Do I really still have him? Oh God, he's so decent. What girl wouldn't be proud to have him? She giggled to herself, what girl wouldn't give her soul for George RedThunder? What a man. Three men packed into one. Would I yearn for him so much if he was not Cooper's friend? Oh dear, this is getting too complex, too introspective. Can it be I want to hurt Cooper? That's crazy.

One thing is for sure. I love Lisa. I'm a rotten mother, but I love her. Oh God, I'm crying. Oh Nancy, you bitch, you're not as tough as you like to think you are. Get out of bed and go home. Go home to Lisa. Go home to your stupid little apartment in that stifling, stinking school. Oh Cooper, why can't you be important, like George is? Why can't you make a lot of money, and fly to Washington? Why can't you be somebody, make me jealous, make me jump to keep up with you? Oh Cooper, how did it come to this? Who could have believed Cooper Morgan would turn out to be dull? Questions . . . dumb questions. "Go home, bitch," she said to herself. Be a mother and wife, if you can still pull it off.

She jumped up, crossed to the bathroom and used the bidet her mother had installed. After cleaning herself, she looked up the next departing train on the New Haven Railroad, called for a cab and did a few household chores. She decided to bring some of her spring clothes to campus and packed a large suitcase full of them.

If it weren't for Daddy, I'd have no clothes, she mused. What a spoiled bitch you are Nancy, she thought. She contemplated leaving the clothes acquired on her father's charge accounts behind. Other teacher's wives get along. She shrugged. But they are not me and I am not them, thank God. She took the suitcase to the front door.

Looking out, she saw that the cab was out front but had locked its front bumper to the rear bumper of the car in front of it. A man was standing on the locked bumpers, bouncing up and down and shouting at the cab driver. The bumpers came unattached. Nancy carried her suitcase to the cab and got in.

"I want to go to Grand Central Station," she said. "The Vanderbilt Avenue entrance, please." The driver turned and stared at her.

"I want to go to Grand Central, at Vanderbilt," she said. The cabbie was glassy-eyed and uncomprehending. She smiled at him, instinctively rising to the challenge. She was accustomed to making her way smoothly and almost any man she encountered was quick to want to help her. "It's at Forty-fourth Street," she said. "Look, you just start going down Fifth Avenue over there, and I'll tell you where to turn."

The cab plunged forward and accelerated into a sweeping left hand turn onto Fifth Avenue. She heard horns honk and brakes squeal, as angry drivers maneuvered to avoid her lurching, speeding cab.

My God, she thought, he's high on something. "Look," she cried. "Here's where I want to get out! It's right here! This is the . . ." Despite her cries to the driver, the cab gained speed. Apparently nothing could stop it—except the rear end of a massive bus standing directly in the hurtling vehicle's path.

CHAPTER 3

Lisa Morgan was a serious little girl. Or so she appeared. She was necessarily self-sufficient for her age. She seemed quiet and a little shy. Often, a sort of secret smile would play across her face. She was as pretty as her mother, but she looked like Cooper. She had his dark brown hair and eyes. Their expressions were very similar and she had his quiet, easy manner.

Lisa attended first grade in the local, public grammar school. Nancy's father had offered to pay her tuition at Miss Emmons' Country Day, but Cooper had declined. This morning, as on most mornings, she was attending to her father's breakfast. Nancy did not get up that early even when she was home, unless she had an early tennis game. Lisa poured orange juice, set out cereal and milk, and set the table in a kitchen-dining nook.

"Hello sweetie," said Cooper who arrived looking fresh in a blue blazer and gray flannels. "Doesn't my little girl look beautiful this morning?" Lisa smiled her secret smile, and sat down demurely at the table, at the same time her father did.

"Did you sleep well, honey?" Cooper asked.

Lisa thought for a minute. She had never been asked that before. "I guess so," she said.

"What I mean is, did you wake up during the night?"

Cooper thought to himself, this is what cheating is all about, isn't it . . . covering your tracks . . . asking little kids how much they know without the kids knowing they're being asked.

"I don't ever wake up in the night, Daddy."

"That's nice, honey. Thank you for getting my breakfast. You take good care of your dad, don't you?"

"I like to," she said. "Especially when Mommy's away. Sherri would like to take care of you, but I told her I'm all you need."

"You sure are. Did Sherri say she wanted to take care of me?"

"Well, she did your laundry, and she vacuumed and dusted, and we did the dishes that were piled up in the sink . . . we did them together. I said babysitters are not supposed to do housework, and she said someone had to take care of you and she was going to do it. And then she read me a story because she said that kids who get read to grow up smarter and I have to be smart because you are, and I have to make you proud of me."-

"Well, that sounds pretty nice, and I am proud of you. And so is Mommy and we both love you very much."

"Sherri loves me, too."

"And do you love Sherri?"

"Oh yes! Sherri is my favorite of everybody. When I'm a big girl I want to be just like her."

Cooper noted that Lisa's dress had been washed. He concluded Sherri had done it.

He smiled to himself at the corny thought that Sherri would make someone a great wife. But she would for all that, particularly in bed. She's really a fine girl, he mused. Yeah, she's a nice girl who's going to screw up my marriage, and my career. Well, maybe. We'll see. Who's at fault here, anyway? You are, Cooper. You are.

He saw Lisa off on the school bus, and walked to his classroom. He was fortunate to have his own classroom without having to share it. Many teachers senior to him at Essex had yet to be accorded that privilege. What is more, he had a corner room, with windows on two sides, the kind that was reserved for department chairmen. Cooper thought of himself as a member of the English Department, and he was. He was also technically head of the Department of Religion, a designation he secretly scorned. In speaking with Nancy he referred to it as, "One of the Headmaster's little games."

There were three teachers of religion at Essex: the Chaplin, the Headmaster and himself. The Headmaster taught two courses, each met twice a week, unless he canceled them. This happened with some frequency because the Headmaster and his fundraising staff were in the process of raising twenty million dollars. He was frequently off campus making speeches and meeting with wealthy prospects among the alumni and the parents of students.

Cooper taught one course in religion and another elective called, "The Bible as Literature." This was listed in the school catalogue twice.

13

It appeared among English Department offerings, and again among the religion courses. The students at Essex regarded Cooper as an interesting teacher, so his Literature course had to be restricted to sixth formers and it was always quickly over-subscribed. Sherri Huff took the course and it was during class, Cooper realized, that he would see her for the first time since last night. He wondered how it would go.

The Chaplin at Essex was Ned Howard. He was a sharp-faced middle-aged man whose movements were quick and eager. Ned was an enthusiastic optimist. He was the coach of the varsity ice hockey team and was good at it. He worked at Essex for a dollar a year and made no secret of his private wealth. He drove a long red Lincoln convertible, which he loved. Ned was loud and energetic in Chapel services. His sermons rarely ran more than seven or eight minutes. Each one told a story that made a point. The fact that he lacked substance intellectually was seldom noticed, because most of the time he had a distinguished guest speaker at Sunday Chapel. Because Ned was an alumnus, and a winning coach, and occupied a central position at the school, he was well known and liked, by the alumni and the trustees. This may have been one reason that the Headmaster did not like him, Cooper thought. In any event, Ned did not hold the position of Chairman of the Department of Religion, and never had, in spite of the fact that he was the only full-time religion teacher at Essex.

Cooper's morning proceeded smoothly. If anyone had already learned of his indiscretion there was no evidence of it. *Indiscretion*, thought Cooper. Adultery is a more accurate word. Or how about *corrupter of children*, he thought. Oh come off it. Just get through the day. Yes, just get through the next period, with Sherri in my class.

When she came through the door she smiled at him the same way she smiled at everyone. Did he miss something? Was there no special look, no secret-shared kind of a glance? None. How did he look, he wondered. Maybe like a lovesick schoolboy? He hoped not. If she can be cool, so can I.

Cooper got the class started. He deliberately avoided calling on Sherri because he was afraid his feelings for her would show. Perversely though, Sherri kept speaking up, contributing to the class discussion, something she had rarely done before.

"Can't anyone here tell me which are the synoptic gospels?" asked Cooper.

"Yes," said Sherri, "Mathew, Mark and Luke because they, unlike John, follow the same sequence of events or storyline. They have more the same point of view."

So it went, through the period. When class was over, Sherri lagged behind, until they were alone.

"Hey, you were really good in class today," he said, because he wasn't sure what else to say.

"As good as last night?" She smiled quickly and then looked at him intently. "Look," she said, "don't worry about anyone finding out. No one will. I care more about you than anything or anybody. I won't ever hurt you."

He stared at her and said slowly, "Why is it I keep getting the feeling that you're the adult and I'm the kid?"

"Well" she said in her soft quiet voice, "We can grow up together."

"I don't deserve you," he said.

She started out the door, turned and whispered, "You can have all you want." She shaped a silent kiss with her mouth, turned and swept gracefully down the hallway.

He rubbed the back of his hand across his forehead.

That's not the way that was supposed to go, he thought. I'm supposed to get us out of this, with minimum hurt for everybody. Now we're getting in deeper.

It was a bothersome thought, but what really bothered him was the knowledge, down deep, that he was thrilled with the prospect that they were not yet through. They would make love again. They would be lovers, until . . . until when?

At midday Cooper walked to his apartment to drop off his mail and some books, before heading to the school dining room, where he was host every lunch and dinner to a mixed group of students at his own table. They would stay with him for a week and then scatter to new groupings at new tables, each presided over by a faculty member. When the week was over, it was likely that never again would that exact same group of people sit together for the rest of their lives. Such was the genius of Oggie "Cyclops" Nosterling, Chairmen of the Math Department, who prided himself on assigning table groupings using a formula that no one else could, or wanted to, understand.

When Cooper opened his apartment door, the phone in his study was ringing. Instead of saying "hello" Cooper always spoke his name quietly and pleasantly into the receiver.

He could hear his father-in-law's voice on the other end, concluding some instructions to an operator. Nancy's dad always had instructions for everyone. Such was Cooper's respect for the old man's knowledge and command of all situations that he half expected the call was about Cooper's recent infidelity.

"This is Blakely O'Brian, Cooper."

"Yes sir, are you calling from Hobe Sound?"

"Yes, but I have just been in touch with New York. Nancy's there. I suppose you know that?"

Did Cooper just imagine a critical tone of voice? Nancy's father had, on an earlier occasion, as much as said, if you had any sense you'd keep her at home.

"There has been an accident my boy. Nancy's been hurt."

This hit Cooper like a blow to the chest. Blakely O'Brian was one for understatement. If he said she was hurt, then she was seriously hurt. "Where is she?" asked Cooper.

"She's at Columbia Presbyterian, Cooper. The best place. The chief of surgery there is an acquaintance of mine. I have already spoken with him. Everything that can be done to help her will . . . well, Cooper, you know . . . he said he'd get the best men on it, and well, I'm counting on him. I don't know what else to do until I get up there. Muffy and I will be on the next plane out. We might even get there before you do."

"How is she? What happened?" Cooper realized he was almost shouting.

"She was in a taxi that ran into a Fifth Avenue bus. The cab driver was . . . well, he's dead. Nancy's condition is listed as critical. She's had a concussion, which is what they are most concerned about. She has a broken leg, some lacerations, a broken collarbone and perhaps a dislocated shoulder. I'm not sure that is precisely accurate, but that is what I was able to learn."

"All right, Dad." Cooper's voice was calm again. "I'll go straight there as soon as I can make some arrangements for Lisa."

"Muffy was hoping you'd bring Lisa with you."

"Not today," said Cooper. "I will probably bring her into the city in a day or two. We'll have to see what's best." Cooper knew that when dealing with Nancy's parents he had to be very firm and show no trace of indecision. Otherwise, they would take over. What had made Nancy first believe she wanted to marry Cooper was the fact that he seemed to be able to hold his own against those two strongly dominant personalities.

Among Cooper and Nancy's friends at Essex Academy were Mike and Sylvia Banes. All four had known knew each other since college. Cooper and Mike were at Harvard together. Sylvia was Nancy's roommate at Wellesley. Sylvia agreed to pick up Lisa at the school bus stop and take her back to Mike and Sylvia's apartment on campus. Cooper left the problem of canceling or covering his classes in the able hands of the school's Assistant Headmaster. Sylvia drove Cooper to the train station. She made sympathetic noises all the way.

"Oh, poor Nancy, and you too, Cooper. Oh, it's all just too awful. It will all turn out OK though. It will. Just you wait. Maybe this will bring you both back together. Oh dear, you know what I mean. Well you know, Nancy has been *gone* as much as she's been *here*. It's been hard for you Cooper, dear. A big, lusty man like you, with no woman to take care of you and Lisa. Well here's the station. Oh, you poor thing. Now, don't forget what I said. I'm your friend. If there is anything you need, anything at all . . . well, give my love to poor Nancy. Call us tonight. You can speak to Lisa. Oh, poor Lisa. Good bye, good bye."

Fortunately he had only a few minutes to wait for the New Haven Railroad's early afternoon express train to New York. As soon as he was seated, he pulled a file folder of students' essays from his small suitcase and began to correct them. He didn't know when he would get another chance, and Cooper set strict standards for doing a careful job. As uncertain as he was about his career and direction, he believed that if he could produce a small cluster of kids every year, kids who really had learned how to write, then his life would have amounted to something worthwhile.

Shortly before arriving in New York, he put away his papers and let his mind dwell on what lay ahead. Critical condition. Face it, that means she might die. She might be dead now. Oh no. She can't. Not all alone. Damnit, I should have been with her instead of . . . the hell with that. Damnit, if she makes it, then we're going to start fresh. We have to, for Lisa if not for us. Eight years we've been together. Married almost seven. Seven year itch. Is that our problem?

He smiled to himself as the train plunged underground with a roaring echo just before arriving at Grand Central Terminal.

CHAPTER 4

1953-1955

Cooper Morgan showed promise as a scholar from his earliest days and might, as a boy, have been sent to Essex Academy because it was only a couple of hours by car to the east of his home in Riverside, Connecticut. His mother thought Essex would be an excellent choice and she felt he could qualify for a substantial scholarship by virtue of his straight A's in public school and the fact that his father was a clergyman.

Cooper's father, Sherman, had other plans. The elder Morgan, having married late in life, was old enough to be Cooper's grandfather. He was Rector of one of the largest and most affluent Episcopal parishes in the country. Since he arrived as a relatively young man, there were few who could remember when St. Stephens had been presided over by another priest. Sherman had started with a relatively small congregation and, by dint of hard work and a forceful personality, had built his church to its present grand proportions. St. Stephens had nine full-time employees, five of whom were clergymen.

Dr. Morgan, as almost everyone called him, had been educated at Lawrenceville School, Princeton University, and General Theological Seminary, and he saw no reason why Cooper should not start out the same way. Therefore, in 1953, having finished junior high school in Riverside, Cooper enrolled as a sophomore at Lawrenceville at age fifteen, after satisfying the appraising scrutiny of the admissions committee.

Sherman Morgan was a regular and popular guest preacher at the school's chapel, so he had a cordial relationship with the Headmaster and was admired by the faculty. Young Cooper had the uneasy feeling that he would be expected to live up to his father's reputation. He was already frightened enough at the prospect of attending one of the nation's top schools where he would be competing with the best, not only in the classroom, but also on the playing fields.

On opening day his parents drove him to New Jersey along with several suitcases full of clothes and boxes containing bedding, accumulated bits of athletic equipment, room decorations and a kit full of writing paper, stamps, and envelopes. They drove the family's large Oldsmobile station wagon and arrived in time for Cooper to register and receive his course assignments and daily schedule. Cooper was assigned to an "old boy" who took him to the bookstore for his textbooks and supplied him with a black tie and a black beanie. Eddie Greaves, his guide, explained, "You must wear the black tie all the time that you normally wear a tie. That is, at meals and classes and chapel. We all wear jackets then too. Now, the beanie, you have to wear that whenever you're outdoors, except during athletics."

"How long must I wear them, all year?"

"Oh, no. Just until we beat the Hill in varsity football."

"Who's the Hill?"

"They're our big rivals. It's a school in Pennsylvania. It's more important to beat the Hill and lose all the rest, than the other way around."

"What if you, or . . . we don't beat them?" asked Cooper.

"Well, you're not supposed to think that could be possible. But, just in case we don't beat them," Eddie lowered his voice like a conspirator, "you have to wear your rhinie tie and beanie until Christmas vacation."

"What's rhinie?"

"A rhinie is what you are, a new boy."

Cooper was to live in Cleve House, one of several dark sprawling brownstone dormitories referred to as "circle houses," because they were located on a great circular driveway. Cooper's father had lived in Cleve. The sons of alumni were usually assigned to their fathers' old houses. Each house had its own colors, and flag, and cheers, and songs, and awards, and fielded a team in every sport recognized at the school. Given this excess of dorm identification, alumni dads took a special pleasure in having their sons represent them a generation later in what amounted to their old childhood clubhouses. Cooper perceived his father's satisfaction in finding the rooms he had lived in forty years or so earlier and in settling his son into the well-preserved relic full of fond memories.

Cooper's mother and father paid their respects to Cleve's Housemaster and his wife, both of whom seemed pleasant enough, and made their departure. Young Cooper felt more alone than he ever had in his life.

Days passed into weeks. Cooper worked hard at his studies, out of fear of doing poorly at first, and then for the joy of it. He realized that for the first time he could remember, he was not the top scholar in his class. However, when the first marking period came around, he made the honor roll. This was a matter of some surprise to his newfound friends, some of whom played with him on the junior varsity football team. At the age of fifteen, Cooper was a skinny six foot three. A natural athlete, he soon won a place as JV quarterback. Combined with his taciturn manner and deep voice, this athletic accomplishment brought him a degree of respect on campus.

"Hey, Coop, you shithead, how'd you make the honor roll? You're supposed to be a fucking football player, not a brain."

The speaker was the boy Cooper most admired in his class, George RedThunder. He was a handsome dark-skinned boy with striking pale blue eyes, which seemed to shine as if they contained an inner light. A star running back, he was the youngest member of the school's powerful varsity football team.

"Don't give me crap, George, you get pretty good marks too." Cooper smiled at him, pleased to be greeted by a campus hero.

"Yeah, I get good marks. I work for them though, not like you fucking smart lazy Wasps. It's hard for the lonely Indian making his way in the white man's world." George looked serious, then winked and laughed and grabbed Cooper by the arm. "Come on, you skinny bastard, let's go to the village and Indian Joe will buy you a hamburger."

"I thought you didn't like to be called that," said Cooper.

"My friends can call me anything they like, and I am my best friend!" George laughed and jumped in the air. "Would you be my friend, Coop?"

"I'd be honored to be your friend, Indian Joe," smiled Cooper.

George laughed again and said, "Good, maybe we can even be blood brothers!"

"Not if it involves cutting my hand with a knife," laughed Cooper.

"OK," agreed George, "No knife. We will become brothers in the blood of a virgin." George clapped his hands with glee, as they walked to the village of Lawrenceville.

"If you can arrange that, George, I'll be your brother and join your tribe and wear feathers on my head."

"You sound as if you're a virgin yourself, Coop."

"Yes," said Cooper, "I suppose I am, and I wish I were not."

"Don't worry about it, buddy. The only difference between you and most of the slobs in this place is you're telling the truth and they lie about it."

Cooper smiled and thought to himself, George RedThunder is the same age I am, but he seems much older and wiser. Maybe that's because he's an Indian. I've never known an Indian. I certainly have never known anyone at all like George. He's probably the best running back I have ever seen. And he wants me to be his friend. That's wonderful. I didn't know he even knew who I was. Seeing my name posted on the honor roll is what impressed him. Before the year is out, Cooper Morgan will be listed on the *high* honor roll.

And so it was. As the year went on the two boys became close friends, even though Cooper lived in Cleve and George lived in Kennedy House. The next year, each was president of his House—making them like minor feudal lords in the greater kingdom that was Lawrenceville. In the winter, Cooper and George played basketball and in the spring they played baseball. George convinced Cooper that he was dangerously thin to play football, and so they worked out together lifting weights. By the fall of their final year Cooper had put on twenty pounds of muscle and was a rangy hundred and eighty pounds. George was a powerful two hundred-pounder and such a threat at halfback that the student body expected an undefeated season. Cooper was now first-string quarterback of the varsity eleven and was voted President of the school. George was Vice President. Life was rich and rewarding for the two boys. They had their undefeated season that fall and scouts from Big Ten colleges came to see George RedThunder eat up the yardage against Lawrenceville's opponents.

Seniors lived together in Upper House, occasionally referred to by underclassmen as "The House of Lords." Cooper and George roomed together and presided over the well being of the school. It was always Cooper, though, to whom others looked for leadership. It surprised him. George seemed much more mature and worldly.

George was, perhaps, too mature and worldly. There was always a part of himself that he held back from everyone, including Cooper. George lived in nearby Princeton. His "guardian" was Emmett Goodhill, partner in a prominent New York law firm. George's mother had apparently been the manager and hostess of the Goodhill household until her untimely death the summer before Cooper came to Lawrenceville. Cooper's father, Sherman, had done some research on the family and had used the word "consort" to describe George's mother in her relationship to Emmett Goodhill. There had been a previous marriage and Goodhill had older children. They were seldom to be seen at the household. If Goodhill had been living with George's mother, which certainly seemed to be the case, then he did not marry her either because he did not want to, or because he was not divorced from his first wife, whom George said he had never met. There were those who concluded that George was Goodhill's bastard son, and that could explain the phenomenon of a blue-eyed Indian. However, George told Cooper that he had been brought to the Goodhill home by his mother when he was little, and he did not know his father. George's mother told him that he was named for his father who was, indeed, a full-blooded Indian. Cooper had seen pictures of George's mother. She was young, petite, and very beautiful. Her name was Maryanne. She was dark complexioned, had Indian features and blue eyes.

George RedThunder's place in the Goodhill household was every bit that of a son, as far as anyone could observe. He had the best early preparation at Princeton's leading day school. He had gone to Lawrenceville in the first form as a day student, and had become a boarder after his mother's death.

And so, concluded Cooper, George RedThunder was not a reservation Indian. He had known only wealth, security and comfort. His upbringing was more elitist that his own had been. Indeed, George had never attended public school. George made no secret of the fact that his references to himself as an Indian were essentially a spoof for his own amusement. Cooper felt that George's dramatic last name, his dark tan skin and his Indian features did not entirely explain the man that he was.

Yes, mused Cooper with a little envy, even at age seventeen, George RedThunder is a man and not a boy.

CHAPTER 5

1955-1956

Cooper's family had a courtesy membership at the Riverside Yacht Club and he had learned to sail there. He had a knack for it and was, for several years, junior champion in small racing boats. The club offered employment to him in the summers. He learned to care for tennis courts, clean the swimming pool, and then he graduated to jobs as a boat boy on some of the larger sailing yachts in the club. He enjoyed the long cruises he got to go on, but they tended to keep him from developing any close relationships with girls.

On the last night of summer vacation before his senior year at Lawrenceville, Cooper at age eighteen went stag to the Yacht Club Labor Day dance. He remembered that he had promised George RedThunder, full of bravado, that he would not remain a virgin. Cooper thought, old George is going to be disappointed in me. I guess I must be afraid of girls. I guess I just don't know how to go about it. I don't even know how to find a whore. Maybe I just haven't put my mind to it. Now, is there any woman here who might let me in her pants? Look around, dummy, there has just got to be someone. There, Terry what's-her-name. She is eighteen like me. Everyone says she's hot to go.

"Hi Terry, would you like to dance with me?"

"Of course I would you big beautiful cold fish!" She smiled broadly at him and fitted her body in close against him. She was a handsome, tall girl, full chested and broad-hipped. She had long, silky, tawny hair. "Does this mean you're interested, or are you just killing time?"

"You don't mind saying what's on your mind do you," he said. "I wish I was more like that." She was silent. "Well, yes, I'm interested. You are a very good looking girl."

"I suppose you haven't noticed I've been trying to catch your attention all summer. I had given up."

"I guess I didn't. You're always with somebody else. You usually go with guys who are older than me. I didn't think . . . that is, I . . ."

"That's OK, you're doin' fine. Keep trying, and tell me, what exactly is on your mind."

"Terry, if I did that you might slap my face."

"Are you trying to say you would like to make love to me?" she said as she pushed her hips into him suggestively. She felt absolutely wonderful in his arms. She looked up into his face and said softly, "If I make it hard for you, will you hold it against me?"

He looked at her closely. He could hardly believe she meant the double-entendre. Seeing that she did, he started to laugh, and she did too. "You have already made it hard for me. Can't you feel it? I *am* holding it against you."

"Of course I can. It feels good. That's why I said that."

"Oh, wow!" was all he could say.

"I'm glad I excite you, Cooper. You excite me, too. Now, try again, tell me just what is on your mind."

"Oh, wow! . . . I, I want to, to . . . make love to you, Terry."

She stood on tiptoe and whispered in his ear, "Does that mean you want to fuck me, Cooper?"

"Oh, yes, more than anything in the world."

"Well, you can't."

"Huh? Hey, you're the one who brought it up!" As he said that he realized he, too, had used a double-entendre. They both laughed at once and drew the glances of people around them.

"Look, my love," she said. "I'm as horny as hell, and I'll do anything close to it but I'll save fucking for the man who marries me." She pushed her pelvis into him again in slow grinds. "If that man turns out to be *you* someday, then you'll be glad I did."

His ego somewhat restored, as well as his erection, Cooper said, "I'm a virgin too, but I'm not as proud of it as you are."

"See? You can do it. You can talk to me honestly. Don't worry. I can make you feel *good. Real* good. I'll do anything with you except let you put it in me. Just remember, anything but that. Don't tell me later that I led you on. OK?"

"OK. Let's get the hell out of here and start doing 'anything but.'" They both laughed again. She squeezed his hand, and they turned and ran from the dance floor.

Later, they lay quietly together stark naked, bathed in the light of a single floor lamp. They were entwined on a big couch in the basement playroom of her house. No one else was home. The two of them looked beautiful and innocent together—young Eve and Adam, before the fall. Cooper began to wonder if he should leave, but he felt too relaxed to move. It had been quite a night. He was afraid RedThunder might not be impressed, but he sure was. He had asked her to leave the light on so he could see everything. Her breasts were perfect. She showed him how to kiss and toy with her nipples. She had even spread her knees and opened the lips of her vulva with her fingers and described every detail to him. He had kissed her there at her urging and he had brought her to a moaning climax. He felt proud that he could do that. She had then relieved him with her hands and caught his semen in his handkerchief. "I'm going to show it to all the girls at Ethel Walker who know you," she teased.

"You wouldn't!" he said.

"No silly, I wouldn't. I'm going to save it for me, and sniff it when I go to bed at night, and get all horny and play with myself."

"That, I believe."

"You should. I bet I can make you come again," she said.

"I would love to have you try."

She sat up and took him in her hands again. He watched her as she bent over him. Her shiny hair cascaded over his stomach, the tips dancing among his pubic curls. Her mouth was warm and smooth. He couldn't believe this was happening. He had been too shy to ask her before. She squeezed with her hand, as he grew hard. Her sucking was the most exquisite thing he had ever felt.

"What the Goddamned *hell* is going on here!" screamed the middle-aged woman standing in the middle of the room.

Cooper was to recall later that he felt the end of the world was at hand. Terry's mother was bleary eyed and raving. Her words were either unintelligible or Cooper was so panicked, as he grabbed for his clothes, that he could understand nothing. He realized that Terry was now screaming too. Her mother was slapping at her with her open hand, but mostly missing and waving in the air. She shouted, "*BITCH, BITCH, BITCH,*" over and over. The word echoed insanely in the room.

Terry, with her party clothes clutched to her bosom, ran naked upstairs past a puzzled man in a chesterfield coat and homburg hat.

While Cooper was frantically tugging on his trousers, he kept trying to think what he should say. I am *terribly* sorry Mrs. What's-your-name. This is all a *terrible* mistake. What you *think* you saw was not what you saw at all.

What was her *name?* Nothing seemed to fit very well, or work. Nipper was the name he read on the sign outside the house. But that wasn't Terry's name, he was sure. Of course! Terry's mother had remarried. Terry lived with her stepfather.

"*Please,*" he shouted to her. She was screaming up the stairs now. Her husband still stood there confused. "Please, Mrs. Nipper, let me explain . . ."

She wheeled on him, further enraged, her face beet red, "*BASTARD!*" she shouted, "*BASTARD, BASTARD . . .*" Then her face lit up with a new thought. "*RAPIST,*" she yelled.

Cooper stopped buttoning his shirt, which had the buttons in the wrong holes anyway. He scooped up his jacket and he, too, ran for the stairs. He passed the man in the chesterfield and homburg who seemed frozen in limbo. He hit the first floor on the run, dashed through the living room, out the front door and into the night. It only took a few seconds.

He did not stop running. It was about three miles to St. Stephens Rectory, and he ran all the way, full out, in his bare feet. At one point, a police cruiser pulled over towards him. Cooper, without breaking stride, cut behind several houses, passed through backyards, skirted a swimming pool, jumped some fences, and did not see the cruiser again.

Cooper was in beautiful condition, and was not even breathing heavily when he sprang deftly into the large paneled hallway of his home. He thanked God it was late, and his parents and younger sisters were asleep.

"Cooper, come in here, please." It was his father's voice from his study.

"Yes, sir. I thought you would be asleep . . ." His father was in his long wool bathrobe and sandals. He looked like an elderly monk. In truth, he looked to Cooper how he thought God must look . . . the Old Testament God.

"And so I *was* asleep, and so was your mother, until we received a phone call a few minutes ago from a somewhat distraught Mrs. Nipper." His voice was crisp but not unkind or unfriendly.

"Jeez," said Cooper. "Oh, wow!"

"You appear to have misplaced your shoes, son."

"Yeah, I left 'em behind."

"You made a hasty exit?"

"Yeah . . . Yes, I did. I left 'em behind." Cooper was aware that he sounded stupid. He could observe himself as though he was a third party looking in. He was stunned. He wanted to tell his father the truth. He wanted to tell him everything, but he was not sure that would be kind to the old gentleman. He surely could never understand. Cooper felt he had no right to upset him. He did not know how to answer, or what to say. He buttoned his shirt and tucked it in. He put on his jacket. He looked around absently for his necktie. He sat down, and tried his most winning smile on his father. "She knew who I was, huh?"

"Yes indeed, she had you identified without a doubt. Although I don't suppose she had ever seen you stark naked before."

"She said I was . . ." He feigned being indignant. He was about to deny it, then thought better of it. "Yes, sir, I *was* stark naked, and so was her daughter, Terry. And there we were, and she walked in and surprised us." There, he said it. He cleared the air. He just hoped the old man could take this. He looked to assess the damage to his father.

The old priest's eyes were sparkling and he was laughing silently. He pulled out a handkerchief to wipe tears from his eyes. Cooper was frozen. He loved his father and now feared his atrocious behavior had caused him to crack up. His father giggled. "Excuse me, son, I don't mean to make light of your embarrassment, but you've got to admit it's a pretty comical situation you're describing."

Cooper was dumbstruck. He could not believe his ears. This was a night for surprises. "You mean you're not mad at me?"

"Well, your mother may be just a bit annoyed. She doesn't like being put in the position of being consolatory to a woman like Mrs. Nipper. She did have to listen to some language that she is not very accustomed to hearing. But, you know, we're both awfully glad to be reassured that you are human."

"I don't understand," said Cooper.

"Well, son, I can't remember you getting in trouble since you were ten years old with that Halloween caper, which, incidentally, I always sort of admired but couldn't admit to you at the time. You work hard every summer earning your money. You help around the house. You go off to my old school and do much better than I ever did., you are president of the student body. I doubt if you know what an achievement that is. Your mother and I, we have been wondering if you are not just a bit too perfect for our liking. I would hate to see you get arrogant or a little intolerant of people with fewer gifts than God has given to you. A lot of things come easy to you, Cooper. You appear to be able to see ahead, act wisely. You have good judgment.

"Well now, I don't know just what you did tonight, but I want to find out, and you are going to tell me. I don't think I approve of what you did, but it is reassuring to see that it didn't all go your way and that you're . . . well, you're human like the rest of us poor buggers on this earth."

Cooper was old enough to see that his father was easing him down, reassuring him, making him feel better about himself. He always had. He seemed to be able to do that with everybody. "Dad, the reason I have done as well as I have is because of you."

"Getting down to the case at hand, my boy, what has led Mrs. Nipper to decide that you are a *rapist?*"

"That's not true, sir. We didn't even do that . . . uh, you know, intercourse. I think Mrs. Nipper was drunk, sir, and she didn't know what we were doing, exactly."

"What were you doing, exactly? Did she not catch you *in flagrante delicto?*"

"If that means what it sounds like, we didn't do that. Terry, she's a virgin. We made an agreement that we wouldn't have intercourse but anything else was OK."

Cooper's father laughed. "Don't you know it is the spirit of the thing that counts? She may be biologically a virgin, but that's all."

"Yes, sir, but that's important to her, and I was so horny, uh . . . excited that I'd rather play with her rules than not play at all! Dad, it was wonderful! I've never even seen a naked girl before. Oh, I mean a grown girl. Not like Kate and Leslie. Dad, she showed me everything and I kissed her between her legs, and she was doing that to me when her mother appeared and started screaming."

"Well now, I think I have the picture well enough. You should know that if Mrs. Nipper ever sees you near her house or her daughter she says she will call the police. Furthermore," his eyes crinkled in a mischievous expression, "she said that everyone knows that the sons of ministers are no good and she has always known you are no exception. And now, sir, I think it is late enough for even rapists to go to sleep, don't you?"

"Yes, sir." Cooper stood and smiled sheepishly.

"One last thing, son. Regardless of yours and her moral confusion, Terry has accorded you a rare honor. It would be ill to repay her gift with loose talk that might do her harm in the community. Do you catch my drift?"

"I understand," said Cooper.

"I believe that with the coming of morning sobriety, Mrs. Nipper will apply the same cautionary thought to her own words and actions, and that we will hear no more from her. Incidentally, Nipper is not the name Terry uses, is it? What is the last name of your beautiful benefactress?"

Cooper's mind raced. Was his father asking him that to test him?

If he finds out I can't remember her name, I will disappoint him. Somehow, that will be the greater sin. I *must* think of it. "Yes, sir, Nipper is her stepfather's name." I can only stall a moment longer.

"Her name is Terry . . . is Terry *Standard!*" It came! Saved at the last minute. "Terry Standard."

"Hmmmm," said his father. "This whole thing smacks of *Pilgrim's Progress.* I hope there is a lesson in it somewhere for you. Tomorrow look up '*in flagrante delicto*' in the dictionary. Goodnight Cooper."

September 5, 1955

Dear Mrs. Nipper,

I hope you will accept my apology for my very poor behavior in your home last night. I do not know what to say except I am sorry.

Your daughter is a wonderful girl. Although you may not think so, she and I are virgins still. I know we should not have been like that, like you saw us. It was my fault. I don't know what got into me. Even though you think the sons of the clergy are . . .

He got no further. He reread it, crumpled it up and threw it into the wastebasket. He went to the telephone, called the local florist and ordered Mrs. Nipper the least expensive floral bouquet they were willing to deliver. He had them sign his name and charged it to his father.

Then he looked up Nipper in the phone book and dialed the number, praying Terry would answer. "Hello, Terry, is that you? Thank God. Well, I was hoping it wasn't your mother."

She laughed. "Did you have a good time last night, Cooper?"

"It was great except for the last part."

"You mean the blow job?" she teased.

"Hey, don't talk dirty. It was beautiful, and you're beautiful."

"Gee, thanks. You left your shoes here and your necktie."

"Yeah, I know. Will you keep them for me until Thanksgiving? I have to go back to Lawrenceville today."

"Yeah, I know. I have to go back to Ethel Walker tomorrow. Can't you come home before Thanksgiving?"

"Maybe, I'm not sure. It depends on our football schedule."

"Can I come see you play, Cooper?"

"Oh, wow. That would be great. Would you come?"

"Sure I'll come, and I'll make you come. I still owe you a blow job."

"It's a deal, and then we're going to see if we can't do something to clean up your language."

"I've still got your handkerchief with all your nice stuff in it."

"You can keep it, and if it runs out I'll send you some more in the mail. You'll be the envy of all the girls."

"Cooper."

"Yes."

"I'm sorry about my mother."

"How is she now?

"Still asleep. She'll be OK when she wakes up. Hung-over but OK. She'll pretend nothing ever happened. But it'll be better if she doesn't see you for a while.

"Terry?"

"Yes.

"Maybe this sounds dumb, but I think . . . I think I love you."

"Wow. You sure now how to make a girl cry, don't you. I've always had a crush on you."

"Terry, will you be my girl?

"You mean not go out with any other guys?"

"Yeah, I guess so."

"Gee, I don't know Cooper, maybe it's too soon for that. I'll think about it. Why do we have to get tied down? Why can't we just have fun together?"

"OK Terry, but I want you and I love you. OK? Goodbye." He hung up with a sigh and turned from the phone to find his two little sisters watching him, spellbound. Leslie turned to Kate, clasping her hands over her heart. "Oh, Kate," she said, "I want you and I love you . . . goodbye."

Cooper leaped and swept them both up into his arms and all three of them shrieked with laughter until they had tears in their eyes.

It was a foregone conclusion that George RedThunder and Cooper Morgan would go to Princeton after their graduation from Lawrenceville. The scholarship offers George received from big universities were most complimentary, but he could only picture himself on a team that had Cooper calling the plays. Their undefeated football season in the red and black Lawrenceville uniform was sweet indeed, and they wanted to perpetuate it. Emmet Goodhill, George's guardian, made it clear to him that he would pay his college expenses provided he attended a college of Ivy League academic rank. As for Cooper, he felt he would disappoint his father if he did not go to Princeton.

With Cooper's very high academic standing and George's exceptional football ability, as well as good marks, the two were confident of acceptance at Princeton. Lawrenceville always sent a large delegation there and the two boys were the pick of the crop.

As spring approached, George grew restless on the subject of colleges and finally confessed to Cooper a growing dislike for the idea of going to college in the same town in which he lived. "I just have to get away, Coop. Things aren't the same at home as when my mother was there. The Old Man has a girlfriend now. I don't fit in. Christ, Princeton is all I know. I need to get out and live in another world. Besides, if I'm going to play pro ball, the Ivy League is not the best fucking training ground."

Cooper told George they were a team and would both go the same college, no matter what. He persuaded him to make no decision until Cooper could talk to his father. Cooper felt confident that his dad would understand and assure him that it was not all that important to go to Princeton, but he felt he owed it to his father to consult him in person and not over the phone or in a letter. He called ahead and arranged to go home for the weekend.

He guessed right about his father, but the conversation held a surprise for him and was more useful than he had anticipated.

"I'm flattered that you came all the way home to address me on the subject, son. There would be a few little pleasures for me if you went to Princeton, but they will be far outweighed if I feel you have done the right thing for yourself and kept faith with your friend." The old man stared intently at him until the silence was overwhelming. Cooper knew from experience that his father did not want him to speak. Most people thought that when his father behaved this way he was thinking. Cooper thought, correctly, that he was praying.

Finally the elder Morgan broke the silence. "I want you to give very careful thought to my advice for an alternative to Princeton. I don't *insist* that you accept my counsel, but I am confident that the right thing for you to do, for you *both* to do, is to go to Harvard."

Cooper looked amazed and was about to speak.

"Let us not analyze my reasons just now son," said Sherman. "Think about it and we'll talk again this evening."

"Uh, could we do it tomorrow, Dad? I have a date with Terry tonight."

Cooper's dad laughed, and patted his son on the back. "We will talk tomorrow."

After a while, Cooper figured out his father's reasoning and agreed with it. He sensed that his father had anticipated this and, as usual, had handled the solution to his needs with wisdom and grace.

He said to himself, RedThunder will accompany me to Harvard, if I have to drag him there.

During another trip back home to Riverside Cooper and Terry were parked on a lonely road looking out on Long Island Sound, which was shining in the moonlight. Their passion spent, they were curled up together on a pile of pillows in the back of the Morgan Oldsmobile station wagon.

"Tell me," she said, "Where did you get the name Cooper?"

"Well, my grandmother's maiden name was Sherman and she named my father that. My mother's maiden name is Cooper, so my father wanted to name me that."

"If you and I had a son, would you want to name him 'Standard'?"

He tickled her ribs. "That would be a lot better than 'Little Nipper' . . . and the next one, we could call 'Exceptional.'"

George RedThunder had accepted Cooper's arguments that in the long run he would be glad he was a Harvard man rather than the graduate of a big football powerhouse. The day after Cooper returned to Lawrenceville, he and George were on their way to Cambridge in a brand new yellow Chrysler convertible that belonged to Emmett Goodhill's girlfriend. They were unprepared for the lack of enthusiasm they found in Harvard's Admissions Office. After a long wait, a young assistant interviewed them. He conceded that the college would like to have more applicants from Lawrenceville, and that George and Cooper's academic credentials were adequate. However, he pointed out that they were embarrassingly late in applying and he seriously doubted if the admissions committee would even care to consider them. This was shocking for George who had been fawned over in a most cloying manner by various university admissions people all year.

"Isn't Harvard interested in football players?" he asked.

The admissions man smiled in a patronizing way as if he did not at all mind being polite to boorish young men who said ridiculous things. "Oh, I am sure that we will have many in next year's freshmen class who enjoy football."

They departed politely, leaving their applications and transcripts behind.

"Well, that was a comedown, Coopie me boy. It looks like we will not be wearing Harvard crimson next fall."

"Not to worry, Indian Joe, we ridum over to Athletic Office, findum our kind of people. We makum big treaty with white man's fancy college." Cooper was right. They were treated like visiting royalty by the Harvard Athletic staff. The two friends returned to Lawrenceville and before the week was out they had letters from the Dean of Admissions assuring them that they would be given every consideration for acceptance and that, further, he saw no reason why they should bother to apply anywhere else.

"How do you suppose they know who we were at the Athletic Office?" said George.

"Because, my fat headed friend," said Cooper, "I asked Coach to call them the day before we left Lawrenceville. Stick with me, buddy, and Indian Joe will be wearing peacock feathers."

George gave him an admiring smile, and said, "Gary Cooper, for a cowboy, you are one sneaky smart white man." George shouted and jumped in the air for joy. "I'll tell you what. Let's sneak out of school tonight. Go to Trenton, celebrate, get drunk. Get laid. What do you say?"

"No way, Jose. Wouldn't that be just great—get caught and be kicked out of school right on the crest of the wave." Cooper looked at his friend earnestly and said, "I know I've broken big rules before, but that was before we were school officers. The Headmaster trusts us. I couldn't look him in the face if I did that. I couldn't look *myself* in the face. We make the other guys keep the rules, at least most of the time. How can we not keep them?"

RedThunder made a pained expression, then grinned. "Do you suppose it's very cold in Massachusetts in the winter?"

Cooper said, "Do you suppose that in that great big college town, there might be one or two sweet young things who might like to keep Indian Joe warm during the winter?"

"Yeah!"

"Yeah!"

They walked off together arm in arm.

Cooper's scholastic average at the end of the year was, for the first time, the highest in his class. A big fuss was made over him at graduation because no one could remember any previous time when the quarterback of the football team, the President of the student body and the Valedictorian were all the same boy. He took most of the top prizes. But it was no surprise that George won the prize for best athlete.

Graduation was a joy unequaled in Cooper's experience. The lovely green campus and majestic old buildings never looked prettier. His whole family was there and they brought Terry. Cooper was proud to show them all off.

How different it is, he thought, from that first day when my parents brought me here. How terrifying it was then, and how I have grown to love it since. He smiled to himself, remembering that his classmates had occasionally teased him by calling him Dink Stover. No one could be that good, he thought, but I must admit that I, like Dink, have come a long way. I never realized before how much I would miss it when it was all over. A big thought roared into his consciousness from deep in the recesses of his brain. This is where I want to spend my life. Here, or someplace like it. Could I be a school master, and coach? Maybe. Maybe.

CHAPTER 6

Cooper was tempted to be a camp counselor that following summer but he knew he could make much more money as a hand on one of the big yachts at Riverside Yacht Club. He knew it was important to fatten his bank account so, when it was offered to him, he accepted a choice berth on one of the most impressive sailing yachts on Long Island Sound. *Apathia* was a graceful and slender fifty-foot yawl. She was past the time of winning races in her class as more modern, but less handsome, hull designs had come along. Her present owner had little interest in racing. Indeed, he was seldom on board but loved the boat for her classic lines, teak decks and brightly varnished mahogany. He spared no expense in maintaining her and each year she came out of the yard as fresh and bright as the day she was launched. Keeping her bright during the summer was Cooper's job. He was the only paid hand and he lived aboard most of the time. The boat's owner was Anthony Kowlicker, the well-known financier who bought and sold professional athletic teams as a hobby and was never without tough, antagonistic comments on everything. Sports reporters loved to quote him on dull days when there was little news.

Kowlicker was a generous employer and, when he and his wife were the only ones aboard, he was always kind to Cooper. He would frequently give him extra days off and suggest that such-and-such a job was too menial and dull for Cooper to do himself and he should get the people at the boatyard to do it, so long as Cooper saw to it that it was done right.

With an audience, however, Cooper's employer liked to play Captain Bligh. Kowlicker mainly used the boat to entertain people and when guests were on board he seemed to love to belittle Cooper, order him around, and swear at him when he, Kowlicker, had made an error in handling the boat. The first few times this happened, Cooper was outraged and suffered in silence—debating with himself whether he should tell the old bastard what he thought of his ability as a sailor, and then quit. He figured out, however, that Kowlicker was merely playing for his audience. He was a small man, lean, dark and leathery. He was spry and fit. Few would guess he was in his seventies. Cooper found it was not hard to ignore the outbursts and regard Kowlicker without emotion. Cooper decided the trick was to neither like nor dislike the man—to be slow in reacting to his moods, either kindly or waspish.

Dorothy Kowlicker was a thoroughbred woman less than half the age of her husband. She was an excellent sailor and Cooper knew that she had been a successful model before she had become the fourth Mrs. Kowlicker. He could picture her more easily on the pages of *Vogue* than of *Playboy* but she had an aura of sexuality about her that Cooper found extremely appealing. But she excited no lust in him, perhaps because she treated him in such a matter-of-fact way. He enjoyed her company, and he strove to be at his best in her presence. She returned his attention by being his friend. She shared jokes with him and smiled encouragingly when her husband was being difficult. She was one of the first adults to invite him to use her first name. He was quick to do so because he sensed that Anthony Kowlicker disapproved of the familiarity. It was pleasant to annoy him a little. Kowlicker never openly criticized his wife in Cooper's presence and probably not anywhere else either.

I wonder how she controls him so well, thought Cooper. I must watch and see if I can figure it out.

He was not long in learning.

Apathia was berthed at a float near the Yacht Club. One evening in late July, Dorothy came onboard unexpectedly and asked Cooper to move the boat from the slip to a distant mooring or anchorage. In answer to Cooper's curious look she said, "I suppose I might as well tell you. It will become obvious soon enough. I'm going to stay on board tonight and I want to be where that bastard can't get to me."

Cooper went immediately to the cockpit to start the big diesel engine and then stepped to the float to unfasten the docking lines. He hopped aboard and eased the big boat quietly back out of her berth. He snapped on *Aphathia's* running lights, put the gear in "forward" and moved the throttle slowly ahead. Gradually they gained speed. The night was still, the black water calm. He could hear the gurgle of the bow wave and, in the moonlight, he could see the navigational buoys that were leading them out of the harbor.

Dorothy came up from below into the cool of the evening having changed into boat shoes, slacks, and a black cashmere sweater. She handed him a mug of steaming hot tea as he stood at the wheel. She had one of her own and she sat down—leaning back on the cockpit coaming and gazing quietly out over the water.

"Trouble, huh?" Cooper said.

She let out a long sigh and said, "It was bound to happen sooner or later. I had a dinner party for some of his business friends and their women. He chewed me out in front of all of them. I told him when we got married that if he ever did that to me I would leave him. He'd never done it either. To everybody else, but not me . . . until tonight."

She did not say anything for a while. Then, as if talking to herself, she said, "Maybe he's giving me a signal, wants me to leave him." She looked at Cooper. "I thought he was going to have a coronary when I walked out. All those people, and then wham . . . no hostess!" She laughed, "He'll never live it down. Oh, how he hates to lose face. He doesn't know where I went and he's got all those guests to deal with. They will have cleared out by now. I just don't want to see him tonight, Cooper. Whether he wants to apologize to me or shout at me, tomorrow is soon enough. It's time I left him anyway." She changed her mood and said cheerily, "Poor Cooper. You don't understand any of it do you? I'm sorry. No more gloomy talk."

Cooper brought the boat to a quiet tree-lined cove and she helped him get an anchor down and set. "No need for two anchors, tonight," he said. "We'll lie quietly here."

"I never did get any dinner," she said. "I'm starved! What have we got onboard?"

Cooper fixed her dinner in the Great Cabin while she sipped a Scotch highball. It was warm below. The cabin still held the heat of the day. He made small talk with her while she ate. He had had his dinner hours before. He washed the dishes and she dried. She said, "Stay up and play cards with me, Cooper, I don't want to go to bed yet. I need company."

Then she asked, "What were you supposed to be doing tonight? Did I ruin your evening?"

"No, I had nothing planned. I was going to read."

"But what do you do for excitement? Do you have your girlfriends come onboard and play house? I know you are a Don Juan, Cooper. I heard the funniest story about you the other day."

He smiled. "What did you hear?"

"I heard that last summer, the night of the Labor Day Dance, you ran all the way from Terry Standard's house to your house, naked as a jaybird. Is that true?"

"Partly true," he said. "I didn't have any shoes on. Where did you hear that story?"

"Terry's mother told it at Bridge Club. She said she caught the two of you playing doctor in your birthday suits in her basement playroom. That's pretty good work, Cooper. Terry has a beautiful figure."

She was teasing him, he knew, and he shouldn't rise to the bait. He should dismiss it with a light remark, but he was nettled to think Terry's mother would say that about her, especially to a whole group of women. He asked, "Do the Bridge Club ladies have little drinky-poos when they meet?"

"Oh, yes," she said. "You guessed it, Madame Nipper was nipping."

"Terry would die if she knew her mother told all those women that. The truth is, Terry is a virgin."

"Oh my, aren't we touchy. And I suppose you are a virgin, too?" She said it lightly, trying to ease the tension.

Sensing her efforts to be nice, Cooper smiled boyishly and said, "If males can be said to be virgin, then I deeply regret to say that I'm one of them. My best friend at school used to kid me about it. I've tried to do something about it, but so far no success."

"Cooper!" she said, "You are being too serious, and you are embarrassing me. But I promise you any man who looks as delicious as you do is not going to have to worry about his sex life much longer."

There was something inviting in the way she spoke. Her reference to him as a man stirred him. In the yellow light of the cabin's kerosene lamps she looked beautiful and sexy. She was warm in her soft black sweater. There was sheen on her skin. Tiny beads of perspiration clung to her upper lip. Her sleeves were pushed back and he gazed longingly at the fine down on her forearms. He realized he could see each individual hair. He tried to imagine what the hair between her legs might look like. His deep voice was thick when he spoke. "How about you?"

She knew what he meant but stalled to think. She was concerned that this was getting out of hand. Although she had wanted to have him in bed ever since she first saw him, she had never intended to seduce him. Still, this situation would make it easy. "How about me, what?" she asked.

He couldn't imagine how he was managing to be so bold. He felt possessed. It was as if he was outside himself, shocked at what he was hearing himself say, but pleased.

Press on, he said to himself. You'll never get what you don't ask for. The situation is perfect. Don't get shy now. Don't back off.

"How about you and me . . . how about me as your lover? You . . . you are the most desirable woman I know . . ."

"Oh Cooper, that's the nicest compliment an old gray-haired lady like me could get, particularly tonight. But no, I just couldn't. Let's not . . . talk about that."

Press on, he told himself. He thought of the name of the Riverside Yacht Club's Race Committee boat, *Press On Regardless*. That's you Cooper. Press on. She's got to say "no" at first. It's only proper. What I'm doing wrong is I'm talking instead of doing. I must touch her.

He reached across the table and took her hand in both of his. He was trembling. "I'm not totally inexperienced. And I'm a quick learner. And I'm well coordinated . . . and I'm gentle. I'll be very gentle with you."

She smiled sweetly and sadly and shook her head from side to side.

Undaunted, he began to talk faster. "Look, the sex experts say that the eighteen-year-old male is at the peak of his potential. That's me! I'm just past eighteen. I'll be *good* for you." He began to falter. "Dorothy, please. Please don't turn me down. I want you so much." He ran out of words.

She cooed softly to him, as she shook her head in the negative, "No . . . no . . . no." A tear ran down her cheek. "Oh, Cooper, I'm so sorry I led you on. I didn't know what I was doing. Don't you see . . . I just couldn't. Not tonight. Perhaps another time, I would love it. I have thought of making love with you, what it would be like. I have, honest. You are an exciting man. I just couldn't make love to anyone tonight."

He stood up, ashamed of himself. "I want to apologize. I was way out of line. I . . ."

"Oh no you don't! Don't you dare back away from one of the best compliments I've ever had in my life." She walked up to him and held his face in her hands. She went up on tiptoe, pulled his face down and kissed him warmly on the mouth. "I'll never forget this night, and how you made me feel good about myself again. Another time, and another place, if you still want to, I'll go to bed with you and keep you awake all night. But tonight I'm going back to my cabin alone." She turned and disappeared through the stern passageway.

Cooper examined himself for wounds. I guess I'm OK, he thought. I'm glad I tried. I'm sorry I failed. I guess I love her for treating me so nicely. I guess I'll love her more, just for pure beautiful lust. Another time, she said. Wow, do you suppose she meant it? She didn't have to say it. She does mean it. Will there ever be another chance? I'll make one. By God, I'll make one!

He left one kerosene lamp going in the main cabin. He went up to check the anchor line to be sure their anchor had not dragged. He felt he was a knight and Dorothy was his queen. He would protect her against anything. He told himself he would die for her. He took a leak over the side because it was much more pleasant than using the head next to his cabin. There were phosphorescent organisms in the water, and they flashed brightly when his urine hit the surface.

Who else do you know, Dorothy, who can piss fire? I should've asked her that! He smiled to himself and went below to his berth up forward.

His cabin was warm. He opened a hatch over his head. Removing his khaki shirt and trousers, he went to sleep in the raw. The stars were bright overhead through the hatchway.

Any good small-boat seaman sleeps lightly when his vessel is riding on an anchor. Cooper was no exception. He awoke unexpectedly in the night, but did not know why. He snapped on a red overhead light. In case he had to go on deck, the red light, unlike a white one, would not spoil his night vision. He checked his pocket compass to see if the boat had swung at her anchor and was lying in a different position. It had not. He heard a noise astern below decks. Instinctively he hopped lightly to the cabin sole and dashed into the Great Cabin, oblivious to the fact that he was naked.

She was there. The golden light from the single kerosene lamp shone on her body. She wore only tiny black panties. They were mostly lace. The sight was breathtaking. Her breasts were perfect—small, erect, the nipples hard and pointed. "Can a lady change her mind?" she asked.

He audibly sucked in his breath.

She came to him and pressed herself against him. She laid her cheek on his chest. The feel of her skin against his was unbelievable. He began to tremble. She whispered to him. "Now we are going to dispel your hangup about being a virgin."

"How are we going to do that?" he asked in mock naivety.

"Come with me, bold lancer." She took him by the hand and led him to her after-cabin.

He was to recall afterwards that it was an almost ethereal experience, rather than biological. She awakened him later in the night and they made love again, more insistently. Then, in the early morning hours, she was ravenous and they stayed in bed together for an hour.

That evening, long after Dorothy had gone home to the Kowlicker mansion in Greenwich, she reached him on the telephone at the club dock. She said she was not going to leave Anthony, at least for now. She said her husband knew about her relationship with Cooper, but that he, Cooper, need not be concerned about that.

Cooper's paychecks kept coming through the mail as they had before. He kept the boat ready to sail all the time. Several times Dorothy came to sail with him by herself. At least once a week she came to him in the evenings and spent the night with him on the boat. Cooper did not see Anthony Kowlicker again for the rest of the summer.

CHAPTER 7

1956-1959

Cooper and George roomed together during their freshmen year at Harvard. They liked their teachers and adjusted to learning in large seminar groups for some of their courses. They were better prepared for the rigorous academic demands than were their freshmen counterparts from public schools. They were forewarned, however, about the hazards of complacency and successfully avoided the consequences of the "freedom shock" of college.

The temptations of Boston's nightlife were tempered by the exhaustion of daily football practice. They both made the freshmen team. Cooper, particularly, was pleased to find that he could make the grade in college competition. George, as in the past, was a standout as a running back. Cooper sustained injuries to both knees and was in and out of play. Despite the team trainer's skill with adhesive tape, he kept reinjuring them. Before the season was over, Cooper had to drop out for knee operations. His surgeon told him that if he kept playing football he might sustain sufficient damage so as not to be able to walk. Without great regret, he gave up the sport and other contact athletics.

Sports were a way of life in boarding school. Success brought the gratification of hero status. In college, however, there were so many exciting things to do that Cooper looked forward to some free afternoons. His marks improved and he gradually found himself moving in the clique of the campus intellectuals. Some of his professors invited him to parties, and he found their world of ideas and the intellect to be more exciting than that of the campus jocks.

If anything, Cooper and George gradually moving into different social groups served to strengthen their friendship. George began to threaten longstanding records for yards gained and points scored in varsity football. George's became the best-known name at Harvard. Cooper found he enjoyed a special prestige because he was George's close friend.

When Terry Standard graduated from Ethel Walker she decided to take a year off before going to college. A few months later she wrote to Cooper telling him she was going to get married to a fellow named Charlie who was in the construction business. She said that she didn't want to go to college and hoped to have babies instead; that she would miss Cooper, and hoped he would wish her luck, and maybe even come to the wedding, if he could. Cooper did both and bought her a toaster for a wedding present. Terry was obviously happy. Cooper found the event depressing and he wished he hadn't come except that Terry was so pleased that he did. She said she hoped they would always be good friends. Cooper left the reception early and called Dorothy Kowlicker, whom he found was in Switzerland for a few weeks. He spent a restless night thinking about Terry surrendering her closely guarded virginity to Charlie, who seemed to be grown-up and a man of substance who had the world, as well as his girl, by the tail.

At college, Cooper majored in literature because he liked it and he didn't quite know what else to do. In the back of his mind he had the thought that he would like to teach English at Lawrenceville. George thought this was silly because there was no money in it and that Cooper was clearly cut out for great things at something far more important. For his part, George decided that he would major in economics and go to Harvard Business School, unless he got a good offer in pro football. Cooper's friends on the faculty said that teaching in a prep school was all very nice but he really should go for a doctorate and teach in college where the action was. Cooper decided that sooner or later he would know what to do and that he wouldn't worry about it for now. Secretly, he expected some unforeseen external power to come along and launch him into a great career in which he would become influential and widely admired. Being a United States Senator from Connecticut would be nice. He took a couple of courses in political science and several in history with that possibility vaguely in mind. However, when invited to become involved in some political activity by his intellectual friends, he found himself unable to get interested.

One of the bright young socialites in Cooper's class was Dexter O'Brian, known affectionately to his friends as Doby, a nickname that came from his initials. Doby was a darling of some of the younger professors and instructors. He was clever and had a good mind for minutiae regardless of its importance. An instructor in a literature course that Cooper took with Doby commented that Doby's brain was an indiscriminate sponge that soaked up perfume and piss with equal speed. Doby was rich, came from New York and prepared at an exclusive New England prep school.

A charming companion and gracious host, Doby had cultivated Cooper's friendship since their freshman year. He had from time-to-time suggested that he fix Cooper up with his beautiful and precocious younger sister. Nothing ever came of that. However, in their junior year Doby's sister enrolled at nearby Wellesley College for her freshman year. She was eighteen years old.

One Saturday evening when there were no parties for them to go to, Cooper, Doby and two other friends decided to have dinner in a downtown restaurant famous for its seafood. Afterward, Doby suggested they go to a slightly notorious club called The Captain's Daughter. The floorshow featured male dancers in drag, or as the master of ceremonies called them, "female impersonators."

They were no sooner seated than Doby said, "My God! There's my sister across the room. Now, at long last, Cooper, you can meet her." He hopped up and moved between the tables with his usual air of confidence and nonchalance.

Doby's sister was even more beautiful in the flesh than Cooper had pictured her. She still had her summer tan, long, straight black hair and looked very chic in a black party dress. Her companions were a dramatic contrast. The men were older than the college crowd. They wore sharkskin suits and silk shirts. The women looked cheap and over made-up. Doby gushed, "Look at you, you pretty thing . . . and you're so naughty to be seen in a place like this." He flashed a broad smile, designed to disarm, at her huge, hard-looking escort.

"Sweetie," Doby said, "you must come over to my table and meet my friends, particularly Cooper Morgan, whom I have told you about." He said the last part with animation and a wink.

"She's goin' nowhere," said the big man, "So fly away, fairy godmother."

Doby regarded the man with that calm assurance of the very rich and drawled, "Bite your tongue, cretin."

The girl, sensing immediate disaster, screamed to her brother. Simultaneously, the giant came out of his chair and a great ham fist crashed into the middle of Doby's face. There was the sickening sound of crunching bones and a "splat" like a mallet hitting a grapefruit. A red spray exploded from Doby's surprised face and blood from his pulverized nose covered his white shirt. A great keening wail broke forth from Doby's throat, as he staggered back. As the big man moved towards him for the killing blow, Cooper raced across the floor. His first thought was that he must restore order by talking reason. As he approached the scene, the huge aggressor sensed a serious threat. The girl was pulling at him. In order to get a clear field to fight, the giant backhanded her as if to brush away a fly. She went reeling backwards across a table amidst a crash of glassware. Seeing this, Cooper knew he had to disable the brute.

As Cooper came up to him, the big man aimed a crushing blow to his head. Cooper ducked under it and drove his right fist with all his strength into his opponent's midsection. The air went out of him in a great "whoosh." As he doubled up, Cooper chopped down at his head with his left. At the same time Cooper slammed his knee into the giant's face. He came up raging and bloody. Cooper landed three fast, hard blows to the big man's eyes, and another sweeping, fierce punch to his stomach. At this point the titan's companions moved cautiously in on Cooper, who hopped back, picked up a chair and brought it crashing down among them with huge force. One lay disabled on the floor, the others backed off. The big man was still on his feet, but he was blinded by blood in his eyes and he staggered off to the side, pawing the air. Cooper knew that he could not sustain his drive against so many antagonists. Every muscle in his body ached. He looked quickly around the room and saw his friends on either side of Doby, supporting him through the door. Realizing he was all alone, Cooper halfway turned to rush for the door himself. But he remembered the girl. She was on her feet. Her huge escort was almost on top of her, still clawing the air blindly. She pushed him in the ribs and he gradually toppled over like a great redwood, crashing in slow motion to the ground. The crash was loud and the big man's companions stared at him in awe and disbelief. Seeing the opportunity of distraction, Cooper dove for the girl's waist, came up with her over his shoulder and dashed for the door.

Outside, the damp night air cooled the adrenaline in his blood. He put the girl down and they ran hand in hand down a side street. He made two quick turns to confuse any pursuers and then decided he had none. Luck was with them, and an empty taxi cruised by. They jumped in. Cooper started to collect his thoughts. "Do you have to go back to Wellesley now? Do they expect . . . ?"

"I'm signed out for the weekend," she said.

"In that case we'd better head for your brother's place. He'll be going there and he'll be worried about you." Doby had his own apartment in Cambridge, which he preferred to dormitory housing.

"Who were those brave guys who let you do all the fighting?" she asked.

"They were taking care of Doby," he said, aware that he sounded defensive on their behalf. He laughed, "I guess they think I can take care of myself."

"I guess you *can*, too." Her voice was husky. She put her hand on his chest and another on his cheek. She stared at his face. "You don't have a mark on you."

"Well, my hands are sort of messed up." He lifted them up to look at and she took them in her hands. Although the cab was dark, it was still apparent that the skin was gone from his knuckles and they were bleeding. She kissed them in a totally unselfconscious gesture.

They found that Doby's apartment was empty, but the doorman recognized Cooper and let him in. Cooper pulled off his suit jacket and crashed on the couch. His shirt was soaked in perspiration. She got some salve from the medicine chest and put it on his hands. Then she wrapped them in cold, wet washcloths. She had a bruise on her cheek, which was swelling. Her hair was in charming disarray and she looked more beautiful than ever. He thought there was an exotic look to the delicate arch of her eyebrows.

She brought a bowl of water and a washcloth and began to unbutton his shirt. She peeled it off him and began to wash his chest and arms. "Jesus, you have hard muscles," she said. "You are really big, aren't you? I like big men."

"So I noticed."

She laughed. "Yeah, well you've got to believe that was my first date with him . . . and last. It was stupid. I was playing the spoiled, jaded bitch. Well, that's what I am. I am. I thought he was exciting. I never knew a man like that before. It was an adventure. You know? A lark. Didn't turn out so well did it? Poor Doby got his beautiful face rearranged. I might have too. Let's not talk about him, let's talk about you, Cooper Morgan."

"How do you know my name?"

Doby told me all about you. Said I'd cream in my pants over you. He was right. My name is Nancy O'Brian."

"I know," he said, "Doby told me I'd cream my pants."

She laughed, "And have you?"

"I guess I started to," he said, "But then I became more concerned with your survival. Now, you're starting to get to me again."

She gave him a hard, straight look. "Don't push it, OK?"

She shook her head, as if coming out of a trance. "Hey," she said, "I'm sorry. It's just that I'm not in the mood. I was really frightened back there. I guess I'm still a little shaky."

She took the washcloths off his hands and looked at his bruised, skinless knuckles. She shuddered involuntarily and went out of the room. She came back with more salve and gauze bandage rolls. She carefully cleaned and dressed the torn flesh and wrapped his big hands in neat bandages.

He held them up to look at them. His wrists disappeared into the white wrappings. There was no sign of thumbs or fingers. "You're a sneaky kid," he said. "Your chastity is preserved. Your knight is helpless and cannot claim his prize."

Her laughter was a shower of tinkling glass. She spun in a circle, singing to herself. "Nancy has tamed the giant killer. At last! I have done something intelligent." She went to Doby's bar and looked in. "Would you like some Scotch, Cooper Morgan?"

"On the rocks with no water," he said. "And find me a straw."

She could not find a straw but she snuggled up next to him and held the glass to his lips whenever he asked for it. He found her close proximity and the perfume of her hair and body intoxicating. He asked her to remove his shoes, and she did. She said he really needed to be sponge-bathed all over. He said that would be delightful. So, she led him to the bathroom and dropped his trousers and briefs. She washed him clinically and without arousing him, but she told him his penis was beautiful and he thanked her. She found a great Turkish towel and wrapped it around him and tucked it so that it went from below his armpits to below his knees. She remarked about the surgical scars the operations had left on his knees and he told her about his terminated athletic career. She went to Doby's bedroom to find something to wear. He stood in the doorway watching her. She found a clean red jogging suit and laid it out on the bed. As she started to get undressed she told him to come no closer, but she didn't ask him to leave. The grace of her lean young body made him take short breaths. When she was bare, she did a slow pirouette for him.

"Nice?" she asked.

"Unbelievable," he replied.

She grinned, threw him a pelvic bump and scurried into the jogging suit like an embarrassed little girl. "Another time," she said.

God, what a wild little witch, he said to himself. She's the most fascinating female I have ever seen!

Doby's apartment had a guest room and Cooper assumed she meant to use it for herself because she pulled down the covers of Doby's big double bed for him.

"Want to sleep with the towel on?" she asked.

He shook his head in the negative, so she unfastened it, and let it drop to the floor. He slid between the sheets with his bandaged hands on either side of his head. She turned the hi-fi to soft music, turned out the lights, and then, to his surprise, she crawled in with him.

She snuggled up to him and whispered, "I can't make love with you, Cooper, I'm still frightened." She slid her hand across his chest and squeezed him. The soft material of the jogging suit felt pleasant on his skin.

"Hold me Cooper," she whispered, "hold me." He could feel her trembling.

In later years, when he looked back, he decided this was the moment when he fell truly, deeply in love for the first time in his life. Her wild streak was dazzling. Her beauty was clean, fresh, and exotic. She was generous—dressed his torn hands even though the sight of them was revolting. She washed him. Showed him her body. She didn't say she would not make love because she was saving it for some guy in the future. Most of all, it was her need, her vulnerability—the fear. That night he lay awake for a while, sexually excited but immobilized, feeling her tremble. Suddenly, holding her and protecting her was the most important thing in the world.

In the morning, he awoke with her astride him. She was tickling him in the ribs and giggling in his face. "Good morning, 'Lone Ranger.' Your fair maiden will get you breakfast. What are your buddies going to say when I tell them I got in bed with you for the whole night and you didn't do *anything*? They'll say 'Cooper's queer, for sure.'"

He grabbed her in his arms, arched his back and flipped on top of her. "Maybe I'll tell 'em the lady threw herself at me, but she just wasn't good enough to turn me on."

She squealed and struggled, laughing. The bruise on her cheek had spread to a classic black eye.

"On the other hand, what makes the lady think she's safe now? It's not too late for the Lone Ranger to shoot his silver bullets."

She twisted and slid out of bed, shrieking with joy. She pulled the covers with her and left him naked. A full bladder had given him a firm morning erection. She pointed to it in mock horror, jumping backwards and up and down. "Jeepers creepers!" she screamed. "How could any woman take *that* monster into her body? Certainly not me." She broke off into gales of laughter and ran from the room.

He struggled to his feet without using his hands, which were stiff and sore. He walked to the bathroom with his erect member pointing the way. He had just emptied his bladder when she came in with his big towel.

"If you had waited a minute, I would have held it for you." She looked up at him with an impish grin. She wrapped the towel around him. She brushed his teeth, and she shaved him, and she combed his dark hair.

"I'm worried about Doby," Cooper said. "I thought he would have come home."

"Let's call up one of your friends who was with you last night," she suggested.

Cooper did that. She dialed for him. He learned that Nancy's brother was at Mass General Hospital. They had decided to admit him when he arrived at the emergency room last night. "He's got to have an operation on his nose, to make it right," Cooper explained to Nancy.

They reached Doby on the phone in his room and agreed to bring him the things he needed from his apartment. They got in to see him. He was surprised to see Nancy's vivid black eye and Cooper's bandaged hands. He told them he and his friends had gone to the police and returned with them to the Captain's Daughter, to find the place in great turmoil. But all of the combatants were gone. Witnesses filled them in on the events. Nancy told him of Cooper's dashing victory and that she spent the night with him in Doby's bed.

"I knew the two of you would hit it off," said Doby in a matter-of-fact tone. "Tell me, Nancy dear, is he a good lay?"

"Couldn't tell you, Doby darling. His hands were too messed up and I just wasn't up to it. Next weekend though, you're going to lend us your apartment, darling, and we're going to find out. Aren't we, Cooper, dear?"

"Huh? Sure, oh yeah, that's what we're going to do," said Cooper.

"Like hell you are," said Doby. "Go find your own fucking place. I need my apartment."

"No, brother dear," she cooed, "You're going to insist that we have your apartment for the weekend. And you are *not* going to tell Daddy that I was at the place where you got your sweet little face pushed in. And I am going to tell him what a hero you were in defending a young girl's honor by soundly thrashing a terrible bully who got in one lucky punch and broke your little nosey for you." Her voice grew firm. "All that's just the way things are going to be, isn't it Doby?"

"Yes," said Doby in a subdued tone. "If that's what you want, honey, you got it."

Cooper felt uncomfortable and said, "I have to get goin' guys."

"Me too," said Nancy.

They headed out in order to find Cooper's friend, Harvard's Athletic Department trainer. Cooper figured he could repair his hands efficiently and well.

On the way, Nancy said, "Don't believe all that bitchy talk back there, darling. I don't really know anything about making love with somebody. I just always seem to have to put on an act for my brother. I'm afraid to go all the way with you, Cooper, but I want to. I want whatever you want. I want to make you happy, and I want you to like me. What do I have to do? Oh, darling, let's be together next weekend. Just ourselves. At his apartment, and I'll do my best for you, if I can, but . . . no promises, OK?"

Cooper smiled at her: "That sounds like the best offer I've got at the moment and you don't have to do anything you don't want to, but . . ."

"But what?" she asked.

"But if you leave me as horny as I am right now, I'll go crazy."

Cooper's friend, the trainer, worked miracles on his knuckles. He left them with only small thin bandages, and the thumbs free. Nancy charmed the older man and told him about the fight. He ventured the opinion that

Cooper could become a great heavyweight. "You're about a hundred and ninety pounds now, right? No fat on ya. And look at that reach! With your speed and reflexes, I could make us both rich. Would you like that, ma'am? You gonna marry this girl, Coop? You could do worse, I'll tell ya! You must weigh in at about one o' five pounds. Can you take care of a big boy like this? Yeah, I bet you can! Well, what are you still doin' here? I got work to do. Get out of here you foolish kids. I love ya."

Monday night, Cooper called Nancy and proposed that they start the next weekend on Friday evening instead of Saturday. She agreed that was a good idea. On Tuesday afternoon, Copper called her and proposed that they study together that evening. It was not a success. All they did was talk and kiss and nuzzle each other and they didn't get any studying done. On Wednesday afternoon, Nancy called Cooper and proposed they cut Friday classes and start the weekend on Thursday afternoon. He thought that was a brilliant idea. Would Doby be willing to get out on Thursday afternoon, as the start of the weekend? Well, with any luck, Doby wouldn't even be out of the hospital by then, because there had been several delays in having his operation. On Thursday morning Nancy called to discuss menus, because she was not prepared food-wise and, incidentally, Doby was going home to New York as soon as he got out of the hospital and not coming back until Monday morning, so they might as well plan to stay together Sunday night too. Also, she wanted him to know that she was a little scared and please not to expect too much of her, you know, at least the first night. Cooper cut his Thursday afternoon classes and picked up his bag that had already been packed for a couple of days. He picked up some Scotch and champagne, and arrived at Doby's apartment. Nancy was there already settled in. She was dressed in an expensive lounging suit. There were candles everywhere and flowers. He gave her a long low whistle.

"I bought it for the occasion," she said. "You like?"

"Cream in my pants," he said.

"I also bought black stockings, a lace garter belt and some very naughty lingerie that I'm embarrassed to even look at, let alone try on!" She dropped her voice. "I also bought some contraceptive jelly and rubbers for the monster."

He swept her up in his arms and kissed her hard. "You're an angel."

She went into a good Mae West imitation, "But I'm gonna be a devil tonight."

He rubbed her nose with his.

Mae West continued, "Put me down big boy, I'm getting so hot I'll burn your hands."

"Why don't we get it over with," he said. "Then we can relax together."

She looked horrified, "What do you mean?"

"Well, gosh," he said, "we're nervous about it now. By evening we'll be crawling up the walls. If we just go on in there to bed and get at it . . . break the ice so to speak, why then we can have some leisurely cocktails and talk about how it was, and then have dinner and then we'll be ready for another go at it. Only then we'll have had some practice, and not be so nervous, and be getting more used to each other as sex partners, and then . . ."

She stamped her foot, "You bastard!" Her voice was high and small. There were tears in her eyes. "If you came here just to get your rocks off and not because you care about me . . ."

"Hey, a bad idea. I'm sorry. I love you, Nancy. This is the first chance I've had to tell you that. So, it's not a time to cry. I was afraid to tell you I love you. I was afraid you'd think I was corny."

"Oh, I love you, Cooper. I love you so much I don't know what to do." She sobbed some more and sniffled. She pulled out his shirttail and wiped her eyes. She slid her hands under his shirt and felt his skin. Then, she reached around him and hugged him. He buried his face in the hair on top of her head. She began to snicker mischievously and tickle him. He put his hands under her blouse.

She giggled and thrust one hand down inside the front of his pants. In a mock deep professor-like voice she said, "And what do ve have here? Vhere did that big monster go? Ah, *here* he is!"

Five minutes later they were in the bedroom. Half an hour later they were dozing. She wiggled in his arms and whispered, "You were right my love. From now on, I know—my love is always right."

His voice was deep and husky, "About what?"

"About how it's better to get it over with and relieve the tension, and then we can do it again, only better."

"It's too soon to do it again. You forgot about having the cocktails, and you cooking dinner, and . . ."

"Who knows how to cook dinner? I like the cooking right here."

"But you said it hurt."

"It did, but then it was wonderful. And I didn't bleed much, did I?"

"You really didn't ever do it before, did you?"

"I told you I haven't."

"Yeah, but sometimes you talk like you've done everything. And I don't know what to think."

"I don't know what took me so long. I have come so close so many times, but I've always gotten out of it at the last minute. And now that I've found out what I've been missing, I'm going to make up for lost time with you darling. OK?"

He stretched and smiled at her. "That's just awful, and I am ashamed of you. *However*, if that's what you really want, I'm going to make an exception in your case. Normally it's just one to a customer, but for you, well, I guess I'm going to have to spoil you. But, now I want a Scotch. And I want you to get it for me because I want to watch your beautiful bare fanny swishing back and forth as you walk away."

She frowned, then smiled, then hopped lightly up and swung her hips in an exaggerated way. As she walked out of the room, she let out a string of hair-raisingly vulgar words in her Mae West accent.

The four days went fast. They spent most of the time in bed. They catnapped day and night. They played games they made up. They explored each other and they tried most of the exotic things they had ever heard of and some they had never heard of. They laughed a lot, particularly at the experiments that did not go well. They managed to prepare a few meals to keep up their strength. Nancy did better at this. She looked radiant as they left the apartment. Cooper looked a little thin. "What can we ever do for an encore?" he asked. "When we get married, what can we possibly do for a honeymoon?"

She smiled at him, "Practice, my love, practice."

They managed to be together almost every weekend through the fall. They utilized hotels and motels, borrowed rooms and apartments. George RedThunder became accustomed to walking in, in the morning, to find Nancy in Cooper's bed. They managed copulation in unusual places: the common room of her dormitory; a cemetery; the back of a bus; a wrestling room in Harvard's gym; in movies, parking lots, the basements of a couple of churches; and in Harvard stadium during a football game, in the rain, under a poncho. They got caught a couple of times and ran and laughed until they had hysterics.

Nancy spent Thanksgiving at the Rectory in Riverside. She made friends with Cooper's mother and she wrapped his father around her finger.

Leslie and Kate caught them in Cooper's bed in the morning, because the girls liked to sneak to his room, rush in and wake him up, and sit on his bed to tell him about their lives. Leslie and Kate woke them up and told them they were naughty but extracted tribute by trading silence for extra attention from the big brother they worshipped.

The day after Christmas, Cooper went to visit Nancy in New York for the rest of the vacation. They went to a lot of elegant parties and Cooper charmed most of Nancy and Doby's friends, as well as their parents.

Nancy had gone to a doctor in Boston to be fitted for a diaphragm. She tried to keep it with her at all times because her lusty escapades with Cooper were so often impulsive, and, therefore, at unlikely times and places. Once, at a crazy party with good friends, it had fallen out of her sleeve where she had forgotten she had tucked it. They had all played Frisbee with it, until it got torn and discarded. That night in Cooper's room, she improvised a contraceptive by shaking a root beer bottle with her thumb over the top and using it as a douche. This left the floor sticky from the sugar in the spilled root beer.

George walked in the sticky place when he came into the room that night, raised hell with them for messing the place up and leaving it like a pig pen, asked who the hell was rooming with who anyway and said if Cooper wanted him to move out all he had to do was say so, for Christ's sake.

Nancy was crushed. How totally thoughtless I have been, she thought. I am an intrusion in the most beautiful friendship I have ever witnessed or been aware of. You're such a complete bitch, Nancy. You not only fowl your own nest, but other's as well. But what can I do? I can't give up Cooper. Cooper is my life, my joy, my buddy, my friend, my lover. Cooper and "the monster" are the fabric of my life. I only study hard and get good grades for him. So he will be proud of me. What can I do?

It came to her as a fuzzy idea at first. Slowly, the idea became clearer. Then, the sure certainty of it produced its own plan just as naturally as night follows day.

Cooper and RedThunder are a team. They are like the Corsican Brothers. There is a bond between them that is exceptional. How stupid for me never to have seen it. I must love RedThunder, too! I must value him as Cooper does. How else could I be worthy of Cooper? How else could I ever hope to keep him?

She mounted a campaign. It was subtle but intensive and unwavering. She cleaned their room regularly. She changed the sheets on their beds. She had never done housekeeping before but she did it with joy and compulsion now. She discovered George's birthday was coming up so she paid for and staged a huge birthday party that the whole class would not likely ever forget. The fact that George was a campus celebrity made it that much more exciting. Cooper was delighted and joined in with enthusiasm.

Nancy fussed over George, looked out for him. She counseled his dates. She did everything humanly possible to make his life go smoothly and well. She gave him back rubs and rubbed knots out of his muscles. She told him she would go to bed with him, if he wanted her to.

"Why would you do that?" he asked.

"Because you are Cooper's best friend. He would do anything for you and, therefore, I would too." she replied.

"Have you consulted Cooper about this?"

"No," she said.

"I think maybe you should, and if he says OK, you're on." He began to snicker. "In the meantime," he said, "How about a hand job?"

"OK."

He broke into a peal of laughter. "You are too much, Nancy. I'm not sure whether you're putting me on or not, but you sure are turning me on. I'd give anything to have a girl like you, but you're Cooper's girl, not mine."

CHAPTER 8

1966

After arriving at Grand Central Terminal, Cooper Morgan made his way directly to the hospital where Nancy Morgan lay in critical condition. He identified himself at the nurse's station and was told that Doctor Taylor, a neurological specialist, was with her. The Doctor came out of Nancy's room and told Cooper that his wife had been conscious when she was brought in, but had slipped into a coma several hours ago.

"It's not a good sign, I'm afraid," the specialist said. "We don't know when she will come out of it."

"Do you know that she *will* come out of it?" asked Cooper.

The Doctor gave him a wistful smile and said, "No. We don't know that for sure. Nothing is certain at this point. But she's young and strong and there's a good chance that she will be all right."

Cooper went into Nancy's room. There was a nurse with her and a machine was monitoring Nancy's life functions. Her left leg was in a cast and was suspended from a trapeze. She had a black eye, much like the one she had the night that Cooper first met her. Nancy's eyes were closed, her face was pale and in repose. Her dark straight hair was combed. She looked quite frail and lovely. He pulled a chair up beside the bed and sat down. He took one of her hands in both of his and quietly looked into her face. He sat that way for a long time. The nurse remained silent. After some considerable time, she stretched and walked out to take a break.

She stopped at the nurse's station down the hall and said, "That is one lucky lady back there . . . if she lives. That gorgeous big male sure is in love with her. He just sits there and stares at her face. It's like he's in a trance. I don't think I ever saw anyone sit so still for so long."

Eventually, Nancy's parents arrived. Cooper greeted them quietly. Nancy's mother fussed with the bedding, and patted Nancy's hair. Blakely O'Brian spoke with the nurse in charge. He determined that nurses would be in her room around the clock. Cooper sought out Doctor Taylor and they had a family conference with him. Blakely O'Brian's friend, the Chief of Surgery at the hospital, came by. He was gracious and reassured them about the quality of care that Nancy was receiving.

Blakely and Muffy O'Brian were a handsome couple. In their early sixties, they were tan and athletic looking. They left the hospital to settle into their Upper East Side house, after getting Cooper's assurance that he would join them there for dinner later. Nancy's brother, Doby, came by towards the end of the day. He and Cooper had a drink together at a neighborhood bar and caught up with each other's news. After a brief, unsatisfactory stint with his father's old brokerage firm on Wall Street, Doby had joined the staff at *Time* magazine. He was now an Associate Editor and was enjoying his work.

Cooper called RedThunder but got no answer. The next day George's office reported that he was in Washington for several days.

Cooper visited Nancy again, and then returned to Essex. On the weekend, he brought Lisa in to see her mother. They stayed overnight with Nancy's parents, but on Sunday he took Lisa home so she wouldn't miss school. Cooper decided it was better to keep busy by continuing to work. He could do nothing for Nancy while she was unconscious. He kept in daily touch by telephone. There was no change.

Sherri Huff took over the Morgan household at Essex. She did the dishes and the laundry. She cleaned and she read to Lisa every evening. The apartment was connected to a dormitory that housed thirty-five boys in the fourth and fifth forms. Cooper was the Housemaster. Also connected to the building was a bachelor apartment that held a young male teacher who assisted Cooper in running the dorm. Cooper usually supervised the evening period just before his boys went to bed at ten o'clock. When he returned to his apartment, Sherri would beat a hasty retreat to the senior girls' dorm. She did her best to play down her curvaceous figure. She wore baggy clothes, no makeup, and she kept her hair in a ragged ponytail.

When Cooper first returned from New York, news of Nancy's accident spread throughout the campus. Sherri had greeted him soberly and said, "I think we had better be good. It was one thing to fool around when she was leaving you alone so often, but now that she's in the hospital and so hurt, I'd feel like a rat to be making love to you."

Cooper nodded and said, "There you are again, being the adult. But you're right. I couldn't do it either. But . . . Sherri, I want you to know that it was wonderful, that one time. I'll never forget. And you will always be . . . always be special to me." Sheri's eyes filled with tears as she fled.

But she came back every day, and she took care of him and Lisa. And they didn't speak of the night they had spent together in bed.

She never called him "Cooper." It was almost always, "Mr. Morgan." But once in awhile when they were alone together she called him "Baby" as she had on that night Cooper remembered so clearly. That was the only sign she gave him that she remembered, or that their relationship was other than student and teacher.

Sherri was a good athlete. She was high scorer the previous fall on the girls field hockey team, and she played fourth on the school's varsity tennis team, which otherwise consisted of boys. She was best known at Essex, however, as the school's leading actress and singer. The stage was her first love and everything related to it was her utmost priority. When speaking, her voice was soft and small. Consequently, when she opened her mouth to sing she bowled her audience over, because she had a rich contralto that could fill any hall with its volume. She sang in the choir, and when she had a solo she could transform an otherwise dull chapel service into an electrifying experience. She also sang in the Glee Club. She sang with the student rock and roll band, her strident, belting voice competing in volume with electric guitars and other amplified instruments. Sherri's mother was a top voice coach in New York for Broadway musical actors. Sherri was one of her star students. Her mother brought Sherri's voice along perfectly as she grew up and it was now beautifully trained. Her gift resulted not so much from raw talent as from the pure joy she took in singing, her remarkable will and determination, and her eagerness to please her mother.

Sherri also loved modern dance and worked hard at it. And she was adept at gymnastics. She saw these things as stage skills, and no stage skill missed her attention. She could even juggle a little bit, and could perform some basic, sleight-of-hand magic tricks. Sherri's father, remarried several times, was a successful director who had made his name on Broadway and was now famous in advertising circles for his prize-winning television commercials.

Her parents expected her to go to college. She had other ideas but, characteristically, she voiced no argument. She merely applied to a college she thought would not accept her, Barnard in New York, and she did not apply to any other. To her amazement, and consternation, she received an acceptance from Barnard the day after she had gone to bed with Morgan. She had failed to take into account the strong recommendation sent from Essex.

Other than the stage, Sherri's chief preoccupation was Cooper. She had never been in love before, but she was now, deeply, and without anguish or bitterness at the barriers that stood between them. Her sense of fairness and sportsmanship kept her from competing for him while Nancy was hospitalized. She reasoned, without any sense of guilt, that Nancy would either die or get well. Then, Sherri would go after him with all the resources available to her. And she expected to win. It occurred to her that a college education might make her more appealing to Cooper, so she decided to postpone her Broadway ambitions.

But before it was time to go off to college, or to win Cooper, Sherri stayed busy with her other love. Elmer Pincer, the talented head of the Music Department at Essex had determined to make the most of his star performer before she graduated. He had written a brilliant, glittering musical comedy as a showcase for Sherri Huff. Spring Musicals were a tradition at the school. They were always well done, but no one could remember a time when they were graced with a singing talent as outstanding as Sherri's.

Spring Term, therefore, found Sherri working hard at rehearsing, at the smooth functioning of the Morgan household, and at a strong academic finish worthy of her acceptance at Barnard.

Lisa and Cooper went to New York to visit Nancy every weekend. At the end of the fifth week, Doctor Taylor told Cooper he was a little encouraged.

"I couldn't be sure at first," the doctor said, "but now I am. There are definite signs of brain activity. The brain waves are getting a little stronger. She's still in a pretty deep coma but sometimes there is something going on. You might say that she is dreaming."

Inside Nancy's room, the nurse jumped to her feet, startled and surprised. "Oh, my dear! You're awake. Can you hear me? Nancy, can you hear me?"

59

"Yes," said Nancy, "I can hear you." Her voice was scratchy. She smiled. Then her eyes grew glassy and she started to close them. She shook her head a little, opened her eyes and focused on the nurse.

"Where am I?" she said.

There was a knock on the door just then and Cooper came into the room. "Oh, my God," he said, "You're awake!" He turned to the nurse. "Why wasn't I told?"

"It just happened. Just now. She just opened her eyes and looked at me."

Cooper dropped to his knees beside the bed. He took Nancy's hand in his. He touched her cheek. "You have been sleeping a long time, my darling," he said. She smiled at him and focused her eyes on him.

CHAPTER 9

The following Monday morning, the Headmaster's office at Essex Academy was a beehive of activity. It was located in an administration building on a central part of the campus across a spacious quadrangle from the Chapel. Architects in another generation had clearly planned the Chapel to be the central building. However, Hyatt Hall, which only housed offices, had for all practical purposes become the school's center. On the first floor, in addition to the Headmaster's office, there was the Admissions Office. The Development and Alumni Offices occupied the basement level. And the offices of the Assistant Headmaster, the Dean, the Treasurer, and the Business Manager were on the second floor. Also on the second floor was a handsomely appointed meeting room known as the Trustees Room.

There were three secretaries outside the Headmaster's Office. One of them had just stepped inside and caught the Headmaster's attention. She said, "Cooper Morgan is here to see you Dr. Frostley." Then, for the benefit of the two men who were earnestly talking to the Headmaster, she added, "You told me to interrupt you when he arrived."

"Quite right." Leighton Frostley nodded his head earnestly and smiled his amiable, almost perpetual, smile. He was a man of considerable bulk, square-shaped and of average height. His white hair was straight and parted perfectly in the middle. He was always meticulously dressed in well-tailored, expensive three-piece suits. This morning's suit was a pearl gray worsted, which he wore with a pale blue, button-down, oxford cloth shirt and a silk Essex Academy tie, in red and blue stripes. A matching silk handkerchief peaked with studied casualness from his breast pocket.

"I must see Morgan on another matter," said the Headmaster. "But while we're all here why don't we ask him about this? He has a good ear to the ground and he's closer to this generation than we are, right?" He chuckled, nodding his head as if encouraging the agreement of his two middle-aged visitors.

Cooper was ushered in. He greeted the Headmaster, addressing him as "sir," and nodded agreeably to the two others who were faculty members and masters of the sixth form boys' dormitory. The two were ill at ease, and Cooper sensed that they were not eager to discuss whatever was on their minds with him.

"Now, Cooper, tell us, have you ever heard of students eating morning glory seeds?" asked the Headmaster.

"No, but I suppose some of them are bound to try it."

"But, why on earth would they do that?"

Cooper said, "A lot of kids think morning glory seeds will make them hallucinate, and to the best of my knowledge there is some truth to the idea. But I don't have any first-hand experience with it. There's a lot of interest in that sort of thing ever since that Harvard fellow came out with what he calls LSD."

"Well, that seems to confirm it,' said Dr. Frostley. "We have a boy, Greg Wheelwright, who seemed to be out of his head last night and jumped out of the third floor window of his dorm. Sprained his ankle is all. Could've killed himself. Damnedest thing. Doctor Hard says he never heard of anyone eating morning glory seeds. Nurse Smith says that's what the boy did. Told her himself. She said he was crazy as a loon when he was brought into the infirmary."

The Headmaster turned to one of the men, putting his hand on his arm. "Tell you what, Bob, pop down to the village, will you? And see who has morning glory seeds for sale. See how many they've got. Buy 'em all up if you can. Then let me know. I'll ask them not to stock 'em. You're doing a first class job. I appreciate it." He herded them gracefully out the door and, as a parting shot said, "I don't think we treat this as a discipline case, fellas. But have that boy, Greg, come see me after his last class today."

The Headmaster turned and grinned at Cooper. "They wanted me to expel that boy. Can you imagine that? Well, I have to admit there is something in the air I don't like. Some of our boys don't want to get haircuts. Think of that! Want to look like those Beatles from England. This generation is getting restless, I tell you. I think it's that damned business in Vietnam. I tell you, we ought to get out of there. Win or lose, but get out."

Leighton Frostley invited Cooper to sit down in an easy chair at one end of the room, away from his desk. There was a large, handsome coffee table there, and an informal grouping of chairs. Cooper realized the Headmaster had something important on his mind when he called a secretary on the intercom, and asked her to bring in two cups and a pot of tea. He remembered that Cooper preferred to drink tea during the day, instead of coffee. Frostley inquired about Nancy and jumped to his feet with enthusiasm when he learned that she was out of the coma, and that her doctors expected rapid progress now.

"Well, that makes what I have to talk to you about all the more interesting," he said. "First of all, I have a bit of nasty business that I must discuss with you, but I just don't quite know how to go about it. It is indelicate."

Dr. Frostley had been Headmaster of Essex since 1935, three years before Cooper had been born. Now, in his early sixties, he seemed alert and capable. Indeed, he was famous in educational circles, widely quoted and admired. He was a bit out of step with the world of young people now, however. Cooper speculated that, while a few years ago he would have been judged as having strong moral standards and a fine sense of decency, he now came off as being a bit prudish and stiff. Cooper smiled at the word "indelicate". It was a Frostley kind of word. So, Cooper was caught off guard by what came next.

"There seems to be a bit of gossip, not much mind you, but, nevertheless, a worrisome sort of unpleasant rumor that, uh . . . Sherri Huff is spending . . . uh, perhaps more time than she ought, at your household. And that your, uh, your relationship with her is . . . is, perhaps . . . ah, not sufficiently professional." Dr. Frostley sighed and said, "I don't think I am making myself sufficiently clear. There is the idea, and I am afraid this may shock you, that you and she are too close."

Cooper said, "Sherri has been babysitting Lisa since Nancy was taken from us. The fact that someone could so grossly misinterpret and add credence to a lie is just awful."

The Headmaster said, "Well, we must put a stop to this rumor. And you must be sure your conduct with Sherri maintains the appearance of propriety."

"I'll do that, sir, you may count on it."

"Fine. Let's say no more about it. I want to change the subject. It is my honor to pass along some exciting news to you, as pleasant as the other is distasteful. I must say though, had your answer been different, I would not have broached this second subject, as you shall see for yourself."

The headmaster cleared his throat and sat back pressing his hands together. "We have talked once or twice about the fact that you might like to seek a headmastership some day, and I hope I have been helpful in exposing you to a number of aspects of school management, such as running the summer school program last year. Well, it has come sooner than I thought it would. I hate to think I might lose you, but I am overwhelmingly proud to think we might lose you to one of the finest schools in the country. I speak of none other than St. Burges School, *the* St. Burges School. What do you think of that?" Frostley beamed at Cooper with fatherly pride.

"Why, I'm overwhelmed!" said Cooper. "How does St. Burges even know I exist?"

"I wish I could take credit for it, but it seems your seminary Dean recommended you to them. The head of their Board of Trustees called me to ask if I would recommend you, and I did, most warmly."

Cooper beamed. "That's exciting. What a marvelous opportunity!"

Dr. Frostley rubbed his hands together in enthusiasm. He said, "Well, I told Bernie about it, and she told me about this Sherri Huff business she had picked up. Therefore, I had to speak to you about that first, of course."

Every weekday morning, there was a gathering at the Headmaster's mansion. All the ladies in the adult community were invited. Those who taught were usually busy. But wives came. Most managed to make it once or twice a week. There were a few regulars who were always there. Little of interest in the way of campus gossip managed to evade these ladies. Nancy thought the whole ritual was ghastly and very seldom appeared.

Cooper said, 'Did Bernie happen to mention where she heard this story about Sherri and me?"

"Oh my no," said the Headmaster. "But, you may be sure, I shall see to it that it is stopped. The thing for you to do is just see that there is nothing that can be misinterpreted. If Lisa needs Sherri, you cannot simply send her away. But I'm sure you can be discrete."

Cooper realized he would be more upset if not for the exciting news about St. Burges. He said, "I thought I was still too young to have an opportunity to be a Headmaster."

"I was only two years older than you, when I came here," replied Frostley. "Besides, if you get it, you will be twenty-nine when you start next year. Others have started at younger ages, including some great ones, such as Verdery at Wooster, and Boyden at Deerfield."

Cooper's mind raced. St. Burges was a beautiful school with one of the largest endowments in the country. If he could get such a distinguished post, he could accomplish some very exciting things. He would certainly feel that he had more than realized his potential as a leader and as a man of consequence. It would vindicate a career decision that many had thought was beneath him and that he, himself, was beginning to have doubts about.

Won't Nancy be pleased, he thought. But then, I might not get it. No, if I set my mind to it, I'll get it. All I need is the opportunity. If I told Frostley the truth about Sherri, I wouldn't have the opportunity. Well, after all, it was only once with Sherri. We've behaved ourselves since. But that's not the point, damnit. This opportunity is predicated on a lie. How am I going to live with that? If I do, I won't be the first—by any means. Is that kind of rationalization going to be good enough? Can't decide now. Lots of time to think about it later.

Cooper asked the Headmaster, "What am I supposed to do now?"

"The head of their Trustees' Search Committee will be getting in touch with you. I just wanted to prepare you for his call," replied Frostley. "Let me know how things go. Come and talk to me if I can help. Obviously, you are free to take time away from your duties here when you need to go meet with the St. Burges people. Keep your head about you. They are sharp. But so are you. Fellow Harvard types." The Headmaster, a Yale man, pretended to be scornful. "A good marriage I suppose, you and all those aristocratic Harvard Episcopalians."

"I'm not part of their world," said Cooper, smiling.

The Headmaster rose, laughing, and patted Cooper on the back. "I know you're not, my boy. I was just having my little joke." He guided Cooper effortlessly to the door. "You'd be a breath of fresh air for those stuffy fellas, Cooper. They'll think you belong, though. You've got a beautiful record at Harvard. Top of your class at General. Oh, you know their language, all right. They'll love you. Keep me posted, now."

Cooper departed Hyatt Hall with a new bounce in his step.

Late that afternoon, Cooper went home to find Sherri had been reading to Lisa from a Nancy Drew mystery, and now they were acting out part of the story. Lisa was Nancy Drew and Sherri was the villain. When Lisa left them to get dressed for dinner, Cooper told Sherri about his conversation with the Headmaster. It seemed the most natural thing in the world for Sherri to be the first to know that he was going to be considered for the Headmastership at St. Burges. She was thrilled for him and said she was sure that he would be their final choice. Cooper went on to tell her about the rumor involving the two of them. He had decided that he would not ask Sherri to stop coming to his apartment. However, he felt she should know that there was a rumor, so that she could be prepared, should she be confronted with it sometime. She seemed to treat the news lightly.

"Baby," she said, "there have been rumors about me, and gossip about my supposed wild sexual adventures on this campus, for the last four years. Almost all of it is fantasy and wishful thinking, by little people whose lives are too dull to suit them. Besides, you and I haven't been foolin' around for weeks. We know it, and that's what counts."

Cooper changed the subject and asked her how the Spring Musical was coming. It was only a few days to the first performance. She said she thought it would be the best ever and told him that her parents were coming. "My father isn't married at the moment, so they're coming together. It makes me want to cry."

The next morning, after breakfast in the school dining room, Sherri watched the Headmaster cross the campus from his house to his office in Hyatt Hall. On an impulse, she walked to his spacious mansion and rang the bell. A maid showed her in and Sherri asked to see Mrs. Frostley.

"Why, Sherri, how delightful that you have come to see me," said Bernadette Frostley, as she glided gracefully into the main living room where Sherri waited. "May I get you some tea? Come sit down, and tell me about the Musical. I hear it is to be a great triumph for you."

Sherri smiled sweetly at the older woman. Sherri's great mop of blonde curls, and her fresh youthful beauty, seemed dazzling in the otherwise drab room. She was like a spray of fresh-cut spring flowers surrounded by dull muted tones. "Mrs. Frostley," she said, "you told your husband you had heard that I was having an affair with Mr. Morgan. Would you please tell me where you got such a story as that?" Sherri stared straight at Bernie.

"Oh, my dear, I couldn't." The older woman was flustered. She had suspected what brought the girl to see her, but she was unprepared for Sherri's poise and directness. "I did hear something about what you say," she admitted. "But, it was expressed merely as a suspicion or a rumor. Not really . . . ah . . . you should not think it was an accusation."

"Is it customary, Mrs. Frostley, for you to deal in rumors? Unfounded rumors, that can hurt people?"

Bernie couldn't decide whether the girl was being impertinent or justifiably forthright. She did know the girl's candor was embarrassing her. She could feel herself blushing. "Oh, Sherri, I don't know what to say. I did not mean to hurt you, or Mr. Morgan. I try not to keep anything from my husband. Anything that affects the well-being of the school. I suppose Mr. Frostley spoke to you about it or, more likely, to Mr. Morgan. Isn't that the right thing to do? When there are ugly things, even untrue ones, shouldn't they be faced?"

"That's what I want to do, Mrs. Frostley, I want to face the person who told this to you."

Bernie held firm and did not reveal her source. She did not want to run the risk of losing any source of information. However, she apologized profusely to Sherri. But she wasn't quite sure why she did. Bernie felt very uncomfortable. She had been told off soundly by a mere slip of a girl. It was interesting that Sherri didn't even deny it. She didn't even condescend to deal with the rumor. What a forceful little thing she was. Bernie realized she had been taken by a real pro. She did not want to be *that* girl's enemy. So she had better do what she promised and put a stop to the rumor. And, she had better start right now. There couldn't be any truth to it, anyway. Not with that sort of reaction from Sherri.

As Sherri walked away from the Headmaster's house, she smiled to herself. I think I won a round for my Baby, she mused. Shall I tell him? Nope. Us girls can't let our men know everything. Huh, does he even know he's my man? Pretty soon, I guess, I'll make sure he knows.

"Hey, Sherri, are you talking to yourself?"

She turned to see a small bright-eyed fourth former with curly red hair. "Hello, Monkey," she said, "How are you doing?"

"Oh, my God, Sherri, don't you call me that dumb name. I thought you were my friend."

"What do you want me to call you, *Crafty*?"

"My name is Adrian."

"Are you still selling marijuana, Adrian?"

"I'll get you some if you want it, Sherri, I can get you LSD, too."

"Thanks, but no thanks, Adrian."

"Sherri, I've got all your songs from the show on tape now. They really sound great. Do you want to hear them? I'll give you the tape, if you want it. I have a duplicate," said Adrian.

The boy with sparkling eyes was an odd sort of loner in the student body. He had come to the school a year earlier and had already established a record of sorts, for flunking more courses than anyone else without flunking out of school. He heard a different drummer, and had some sort of learning disability that could not be defined or explained by the best experts. For all this, he was romping through the most advanced math courses with straight A's and he was an electronic genius. Monkey, as almost everyone called him, was invaluable to the Dramatic Department. He was a wizard with stage lighting and sound amplification.

He lived in Cooper's dormitory, and it was only through Copper's persuasive arguments in faculty meetings that he was still at Essex. So far, Cooper had managed to convince most of his colleagues that a school with high standards still ought to have room and flexibility to accommodate a talented student who did not fit the mold. The faculty would have been more distressed if they knew everything about Monkey Craft that Cooper knew. For example, Cooper had been plagued for months by stealing in his dormitory. He finally caught the culprit, Monkey, but he didn't report him. Housemasters were allowed discretion in matters of discipline by school policy. The Dean practically never got a discipline report from Cooper's dormitory. Cooper handled it effectively from within. The Dean had no complaints. He had enough to do with the teachers and dorm people who could not manage proper student behavior without front office backup.

Cooper was determined to bring out the best in Monkey. He knew if he were expelled, no one else would solve the boy's problems. As near as Cooper could tell, Monkey did not steal again. He did not know that Monkey had become a drug dealer.

"Oh, Adrian, you are an angel! I'd love to hear the tape, and I'd love to have it to keep. Will you play it for me this afternoon, after rehearsal?"

"Sure I will, anytime you want. Anytime."

CHAPTER 10

Nancy was thrilled when Cooper reached her on the telephone. Her father had it installed in her room as soon as she was out of the coma. Cooper told her about the St. Burges School possibility and she told him it was wonderful.

"I'll do my best to be a good headmaster's wife, darling," she said. "But I have my own ideas about how a headmaster's wife should be."

"I bet you do. Well, I have some ideas of my own about running a school that some might find a little different."

"Cooper, do headmasters fool around in bed with their wives?"

"If they don't we're going to change the rules about that, too."

"Oh, that's nice, love. I got the cast off my leg today, so I'll start practicing my bumps and grinds. Do you know what? They told me my collarbone was broken and I never knew it. It's all well now, and they say my leg is good, too. The Doctor spent an awful long time feeling my leg, Cooper. Do you think that's nice?"

"You don't want a dumb doctor, do you?" Cooper asked. "That just proves he's a smart fellow and knows a good thing when he feels it."

"Darling, do charm those St. Burges people when you see them. I'd just love to get away from Essex. It could be a new start for us. Do you know what I mean?"

"I know what you mean, Nanny. I'll do my best."

The call came the next day. It was from the president of one of the leading Hartford based insurance companies, Edward P. Janes, who was head of the St. Burges Trustees' Search Committee. After a few pleasantries, Cooper told Janes he was eager to interview for the Headmaster position.

"That's just grand, Mr. Morgan," replied Janes. "It was a great shock to us to lose Father Windsor this past winter. We are prepared to operate next year with a temporary head but we hope to start next fall with a new headmaster. That would be so much better. If you were our choice and we yours, do you think Dr. Frostley would release you from your commitment to serve Essex next year?"

Cooper said he thought Dr. Frostley would go out of his way to be gracious to a sister school, and helpful to a colleague on his faculty.

"Are you familiar with St. Burges?" asked Mr. Janes.

Cooper replied that he had been a guest speaker at Sunday Chapel there, and had traveled to the school with Essex teams he was coaching. "I even played football against you years ago, when I was a student at Lawrenceville."

"Ah, now I know why your name is familiar to me. You were quarterback of that incredible Lawrenceville team that swept the league. You had that Indian fellow, RedThunder, running all over us."

Cooper said it was nice to be remembered as an athlete. It had been a long time. He explained why his football career was cut short and what George RedThunder was doing today, and acknowledged that, yes, they were still very close friends. He detected that Mr. Janes was a characteristically avid Ivy League sports fan, and he was amused to suspect that it was his friendship with RedThunder that most impressed the St. Burges Trustee.

They set a date for a meeting in Harford. Janes asked if Cooper could bring his wife. Cooper explained that she was recuperating in a hospital in New York, but he expected she would be released soon and said he knew that Nancy would be pleased to meet some people from St. Burges as soon as she could. A little more skillful prying on Janes' part enabled the trustee to discover that Nancy's father was Blakely O'Brian, the financier. Janes not only knew him, but Blakely was a Director of Janes' insurance company.

It's a tight little world, Cooper said to himself after hanging up.

Cooper normally strolled the halls of his dormitory at ten o'clock in the evening, while his prefects, who were handpicked sixth formers, supervised the boys in the dorm as they prepared for bed. The two prefects were top leaders in the school and managed their job with ease. Nevertheless, it always went smoother when Cooper was on hand, chatting with his charges, checking up on the dozens of little details that impinged on their lives.

"Donnie, I have a slip here that says you missed athletics today because you were at the infirmary. But there's no note from the infirmary that says you were there. Where were you really? OK, I didn't say I don't believe you, but you have to get a slip from the infirmary. Get it to me tomorrow, or you'll get an official absence from athletics.

"Hey, Knobby, come over here. Have you heard from your brother yet? Well, if you don't, then maybe you had better take a special weekend to go home and see your mother. I'll arrange it. It's OK, I've got pull with the Dean, and we'll get you sprung."

"Fred, my friend! Have you done that make-up paper for Mr. Jones? Oh, Fred, you promised me you'd do it today. Look, pal, you're going to break your father's heart if you don't get accepted at Dartmouth, and you'll never make it if you don't start building a better looking academic record. Yeah, now. You're going to be sorry when you're a sixth former, if you don't start working harder right now. I'm going to give you late lights tonight. Show me that paper at breakfast, or I'll run you up the flag pole, feet first."

"You want late lights, too, Adrian? You got 'em pal. Do your English, not the math, OK? Do that word list I gave you, too."

When he returned to his apartment, Cooper found Sherri there. "Hey, it's late for you," he said.

There was something different about her. She had on that marvelous perfume he remembered from the night they had gone to bed. Her hair was brushed out and glistening. When she moved, the light caught her thin cotton blouse and he could see that she wore no bra. Her nipples were hard and they made shadows where they pressed against the white blouse. He could see faint pinkness through the material. "Oh, my God," he breathed.

Sherri said, "Nancy's OK now. The truce is over." She pressed herself against him and put her arms around his neck.

He crushed her to him and whispered, "This is a big mistake."

"No, Baby, no mistake. I love you and I'm going to show you just how much I love you." She trembled as she hugged him.

Cooper decided he should look as mature as possible for his meeting in Hartford with the St. Burges people. He wore a three-piece suit and a striped blue shirt, with a conservative, small-print tie. He met Mr. Janes at the Hartford Club in a beautiful dark-paneled reading room. His host led him to a spacious private meeting room where he was introduced to four more of the school's Trustees. They were all middle-aged. Two were businessmen who had come from New York for the meeting. A third was a well-known heart surgeon from Boston. The fourth was a professor at Trinity College, Dr. Hooper. The latter was bright, quick and urbane. Cocktails were served. Cooper nursed one Scotch and water while Mr. Janes had a third martini. Janes led the conversation. He was a gracious and attentive host.

"Do you think advanced placement courses at Essex are serving their purpose, Mr. Morgan?" asked Dr. Hooper.

The others joined in.

"What about the practice of bringing in a few post-graduate athletic stars, which so many of our good independent schools do? Is that a good thing or not?"

"After you received a Bachelor of Divinity degree at General, Mr. Morgan, why did you not take the next logical step and become ordained?"

Cooper was enjoying himself. The company was good. He was at ease as the center of attention. He enjoyed the questions, which were woven graciously into casual and pleasant conversations. Only Hooper's last question bothered him, and he chose not to answer it. He merely said that a parish ministry was not something he chose to do and, since a career in education did not really require that a man be ordained, he had, for personal reasons, decided against ordination.

They moved to an adjacent private room where a table was set with white linen and plated silver. A delicious dinner of filet mignon was served. After dessert, Cooper declined a cordial, accepted a cigar, and chatted for forty minutes. Then Mr. Janes rose and thanked Cooper profusely for coming. As they were leaving, Janes drew Cooper aside and chatted with him. Then, as they were leaving the club, Hooper fell in step with Cooper and asked if he might visit him at Essex. Cooper said he would be delighted, and they agreed on a date Dr. Hooper could visit his classes and follow him through his typical routine. The erudite professor suggested explaining to the curious that he was a friend who was interested in learning more about Essex. Cooper laughed and asked, "Can I conclude from this that at least I have not been eliminated from the race?"

"Indeed, no," replied Hooper. "It appears that you have impressed our Chairman very much."

The Spring Musical was a smash hit beyond anyone's expectations. The campus was knocked on its ear. After the first performance, the audience, consisting of the student body, faculty, staff and friendly neighbors from the town, demanded four curtain calls and kept on cheering after the last. Finally, Elmer Pincer, who had written the words and music, climbed onto the stage, delighted and flustered. He called Sherri out for a final bow all by herself. Hugging an armful of flowers, she threw kisses to the audience, which went wild and spontaneously leaped collectively to its feet. They stomped and cheered and shouted, "Encore!"

At this point, things could have gotten out of hand because this kind of response was unprecedented. However, Adrian "Monkey" Craft kept his head, and gradually dimmed the house lights. The director called to the two piano players, who constituted the orchestra. He signaled them to play Sherri's main solo, which was the theme of the play. She sang it again, to everyone's delight, and the happy Essex community finally filed out of the auditorium, hushed and spellbound.

The musical was about a fictitious country in South America presided over by a benign, and easily hoodwinked, president who bore a resemblance, in mannerisms and speech, to Headmaster Leighton Frostley. There was an evil deputy who took over, and worked much devilment in the name of the ignorant president. The peasants staged a coup and elected a barmaid, played by Sherri, as president. She turned out to be a wise and skillful administrator, who solved the little country's problems using a set of cleverly humorous stratagems that benignly parodied life at Essex. Several of the play's characters bore resemblances to real members of the Essex community, but the spoofs were in reasonably good taste and not even the Headmaster was annoyed.

The next day was spring Parents' Day. That evening, the musical's second and final performance played to a packed audience of parents. Also, many in the school community came to see it again.

There was the usual cast party, but several days later Bernie Frostley threw another party for the cast and crew, and the faculty who were involved. She included several Trustees. Bernie made a point of making a great fuss over Sherri in front of everyone. It was clear to Sherri that Bernie wanted to make amends. Sherri received the heaped-on praise gracefully and, after having been toasted by all assembled, made a little speech of thanks to her hostess.

Sherri spoke to Monkey Craft at the party and thanked him again for the tape he had made of her songs in the show. The little redhead beamed with pleasure at receiving attention from the campus heroine. "You sure are a good sound man, Adrian," she said. "Even if you never graduate from Essex, you can have a great career as a show business technician."

"Sherri, I've made another tape with special sound effects that you are going to like even better. I've dubbed your voice, quadrupled it so you sound like a close-harmony quartette. You're going to love it."

"Oh, Adrian, you doll! When can I hear it?"

"How about tomorrow after dinner? There won't be anyone around the stage then. We can go back in my sound room and play it, OK?"

"That's super, Adrian. I'll see you there."

The ruse about Dr. Hooper being a friend wanting to learn more about Essex didn't work. A forthright girl in Cooper's Sixth Form English Class asked Dr. Hooper straight out if he wasn't really a spy from St. Burges, come to check out their teacher. Hooper laughed and admitted he was pretty much what she had guessed. Students kept insisting on testifying to what a great teacher Cooper was. They asked Hooper many questions about how a school decides on a headmaster. He answered their questions well. Two of the students in the class had been accepted at Trinity College and Hooper persuaded them to enroll there in preference to other colleges where they had been accepted.

At the end of the day, Dr. Hooper confided to Cooper, "At our meeting in Hartford, I was the only one you didn't snow. But now I'm on your side, too. I hope you get the job. You certainly appear to have made a good name for yourself here."

Cooper thanked him, and ventured the opinion that they must have some pretty impressive candidates with more experience than he had.

"Sure we do," said Hooper, "We have three candidates who are headmasters now at other schools. However, this is going to be a young man's game in the next few years. I think rapport with students and lots of energy is going to count for more than experience and wisdom."

"How come?" asked Cooper.

The shrewd Professor laughed and said, "I think you already know. Our society is ready for upheaval. There's a revolution in attitude coming right now and our students are in the forefront. Teaching is going to get interesting, and it's going to get frustrating, and it's going to be real hell for a lot of complacent administrators who are living comfortably within the status quo."

"You'll get the brunt of it in colleges, though," said Cooper. "Our kids at the secondary level are easier to manage. For one thing, schoolmasters are a lot closer to their students than you guys in colleges are."

"Some schoolmasters are, and you're one of them. That's why you'll make a good headmaster. Good luck. I don't envy you."

"You sound like you're offering me the job."

"That's not for me to do. But, I hope you get it. If you don't, it's only a matter of time before some other school grabs onto you. If you want to be a headmaster, Cooper, I'm sure you'll get your chance."

"As long as it's for the right reasons," said Cooper.

'What do you mean by that?"

"Oh, nothing, I guess. I was just thinking about something my father said to me once. He said, don't let yourself get promoted unless it's for the right reasons. One good reason is for the chance to grow."

"I'll drink to that," said Hooper. Then he said his goodbyes and left.

All was right in Sherri's world. Her parents had admitted to her that maybe she had a chance as a professional entertainer. Her performance had even impressed these two veterans of the Broadway scene. But she was going to try college life at Barnard, mostly for Cooper's sake, and she was looking forward to it. She had none of Cooper's misgivings about their affair. She enjoyed it for its own sake and simply ignored the frustration of having to keep it a secret. She had not tried to make love to him since the delightful evening of the week before. She felt she had needed to reassert herself as his lover after more than a month of abstinence in deference to Nancy's perilous condition. Now, in order to save him from the possibility of scandal, she decided she would not throw herself at him again, at least not until after graduation and the end of the school year, which was now only a week plus a few days away. Nancy would be home soon. Sherri decided she would just have to wait to see what happened.

Sherri was humming a tune to herself as she walked to the backstage area in the school's auditorium. She found Monkey Craft in his sound room surrounded by control boards. From here he could control most of the stage lighting, produce sound effects, amplify the orchestra or a soloist, and monitor all sound on the stage.

"Hello, Adrian, what wonderful thing do you have for me to listen to now?"

Without saying a word, Monkey turned dials and threw switches. Sherri heard her own voice singing the opening bars from one of her numbers in the Spring Musical. Then, the dubbed in repeats of her voice came in. Her clear contralto was as smooth as syrup. She knitted her brow at some of the little vocal tricks she had put in at the ends of phrases, and wondered if they were not just a little overdone. She made a mental note to talk to her mother about it.

Monkey's equipment was excellent. Her voice, sounding like a quartette, filled the room. The amplification was near perfect, and she could hear no distortions. When it was over, she grinned at him. "Oh, Adrian, you are a genius. How can I ever thank you enough?"

"Don't you know why I've done it?" said Monkey.

"No, why have you? Because you're my friend?"

"No Sherri. Because I'm in love with you."

CHAPTER 11

Sherri smiled at him hesitantly. His intensity was a little unnerving. "But Adrian, you can't be in love with me. I'm too old for you."

"No!" he said, raising his voice in anger. "I am older than you think. I have had to repeat some grades and now I am eighteen. Oh, I know half the boys in this school have the hots for you. You wouldn't like to hear how they talk about you sometimes, and what they'd like to do to you. Some of them say they have. I'm different though. I really love you." He reached out quickly and grabbed her hand. His eyes were pleading.

"Adrian, I don't know what to say. I'm sorry. I believe you, but . . . I think of you as a friend."

Monkey's face showed extreme annoyance. "You don't understand. It's driving me crazy. You are all I can think about. I dream about touching you and kissing you." He held her hand tight in both of his. He rubbed it intensely with his fingers.

The little redhead was strong. Sherri thought perhaps he was crazy. They were the only ones in the whole building. She knew she had to talk her way out of there. She did not panic. She knew she had this effect on males. She had been in tighter spots and gotten out of them.

"Gee, I'm sorry," she said. "But it's going to be all right, Monkey . . ."

"Don't call me that!" he screamed.

She whispered, to counteract his excitement, "I'm sorry. I forgot, Adrian. Now take it easy."

"Don't you understand? I've got to touch you. I've got to feel your body. I've got to . . . you're driving me crazy. I can't even think. I *love* you. I've never done this before. I haven't ever had a girl. You can show me. You will, won't you Sherry?"

"No, Adrian, I won't!"

"I'm not good enough for you, huh? Not big and strong like . . . like some people?"

"That's enough!" She began to show anger, hoping she could back him off. "Don't start saying things you're going to regret. Now, we can still be friends. I'm sorry. But I didn't lead you on. You're going to have to find yourself another girl. I'll help you, OK? I'll teach you how to catch yourself a girl. OK?

"I don't want a big sister, damn it, I want you." He began to cover her hand with kisses. "You put out for other people. You're going to do it for me."

"What do you know about me? Nothing," Sherri said.

"I know plenty about you. You peddle your ass for that bastard Morgan. What do you get for that Sherri? Good Grades? Does Morgan give you A's for spreading your legs? Do you fuck all of your teachers Sherri? Well you're going to put out for me, too. Do you know why? Because you don't have any choice. Everybody thinks I'm dumb. Monkey, do this. Monkey, do that. Well I'm not so dumb, and I've got you by the short hairs, Sherri. I hoped I wouldn't have to do this, but you forced me. Listen to *this*, and you'll see what I know!"

He released her hand and jumped to his control panel. He flipped a switch, and turned a dial. Sherri heard Cooper Morgan's voice coming though the amplifier.

"Hey, it's late for you." There was a pause, then, "Oh my God."

Sherri heard her own voice say, "Nancy's OK now. The truce is over."

Cooper said, "This is a big mistake."

Sherri heard herself say, "No, Baby, no mistake. I love you and I'm going to show you just how much I love you."

Sherri turned on the boy, her voice seething, "You slimy little bastard!"

Monkey turned the switch off. "Don't you want to hear the rest?" he asked. "I've got it all. Even the squeaky bed springs. You're a heavy breather, Sherri. The best part is when you come. You really have noisy orgasms, Sherri. Do you think I liked listening to that? When I'm the one who loves you? He doesn't love you. He's just taking what he can get. But, I love you Sherri. You're giving it to the wrong person. Now, that's going to change. Now you're going to love me." He said it triumphantly.

"And if I don't?" asked Sherri.

"If you don't," said Monkey, "This tape appears in a tape player on the Headmaster's desk, with a note telling him which button to push.'

"You have it all worked out don't you?" asked Sherri. "I can see I've really underestimated you, Adrian." Sherri felt a little horrible fear in the pit of her stomach. Her fear was for Cooper.

What have I done to my Baby, she said to herself. It does no good to go along with blackmailers. It stands to reason he's made at least one copy of the tape. I must stall for time. There has to be a way to deal with this clever little creep.

"Yes, I have it all worked out," said Monkey. "I put seven bugs in Morgan's apartment. So I would get every word, every groan. It won't do you any good looking for them. I took them all out. I didn't want to have to threaten you, Sherri. I want you to love me because I love you. But you'll learn to love me. You will.'

"You're wrong, Adrian. You're very wrong. I love Cooper Morgan. He's the only man I have ever loved, really. Loving him is a beautiful thing. You've made it ugly. You have done a really rotten thing. You think that's going to make me love you? You're nuts! You must have worked for weeks to get that tape, to get just what you were looking for. That's really *weird*."

Monkey laughed. "You know what? Morgan gave me late lights so I could get that tape." He mimicked Cooper, "'Do your English, Adrian. Don't do your math. Do the *word* list I gave you.' I saw you go in his apartment that night. It was late. I could tell something was up. I watched you Sherri. I watch you all the time."

"You're sick, Adrian."

"Yeah, I'm sick. I'm sick because of you. You're a cock teaser, Sherri. You drive me up the wall. Look at the way you dress. The way you move your beautiful blue eyes. Every time you speak to me I get a hard on. Well, you're not going to tease *me* anymore. You're going to put out. You're going to do everything I want, just the way I want it. We're going to do it *all*, Sherri. Everything I ever dreamed about." Monkey leered at her. His eyes were glossy.

"You're wrong. Things don't work that way. It wouldn't be the way you think. I wouldn't be good for you because I'd hate every minute of it. You can't just *make* somebody love you, Adrian."

"Stop stalling," said Monkey. "I worked hard for this. Open up your blouse, Sherri, I want to see your beautiful big tits. Do it now!" He began to advance towards her.

"No, Adrian, I won't."

"You won't? You want Frostley to listen to that tape? Think about it, Sherri. I'll do it. You know I will. My, won't old Frostley be surprised? He'll choke. He'll turn blue. Do you remember what you whispered while Morgan was fucking you, Sherri? Do you want to hear it? That was dirty, Sherri. I never heard any girl talk that way. Use those words. You love it! Don't pretend. If you can do it with Morgan you can do it with me. Otherwise, it's bye-bye diploma. They'll throw you out, Sherri. Is it worth it? Come on. Open your blouse. I want to see 'em. I want to feel 'em."

Sherri backed towards the door. "How about Morgan, would you do this to him? He's the best friend you've got in this school. Do you want to hurt him?"

"I don't give a *shit* about Morgan. I hate Morgan's guts. Everybody thinks he's so great. You're giving it to him. I heard it. I heard it all. Did you suck him off? Did he like that? Well, you're going to do that to me." He screamed at her, "Get on your knees!"

Sherri was thinking as fast as she could. At first she couldn't believe that Monkey could get away with what he intended. There is no senior in any school who thinks a lowly little sophomore can control him or her. The notion took some getting used to. She couldn't believe there wasn't some way out. Now, however, she was beginning to wonder.

It's like chess, she thought. Your opponent says, "Check," and you go to move out of it, and you try this and you try that, and nothing works, and gradually, you realize its checkmate. You never saw it coming, then pow . . . checkmate. How could this little creep do this to me? Do I have to give in? Do what he wants? I couldn't stand it! But I can't find a way out. The slimy little bastard doesn't even realize why he's got me. I wouldn't put up with blackmail just to keep from getting kicked out. No, it's Cooper. He'd be fired. He wouldn't get to be the Headmaster of St. Burges. His whole career would be ruined. It would all be my fault. He didn't even want to go to bed with me. I made him. Why do I affect men this way? I guess I'd be a great whore. I guess I'll find out what that's like with Monkey. Not yet, damn it. I can at least stall him. I can do that.

"OK, Adrian, you win."

He grinned. His face showed so much happiness, she almost felt sorry for him. He reached for her.

"Hey, not now, stupid," she said. "We'll get caught. The people in my dorm know where I am. I'm supposed to be back there. They'll come looking for me here. Besides, it's no good here. We need a bed, a big bed.

Don't you know how to do anything right? What kind of a girl do you think I am? If we're going to do it, we're going to do it right. If a guy gets me, he gets the *best*! You're not going to believe it. You think that was good with Morgan? You haven't heard anything yet. Have you ever heard of whips? Wait till I show you *that*!"

Monkey's joyful expression turned to suspicion. "You can't trick me. I won't wait. I want . . ."

She could see the confusion in his face. He wanted to believe her.

She thought, my God, what *is* it about me? Well, I'm going to win this round.

She pushed him away gently and opened the door to the sound room. She said, "Take it or leave it, lover. We're either going to do it right, or the whole fuck is off! I'll let you know where and when. You will not be sorry." She blew him a kiss and fled.

He may suspect me, she thought. He may be almost positive I'm lying to him, but he will wait to find out. He'll have to. When you've got them hooked, hope springs eternal. They will put up with a lot. But it won't work forever. How did I hook that little shit? Oh my, Sherri, why did God make you so sexy? Yes, he'll wait for a while at least. He may even have believed me. He thinks everybody is as rotten as he is.

When I tell Cooper, he'll know what to do. He will handle it.

Checkmate? How can anyone handle checkmate? Not even Cooper. Hey, Mr. Morgan, we've got this little problem. You know how much I love you, right? Paraded my little ass back and forth in front of you till I got you hooked, right? Pushed you in bed and got you to do this neat little adultery thing. Messed up your sense of decency and made you miserable, right? Well, you haven't heard anything yet. I love you so much that I drove a fellow student into making this swell recording that's going to screw you like little Sherri never dreamed of screwing you. How do you like them apples, man? Makes you really want to love little Sherri, right? Right. Throw out sweet little Lisa's mother and run off with little Sherri into the fucking sunset. What a lucky man you are! Oh, *shit*!

I guess I can't tell Cooper. He'd want to save my honor. He'd just tell Frostley, resign his job and take crafty Monkey Craft with him. Spend the rest of his life trying to rehabilitate that little redheaded bastard and get as far away from me as possible, just as fast as his big beautiful, muscular legs can take him. It would be a lot easier just to turn the trick for Monkey. I might even like it. Yeah . . . Yuck! Like kissing rattlesnakes, I'd like it.

Sherri went back to her dorm. She had exams to study for, but exams no longer held any fear for her. She had a term paper that was long overdue. She kept getting extensions of the due date because of the musical. Her mighty triumph seemed like a hundred years ago. She couldn't think about a term paper now. Some of her buddies came to her door for a gossip session, but she begged off.

Thank goodness I don't have a roommate. At least I can be alone. I guess I'm not hungry. I guess I'm sick to my stomach. What will I feel like if I have to put out for that creep? Probably throw up all over him. She laughed. She remembered her mother's advice if she was ever in danger of being raped, "Just shit in your pants dear. Nothing so squelches the male erection as a little feces."

She put on a soft clean sweat suit, went down the hall to the bathroom and washed out her underwear. She hung them up to dry on a towel rack in her room. She sat down with a pencil and paper. Sometimes that helped her solve problems. She made a list of all the boys in school who would beat Monkey senseless for her if she asked them to. It was quite a long list, and she could really have thought of more. She crossed out the names of those who would want some sexual favors in return.

Out of the frying pan and into the fire, she mused. After all, Monkey's pecker is probably too small to hurt very much, she giggled to herself. I'm getting slaphappy. There aren't many names left. Now, let's cross out the ones who would want to know why they should beat Monkey into oblivion. Now, all the names are crossed out. Hmmm, go back and circle the ones I could pretty easily lie to about it. This is good. This brings back a few. But Monkey would probably tell them about it before they beat him senseless. He'd let them hear the tape.

She crumpled up the paper and threw it away. Now, let's analyze Monkey. Maybe that will get us somewhere. He's a loner. He probably hasn't told anyone about the tape. He has no friends. He never tells anyone about himself. He's confessed more about himself to me today than I think he's ever told anyone else. He is bound to have copies of the tape, well hidden. He is clever and resourceful. If he promises to destroy all the tapes if I do what he wants, he'll almost certainly cheat and not do it. However, after graduation, he won't think he has anything on me anymore. I sort of think he doesn't realize how much he can hurt Cooper. Also, Cooper probably doesn't have anything he wants. I don't think he realizes he can get to me by threatening Cooper. If I can stall him ten days, I've got it made. Hey, that's good. No, he'll never let me stall him that long. Yeah, after I stall him for a while, he'll catch on and give me a deadline. If I play my cards right, I can stall him down to the wire, then go to bed with him once, give him a hell of a good toss, then bang . . . graduation. I'll convince him his tape is worthless after that. I won't even ask him to give it to me. Well, that's the best I can think of for now. Got to go to bed. New ideas in the morning, maybe. Hope so. Not so bad, Sherri old girl. You'll live through it. You've had worse problems. What? Think about that in the morning too.

"Hello Mr. Morgan, Ed Janes here. I'm sorry to be calling you after hours, but you are hard to catch in the daytime, off to your classes and coaching and all that sort of thing, I suppose."

"Right, Mr. Janes, I'm glad to have you call me in the evening. It's the best time to catch me."

"Fine. That's fine. Say, George Hooper had an absolutely marvelous time with you down there. He gave me a full report. He thinks you are an exceptional fellow."

"Well, that's very nice of you to say. Nice of him, too. We did have a good time. I am afraid my students are eager to get rid of me. They are determined to pass me on to you fellows, so they gave Dr. Hooper a big sales job. It was a little embarrassing, but I survived."

"You are too modest, sir. The people at Essex clearly think very highly of you. Nobody fools George Hooper, I assure you. He is quite a fellow, don't you think?"

"Yes, I do. I like him very much. He's a great credit to Trinity College and to St. Burges, too."

"Yes, sir. Speaking of St. Burges, I wonder if you would be willing to visit the campus this weekend. The people there are eager to meet you. We have two committees that are advisory to the search committee. One is made up of faculty members and the other of students. These committees would like to meet with you separately. Your host and hostess would be Dr. and Mrs. Carl Sainely. Batty Sainely is Vice Rector for Studies and currently Acting Rector and, uh, Headmaster. They would have a reception for other members of the school to meet you. Then, you would, of course, be free to visit classes, go anywhere you care to, ask any questions of anyone you choose, that sort of thing."

"Mr. Janes, would it be possible for me to do the same thing during two weekdays? The weekend is the only time my daughter and I get to visit my wife in the hospital in New York. Now that she's better, it means a lot to her to have us there."

"My good fellow, excuse me. Say no more about it. Of course we can do it during the week. Next week, I hope?"

Cooper arranged the trip for Wednesday and Thursday of the following week. Edward Janes explained to Cooper that they had started their search with more than sixty candidates. They had preliminary meetings with thirty. The Committee had, that very day, narrowed the field to three and he, Cooper, was one of them.

"Incidentally," said Janes, "I wonder if, while you're in New York this weekend, you could arrange to meet with the President of our Board of Trustees. If you have any free time at all, I'll suggest that he call you and arrange a time and place to meet with you. He's Stokley Ramsey, the publisher. I imagine you know of him?"

"Yes," said Cooper. "I guess most people have heard of Mr. Ramsey. It certainly will be a pleasure to meet him."

"Good, it's all set, then. I'll ask Stokley to call you, perhaps tonight, if I can get to him. In the meantime, please give my good wishes to your father-in-law, Blakely O'Brian. I have great admiration for him. Also, ah, I would consider it an honor if you would call me Ed, and, if I might, I would like to call you Cooper."

"Thank you, Ed; I'd like that very much."

Janes said goodbye and hung up and Cooper smiled to himself. For the first time, it hit him that this was real. There was a very good chance that he would be the next Headmaster of St. Burges School. That sounded odd, he thought. Of course, the recently deceased head of St. Burges, Father Windsor, was always referred to as Rector, not Headmaster. To the best of Cooper's knowledge, all of the school's leaders had been high church Episcopal Priests, were referred to as "Father" and carried the title, Rector.

I wonder why, he mused, they are now considering a layman. Maybe they're counting me in because I've been to seminary. I hope they wouldn't want to call me Rector. That was my father's title. I can't have it.

Cooper knew a lot, of course, about the Episcopal Church. He knew that the title Rector merely meant ruler. One did not need to be ordained to be called Rector.

He checked his watch. It was still early enough to call Nancy.

She'll want to know I'm a finalist. What if they choose me? I want them to, but, then, I really don't. What's that all about? It's a contest. I love to win. I always jump through hoops to win any competition in sight, whether I want the prize or not. Why aren't I more excited about the prize? Because I lied to Frostley. If I hadn't lied, he would have withdrawn his endorsement, and bye-bye headmastership. You're being too sensitive, turkey. It's a tough world. Most of us just can't afford to be that pure. But I can. Can't I? Worry about it after you get the offer. Don't cross the bridge until they say it's your bridge.

Nancy was thrilled. "Knock 'em dead, tiger. Charm the shit out of them," she said.

Then she told him she would be out of the hospital in time to attend graduation at Essex. She loved graduations because there were always a number of students she wanted to cheer for.

"Of course, I can't overdo it," she said. "If I rest before and afterwards, then I can attend the Commencement ceremony. Thank God you backed out of running the summer school again. We can both go to the house on the Cape with Dad and Muffy." Nancy and her brother, and Cooper, usually referred to Mrs. O'Brian by her nickname.

"Whatever you want is OK with me Nanny. Of course, if they offer me the St. Burges job and I take it, I'll want to be spending a lot of time there learning the ropes. We'll have to organize our gear and move it, too."

"What do you mean by 'if I take it'?"

"Oh, I don't know. Let's worry about that if they make the offer."

"Cooper, sometimes you're awfully silly. Of course you'll take it."

After Cooper finished talking with Nancy, St. Burges' prominent Board President, Stokley Ramsey, called. He was completely charming and at-ease on the phone. He invited Cooper for lunch at the New York Yacht Club on West Forty-Fourth Street the following Saturday. Cooper decided if Ramsey was a yachtsman, they should hit it off just fine.

CHAPTER 12

"Hey, Sherri, stop trying to avoid me."

"There you are Adrian. I'm not trying to avoid you. I've been looking for you."

"Yeah, sure. I'd like to believe that."

"I really have. Now that I've thought about it, I've decided it's going to be a whole lot of fun making love to you. We're going to have a blast, right?"

"Yeah? You really want to? That's great. When, tonight? Where will I meet you?"

"Well I thought you were going to tell me that, Adrian."

"No, no, you said you'd tell me where and when."

Sherri looked peeved. "You mean you haven't made any arrangements at all, huh? Well if you aren't a big disappointment. You've got these grown up urges, but you don't know how to make any arrangements. The woman is not supposed to make the arrangements!"

"Cut it out, Sherri. I'll make the arrangements. I just didn't know I was supposed . . . oh, what's the difference. What kind of arrangements did you have in mind?"

"First of all," said Sherri, "who else knows about this?"

"Nobody. If you keep your end of the deal, I won't tell a soul. If you don't, you know what's going to happen."

"OK, Adrian, but remember if you tell anyone at all, the whole deal is off. I'm not getting in the sack with a blabbermouth. Keep quiet and you'll get my end of the deal."

"OK, don't worry. Where shall I meet you?"

"Why don't you get us a room at the Fairlawn Inn for this Saturday? We'll have plenty of time Saturday evening before you're due back at your dorm."

"The Fairlawn Inn? That's right next to the school! Somebody will see us. How am I going to get a room at the Fairlawn?"

"Nobody will see us, dummy. Do you expect me to walk to the other side of town? Tell 'em you want a reservation for your sister who's visiting you on Saturday. Then, Saturday afternoon, go register, pay for the room and get a key."

"OK, I guess."

"That's a good boy."

"I don't want to wait till Saturday."

"Well, I have a meeting of some sort every night. Study for your exams. Let me know when you've got the room. Get champagne, too. I like champagne when I do it. I'll bring the whips."

"Hey, Sherri, I don't know about those whips."

"OK, scratch the whips. Gee, I wonder if you're going to be any fun at all."

"Tell me, would you accept the job if it's offered?" asked Stokley Ramsey. The man was very charming and very quick. They had chatted about boats and about schools. The meal at the New York Yacht Club was excellent, and the atmosphere was captivating for anyone who enjoyed boats. The beautiful wood-paneled walls were adorned with a profusion of fine paintings and of carved half-hulls. On entering, they stopped to admire the America's Cup in its case and marvel at the fact that no other nation had yet been able to win it away.

Ramsey asked Cooper only a few questions. None of them were repeats. It was clear that he had been briefed in detail about Cooper. As for accepting the job if it was offered, Cooper laughed and said he couldn't guarantee that. His host seemed to be impressed by that answer. Then Ramsey asked Cooper if it was for a lack of faith in Christian doctrine that he had declined ordination. Cooper said no, that was not the case. While a fundamentalist might find fault with the nature of his belief, he, Cooper Morgan, felt his faith was compatible with Episcopal Church standards for joining the priesthood. Then, to draw Ramsey away from the next logical question of why, then, had he not chosen to join the clergy, Cooper launched into a philosophical discussion about faith.

"I believe that Jesus is The Christ, the Son of God. I believe on a different plane of understanding than the one that leads me to believe that if the soup is hot I will burn my tongue, or that I will get hurt if I step in front of a fast moving car. I have burned my tongue on hot soup. I have not ever stepped in front of a fast moving car. I believe both conclusions, however. Just as each conclusion calls for a different level of belief than the other, my faith in Jesus Christ is belief on still another level or plane. This level is higher, if you will. It doesn't depend on what many people would call reality or scientific truth. But, it is very real, nevertheless. It is just as real as the knowledge that something or someone is beautiful. Say, a fine tall sloop beating in a fresh wind, or that blonde woman at the table over there. Our knowledge of beauty is so sure it is beyond challenge. Yet, we can't prove it or even explain it. The plane of understanding that leads me to believe that the resurrection is true is, I think, a different plane still than that which gives us simple truth. Cooper laughed and said, "And, I believe I am lecturing you as if you were an insensitive schoolboy. Excuse me, I got carried away."

"Don't stop," said Ramsey. "I am fascinated. You have just given me an insight that I don't think I have ever heard before. You make it so logical. Why doesn't the Rector of my church ever talk that way? He'd have more people in the pews if he did."

"Some of the clergy talk that way to their parishioners," said Cooper, "but most are afraid to. Afraid they will shake 'em up, surprise them. Make 'em mad. How people come to believe is almost a taboo subject, like what one talks about to his wife while copulating."

Ramsey chuckled. He said, "What you said there about planes of understanding, is that your own idea?"

"Not really," said Cooper. "It is only my way of talking about it today. Plane of understanding is a metaphor taken from our concept of space and applied to something that is eternal, or spiritual. Paul Tillich refers to a 'dimension of depth.' Reinhold Niebuhr talks about one's life and its sequence of events in time as a two dimensional canvas painted with symbols and distortions so it will look real. Man's religious nature gives the third dimension to our understanding."

"Fascinating," said Ramsey. "You're a born teacher, aren't you? 'No wonder those kids at Essex are crazy about you. You help them learn. Not many teachers really do that."

"Oh, sure they do," said Cooper. "That is just what good teachers do. You've been away from it too long. There is something more important, though, and that is to love them. I like to work with students at this stage of their growth because I find it very easy to love them, and a great joy.

And that is what I think believing in Jesus is really all about. His teaching, what he represents, all summed up is, love . . . agape. Christians don't have an exclusive claim on it, but the real Christian puts his emphasis in the right place, and that is his strength. Sermon over. My, I'm feeling pompous today."

"No you're not," said Ramsey. "That was just great. Thank you for opening yourself up to me that way. I would like to sit in on your classes."

The rest of the meeting went well and Cooper successfully avoided being asked why he was not ordained in the Episcopal Church.

"Sherri, it's all set. I have the room and the champagne. Hey, that stuff is expensive. Sherri, you won't believe how scared I was reserving that room. I almost died! Me, who can lie to anybody without blinking an eye. But, oh, it was worth it. I can't wait till tonight. You don't know how much this means to me."

They were outside on the quadrangle in front of the Dining Hall. Sherri said, "Adrian, lover, we have just run into a terrible piece of bad luck."

"What? What's the matter?"

"I can't believe this has happened. I can't stand it. After you spent your money and all, and I was looking forward to it so. I have the curse. It came early."

"You have what?"

"My period dummy, don't you know anything? I am menstruating. Bleeding, got it?"

"Oh my god."

"This is not an act, Adrian. I'm not trying to stall you. I'll show you if you like. If you can stand it."

"No. Uh, what will I do?"

Monkey Craft was caught up in the witchcraft and mystery of female lore. He knew somehow that this woman was taboo, taken away before he could sample his hard-won prize. She was unclean, undesirable. So his culture had taught him.

He said, "When is it over, when can we . . . ?"

"It takes me five days," said Sherri, "sometimes six."

"But, that's next Friday! Graduation is Saturday. I'm not supposed to be here after Thursday. Sophomores don't even stay for graduation. Sherri, you did this to me! You stalled me till now. I'm going to get even." His eyes were blazing. He was furious. His face turned red.

"Take it easy, will you?" Sherri said. "I have an extra Commencement invitation. I'll give it to you. You can stay on if you have a reason to stay. Several fourth formers are staying, the ones in the choir, and those who are staying for kitchen duty. Go cancel your room. Tell 'em your sister can't make it, but she'll be here Friday. They might be full Friday because of graduation, but maybe not. If they are, we can go somewhere else. Count on it, lover. I'll take care of you on Friday night. Things don't always go the way we plan, but you're going to get it all. Just be patient. Now, go on down to the Fairlawn before they charge you for tonight. I'll see you later. Save the champagne, ok?"

"You look wonderful, darling!" Said Cooper.

Nancy held up her arms to him, to kiss him again. Her parents had just hurried off after delivering her at Essex. Whenever Blakely O'Brien decided to drive anywhere, he rented a limousine and driver, and that's the way they had brought her home. She had spent the night at their East Side brownstone, after she was discharged from the hospital, and Cooper had spent that same night at St. Burges in Massachusetts. He arrived home just ahead of her.

"Oh, my, you look delicious," Nancy said.

"It's been a long time."

"Well, my love, why are we standing here in the hallway when we ought to be upstairs in bed?"

"Did your doctor say sex is all right now?"

"I don't know what the hell he has to say about it."

"I don't either," said Cooper with a devilish grin. He scooped her up in his arms and started to carry her upstairs.

"That's a little more like the lover boy I used to know," Nancy whispered in his ear, snuggling close to him.

"Hmm, we have some rare exotic perfume on this afternoon, don't we?"

"Follow your nose and see if you can discover the places where I dabbed it."

"Ah, I love a treasure hunt."

"When you find the treasure you'll have to brush the cobwebs off of it. But you'll find it is getting wet and swollen."

"Daddy will kiss it and make it well."

"Yes. Do that!"

Cooper laid her down on their bed and said, "Do you know what?"

"What?"

"Lisa is due home any minute now from the Banes's house."

"Then we better hurry."

"Last one with any clothes on is a rotten egg."

Lisa didn't come in for an hour, but when she did they were still in bed. Sylvia Banes brought her and followed Lisa upstairs into their bedroom. Cooper heard them coming and thought about hopping into the bathroom but he was too comfortable where he was. He just pulled the covers up over them.

"Well it didn't take you two very long," said Sylvia. "Does everything still work?"

Nancy and Cooper nodded their heads, smiling foolishly. Lisa jumped on the bed and hugged Nancy.

Sylvia said, "Come on Lisa, honey, let's go downstairs and start dinner for Mummy and Daddy, and they'll be down in a little while. Isn't that a good idea, Mummy and Daddy?"

At dinner Nancy asked if all their Thatcher House boys had gone home for summer vacation. Cooper told her that only a few were left, those who had some function at the Commencement ceremony in two days. He said that Adrian Craft was staying just to see graduation.

"Now, save next Tuesday to take me back to New York to see Dr. Taylor. He wants to do a test and he wants to talk to you, as well as me. I don't know why, but he does."

"Is he the one who likes to feel your leg?"

"He acts as though he might like to, but it's another one who did, the orthopedic man. Now, you still haven't told me the rest about your trip to St. Burges. Give."

"I had a good time. It's a lovely school, but really no better than this one."

"Oh, I think it's more 'in,' don't you?"

"Sure. They've got a bigger endowment by quite a bit. It's fashionable, but it's all boys. I kind of think a co-ed school like Essex works better and I also think it's the coming thing."

"Did they like you?"

"Yeah, I think they did. They've heard me in Chapel there. I know some of the team coaches. That helped. I suppose I hit it off best with the kids. I told them I didn't think their strict dress code was very important, and if they wanted to change it they ought to be able to. Some of the old guard faculty didn't like that, including my host, Batty Sainely. He was polite, though. I suppose some of that very conservative element thinks I'm too young and they don't think a layman should head the school."

"So why don't you get ordained?"

"Hey, come on, Nancy, we've been through all that."

"Sure, but you never had a reason to be ordained before. Now, you do."

"It's not just that. It's something that happened. I just don't think I deserve to be a priest."

"Don't you think it's time you told me what happened?"

Cooper looked at Lisa and suggested that she help him do the dishes while they let mommy rest on her first day out of the hospital.

"This d-damned key doesn't fit the lock!" Monkey said.

"Oh, sure it does. Let me try," said Sherri. She opened the door and ushered Monkey in. "See, it works fine. If you're so nervous you can't get a key in a keyhole, what makes you think you can get your pecker into me?"

"Shut up, Sherri. Just stop wising off at me. I'll be all right."

"Do you have some champagne in that bag? Is it cold?"

"How was I supposed to get it cold?"

"Adrian, you are such a klutz. You're about as romantic as a dead fish. Honestly, I had better lovers in the third grade. Go out and ask somebody where the ice machine is. They've got to have an ice machine. That's what this paper bucket here is for. Put the ice in the bucket and bring it back here. *NOW!*"

"All right. All right. Don't let's fight, Sherri. I want this to be nice. It's my first time. A guy's first time ought to be special, shouldn't it?"

"A guy shouldn't be having his first time when he's still a baby. You probably ought to be in diapers. You looked like you were wetting your pants when the manager spoke to you down in the lobby."

Monkey groaned and went out the door with the ice bucket. Sherri thought to herself, I didn't know I could be so bitchy. Honestly, I don't know why he puts up with it, the poor little bugger. He ought to walk right out. Would serve me right. Don't I wish. As she ruminated, she went around the room turning on all the lights. Got to make it as unromantic as I can. Too bad it's a warm evening. It would be good to make it cold in here.

"Ok, here's your ice," said Monkey when he returned. "I don't think anyone saw me out there."

"All right champ, put the bottle in the bucket with the ice. You got glasses?"

"There are glasses in the bathroom."

"That's a blast. Champagne in water glasses," lamented Sherri.

"I'll get 'em. I have to go to the bathroom anyway," said Monkey.

"Oh, good, Adrian, I'd like to watch."

"You what?"

"You know, watch. Watch you pee. If we're going to be intimate, can't I watch?"

"You know what, Sherri? You're crazy. Do you know that? OK, you can watch."

"Oh good, I never watched a boy pee before. Oh, look, it's not very big is it?

"It's not supposed to be big now. It isn't hard yet."

"I know, but it's still not very big. Why don't you go ahead?"

"I don't know. Nothing seems to come out. I know I have to go, but it just won't come out."

"I still say it's not very big."

"Will you stop saying that? It's plenty big enough."

"How old are you, Adrian?"

"Damnit, I am eighteen. I was eighteenteen last month! I have had to repeat two grades"

"Why don't you pee?"

"I don't know, damnit. Stop asking me that. It's probably because you're watching."

"I want to watch."

"OK, OK, so watch! But, I'm not going to do anything."

"Here, let me hold it. There, does that feel nice?"

"Oh, Sherri, that's wonderful. Now, you see, it's bigger. Better stop doing that or I'll come. I don't want to do that yet. Hey, stop. Oh . . . oh my god! You made me do it. Look, you got it all over my pants. Oh, what a mess."

"You sure have a quick trigger. I never saw anybody shoot so fast."

"Yeah, but I wanted it to last longer. You shouldn't have done that."

"Is that so? What did you come here for, to play checkers?"

"No, but don't you see? Now, I won't be able to get hard again for a while. I won't be able to do anything for you."

"That's OK. Let's go back to school."

"Are you crazy? I don't have to be back until eleven. I haven't got what I came here for yet, and we're not leaving till I do."

"OK, it's up to you."

"I haven't even seen you yet. I want to see those beautiful big, uh . . . I want to see your chest. I'll be all right in a while, Sherri. I brought rubbers. I won't get you pregnant."

"I didn't think they made rubbers for dicks that small."

"Damnit, Sherri, stop talking like that, please? Come in the bedroom and we'll open the champagne."

It was almost eleven o'clock when Monkey and Sherri left their room at the Fairlawn. Monkey's eyes were bloodshot as if he had been crying. He looked pleadingly at the beautiful blonde girl and said, "I'm sorry Sherri. It wasn't very nice for you either, was it?"

"That's all right, Adrian. Don't worry about it," she said with a little secret glint of triumph in her eye.

"I don't know why I couldn't do it. Do you think there's something wrong with me?"

"No, honey," she said, "you're going to be OK. You just went about it all wrong. You can't blackmail a girl into bed with you. It doesn't work for her, or for you either. You have to win your lady. Try somebody else and be nice to her. Send her flowers. Take her to dinner. Pet her and compliment her. First thing you know, you'll both score and feel great about it. Sex with girls isn't really the way the boys talk about it. It's not a matter of you getting her. It's you both getting each other. See?"

"I guess. Sherri, you won't tell anybody, will you? You know, that I couldn't do it?"

"No Adrian, it will be our secret. Just do me a favor and throw away that tape. Erase it or cut it up."

"I'll give it to you."

"No. Just get rid of it. It will be a bad memory for you if you keep it, and I don't want it."

"OK, I will. Just please don't tell anybody the way it worked out."

"It's a deal."

When Sherri got back to her dormitory, most of her girlfriends who were about to graduate the next day were having a party. Sherri was laughing to herself when she came in, and she was elated and giggly for the rest of the night. Some of her friends thought it was more than the happy anticipation of graduation, but she would not tell them a thing. She just acted silly, giggled, and ate more pizza than she ever had in her life, or, for that matter, ever would again.

CHAPTER 13

"Congratulations, Sherri," Nancy said. They were standing on the quadrangle outside the Chapel, with all the new graduates and their families. The day was clear and bright and warm."

I just love graduations, and this one was the best, because of your beautiful solo with the choir. Honestly, Sherri, someday you are going to be famous and we all are going to brag about how well we knew you when you were in school."

"Oh, thank you, Mrs. Morgan." Sherri beamed and pecked Nancy on the cheek. "You just look wonderful, as if you hadn't had an accident at all, like you're ready for three sets of tennis."

"Not with you, my dear. You're too good for me. Sherri, I'm so sorry I missed the Spring Musical. I hear you outdid yourself. And with all that rehearsing you still found the time to take care of Lisa and Mr. Morgan."

"Oh, I took good care of Mr. Morgan, didn't I?" said Sherri, looking intently at Cooper.

"Indeed you did," he said. "Before you leave today, Sherri, stop by Thatcher house. Lisa and I bought you a graduation present. It's to say thank you."

"OK, it's a deal, but don't forget you also promised me champagne, my first *legal* alcoholic beverage on the Essex campus."

Cooper laughed. "Do me a favor, Sherri, don't tell me about the illegal ones. Your champagne is cooling, and it's not domestic. It's the genuine article."

"Oh, goody! May I bring my parents with me? They're seeing a lot of each other because of me. Isn't that neat?"

As a graduation present, Cooper gave Sherri a lovely, delicate watch that was no wider than its intricate fourteen-karat gold wristband. Sherri saw that on the back it was engraved: "To Sherri with love, C.M." No one else saw that, and she promptly fastened the watch to her wrist so they would not. She smiled at Cooper with a special, intent look in her eye. Her silent communication was interrupted by Nancy calling Cooper to the telephone.

"Ed Janes here, Cooper," said the voice on the other end of the line. "I have some pretty exciting news for you. It is an honor to tell you that you are our choice to lead St. Burges School."

"Gosh, Ed, I'm overwhelmed. I don't know what to say."

"Don't say a thing. But let me come down from Hartford to talk to you about it. I'd like to do that as soon as it is convenient for you. For example, if you're free this evening, I'd love to drive down."

"I guess this evening would be OK. You can meet Nancy, if you don't come too late. She's home with us now."

Cooper invited Janes to dinner but he declined and they settled on his arrival around seven o'clock.

When Janes arrived, Nancy served espresso and fancy cookies and thoroughly charmed him. She had been bubbling with high enthusiasm ever since Cooper told her the news.

After an hour of animated small talk about St. Burges and its traditions and folkways as a church school, Nancy excused herself, explaining that she still got tired quickly, and went up to bed.

When they were alone, Janes turned to Cooper and said, "Cooper, the job pays thirty thousand a year. Of course, you also get the Rector's house with all utilities paid and a cleaning lady. The school will put three thousand dollars a year in your pension fund. You would match that. We have TIAA-CREF, as you know. I suppose you and your family would take many of your meals in the school dining room, and that, too, is at no cost to you. You'll have an expense account and a discretionary fund of five thousand a year. Have I forgotten anything?"

"Well, I'm not really concerned right now about the detail. That all sounds fine. Very generous, and a lot more than I'm making now."

"Well, I have one more piece of very good news. At least, I hope you'll agree it is good news. You know, of course, that St. Burges, being a church school, has always been led by a priest. The Trustees decided that we wanted the best possible man whether he was a priest or not, as long as he is an Episcopalian. We have right along hoped that the best man we could find would actually be a priest. Well, now comes the good news. The Bishop of Massachusetts, bless his heart, has said that he would be glad to ordain you in a special ceremony, right at school. What do you think of that?"

Cooper was quiet and thoughtful for a long pause. An old family friend might have remarked, "He gets more like his father every day."

Finally, Cooper broke the silence, saying, "Is accepting ordination a condition to your job offer?"

"Well, that's an odd way to put it. We were hoping that you would want to serve the school in the best way possible. The fact that you were such a distinguished graduate of General Seminary was not lost on us when we voted to extend you the offer."

Cooper smiled warmly at him in a most engaging way. He said, "Ed, I am very pleased to have made your acquaintance through this business. Whether I join you at St. Burges or not, I would like to feel you are my friend and I'm yours."

Janes nodded with enthusiasm.

Cooper went on, "Then tell me, as a friend, would the Board still like to have me as the school head, if I elect to remain a layman?"

"I guess some would and some wouldn't."

Cooper entered into another long silence. Janes became nervous but sensed that he ought to wait quietly. Was Cooper praying as his father did in the midst of conversation? Cooper probably could not have said himself, if asked. He was talking to his God, but there were no introductory clauses, no ritual, no memorized phrases.

Cooper had his answer. He knew what he was going to do. And he knew it was the right thing. A feeling of wellbeing came over him, a feeling of elation. He felt a burden had been lifted.

Cooper spoke gently and quietly, "It had been my intention, Ed, to ask you for a week to ten days to think it over, even though I know St. Burges' commencement is tomorrow and Stokley Ramsey would dearly like to make an announcement at that time. You were gracious not to mention it, but I'm right, aren't I?" Janes's sheepish grin confirmed Cooper's shrewd speculation. "Well, Ed, I don't need to think it over. You deserve a straight answer, now. You have paid me the best compliment I have ever received, and I thank you. I thank you profoundly. I'm not right for St. Burges. I'm sure of it. I should have known it sooner, but I wasn't sure. It just wasn't meant to be. I don't think you can know how I hate to say this, to pass up an opportunity that . . . that I have wanted badly. I can't do it and I won't change my mind. It's not just the ordination thing. Don't worry about that. The shortcoming is mine. It won't work and I can't tell you any more."

"But, surely, you ought to sleep on it. Talk to Nancy . . . think about it . . ."

Ed Janes's voice trailed off. His expression was incredulous. He managed, "Why don't you at least talk to Dr. Frostley first?"

Cooper smiled with kind eyes. "Thank you, Ed. Thank you for caring so much. I can't explain it to you. I know I am doing the right thing. I know Mr. Ramsey will call me, perhaps Dr. Hooper will too. It's no use. My mind is made up."

Janes's self-assurance gradually returned. He was once again the chief officer of one of the nation's top financial institutions. He thanked Cooper for his straight talk, sincerely wished him well and left.

Cooper did not pause for even a moment of regret. He said to himself, I hope Nanny's asleep. I'd much rather face her with this in the morning.

He found she was, indeed, asleep. And she was still asleep when Cooper arose early to have breakfast with Lisa. He told her that they would not be going to St. Burges. Lisa said she was glad. "I wanted to stay here with all my friends and to go to this school when I get old enough."

I just wish Nancy would take it as easily as that, thought Cooper.

The phone rang and Stokley Ramsey greeted him in cheery tones. He asked if there was any basis at all on which Cooper would change his mind. Cooper said there was not. Cooper thanked him, told him he had great respect and admiration for St. Burges but that he was convinced he was not the right man for the school. He told Ramsey he still wanted to be a headmaster but not until he felt he would fit into the prospective school just right. Ramsey was very cordial, did not pressure him, wished him well and offered to be of service whenever he could.

When Cooper hung up the phone he found Nancy had come downstairs. She looked rested, although her cheeks were still a little hollow. She looked quite lovely in the morning sunshine streaming through the windows. There was a rich, earthy smell of spring in the air. In a few hours it would be more like summer. Nancy had on a pretty new sea green quilted bathrobe that matched, and seemed to intensify, the green in her eyes. She said, "Did I hear what I think I heard you say on the telephone?"

Cooper looked grim but firm and nodded his head. "I'm sorry you found out that way. I had hoped I could break it to you a little easier."

She sat down, her lower lip protruding just the tiniest bit, a sure sign she was angry. Her voice was a whisper. "Why, Cooper? Why, why . . . why?"

"I'm so sorry I've disappointed you, honey. I just couldn't do it. It was all wrong. It felt wrong even at the start. That faculty is not ready for someone like me. My gut feeling when I went there was bad. Then, what clinched it was they wanted me to be ordained. Even had it all set up without asking me."

Nancy glared at him. "Just what the hell is it you think you've done to make you unworthy to be a priest? Damnit, I have a right to know. I think you have set strange special standards for yourself that you don't expect of anyone else. What do you think you are, some kind of saint? Is it because of our sexual adventures before we got married? What do you call it? Fornication, is that it?"

"No, Nanny, I have never thought loving you was a sin, quite the opposite. It's nothing connected to you. I didn't intend to keep it from you but I never told you. I didn't want to burden you with it. I've never told anyone. It is . . . well, it was the main reason I took that scholarship to go to Seminary. I thought I owed it to my father and God, and everybody, to give my life to the church. But my studies in the Seminary changed my understanding about God and about the church, significantly. In the final analysis, it's what you know, or think you know . . . what you believe, that leads you to decisions. Then, after I had learned so much, I came to believe that I should not represent God as a priest. Of course, it wouldn't matter to others because they don't know, but I know, and I'm sure I should not represent God in that way. I'm not saying others shouldn't, but it's not right for me. I can give my life for others, and I should, but not as a priest."

"So, tell me what you did. I want to know. I want to understand you."

Cooper said, "Man sins and God forgives. I believe that. I believe God has forgiven me. Nevertheless, I think God's representative on Earth should probably be without experience of, at least, the worst sin. I'm speaking of a sin against the Sixth Commandment."

Nancy said, "Give me a break, love, I never learned them by the numbers."

Cooper said, "The Sixth says, 'you shall not kill.'"

Book Two

Book Two

CHAPTER 1

1959

At the conclusion of Cooper's junior year at college, his father began urging him to give thought to choosing a career. "I have thought about a lot of things," he told his father. "Particularly things I thought I 'ought' to do. But they don't mesh with the only thing it's ever occurred to me that I 'want' to do."

Cooper admitted that the one thing that excited him was the idea of being a teacher in a boarding school. He knew it did not pay well and that it might be a poor way to fulfill the considerable promise of his talents.

But his father ventured the opinion that a man could go a long way with that sort of a career, perhaps accomplish more in the long run than he could as a stock broker or statesman or diplomat. "Use your imagination," he said, "You could be headmaster of a great school, or how about State Commissioner of Education? You could be an author and spokesman for education.

"One of the major keys to success," Sherman Morgan said, "is to do what you really enjoy doing. My boy, I think a man can go a lot further in a calling that appears limiting but is, nevertheless, exciting to him."

Thus encouraged, Cooper consulted his old Headmaster who suggested he try out his interest by working in a boarding school's summer session. He said that Essex Academy ran a superb summer school and he would recommend Cooper warmly to the Headmaster of Essex, who was a friend and would, no doubt, make a place for him.

Cooper did, indeed, receive an offer to help teach some of the English program, and run some recreational activities in the afternoons. He accepted the job.

Nancy proposed that she rent a cottage on the nearby Connecticut shore, so they could live together. "No one would need to know," she said, "and it would be like we were married." She slipped her arms insides his jacket, hugging him, stood on her tiptoes and looked up into his face.

"The only problem with that is I'll be living in a dormitory, taking care of a bunch of kids every night. I have to be there. I can't leave."

She pushed herself away from him. Scowling, she stamped her foot. "Is this fucking school going to own you all summer?"

"Not on the weekends, honey, the weekends will be all for us."

"And is that what you want?" she demanded.

"Yeah," he grinned at her. "I want to build up my strength for five days, then screw you for two straight. Five off and two on, every week."

Nancy saw that it was pointless to argue with him. Still, she had reservations about the whole idea. But she kept her negative feelings to herself, put on a cheerful face and made the best of it. Her family had a summer place on Cape Cod in the town of Falmouth. It was a huge Victorian house on the shore facing out toward Nantucket Sound. There was room there for twelve guests. Nancy resolved to spend the summer weekdays there. She was majoring in Biology at her college because she had a halfhearted sort of idea that she would go to medical school. She got a volunteer job at the marine biology research station nearby for the summer. It not only kept her busy but the work was exciting. She felt it was more satisfying than whiling away her time with the country club set. It gave her something interesting to talk about with Cooper when they met on the weekend. The fact that he was impressed was enough, all by itself, to make her feel good about it.

Cooper found his experiment at Essex Academy better than he had imagined it could be. Some students were there to make up courses they had flunked or to strengthen basic skills such as reading, writing, and mathematics. Most, however, were bright students who wanted to take interesting courses just for the fun of it. Most of their parents had in mind that the summer program would improve their children's chances of admission to leading colleges. The courses for these ambitious students were referred to as "an enrichment curriculum."

Essex was one of the few prominent boarding schools that were co-ed and Cooper found he liked the atmosphere. He had always liked kids and had a knack with them. For a number of summers he had run informal classes in swimming for children at Riverside Yacht Club. They trusted him instinctively and they learned to swim. The students at Essex, although older, flocked to him. His afternoon recreational activities were voluntary and he had no adult help. When the activities began attracting too many takers, he enlisted some of the older students to assist. There were a number of good athletes making up courses and they fell all over themselves responding to Cooper's appeals to their egos. Before the summer was over, Cooper was managing an extensive afternoon program: tennis, softball, volleyball, swimming, soccer, lifesaving, first aid, badminton and special football skills.

Cooper initially hoped he could help teach enrichment courses and avoid the dull drill involved in teaching basic English skills. He found, however, that the professional teachers felt the same way and they outranked him. But he discovered that teaching grammar and basic writing to some of his afternoon athletic field friends could be rewarding. Watching the light dawn on a student was often thrilling. Cooper discovered that real teaching wasn't easy. He was amazed to find that he had almost no guidance, and could find little. So, he experimented. He worked every night, reading and making out plans to solve each of his student's problems. He seemed to understand their problems intuitively. He was quick, and had a rare instinct for knowing just what was holding a boy or girl in a state of confusion. He soon worked out techniques to teach them what they needed to know. He broke up little mental logjams by the dozens that summer.

Smoke Johansen, who ran the English program, told the Headmaster that if he hired Cooper Morgan as a permanent member of the faculty it would be one of the smartest moves he ever made. The Headmaster, already impressed with Cooper's afternoon recreational program, said he would do his best, but they really ought to let him finish college first.

So, Cooper went back to his college for his senior year with what he thought at the time was a clear idea about his career intentions. Whenever he thought about a life as a teacher, he pictured himself in secondary school, specifically in a boarding school. But several of the faculty members that taught him had recognized in him a potential for fine scholarship and had urged him to consider college teaching. It was clear to Cooper that they, perhaps unintentionally, felt superior to their brothers who labored in the vineyard at the secondary level of education. This amused Cooper because he personally placed a higher value on the life influence of his teachers in his prep school than he did on those who taught him in college. That feeling, however, was not what led him to his decision. He simply was much more excited by the "process" of teaching than he was by the subject matter being taught. He reasoned, correctly, that the college level teacher was far more concerned with expertise, knowledge and thought in "his field" than he was in pedagogy itself.

There was something else. He conceived of the boarding school community as perhaps the most interesting life of all. It would not be a bad thing, he thought, to end up as the headmaster of such a community. Certainly his family and friends and teachers, or he himself, for that matter, could find no fault in such a lofty ambition or its achievement.

When the only headmaster he had ever known was his own boyhood headmaster, Cooper had shied away from any thought that he could ever fill such giant shoes. However, the leader of Essex Academy, seen from the vantage point of Cooper's twenty-one years, did not seem to be a titan or a particularly remarkable man. He had served Essex for many years. And the school was highly regarded. In other words, a competent but not unusual person could do the job. Therefore, Cooper reasoned, he might keep that goal in mind as an eventual career achievement.

Destiny, however, sidetracked Young Morgan for several years from his intended career as a schoolmaster.

That summer, more often than not, Nancy picked Cooper up on Friday in the late afternoon and they drove to Riverside to spend the weekend with his family at the Rectory. It was a large old house, purchased by the Vestry of St. Stephens and situated across the road from the huge church that was built to accommodate Dr. Morgan's fast-growing congregation. That was in the early years of his ministry in Riverside. The house had a back wing with a large kitchen and several pantries. The two floors above had been designed for servants' rooms. When Cooper entered Junior High School, his mother, Elizabeth, celebrated the event by allowing him to take over the very private suite of rooms on the third floor of the back wing. Consequently, he became the envy of his friends, with three small rooms and a private bathroom all to himself. He used one room for a playroom, one for a bedroom and one for a study. On the second floor, below him in the back wing, there were three identical rooms, which Elizabeth had set up as guest rooms. Nancy always stayed in one of these. There was a back stairway that connected the kitchen area with the two floors above.

Cooper wondered, from time to time, whether it had ever occurred to his parents that he and Nancy could sleep together unobtrusively, because of the special privacy afforded by the back wing. Could it be, he mused, they think we are so upright as to be incapable of fornication? Probably not. Could it be they think it's a decision for us to make, and none of their business?

Amazing as that thought was, Cooper decided it must be the case. That did not square with Christian doctrine as he understood it, however. Yet maybe it did. His study of philosophy at college had taught him that there were many subtleties to right and wrong, and he knew that different Christian spokesmen interpreted doctrine in very different ways. He was instinctively suspicious of interpreting scripture to suit his own purpose. He wished he could talk to his father about it, but felt it might be wisest to let well enough alone.

There were many things he could talk to his father about, and he found he enjoyed doing so. Both his parents had the knack of letting Cooper find his own way. They always had. They cared about him, and they were there to help when he needed it, but there was no intrusion when he didn't. Now it occurred to him that most of the time they treated him with the same deference they treated their friends. He began to respond in the same way. He understood his parents' foibles and idiosyncrasies as he never did before and he liked them as people. He began particularly to enjoy conversations with his father.

The man always seemed to have a fresh liveliness about him. He was forever developing new interests. For example, he had a parish member who was sent to prison. He went to visit him. Then he started to visit other prisoners. He obtained the Warden's permission to lead a discussion group at the prison. He conducted services there. He instigated a legislative movement to increase appropriations for better prison facilities. He enlisted a network of lay Episcopal businessmen to provide jobs and training for discharged prisoners. His door was always open to ex-cons. Many came to see him for help of various kinds. They came because they got the help they sought. Sherman Morgan had influential friends who would usually do the things he asked of them on behalf of others.

Sherman got excited about Cooper's summer school teaching adventures. He apparently got as big a kick out of them as Cooper did. He got involved in his son's experiments in how to communicate skills to reluctant, or mentally awkward, adolescents. He was eager to find out how some ideas they talked about had worked out in practical application.

When Cooper decided to work towards becoming a headmaster his father agreed that might be an excellent goal. "However, son, I hope you will always beware of advancement for advancement's sake," he said.

"I guess I'm not entirely sure what you mean." replied Cooper.

Sherman Morgan placed the tips of the fingers of each hand together, in a characteristically thoughtful attitude. He said, "When an opportunity for promotion comes along, analyze your reasons for wanting to take it. Make sure they are good reasons. If they are flimsy, then your step forward might end up being a bad one for you or for others. Be sure where you think the new opportunity will take you. Don't worry about whether you think you can handle it. Jumping in over your head is what makes you grow. Just make sure you are doing it for the right reasons."

"Is that why you've always turned down the opportunity to become a bishop?" asked Cooper.

"Oh, I suppose there might be something to that," said his father. "Your mother and I like it here. It is a good place to raise children. I think I can still give something to St. Stephens. There are so many good men to fill the places of bishops. I sort of prefer to see others get the recognition. I have been given a lot of things, Cooper. The money my father left has enabled us to be comfortable. I have been given more than enough for one man."

The summer weekends enabled Cooper to get to know his father on a new level. Later on, he was particularly grateful for those weekends, when he realized their time together had been drawing to a close that summer.

It happened in early autumn. An emergency phone call brought Cooper home. His father had been found shot and killed, in his study. No one knew why.

Kate was eleven years old then. Leslie was ten. They were devastated and they needed their big brother badly. Cooper found his mother withdrawn and quiet. Elizabeth had always been strong and seldom showed emotion. But, she seemed slimmer and there were dark shadows under her eyes. He was startled to observe how pretty she was. He had never thought about his mother in terms of being a desirable woman. Suddenly, he realized she was. Elizabeth was just past forty, twenty years younger than Sherman. It was widely known that she was bright and scholarly. She was inevitably cool and poised. She never gossiped and rarely committed herself. Hence, she was held somewhat in awe. People were inclined to be careful what they said in front of her, and to worry a little about whether she approved of them. As a matter of fact, she did not approve or disapprove of anyone. She understood almost everyone.

Cooper learned that one of the staff members at the church had found Sherman. Elizabeth and the girls were not home. Dr. Morgan had left his office at the church to meet someone at the rectory, but no one knew whom.

"Have you looked at his appointment book?" asked Cooper.

"Yes," said his secretary. "The police asked that, too. There was nothing in the appointment book, but they took it with them anyway. "She looked embarrassed. "Cooper, I've been so upset, I don't know who's doing what. I just haven't made any sense. None of this makes any sense. How can the nicest man anyone ever knew be murdered? How could any human being do that to him?" She started to sniffle and swallow her words.

He patted her reassuringly and spoke gently to her. After he left, she stared at the door he had gone out of and said to no one in particular, "He's just like his father. He makes you feel good about yourself."

Cooper drove to the town police station. He had not been inside since he was ten and had been apprehended for some Halloween pranks. Nevertheless, he remembered the interior in great detail and, for a moment, he felt like a scared, small boy. He shook that off. His height and deep voice caused most people to treat him with more respect than a twenty-one-year-old would normally command. Consequently, Cooper carried himself as one to whom respect was due. It amused him when he thought of it.

As soon as Cooper identified himself, a man who said he was "the investigator" invited him into a small room. The officer was polite, said he knew Cooper's father and admired him, as everyone else did. He offered his sympathy and, in neatly phrased sentences, admitted that there was not a single clue as to who Dr. Morgan's assailant was. Cooper asked if other police officials would become involved. He pointed out that his father knew many ex-convicts living both in and out of the state. He was told that no other investigative forces would come in unless some as yet undisclosed evidence created a reason for that.

Cooper was outwardly calm. He hung on to the idea that he must take things slowly and calmly, otherwise he might scream. Last night, late, he had cried in his bed. He didn't feel ashamed and he didn't mind. He felt his father deserved it. He resolved, however, that no one else would see his emotion. He thanked the courteous policeman and stood to leave.

But he felt stirrings of anger. Someone killed my father, blew him full of holes. And he's going to get away with it. Well, it's not this fellow's fault, Cooper, he told himself. Be polite and get the hell out.

Elizabeth did not know how to choose among the several priests in the parish, so she asked the Bishop to officiate at Sherman's funeral service. He was a good friend and she supposed the congregation would expect it. The Bishop asked Cooper to read the lesson in the service. Cooper saw his mother was pleased at that suggestion and so he readily agreed. He had performed a number of ritual parts in services in the big church over the years, and felt at ease in a cassock and surplice.

RedThunder came down from Boston with Nancy on the day of the funeral. Their arrival warmed Cooper and pleased him more that he would have thought. At his urging, they agreed to stay a couple of days. Nancy threw her arms around Elizabeth and the two women cried a little. It was the first time Cooper had ever seen his mother cry. He noted that Nancy was very special to his mother and that, too, was consoling. RedThunder kissed his mother and she hugged him. Cooper, embarrassed by the big Indian's display of affection, was about to kid him for slipping out of the stereotype of the strong silent red man, when he saw that George had tears in his eyes. A lump rose in his own throat, so he embraced his friend to cover his confusion. George's massive torso felt like a rock with a shirt and suit draped over it.

Cooper stayed with his sisters almost constantly because he knew they needed him. He left them only to join the solemn procession of clergy and choir, waiting to enter the church. Elizabeth, Kate and Leslie were the last to enter before the procession. Although he had told them it was all right the girls had, nevertheless, promised him they would not cry. But he could tell they were not going to make it. They walked down the long center aisle and took their places in the front pew just ahead of relatives who had gathered from far and near. St. Stephens was packed and people were standing in the back and along the side aisles. Even the huge balcony was packed. The great organ, ranked as one of the best in the United States, was booming and rolling out the massive bass notes of a Bach chorale favored by his father.

As Cooper entered the long aisle he saw a dark, mahogany closed-coffin in the front of the church. It was like a weight hitting his chest. Oh my God, my father is in there. This is real. He's dead. He's gone.

Cooper suppressed a sob in this throat. I can't control myself, he thought. I can't read a lesson. How could anyone think I'd have the poise and guts to do that? Dad could have done it. He could do it if it was me in that coffin. But he's grown up. I'm just a kid, a kid like Katherine and Leslie. We've lost our Dad!

The procession was almost in place. Cooper took a deep breath. He looked at his mother. She gave him a little wistful smile. Ever so slightly, she moved her jaw out. It said, hang in there, we're all together.

The Bishop raised his voice:

> I am the resurrection and the life, sayeth the Lord: he that believes in me, though he were dead, yet shall he live: and whosoever lives and believes in me, shall never die . . .

For no good reason, Cooper thought of a story he had read earlier in a New York paper. It was headed: "Prominent Connecticut Clergymen Gunned Down." It was as if his father was a gangland chief. There was the implication of scandal. The story seemed to pose the question, what sort of games was this so-called priest playing to get himself all shot up? Recalling the story now, the anger he had felt in the police station welled up again. Its effect was to steady his nerves. The urge to weep disappeared. He clenched his fists tight together. He jutted his jaw out just a bit. Elizabeth smiled with her eyes, and he returned it. He resolved to himself that he would get to the bottom of the mystery. He would dispel any inference that Sherman Morgan had any improper relationship with criminals. If he had to wring a few necks to get the truth, he would do it. His father's murderer would not get away untouched.

The Bishop was finishing the one hundred and twenty-first Psalm. He gave a look to Cooper, who turned and walked to the lectern. Cooper stood there looking even taller than his six feet three inches. The vestments he was wearing exaggerated his big frame. He looked calmly out at the sea of faces in the great church. He knew most of them. He stood silent for what seemed a long time. The muscles in his jaw were tight, revealing his anger; the huge congregation was deathly quiet. Every eye was on him. He turned his head and looked at the coffin. He smiled slightly and, as if he were addressing his father, his deep, resonant voice rolled out through the huge church in a conversational tone, "Here now, the words of St. John:

> Jesus said, 'Let not your heart be troubled: ye believe in God, believe also in me. In my Father's house are many mansions: if it were not so, I would have told you. I go to prepare a place for you. And if I go and prepare a place for you, I will come again, and receive you unto myself; that where I am, there ye may be also. And whither I go ye know, and the way ye know.' Thomas sayeth unto him, 'Lord, we know not whither thou goest; and how can we know the way?' Jesus said unto him, 'I am the way, the truth, and the life: no man cometh unto the Father, but by me.'

Cooper had not once looked down at the lectern. He had not intended to memorize the passage when he had read it to himself earlier. He simply had the kind of mind that retained what he read without any difficulty or design. Every word he said had been heard. To many who were familiar with the passage, it was as if they understood it for the first time. Cooper left the lectern as the Bishop announced a hymn. The congregation was quiet and then sang forcefully.

After the service, Cooper stood outside with the Bishop at the top of the church steps to greet the people. Everyone wanted to shake young Morgan's hand, and be close to him. "You'll make a fine priest," said his great-aunt, who was the first to seize his hand.

There were repeated expressions of this sort. "What a dynamic reading, Cooper. You're going to make one hell of a preacher."

"Make your Dad proud."

His mother and the girls went straight to the rectory to receive friends and relatives. Cooper stayed and greeted every person who had come to the service. Afterward, the casket was to go to a crematorium.

"Well, Cooper, this congregation seems to have chosen a career for you," said the Bishop.

"Curious," said Cooper, "I've never even considered the idea, not seriously anyway."

The Bishop smiled at him, "I know." Cooper looked questioningly at him. The Bishop went on, "I spoke to your father about it only a couple of months ago. He told me you hadn't given the slightest thought to it and he regretted that. He agreed with me that the Church needs men like you."

"My father said that?"

"Indeed he did," said the Bishop.

"But he never . . . to me, he never . . ."

"I know, he said it would have to come from you. He would not steer you to it. He thought that would be a mistake. He was right, of course, but I have no such finely developed sense of the fitness of things. I speak my mind, and I tell you the Church needs strong bright people like you. You heard what they said today. It's not just that you read a lesson well. I know you were talking to your father and I haven't the slightest doubt that he was listening to you. Now, Cooper, *you* listen. Look for a sign. Yes, that's a corny idea, but don't sell it short. Just keep your mind open. Come talk to me, if you ever want to. As a matter of fact, Cooper, come see me any time you want."

The Bishop paused and said, "It would be an honor to help Sherman Morgan's son in anything. I think you know I admired your father tremendously. He far outreached me in all things, except pride. I don't know that God had a finer servant in our time and in our world."

Late that night, Nancy came to Cooper's room in a long flannel nightgown. "I don't want to fool around, honey," she said. "I just want to hold you, OK?" They lay quietly in each other's arms and slept. During the night, Cooper's subconscious brain sorted out data and dealt with his confusion and anguish. He awoke fresh and clearheaded. After breakfast, Cooper drew RedThunder aside. "I'm going to find out who did it. Will you help me?"

"What do you mean?" asked George. "If the police don't know anything, then how can you?"

"I know my father," Cooper said with a matter-of-fact look of confidence. "He kept a lot of confidential files in his study here in the house. I think we can get some leads from them. We can take it from there."

In the study, Cooper retrieved a key from its place on a nail, out of sight in a wall of bookshelves. He went to a four-drawer file, and opened it. The top drawer contained personal checking account statements and copies of income tax returns. In the next one was payroll information relating to the staff at the Church, and other personnel files. The third drawer had alphabetical dividers and files with the names of people on them. In the back, there was information about gifts to the Church and about fundraising. The bottom drawer had vertically stacked files and pamphlets in it.

Cooper said, "George, would you look through these files and see if you find anything about men in prison or ex-cons? I'll look through the check book and bank statements for anything unusual."

Nancy came in, discovered what they were doing and insisted that she could help. She said, "Don't you turkeys realize you need a woman's point of view for really effective research? Besides, I have a hundred and fifty-five IQ and you dummies need some brains on the team."

After half an hour of poking around and reading, RedThunder pointed out a stack of files, all on ex-convicts, and suggested they could save time by dividing the stack in thirds and reading them through. They agreed.

"What are we looking for?" asked Nancy.

"I'm not sure," Cooper remarked. "Perhaps information that might be dangerous to someone if it got out. I don't know, I think we should just read them with an open mind and look for ideas."

They read for more than an hour and then Nancy said, "Here is an interesting fellow, Thomas Stephen Yiping. Called Tommy. Can't hold a job, paranoid, very suspicious of your father and his motives, terrible temper . . . and look here, he's done time for armed robbery, which means he's probably familiar with handguns. What do you think?"

"I think that's brilliant," said RedThunder, "Do you know why? His initials are on this note pad on the desk. Look, 'T.Y. 10.' That could mean 10:00 a.m. That would be about right. I think your dad was found here just before noon.

"That's good," said Cooper. "Is there anything there that might be a date?"

"No, but it's right here on the top sheet on the pad. It has to be pretty recent."

Cooper and Nancy looked at the note pad. They all read everything in the file on Tommy Yiping. Then they agreed to finish reading all the files to see if any other suspects emerged. When they were through Cooper said, "Well, at least the stuff on Yiping ought to be interesting to the police."

RedThunder said, "Before we see the police, why don't we go one more step. The guy's address in New York is right there in the file Let's go see him."

Cooper's eyes danced with anticipation, but he said what he thought he should say, "We don't have any experience in this sort of thing. Wouldn't the police be apt to do better with this information?"

RedThunder said, "The police here would have to hand it over to the New York police. They could care less. Just routine for them. We know your Dad. We know the situation. There's no real evidence here. I bet we could squeeze more out of this character than the cops could." He smiled with a knowing look and struck his fist into the palm of his hand.

"George is right," said Nancy. "They might handle it right, but all I've seen from public servants is double talk, stalling and 'wait till tomorrow.'"

"OK," said Cooper, "We'll have a go at it. We can always give it to the police later, maybe with some more evidence."

CHAPTER 2

As Cooper and George mounted the stairs of a broken down apartment building on New York's Lower West Side, they could have passed for a couple of high-priced gangland enforcers. George had suggested they discard their usual button-down shirts and tweed jackets in favor of suits, dark shirts and brightly patterned ties. "I feel like it's Halloween," Cooper had said as they dressed for the hour's drive to New York.

Loafers and young punks hanging around the lower hall of the building scattered when George and Cooper entered. His suit could not hide RedThunder's 220 pounds of rock-hard muscle on his six-foot frame. His dark features looked hard, and his distinctive pale blue eyes were chilling. If this man looked like bad news to the local residents, his taller companion offered no reassurance or comfort. As a pair, they looked so big and powerful one had to assume their purpose was to intimidate or destroy.

Yiping's name was on the mailbox downstairs, with the apartment number next to it. They stopped at his door and knocked. Cooper called out, "Delivery for Mr. Yiping."

The door opened the few inches allowed by its safety chain. A voice said, "Delivery of what?" Cooper caught a glimpse of a tall man with a narrow hawk-like face.

As Cooper's mind raced for a good reply, RedThunder seized the initiative by kicking the door in. There was a ripping sound of splintering wood as the chain pulled out of the jamb. Fortunately, the door slammed into hawk-face knocking him down, because he had a short barrel revolver in his hand. Seeing the gun, RedThunder reacted the way a football player would with a fumbled ball loose in the backfield. Without pausing, as the door flew open, he threw himself headlong at the falling man, both of his hands grabbing for the pistol. He seized the hand that was holding the gun, squeezing and twisting it. The revolver was thrown aside and the man screamed as bones in his hands broke.

It appeared to be a one-room apartment with only hawk-face in it. RedThunder, now sitting on the helpless man's chest, stopped his screams by the simple expedient of squeezing his windpipe flat.

Cooper and George had agreed to present themselves as totally ruthless in order to get Yiping to talk. So now Cooper said to RedThunder, "Hey, Animal, take it easy. We don't necessarily have to kill this guy. Maybe he'll want to cooperate."

Morgan shoved the door shut. He grabbed a frail chair by its back, flipped it around in front of him and sat down on it backwards, right behind hawk-face's head, so that as he bent over it, he appeared upside down to the man on the floor. His deep voice sounded oily and sinister as he said, "You want to cooperate with us, don't you Tommy?" As he said this, Cooper reached down and lifted the man's arm, with the injured hand, straight up in the air. He held the wrist in a vice-like grip. With his other hand, Cooper began to slowly squeeze the broken bones together.

By this time RedThunder had released the man's windpipe. The choking and gurgling changed to another scream muffled this time by the Indian's big hand pressing down over Yiping's mouth. Yiping's face was white, and shiny with perspiration. He was slobbering and his eyes bugged out with fear. A strong odor revealed that his bowels had let go and he had fouled his pants. A look passed from Cooper to George. It said, he's ready to talk.

"How about it, Tommy, are you going to cooperate?" asked Cooper. There was an urgent nodding of the head.

Cooper thought to himself, at least that means he *is* Yiping. Thank goodness we have the right man. It's awful to think that he might be an innocent bystander. My God, I have never hurt anyone deliberately before in my life, at least not in a cold, bullying way like this. Of course, he *did* have the gun. He probably was already afraid of something before we got here. George looks like he's enjoying this, Cooper thought. I hope he's just acting. Maybe he's wondering the same thing about me.

Cooper's thoughts were interrupted by RedThunder's voice, "Why did you kill the preacher, Tommy?"

The man's eyebrows shot up in surprise. A new wave of fear shone in his eyes. His reaction certainly showed he knew what George was talking about. He started to cry. Then he simpered, "You bastards know I didn't do it. Tinker sent you here. Yeah, I know, Tinker." Yiping looked desperate. His eyes darted from side to side, fruitlessly trying to seek escape. He looked intently up at RedThunder. He seemed to focus for the first time on the massive shoulders and bull neck. "What are you trying to do?" he hissed.

Cooper sensed they had better not risk tipping their hand, at least for the moment. He tried to sound as evil and nasty as he could when he said, "What do *you* think we're trying to do, Tommy?"

"Tinker thinks I'll talk, don't he?" pleaded Yiping. "I won't! I swear I won't say nothing. You're gonna say I shot up the priest, I know. But I ain't gonna talk, honest."

Cooper noted that Yiping had proved beyond a doubt that he knew the facts. George had used the word "killed." Yiping said, "shot." Cooper quickly thought, apparently someone named Tinker did it. At least it sounds that way.

He decided to take another step. "The trouble is, Tommy, you were there."

"Yeah," said Tommy miserably, "I was there."

"And there wasn't nobody else there, was there?" asked Cooper. George made a face at Cooper, as much as to say you are really getting into it now, aren't you.

Yiping said, "No there wasn't. But I'll never tell, never." He stretched his neck, looked up at Cooper and whined, "If you guys was gonna kill me, you'da already done it. Now, don't hurt me no more. I ain't never gonna talk. You can count on it."

Cooper thought to himself, you're talking pretty well right now you smelly creep. How can I keep you talking without you knowing you are?

He decided he had best keep trying to draw Yiping out until he realized they were not who he thought they were. He took another crack, "You mean you ain't going to tell anybody that Tinker shot up the priest, shot up Morgan, and killed him?"

"I won't tell, for God's sake, honest I won't," groaned Yiping.

"Then say it," demanded Cooper. "Say what you won't tell nobody!"

Yiping sounded exhausted as he whined, "I won't tell nobody that Tinker killed Morgan."

"Tinker who?" demanded Cooper.

The helpless man gave Cooper a wary look. He stared at RedThunder, panic in his face. Cooper squeezed the crippled hand and the man let out a blood-curdling scream.

"Tinker who?" Cooper shouted at him.

Choking and blubbering the man gasped, "Tinker the Pimp." Then he passed out.

RedThunder grinned at Cooper and said, "Goodness gracious, I had no idea you were such a sadist."

Smiling, Cooper said, "I thought the same thing about you."

"I think he's on to us now," said George, "What's next?"

"He stinks," said Cooper, "Let's strip him and throw him in the shower. We can clean him up and wake him up at the same time."

As they carried Tommy Yiping to the bathroom, Cooper said, "I think we do better scaring him than hurting him anymore."

Yiping was out cold as they took off his clothes. A large switchblade knife fell out of his pocket and Cooper retrieved it. They laid him naked in the bathtub and turned on the cold water to the showerhead, which stood at the top of an old-fashioned pipe going up the wall from the tub. Yiping sputtered to consciousness as Cooper threw a wink at George and said, "If Tommy doesn't tell us everything, then we can kill him, right?"

RedThunder giggled insanely and said, "Yeah, but let's do it slowly. I love the way this one screams."

"I know," said Cooper, "Let's do the ice pick routine on him. That lasts a long time." Cooper then seemed to have just noticed that Yiping was conscious. He snarled at him, "Wash the shit off yourself, creep. Then come out of there! We got a lot to talk about."

"I hope you won't talk," snickered RedThunder, "then we can have some fun with you." He broke off giggling to himself.

Tommy came up out of the tub, shivering and hugging himself. They spread Tommy across a table and, with a clothesline Cooper had cut from the wall, they tied his feet and, running the line under the table, fastened his hands at the other end. Cooper waved the switchblade. Grabbing Tinker by his balls, he laid the knife against them, saying, "Tell the truth or I'll cut." Tommy darted nervous looks at his two tormentors. Between chattering teeth he sputtered, "Who are you?"

George said, "We are the Christian killer squad." Cooper made a hand signal. It said, easy now, cool down.

He told himself, we're getting close. Let's get on with it. I'll decide later if we've done the wrong thing.

Those thoughts had taken but an instant, Cooper realized. Yiping was so terrified he probably would believe anything, even something more outlandish that what George had said. Maybe he hadn't even heard it. Cooper cleared his throat, "All right now, Tommy, tell us about Tinker the Pimp."

"What do you want to know?" gasped Yiping.

"Everything, damn you. Start talking. Do you want the knife?"

"No, no," Yiping whimpered. He was trembling uncontrollably. "Tinker went with me to see the Priest. I didn't know he was going to kill him. He shot him over and over again. It was awful. I . . . I don't know. I . . . Tinker thought the Priest would rat on him. See . . . he knew. That is, he knew . . . I told him about the girls . . . ah, how Tinker got the young girls . . . ah, got 'em and, and made 'em be whores." His teeth started to chatter so badly he couldn't talk.

Cooper said, "Hold it a minute." He yanked a blanket from Yiping's bed. He threw it out over the table so that it spread in the air and then settled over the trembling man.

Lest Yiping change his mind and get tricky, RedThunder said, "Keep talkin' and talk straight or we'll cut off everything you've got and shove it up your ass."

"OK, OK," gasped Yiping. He talked on and on. He seemed afraid to stop. He told a sordid story of teen-age prostitution. Of Tinker, the manipulator, how he ran it and made money on it. Yiping was his part-time enforcer, and errand boy. Yiping admitted under pressure that he had tortured girls, and killed one of them accidentally by going too far. He'd told the Priest that he wanted to quit the racket and go straight. The priest had helped him before. Then he decided the Priest was out to get him. He told Tinker what the Priest knew. Tinker had him set up a meeting with the Priest, and then Tinker came along with him, unannounced. After he saw Tinker kill the Priest, he was afraid Tinker would decide to kill him to shut him up. That's why he had a gun in his hand when Cooper and George found him.

By a sideways toss of his head, Cooper signaled George to step out of earshot. Then he said in a low voice, "What do you think? Can we take this to the police?"

RedThunder thought a minute and said, "I don't really think we should. I feel certain the creep is telling the truth, but I don't think the way we're getting it is legal or admissible. This slimy bastard will change his story fast in front of the cops, with no knife on his balls."

"That's what I think too," said Cooper. "So we try to get him to lead us to Tinker, huh?"

"Yeah, let's find out what Tinker looks like, and where we can find him," replied RedThunder.

"One more thing," said Cooper, "We've made some noise up here. Do you think anyone in the building knows what's been going on?"

"Can't be helped," said RedThunder. "But I don't think anyone will poke their nose in. This is the kind of neighborhood where nobody knows anything."

"OK," said Cooper, "Let's take Tommy for a walk."

The two approached Yiping again, whispering in a most sinister way. They outdid each other telling him how they would enjoy doing unspeakable things to him if he lied to them, even once. They released him from the table and got him dressed. His hand was beginning to swell and discolor, but there were no signs of significant internal bleeding. George took the laces out of Yiping's shoes to make it difficult for him to run. They left the building with him between them. They saw no one, but Cooper sensed there were eyes on them.

They walked until they found a cab. Yiping gave the driver an address. They moved off. There was a chill in the air, as night settled on the city. They arrived at a club advertising a nude girly show. The bar was open but it was too early for the entertainment. Only three customers were inside. Tommy told the bartender he was going in back to see Tinker. Tommy and his new companions went through a door at the back of the room, into a hallway. Tommy nodded to another door. RedThunder tried the handle. It opened and all three stepped in. It smelled of garlic and stale cigarette smoke. Against one wall there was a pale man picking his teeth. A big, bald fellow with deepset eyes had his feet up on a desk and was just hanging up a telephone.

"What the hell is this," said the bald man.

Tommy stuttered and finally said, "Tinker, these guys know about the Priest. About Morgan . . . in Connecticut."

Tinker jumped to his feet. "Are they cops? You bastard! You squealed. You brought the fuzz down on me!" He pulled open a drawer in the desk and started to reach inside. He shouted at Yiping, "You're going to get the same thing. I'm going to blow you away, you sneaky son of a . . ."

Everything happened at once. Cooper moved fast across the room, grabbing Tinker's arm as his hand closed on a gun in the drawer. The three "bar customers" appeared at the door. The first one grabbed for RedThunder. The pale man dropped his toothpick and drew a pistol from a shoulder holster. Cooper slammed the drawer shut on Tinker's gun hand and pivoted behind him, screening himself from the pale man. Paleface, finding no target, turned his weapon towards George. At the same instant, the man who had grabbed George came hurtling through the air toward Paleface, knocking him down. Cooper grabbed Tinker by the seat of his pants and his collar and threw him over the desk. Then, in two steps, he placed a perfect punt into Paleface's gun hand. The wrist broke with a snap almost as loud as a pistol shot. As Cooper turned to assist George, Tinker ran from the room, through a door that appeared to lead outside to an alley. Tommy ran out the door they had first entered.

The man George had thrown at Paleface now flung himself on Cooper, who drove a hard left and then a right with his big fists, into the man's midsection. The fellow reeled back against the wall then bolted for the door through which Tommy had just escaped. Seeing that RedThunder seemed to have the upper hand against his remaining two assailants, Cooper rushed for the alleyway into which Tinker had escaped.

Deep down the alley, away from the street, Cooper could just make out Tinker getting into a big car. A moment later, the engine roared and the headlights flashed on, blinding Cooper for the moment. He knew the car would be hurtling down upon him within seconds, but adrenaline was coursing through him and, rather than retreat, he seized a big garbage can beside him and lobbed it through the air towards the vehicle. The can was full and heavy, and came crashing through the windshield as the car raced forward. The car swerved as Cooper jumped to the side. It roared past him and crashed. Tinker staggered out of the car drunkenly, a pistol in his good hand. Cooper could see him silhouetted against the light of the street. Tinker came back towards Cooper with his pistol raised. Cooper crouched down, realizing that for the moment he was hidden in the darkness from the slowly stalking killer. As he came down into his crouch and his hand touched the ground, Cooper felt the edge of the garbage can lid. Without stopping to think about it, Cooper came out of his crouch like a coiled spring, throwing the lid hard towards Tinker.

It sailed, spinning. The gunman saw it too late. He threw up his hands, but the lid caught him full in the mouth. The gun went off in his hand. The explosive sound was ear splitting. In less time than it took for Tinker to taste the blood in his mouth, Cooper was on him. He drove his left fist into the killer's stomach and came up into his jaw with a right uppercut, with all the strength that Cooper had in his arm and back. The blow was shattering. Tinker's head snapped back with a loud crunching sound. The big bald man sank to the ground. Suddenly, RedThunder appeared and crouched beside Cooper, examining the now lifeless form on the alley pavement.

"My God, Cooper," said George, "he's dead. His neck is broken." The faint light seemed to glow on the killer's face. The deepset eyes were open and sightless. The head hung at a strange angle. Urine from the relaxed bladder seeped out on the pavement.

"Come on, buddy, it's time to go," said RedThunder softly. He put his arm around Cooper and pulled him to his feet.

Cooper put his hand out to the wall to steady himself. "No," he said. Then he choked, and gagged. He bent over and threw up. George held his forehead. Cooper forced out the words, "Got to stay. Wait for police."

"Hey man," George said urgently, "those goons back in there have guns! They'll be out here any second."

Cooper sprang to life. He nodded his head. They ran out of the alley, stopped, looked both ways, and walked quickly around the corner, disappearing among other pedestrians. Eventually, they hailed a cab. George gave the cabbie an address and they quickly arrived at their parked car. Cooper collapsed on the front seat as George took his place on the driver side.

"We've got to find a police station," Cooper said.

RedThunder smiled at him and said, "Relax Gary Cooper, just settle back and close your eyes for a few minutes. I'll take care of everything."

George's suggestion was a good one for Cooper. He let himself go limp and rested his head on the back of the seat. "Wow," he said, "I thought I had been keeping myself in shape, but you seem to take to this sort of exercise better than I do."

"Yeah," George replied, "just the same, I'm glad I'm on your side. Did you ever consider a career as a prize fighter?"

Cooper didn't say anything and appeared to have gone to sleep. However, in a while he sat up and said, "Hey, where are we? This looks like the West Side Highway. We can't just bug out, Indian Joe. I've killed a man!"

"OK, take it easy. Let's just talk about it first, all right?" George turned the car up a ramp toward the Cross Bronx Expressway, heading back to Connecticut.

"Now just listen to me for a minute," said George. "Let's consider the situation. You didn't premeditate it. This guy, Tinker, and four other guys attacked us. He attacked you with a gun, and then with a car, and then with another gun. You took him on bare-handed there, in self defense, even though you've got Tommy's gun in your pocket, right?"

Cooper looked startled. "I'd forgotten about that gun." As he spoke he drew it from his pocket.

"Wipe off your fingerprints," George said. "We're going to make a little detour and toss that baby off the Whitestone Bridge. Keep listening. I haven't finished. You and I know beyond any doubt that Tinker murdered your dad. Tommy told us the truth, and Tinker admitted it by what he said. Now Tinker's dead and he can't tell anybody anything. Unless I miss my guess, Tommy Yiping is on his way underground, way underground where you, me, the cops, and Tinker's playmates can't find him. He's the only one who could testify that Tinker killed your dad. I don't think he'd do that even if he could be found. Now, anyone who knew the facts would say that Tinker's death was the result of self-defense, unpremeditated manslaughter, and they would let you off. You and I know beyond any doubt that's true. But can we prove it? I don't think so. I don't think we can substantiate a damned thing. The question is, are you going to put your mother and the rest of your family through the agony of this mess, including the awkward detail of having a loaded gun in your pocket, or are you going to do the decent thing and shut up? Are you big enough to absolve yourself and forget it, or do you have to go through hell, dragging your family with you, in the hope that an imperfect society will do the right thing and absolve you? I know you. You think protecting yourself is immoral. Well, this time you're full of shit. Now get this, I'm no dummy, and I know the facts. I absolve you. Tonight's events are a secret I'll take to my grave, and I'll do it with a clean conscience."

Cooper smiled at him and said, "For a big muscle-bound ape, you sure are an eloquent son of a bitch. I never knew you could be profound. You're right, it's a moral dilemma. There's a lot involved. I'll agree with you for now. We'll keep a lid on it for the moment, but I've got to think about it."

George said, "For God's sake don't tell Nancy or your mother. You can't ask them to carry any part of this. Don't put them in a position where they would ever have to lie about it. You've got to carry this by yourself."

"With you," said Cooper.

George laughed, "Yeah, buddy, with me."

RedThunder believed more in action than in words. He felt better when, as they were passing over the Whitestone Bridge, Cooper handed him the revolver when he asked for it. He knew then he had won Cooper over to his point of view. George opened his window, slowed down the car, and threw the gun, spinning in a high arc, over the guardrail into the night. It disappeared into the dark, falling into that wide part of the East River as it opens into Long Island Sound. It was so far away when it hit, he couldn't see or hear a splash. "Now, I'm really an accessory to the deal. If you decide to talk, you'll get me in trouble too," said George.

"I know," said Cooper. "I've never said this before, although I've thought it. It's nice to have you as a friend. It's even wonderful to have you as a friend."

George was embarrassed. "Well, I think it's pretty stupid being tied up with a sentimental old lady. I don't know why I've put up with you all these years. I only hang around because I want to get into your girlfriend's pants."

Cooper grinned. "I guess I can't blame you for that," he said mildly. Then his face grew serious. "Look, George, I've thought about it. You're right. There's no way we or I can be traced to the death of Tinker-the-Pimp. There is no sense in going to any authorities now. But, what I did was wrong. Nothing you can say can change my mind about that. I've avenged my father, and maybe I should feel good about it, but I don't. I feel rotten about what we did to Tommy Yiping too. I'm sorry now we didn't go to the police in Riverside. They are good, competent people. It was their job, not mine."

"You may be right," said George.

"I just hope my father doesn't know about it, but I'm afraid he does."

George turned and gave Cooper a hard look. He returned his eyes to the road and said, "If he knows about it, then he'll forgive you. You can be sure of that."

"Yes," replied Cooper, "I can be sure of that."

CHAPTER 3

"I'm going to be fine, and so will the girls," said Cooper's m other. They were chatting together in the big friendly living room of the rectory. It was the night before Thanksgiving. Cooper, Nancy and RedThunder had come down from Boston that day to spend the vacation with Elizabeth, Kate and Leslie. It was six weeks after Sherman's death. Everyone but Cooper and his mother had gone to bed.

"I've found a house I'm going to buy here in town," said Elizabeth. "I want to show it to you tomorrow. I have some municipal bonds I'm cashing in to pay for it. I'll have your father's investment income, his life insurance, his pension . . . I'm going to be really well off. I'm going to grieve for my husband, whom I loved totally, for as long as it takes. When the sting is gone, I'm going to find myself another man. I'm too young to be widow for the rest of my life. Does that shock you?"

"No, Mom, that's OK. I hope you do. Maybe you can have a double ceremony with Nancy and me." Cooper laughed.

"Is this an announcement?"

"Oh, we haven't set a date or announced a formal engagement, but we love each other and we figure we'll get married sometime."

"Good, I'm glad you want to make an honest woman of her."

Cooper gave his mother a shrewd look and smiled. "With that I think I'll head up to bed."

Cooper had decided that George's advice was just right about not telling his mother or Nancy, or anyone else, that he had killed his father's murderer. He had confirmed the death when he read about it in a New York newspaper. He missed it at first because he didn't known Tinker-the-Pimp's real name, but closer reading of a news item chronicled the death of

Heindrich M. Pinnstitch, a gangland figure known as Tinker-the-Pimp. The killing was assumed to be an "assassination" by a rival mob. The paper made much of a presumably very powerful hit man who had deliberately broken his victim's neck.

CHAPTER 4

1966

"I guess that's all there is to tell. It must have been seven years ago, but I don't suppose I will ever forget a moment of it," said Cooper as he looked over the breakfast table at Nancy. It was the day after the class of 1966 graduated from Essex Academy. It was also the day after Cooper had been offered and had refused the headmastership of St. Burges School.

"Does the memory of it bother you?" asked Nancy.

"No, but I wish it hadn't happened. I took the law into my own hands and they came out bloody. I don't like it, but there isn't anything I can do about it."

"That's quite a story. Do you remember I'm the one who found Tommy Yiping's files? You and George told me you had gone to see Yiping in New York. You said he proved to you he had been in Florida when your father was killed. You bastards lied to me."

"Yes, but it was for your sake. I didn't want you to have to lie if, for some reason, you got questioned about it. Don't you see that?"

"Oh, sure," said Nancy, "I understand why you did it. Good old noble Cooper Morgan. But, I wish you had told me at the time. Maybe I could have helped you not feel so guilty. I think what you did was great. You solved the mystery. You avenged your father, and you rid the world of a jerk who didn't deserve to live in it. Wouldn't a jury and judge who knew the facts say the same thing?"

"Oh come on, you know the answer to that, Nanny. I don't have to spell out the details. You're a smart girl."

"OK, I dig it. Are you going to carry a cross your whole life?"

128

"No, I'm not carrying a cross. I just don't think I have the right to be symbolically designated as God's minister. So, I lose out on St. Burges. It's my decision. I can live with it."

"That's nice, but I'm not sure I can."

"What does that mean?"

"It means I'm not sure I want to be married to a man who isn't willing to make some sacrifices in order to get somewhere."

"Hell, Nanny, there will be other schools. I'll get the right chance."

"When?"

"Maybe as soon as a year. Now that I know a search committee will consider me despite my age, I'm going to register with an outfit that recommends headmaster candidates to schools. It might not be a year. It might take longer. I'm sure there are no openings left for next year. It's too late for that."

Nancy stood up with a determined expression and started to walk out of the kitchen. Over her shoulder she said, "Well, give me a call when you get your act together. If I don't have anything better going on, I might join you."

CHAPTER 5

"Hello, Baby, do you miss me?"

"Sherri, is that you? Where are you calling from?" asked Cooper.

"From New York, silly. That's where I live. Answer my question. Do you miss me?"

"I guess I'd be lying if I said I didn't miss you."

"How's my buddy, Lisa?"

"Lisa is with her mother in Europe, Sherri. I haven't seen either one of them since the day after you graduated three weeks ago. I've talked to Lisa on the phone, but Nancy won't talk.

"You mean that bitch has left you again?"

"I made her pretty angry, Sherri. I was offered the headmastership of St. Burges and I turned it down.

"Crazy! Why did you do that?"

"Because they're not co-ed and I couldn't get along in a school without gorgeous little blondes running around."

"Yeah, I bet. Is that why you didn't let me know that the Dragon Lady had gone away?"

"Well, I sure have thought a lot about it. But, you have your own life to lead, honey. You don't need an old school master chasing you."

"Baby, since when have you chased me? You are the hardest guy to seduce I ever heard of. So, can I come out and take care of you? I'm not doing anything here."

"How many times have I told you it's 'may I', not 'can I'? And you may not. I'm going sailing. I just bought a small sloop and I'm going off to lick my wounds by myself. I only came back here today to pick up some clothes. I want to be by myself and think."

They talked further and Cooper told her his boat was a twenty-six foot Folkboat, with a varnished teak hull, built in Hong Kong, that he had bought it from a friend and that he was leaving tomorrow from Old Saybrook where he had it berthed. Sherri did not seem too put out by Cooper's refusal to see her. She told him what she had been doing, what some of her classmates were doing, and then she wished him well and hung up.

Cooper's plan was to sail east though the Cape Cod Canal, and then to head for the Maine Coast. He arrived at the boatyard early the next morning. A fresh July day was in the making. The air was clear and the sun had risen in a cloudless sky. Cooper had a large duffel bag slung over his shoulder and he carried a cardboard box filled with canned goods, fresh fruit, coffee, tea, raisins, and chocolate bars. He walked towards the float where his boat was tied, puzzling over the words he had just heard from a boatyard employee who said, "Mrs. Morgan is on board waiting for you. She's been there since last night."

Nancy couldn't be there, he thought to himself. She doesn't even know I bought the boat. Maybe it's somebody who's on the wrong boat by mistake. Or, his heart leapt with excitement and anticipation, it could be . . .

"Hi there, Captain, I hope you have some Champagne in that box. It's going to be a long cruise, and I get scurvy without my ration of grog."

"It's fruit that prevents scurvy and songbirds are not supposed to like Champagne," he said. "We'll pick up the bubbly at the next port, and if any one of the crew tries to give orders on this vessel, she gets a taste of the cat."

"OK, Baby, just don't say I can't go with you."

"You shouldn't be here, Sherri. But, I'm awfully glad you are. I don't really like being alone all that much. And, I have to admit, there's something about you that is kind of exciting to a lonely old sailor." He kissed her lightly on the mouth and then held her at arms length. He slid his hands up against her breasts. "Tell me," he said, "What do you have hidden under this tight sweater, two fat puppies?"

"With pink noses," she said as she nuzzled close to him.

"I think we had better go down below," he said.

"Aye, aye, Skipper. What would you like me to do down below, stow the chow?"

"Later, my love, first show me the puppies."

"You know, I think you're getting easier to make. Before long you might even get to be a pushover. Now, me, I'm your basic round-heeled sailor lady." Sherri pulled off her sweater. She had no bra on underneath. She said, "I can just barely stand up down here, and you certainly can't at all."

"There's no headroom, but I can stand up when you take your clothes off. Bring me the puppies."

She held her breasts up to him as he sat on one of the berths in the cabin. "The puppies' pink noses are getting hard and starting to stick out. These noses are like Pinocchio's. I guess my puppies must have told a lie."

"Oh, Sherri, you are so beautiful!"

"You ain't seen nothing yet, kid, just wait until I drop the blue jeans."

"Do that." Cooper kissed her breasts slowly and tenderly. As he did, Sherri unfastened the belt and zipper on her jeans. Cooper tugged on them to pull them down, saying, "These pants are a tight fit."

"Well, they have my curvaceous little fanny all tucked tight in there."

He said, "It's probably the loveliest derriere on the Atlantic Coast."

"It's definitely one of the two best on this boat. I kind of like yours. It's nice and tight with hard muscles. I'd say it's an athletic ass."

Cooper pulled her over on top of him and kissed her on the mouth. "You like to talk dirty when you're horny, don't you?"

"Yeah, it's a bad habit. Somebody else might be listening."

"Who else could be listening?"

"I don't know, Captain. It's an electronic world we live in. Snooping devices can be anywhere. I think I had better look for them." She unbuttoned his soft cotton chamois shirt and peered inside. "Nothing in here. I guess I had better check the pants."

He laughed and slapped her panty-clad fanny.

"Ow! That hurts. What the hell is this, a slave ship? I'll fix yer bloody arse for ya, Captain Bligh." She tickled him mercilessly in the ribs.

Roaring with laughter, Cooper twisted around and scooped her up and carried her to the forward berth, which formed a V-shaped double bed. The pointed end was up towards the bow, the point being cut off by the forward-most compartment, which held the anchor line and chain. Both were fed up through a hole on deck. Sherri kicked off her jeans, which were hanging on her feet. He laid her gently on the berth with her feet towards the bow.

"This is where I slept last night," she said. "I think this is the most beautiful room I have ever seen. I'm glad it's all together and not cut up into separate cabins. This wood is so golden. What kind of wood is it?"

"It's teak. The whole boat is made of teak, all but the mast and boom. It is the finest marine wood there is. It doesn't swell or shrink. It resists marine borers. It costs a fortune here, but it's cheap in the Orient, where this boat was made."

"Why are there dragons carved on the walls?"

"Those are called bulkheads. The dragons are a sort of trademark of the builder, the Cheoy Lee Boatyard in Hong Kong. Lots of people think they build the finest yachts in the world. They certainly are exceptional for the prices they charge. They have highly skilled but inexpensive labor."

"Well now, ask the teacher a question, and you get a lecture. There are guys who could think of other things to do with me lying beside them with nothing on but my little white lacy panties."

"Every guy in the world," he said. "And me too."

"There are some guys who don't care for girls."

"That's because they haven't met you."

"You're a sweet talkin' devil when you want to be," she said, hugging him. Sherri raised herself to a sitting position and began to methodically remove his clothes.

Cooper said, "Can I expect this kind of service for the rest of the voyage?"

"It's not 'can I', dummy, it's 'may I,' and you're not going to be allowed to have your clothes on for most of this voyage. They get in the way of my lovin.' You see, I said lovin' instead of fuckin.' I'm cleaning up my act, not talking dirty any more."

"That's nice. I can see you are refined little girl."

"I may be small, but I got a big voice, and I got big tits."

"So, I see. They don't sag either. They are truly spectacular. And, your voice is nice too."

"You don't seem to have any sag in your anatomy, either. This post is tall and straight."

"I told you I could stand up down below."

In one smooth, fluid motion Sherri shed her bikinis. She put her knee across and straddled his torso and she dropped the panties on his upturned face. "Those panties are drenched because I am so excited," she whispered.

"They smell heavenly," he said.

He held the sides of her hips, one in each hand, as she sat upright and slowly lowered herself onto him. As he entered her, she sighed deeply and said in a husky voice, "That feels good." Cooper raised his hands and rubbed his thumbs across her nipples.

As her buttocks settled down on his pelvis, Sherri grinned and said, "I may be small, but I have all of you inside me. I have never felt so filled up in all my life. I have just joined the Ladies-On-Top Movement."

Later, they cleared the harbor under the power of the boat's one cylinder Volvo Penta diesel engine. They pulled a little eight-foot dingy behind their graceful sloop. "That 'thunk-a, thunk-a, thunk-a, thunk-a' of the engine sounds like movies about pirates on the China Sea," Sherri said. The morning had already turned warm and she had on a thin, white turtleneck shirt and her white panties, which she had washed out and put on wet. They clung tight to her bottom and the wetness made them almost transparent.

"Judas! Can't you wear something a little more modest?" said Cooper.

"They'll dry out soon, and there aren't any boats close by, and I don't want your mind to wander."

Cooper laughed. "OK, even though I am satiated, you have my full attention, callipygian princess."

"I think I have just been insulted. Talk English, Morgan."

"Callipygian is an adjective that means having a beautiful fanny."

"Is there really a word that means that?"

"Yep, that word does."

"Hey, you are a sweet talking brainy guy."

Cooper told her it was time to raise the sails. He had her take the tiller and showed her how to be sure they were headed into the wind, while he wound up the halyard cables on drum winches which raised the main sail and the jib.

"Hey, that sail up forward is a big mother," said Sherri.

"It's called a Genoa jib, or a jenny for short. The boat is heavy even though she is slender. She's deep and she has a heavy keel, so she can carry a lot of sail unless it's blowing awfully hard."

Cooper instructed Sherri to head off to the east while he trimmed the sheets that set the sails. The boat heeled a bit and her bow lifted as she got up speed. Cooper leaned down to the engine throttle, which was located low in the cockpit. He pulled it all the way back, shutting off the fuel. The starved one-lunger choked and reluctantly hammered to a stop. The silence was beautiful.

"The wind drives us faster than the engine," she said.

"Right. This is a wind vessel, little doll. The best there is for her size. Sailing is the only way to go."

"I can see why you love it. Let me ask a silly question."

"Shoot."

"What is the boat's name?"

"*Barbarian.*"

"That's an interesting name. Is it because it's from Hong Kong? Are there barbarians in Hong Kong?"

Cooper laughed, "I suppose there are barbarians everywhere. The fellow I bought the boat from has a wife named Barbara. Barbara is a derivation from barbarian, so that's why he named the boat *Barbarian*. I, however, while wanting to keep the name, have decided on a secret nickname for her."

"Which is?" Sherri prompted.

"*Callipygian Princess.*"

"For me?"

"Right, Sherri, for you."

"You are a charmer, Cooper Morgan. I love you."

"I love you, Sherri."

"How about Nancy?"

"I love Nancy, too. Now don't ask me which one of you I love the most, because that's a question that doesn't have an answer. I hope she comes back to me, though. I'd like us to stay together for Lisa's sake, if for no other reason."

"That's OK, Baby, I understand. I don't want Lisa to be hurt, but remember one thing, OK?"

"What's that?"

"If Dragon Lady doesn't come back, I can take care of Lisa. I love Lisa. And, I love . . ." her voice cracked, "I love you." Her eyes brimmed with tears. He held her tight with one big arm and took the tiller from her to keep *Barbarian* on course. Sherri buried her face on his chest and sobbed. As a teacher, Cooper had seen a number of young girls cry, but never Sherri. She was always in control, always belittled sentimental situations with a wisecrack. He patted her gently and made soothing noises. She grew quiet. She dried her eyes on his shirttail. He gave her a tissue and she blew her nose. She sat upright, her back ramrod straight.

"You didn't need that, did you, Baby?" she said. "Poor Captain Bligh, your crew just doesn't know how to behave. I won't do that again. Now, you beautiful big bastard, give me back the stick you steer with and get me something to eat. I haven't had any breakfast. After you teach me how to work that little stove and everything I'll get the meals, but now I'm starved and if you don't feed me fast, I'll bite your dick off!"

Cooper looked at her with surprise. His mouth hung open. Then he began to laugh and laugh until tears came to his eyes. He left the tiller and went down the companionway, still laughing. "Life with you is never dull is it, Sherri? You really are wonderful. The stick you steer with is called a tiller and you just steer so the sails stay full."

In a while Cooper handed her up a can of cold pineapple juice. Then he produced a plate with toast, English marmalade, and two perfectly fried eggs. Last, came a big mug of coffee with milk and honey in it. It was steaming and delicious.

Sherri ate ravenously while holding the boat on the right course in relation to the wind. She seemed to have an instinct for it. "On second thought," she said, "I think I had better be the Captain and you cook the food. I could never do this well."

"Whatever you do will be all right with me," Cooper said.

"Oh, yeah? Who cares what you think? Just do what I tell you to do. I'm in command here. Now get your ass up on deck and give me a kiss."

Grinning broadly, Cooper did as he was told. He pointed out Fishers Island to her, twelve miles ahead. He told her that although it was just off the Connecticut shore, curiously, it was part of New York State. "Keep it on your right," he said, "Head for that low-lying, sandy area beyond. That's Watch Hill, the first town we will see in Rhode Island."

"Will we get that far today?"

"Sure, the wind is picking up and we have a nice broad reach. I'm hoping we make Point Judith by sunset."

"Will we sail all night?"

"No, my love. We will anchor in a delightful, lonely area known as The Harbor of Refuge. We will there partake of a fine bottle of red wine and eat a fresh salad, Dinty Moore stew and Italian bread. We will watch the sun go down. We will listen to soft music on the radio. We will go to bed and make love. How does that sound?"

"What, no television?"

He smacked her on the fanny. "Foolish child," he said, "You are a peasant. And now, my love, I recommend you cover your lovely legs, because even though you have some tan, the sun is getting high, and the sun on the water can fry your skin."

At noon they were in Fishers Island Sound approaching Napatree Point at Watch Hill. Cooper rigged a rubber shock cord and a piece of line to the tiller so they could leave it and go below. He showed Sherri around the galley area and where things were kept. They had peanut butter and jelly sandwiches and Coke for lunch.

The day was hot with a bright strong sun, but the breeze off the ocean was cool and pleasant. Gradually the wind shifted from the south. Cooper tapped the barometer in the cabin and found it was falling. Block Island, off on their starboard beam, became less visible in the haze on the horizon.

The wind freshened. It came from the southeast. As the wind came more and more from in front of them, Cooper sheeted the sails closer, explaining to Sherri what he was doing and why. *Barbarian* heeled a great deal more to port so that the rail along the deck was almost underwater. Cooper went forward on the leeward side. Reaching out for the shrouds, he laid himself against two of them so that he was suspended at an angle out over the water. In this position he relieved himself over the side.

Sherri said, "That's a pretty neat trick. What is a girl supposed to do? I've been meaning to ask you."

"Didn't you know there's a head down below? Didn't you use it this morning when you got up?" asked Cooper.

"No, I went ashore and went out behind one of the buildings in the boatyard."

Cooper smiled. "Come on," he said. He guided her down below and lifted up the center section of the forward V berths, including the cushion. There was a neat small toilet looking somewhat different from the usual one in a house. "I'll show you how to work it," he said. "There is a pump to bring seawater in and a flushing handle that pumps everything out."

"But there's no privacy," said Sherri.

"Not much," agreed Cooper. "However, there is this canvas curtain that hangs down when you undo the snaps. That gives you a little visual privacy, anyway. Small boats just don't provide much privacy."

Sherri said, "The mast seems to be in the way."

"Not really. When you sit down the mast is between your knees. Sometimes, such as now when the ocean is rough, it's nice to have the mast there to hang on to."

"OK, Captain Bligh, when I use this thing. I want you up on deck and out of the way."

Cooper said, "Sure, I'll even close the hatch, if you like."

Later, when Sherri came up, the sun had become shrouded in clouds and mist. Cooper asked her to bring him a sweater and suggested she dress more warmly. After a while he went below and brought up the chart of the area in which they were sailing. He began to take compass bearings and mark them on the chart. He explained that they might soon be surrounded by fog, and they would be required to find their way by compass and the sounds of various navigational aids that were located in various spots and described by symbols on the chart. He showed them to her and explained what they meant.

Cooper then went below and came up with a sail bag. While Sherri held *Barbarian* into the wind, Cooper went forward and dropped the jenny and then hoisted a working jib. It was a much smaller sail and, as soon as they resumed their course, the motion of the boat was easier, and they were not heeled over quite as much.

"I like that better," said Sherri. "This is less frightening."

"Were you frightened?"

"Well, I saw that you weren't, so I decided we were OK. It is exciting. Could we turn over?"

"I think the worst thing that could happen in this boat is a knockdown. That's a situation in which the deck is perpendicular to the water and the mast . . . the mast hits the water. Then the tremendous weight in the bottom of the boat, on the keel, makes the boat turn upright again. So, when that happens, just hang on and wait. We'll come back up. Then the water in the cockpit will drain out, because this is called a self-bailing cockpit. The cockpit sole, that is, the floor, is above the level of the water line. These drains, or scuppers, allow the seawater to flow out. A knockdown is very rare. It can only happen if we have a very sudden gust of gale-strength wind and we are unprepared for it. With only a second or two of warning, all you have to do is yank the main sheet out of the cam cleat here and let it go. If winds are very strong, we'll be shortening sail, taking a reef or two in the main. Does all that make you feel better?"

"Yes, I guess it actually does. You explain things rather well, Cooper Morgan. Have you ever considered being a teacher?"

"You know, Sherri, I really love teaching. I love almost everything about schools, particularly boarding schools. Nancy doesn't, and she doesn't like me being a teacher. Am I being selfish?"

"Hey, Morgan, don't talk to me about your wife. She's my rival. Don't you know that? Do you think I go to bed with you just because I have hot pants? I love you, you turkey. And I think being a teacher is a great thing to be. I also think you'd make one hell of a neat headmaster. So, do what you want to do, Baby. It's your life."

"Do you realize we have only about one hundred yards of visibility? Where did this beautiful day go? Do you see those numbers on the compass right there? Steer as close as you can to eighty-five degrees. It's important to sail a straight course now. It's the only way to know where we are and go where we want to go."

"Maybe you should steer. I don't want to mess this up. How do you know where we are now?"

"You are a damned good helmsman, Sherri. I've been watching you. You have a natural instinct for it. I think you are better at it than I am. You steer and I'll keep lookout. If the fog gets any denser, we'll have to start blowing our horn. I know where we are, because I've been watching the shore until it disappeared in the fog. See, we are right here on the chart. We're making about five knots. We're just two miles from this red nun at Nebraska Shoal. So, we should see it in about twenty-five minutes. You are holding us on course quite well. You're only varying about five degrees on the compass there and you're averaging right on eighty-five degrees. That's as good as anyone can do it and better than a machine can. Just keep concentrating. Don't let us wander off. If we go in a straight line, we'll come right up on that nun, number two. It will say '2NS' on the side of it."

"OK, Baby, you can count on Aunt Sherri to see us though."

"The waves have been getting bigger. They must be six or eight feet high. Is your tummy OK?"

"I got a little light-headed when I was down in the cabin on the head, but I'm all right up here."

"I think our visibility is continuing to deteriorate. Can you hear that siren? Can you tell where it's coming from? It should be dead ahead, four miles. It's right at the entrance to the Harbor of Refuge."

"I thought sirens flew around and tried to lure sailors onto the rocks."

"Oh," said Cooper, "I love a girl who knows her mythology. Sirens are half-birds and half-women, I believe. Do you think that's a female sort of thing to do? Lure sailors onto the rocks?"

"I think it is very male of you to think that."

"I didn't say I think that."

"Poor old, big, sexy Cooper Morgan! You have been lured a few times, haven't you, Baby. I'm not surprised if you see females as lurers. I guess I'm one of them, huh?"

"You are an alluring woman. I was going to say I knew you when you were a girl, but actually you have been a woman for a long time. How come you're so grown up, Sherri Huff?"

"Mommy and Daddy fighting and getting divorced makes a little girl grow up fast. She has to learn to take care of herself. Maybe that is a good thing. Maybe not. I didn't have a choice."

Cooper lifted the cockpit seat opposite him and brought out a foot-long cone-shaped, galvanized metal horn. "Going to blow this with one blast about every minute. That will tell other vessels that we are a sailboat on the starboard tack."

"It is nice of you to tell them that, Morgan. You are one hell of a nice guy. While you're at it, tell them not to run us down."

Cooper blew the long blast on his horn. Almost immediately it was returned by a much bigger, power air-horn, which sounded as if it were right beside them. Both Cooper and Sherri jumped in surprise. They could now hear the sound of a big diesel engine. It seemed to come from everywhere. Cooper blew his horn again. They peered into the surrounding gray mist, expecting at any moment to see the huge bow of a ship bearing down on *Barbarian*. Cooper told Sherri to hold steady on her course. The sound of the big vessel's engine began to fade and then disappeared.

"They may have seen us, but I sure didn't see them. They were damned close, though," said Cooper.

"What kind of ship do you think that was?"

"A big dragger, probably heading the same place we are. This fog is really thick."

"Is that our nun?" said Sherri pointing.

"Damned right," Cooper said. "What a good helmsmen you are! See, it says '2NS' on it. That stands for Nebraska Shoal. That took just twenty minutes. So, we're making six knots right on the nose. Hold your course on eighty-five degrees. In twenty-eight minutes we'll see a flashing white light on a tower that's thirty-five feet high. That's almost as high as our mast. There will be a flashing red light off on the right. The siren is on the tower with the white light. You can hear it clearly now when you listen for it. It's right straight ahead."

"I got it," said Sherri. "Why do they call it a nun?"

"I really don't know unless it's the shape of the silhouette, tapering at the top and cylindrical under that. It could be the outline of a nun in her habit."

"I'm cold and wet, Baby."

Cooper brought up a yellow slicker for her and slipped his arm around her. He nuzzled her ear and whispered, "This morning you were hot and wet."

Sherri grinned at him and kissed him lightly on the mouth. "Perhaps I'll warm up for you again, Captain, if we're not run over by any draggers."

After a while the sound of the siren was very clear and Sherri was able to steer right for it. They came on the tower with the white flashing light right on time. It looked ghost-like in the blowing fog. It stood on a high ridge of dark rocks. The waves threw a spray in the air as they hit the rocks.

"What now, Skipper, where's the red blinking light?"

"It's a quarter of a mile on our starboard beam. In a minute we'll come about and head down towards it."

They shot past the tower and the rocks at the end of a long breakwater. Suddenly, the water was almost calm. The waves were gone and, in their place, there was choppy water in which *Barbarian* glided smoothly. Cooper showed Sherri where they were on the chart. They had gone past the top of a breakwater shaped like a "V," and Cooper indicated they would sail south toward the bottom of the "V" and anchor in the lee of the breakwater where the water would be the smoothest. They came about neatly onto the port tack, and sailed past the flashing red light, keeping the giant rocks of the breakwater on their right and in sight. They arrived at their anchorage. Cooper had everything ready. Sherri pointed the boat up into the wind as Cooper dropped the jib. He quickly stowed it in a canvas bag, while it was still attached to the head stay. Just as *Barbarian* lost momentum and lay dead in the water, he lowered the anchor. It took hold readily in a muddy bottom. Cooper noted he had let out thirty feet of chain and line. He let out sixty more feet as they drifted downwind. Then he cleated the rode fast and lowered and furled the mainsail.

Returning to the bow, Cooper checked the tautness of the anchor rode. It assured him that the anchor was holding fast, and they were safe. He went back to the cockpit and stood there with Sherri as they looked around them. The breakwater was now out of sight. They were totally alone in a world of whirling, wispy fog. Only *Barbarian* was real. Nothing else existed.

Sherri asked, "Why doesn't the wind blow the fog away?"

"I guess it does, but it brings more with it. Out to sea there, the fog is forming just as fast as this brisk wind can bring it along. It is our cocoon."

The top of Sherri's head did not quite come to the top of Cooper's shoulder. She snuck under his arm and snuggled against his chest, laying her cheek against the rough wool of his sweater. Little beads of moisture clung to the fibers of the wool. Inadvertently she shivered.

Cooper said, "*Callipygian Princess* is our little island. We are safe here. We have our refuge. When we get the stove going, we will be warm and dry and cozy. And then, I will predict your future. It will be long and full of glorious triumph."

His voice was quiet and seemingly came from far away. Sherri looked up at him with wonder in her eyes and serenity in her innocent young face.

My man is in a trance, she mused to herself. I must not jar him awake. He has depths in him I can't fathom.

Later, when their meal was complete, the little cabin was, indeed, warm and inviting. The teak interior glowed in the soft light of two kerosene lamps. One burner of the kerosene stove was on and turned low. Cooper reclined on cushions on one of the quarter berths with his feet up. Sherri was perched between his legs and curled up against him. On a little table beside them was the remaining half bottle of red wine and two steamed pewter cups. The enchantment that had come upon Cooper when they anchored now enveloped their small low-ceilinged room. Sherri was as much charmed by it as he. The light gray, cottony fog that enveloped the little yacht and all the other vessels on the New England coast that evening gradually grew darker with the onset of twilight. They watched it happen through the small ports in the cabin bulkheads. They spoke together in subdued tones, their mouths just inches from each other. They spoke of things mundane and things poetic.

"How much did you pay for this beautiful boat?"

"Four thousand dollars."

"Where did you get the money?"

"From a trust my father left me in his will."

"Would your father approve of us being here together?"

"Perhaps not, but I'm not sure. My dad wasn't much for judging people. He was long on loving them."

"I'm long on loving you."

"Where do your parents think you are right now?"

"My father would not know but my mother thinks I'm on your boat with you."

"Does your mother approve?"

"Oh, my no, but she gave me her contraceptive pills and kissed me goodbye."

"Nice mom."

"She taught me to sing."

"Your voice is the most beautiful sound I have ever heard."

"Tell me about it."

"Sometimes listening to you sing in chapel brought tears to my eyes. Sometimes hearing you sing jazz made me hot and lustful. Listening to you talk now makes me feel light and warm. There's a vibration in your voice that my guts are tuned to. That vibration makes me buzz inside. The buzzing is good, exciting. It makes me think something important and special is going to happen."

She laid her cheek on his and purred. She put her lips on his ear. "Tell me more."

"You're a good siren, little darling. Your alluring voice makes the lonely sailor dream mighty dreams. Your voice is liquid energy. You are pure and clean. You are my shining golden girl, Jason's quest. From your mouth come deep shimmering bells, from your vagina sweet musk to arouse a Zeus. You are my Leda."

"Shucks, Captain, you swans say that to all the girls."

"I am your Zeus, and I can shoot thunderbolts in your belly."

"You sure know how to charm a girl's pants off."

"I don't want your pants off. I am not asking for gratification. Somehow that doesn't suit how I feel. I only want to hold you, to feel your breath on my face, to tell you I love you, to sleep with you in my arms."

Sherri was quiet. He brushed his lips across her cheek and tasted the salty wetness of silent tears.

CHAPTER 6

In the morning, Sherri slowly rose to consciousness. Her hand reached out and touched the smooth, polished teak of the bulkhead. She opened her eyes and then remembered where she was. Cooper was nowhere to be seen. An old, gray, enameled porcelain coffee pot was perking over a low flame on the stove. Sherri stretched, then tumbled out of the double berth and poked her head out of the aft companionway. They were still surrounded by the cocoon of moist fog, but it was almost milky white now. She could feel the warmth of the morning summer sun. Cooper was naked. He was perched on a seat in the cockpit with a mirror on his knees. He was scraping away the last of beard stubble and shaving cream lather on his face.

"Good morning, my lovely sea nymph," he said. "Did you sleep well?"

"Hmmmm, I slept like a stone in my lover's arms." she cocked her head to the side and gave him a happy smile.

"I think we ought to stay here until the fog lifts," Cooper said. "That might be later today, or tomorrow, or perhaps not until the next day. I have some interesting ideas about how we might while away the time, but first, would you like to go for a swim before breakfast? The fog has its compensations. We can skinny dip in privacy."

"You're on, Cooper Morgan; I can probably swim circles around you."

"You can try, Blondie, but you will not succeed."

Cooper lifted up a cockpit seat and brought out a short ladder made of wooden steps connected by two stout lengths of rope on each side. While he suspended this contraption over the side, Sherri brushed her teeth over the little galley sink in the cabin. Cooper gave a low whistle of appreciation, as she climbed up the companionway steps, nude and golden. Her skin was a smooth tan except for the white triangles a bikini swimsuit produces. That and a little tuft of dark yellow pubic hair drew Cooper's rapt attention. Sherri felt herself starting to blush. In an effort to regain her composure she mimicked the movements of a burlesque queen. She gave him a slow smile under lowered eyelids and arched her back so as to stick out her chest and fanny at the same time. She swung her hips in a slow gyrating circle, placing her hands behind her head, and she sang a childhood ditty in her full, low voice, "Oh, they don't wear pants in the southern part of France . . ."

"You're a real blonde, all right," said Cooper, grinning. Then, with a straight face, he whispered, "And you are beautiful beyond all description."

He stood up. He took her hand and held it lightly over her head and led her up on deck and onto the bow of the boat as though she were a ballerina. They stood poised, hand in hand, feet on the rail, silent. They took deep breaths, standing on their tiptoes. They appeared to be the essence of man and woman, the culmination of evolution, exaggerated by a romantic artist. Still hand in hand they dove gracefully into the deep, dark, green water of the Harbor of Refuge.

Cooper broke the surface first. Sherri's body shot past him in a blur under the surface. She took several quick underwater strokes and then exploded to the surface in a spray of water and bubbles. "Morgan, you bastard," she shouted. "Why didn't you warn me how cold it is?"

"Oh, no, little Long Island beach girl finds it too cold, huh? Wait until we get to Maine. Then I will show you cold. I'll race you around the boat to the ladder," he challenged.

Without replying, Sherri shot off like a fish, turning around the bow ahead of Cooper. However, down the port side towards the ladder, Cooper, racing hard, passed her by. As he was about to grab the ladder, Sherri broke the surface in front of him and seized the ropes, having swum under him. Sherri started to scramble up the ladder, but Cooper seized her about the middle with both arms wrapped around her. "You cheated," he giggled.

Sherri shrieked and twisted, but Cooper hung on and pulled her back in the water. Their laughter turned to bubbles as they submerged, twisting. They broke the surface face to face and Sherri sprayed a mouthful of water straight at him. "I'm the swim champion here," she shouted. Cooper nodded and spinning her away from him, lifted her back on the ladder. As she climbed up, she laughed and shrieked, "Stop goosing me, Morgan. The loser shouldn't goose the winner."

Cooper followed her up and back onto the bow. There he produced a dark green cake of saltwater soap. Sherri said, "Show me how it works, Morgan." He rubbed the cake around and under her breasts and down her belly.

"It works like this," he whispered. "Does it feel good?"

"It feels wonderful. Don't stop." She pressed herself against him. "Now, do my back please. Mmmm, that's nice. Hey, get your fingers out of there. Why are you always goosing me?"

"I can't resist your pretty fanny."

"It's about time. Let's go back to bed."

"We'd better rinse off first."

"OK, but let me wash you now. Oh, my, look how big you've gotten. It will take a long time to wash all that."

"All right. Mmmm . . . hey, don't stop."

"Nope. Time to rinse off," she laughed. "I'll race you again. You won't be able to go fast with that big anchor sticking out in front of you.

Wordlessly, they took one another's hands again, looked out into the swirling fog, took deep breaths, arched and dove gracefully in. They broke the surface still hand in hand.

"Oooh, it's nicer this time," she said. "Doesn't feel as cold as before."

She twisted gracefully in the water to face him up close. She kissed him on the mouth, and reached down with both hands and grabbed him. She expelled her breath and sank slowly down in front of him, then took him into her mouth. Through the water, her yellow hair looked like a pale green cloud beneath him. The water was a blur where the soap that was in her hair drifted away. He arched his back and took a stroke backwards, bringing his body and Sherri's to a horizontal position on the surface.

After a long pause she lifted her head and took a breath. She gave Cooper a slow devilish smile. He said, "I seem to have picked up a remora."

"Does your remora feel good?" she asked.

"Fab," he drawled, mimicking an Ivy League accent. "Fabuloso. It beats anything else I ever did in the water."

"All over," she said releasing him. "It's time for the big race."

Cooper reached quickly to grab her, but she was away, taking swift sure strokes towards the boat. Within moments, he caught up. He grabbed her and hung on. She giggled and twisted to slip away, but he hung on tight and they sank several feet before bobbing up again to the surface. They took deep breaths as he pressed her to him. They clamped their mouths together and sank again, leaving a trail of bubbles. Kicking, they surfaced again and Cooper said breathlessly, "It's time to go aboard, my love."

Her blue eyes were wide and intent. "All right, Baby," she said in her husky, mellow tones.

Late that afternoon the fog began to thin. The massive granite blocks of the breakwater came into view. After dinner, Sherri and Cooper discovered the fog was gone and the horizon was clear and sharp. They went up into the cockpit to sip cups of coffee quietly and watch the setting sun paint the western sky with streaks of yellow, pink, red, and finally, as the light faded, purple.

The next day they sailed past Newport and arrived at the western edge of Massachusetts, anchoring in Westport Harbor for the night. Then they sailed into Buzzard's Bay and into a village, where they could shop for more groceries and replenish their supply of ice.

They passed through the Cape Cod Canal propelled by sail and engine combined. At the eastern end there is a snug basin for yachts. Although it was early in the afternoon they decided to stay over, because there was no shelter on the way north to Plymouth, where they would make a later arrival than they cared to make. They stayed in Scituate the next night. Then they passed Boston heading due north across Massachusetts Bay to Gloucester. They took the Cape Ann Canal and the Annasquam River and sailed straight for the Isles of Shoals, out in the Atlantic east of Plymouth, New Hampshire. They had mostly fair winds from the southwest. They had rain and sunshine, cloudy days and brilliant ones. Their hair bleached lighter and their skin turned brown. Sherri delighted in going nude when it was warm and they were alone on the ocean. She lost the white patches made by her bikini. She told Cooper that it was the first time in her life that she could tan all over.

Their days were simple and joy filled. They learned *Barbarian's* little eccentricities. Sherri picked up the knack for sailing quickly, and worked steadfastly at learning the whole new language of boating. A water map was a chart. A rope, once on board, became a line. Then it became another word that described its use: sheet, halyard, painter, pennant, stop and so forth. They prepared simple meals. Mostly, they went to bed at nightfall and arose at dawn. They played with each other's bodies, slept in each other's arms. Their love for each other deepened and they did not mention the future.

Each day offered its delights and experiences, its obstacles, hazards and challenges. Once, they saw a whale not twenty feet from the boat. Occasionally porpoises swam beside and ahead of them. They confronted occasional heavy seas and sometimes, dead calms when they would run the little engine. It consumed less than a quart of diesel fuel in an hour. It would pound away with its own special rhythm, setting up a vibration in the stainless steel of the standing rigging, which sounded like a drum from down below. The propeller snared the line of a lobster pot in Gloucester Harbor, killing the engine dead. Sherri, who had been preparing dinner below, popped her head out the companionway. "Why'd we stop?"

"Have to attend to the screw," Cooper said.

"Can't you wait till tonight?"

He smiled at her and explained what had happened. He explained that the lobster warp would be wound so tight around the propeller shaft that he would have to dive with a sharp knife and literally carve it off. It took nearly an hour, with the need to return frequently to the surface for breaths of air.

They encountered friendly people along the way, in shops along wharves, in fishing boats and yachts. In anchorages they occasionally accepted invitations for a short visit aboard another boat, usually for a cocktail at the end of an afternoon. *Barbarian's* tall rig and slender, varnished teak hull always attracted admiring interest. When they encountered people, Sherri found it amusing to introduce herself and Cooper with different names, usually outlandish ones. Each time she had a different story about who they were, where they came from and where they were going. Cooper was sometimes annoyed and sometimes delighted with her fabrications, but he always played along, because it was expedient. He found the truth too awkward.

The passage to the Isles of Shoals was a long one on a gray day. They had headwinds and heavy seas all the way, which slowed their progress to a crawl. By nightfall the air was misty, damp and cold. Finally, they saw the eighty-two foot high lighthouse, flashing its white light every fifteen seconds, on White Island, which is the first landfall at the Isles. Cooper timed the intervals between flashes with a stopwatch to be sure he was identifying his landfall correctly. By the time they eased their little vessel into the welcome security of Gosport Harbor, night had fallen and wisps of fog were drifting past on the wind. The pleasant and lonely harbor was a manmade creation. There were granite block seawalls connecting three of the little islands together. They created a snug basin that was open to the west. Sherri looked up from the chart with a delighted expression. "Did you notice the name of the island over there? Smuttynose, isn't that quaint?"

"I don't know why it's called that," said Cooper. "There are lots of wonderful legends here. White men settled these islands before they settled Plymouth. Pirate treasure has been found here and there is a story of an awful double murder on Smuttynose, late in the last century."

"Let's stay here tomorrow and explore."

"OK, we'll probably be fogbound anyway. And this is a nice place to be as long as we've got all the supplies we need with us."

Cooper's prediction came true. Morning found them in a thick fogbank, when he came awake. Cooper heard the mournful sound of the foghorn at the lighthouse on White Island. Going up on deck, he found that visibility was limited to about thirty or forty feet. A black-hulled sloop had anchored so close to them sometime in the night that he could make out its ghostly outline off their starboard beam.

"Good morning!" came a friendly hail from the other boat. "We did not mean to intrude on your privacy by anchoring so close, but our engine failed right here, so we found the expedient thing was to drop anchor forthwith." The cheerful voice of the speaker was reminiscent of a lordly British accent. "I say," he continued, "You wouldn't by any chances have some familiarity with engine mechanics, would you?"

"What kind of an engine do you have?" asked Cooper.

"Why, it's a Volvo. Diesel, you know. For anything more I'll have to put you in touch with my partner, who's down below just now. He understands the bugger better than I do."

"Tell you what," called Cooper. "None of us will be going anywhere in this fog for a while. We'll have our breakfast over here, and then I'll come over in our dinghy and have a look for you. I'm not a mechanic, but perhaps I can suggest something."

The stranger expressed his thanks and each of them went about his business aboard his boat. Later, Cooper put his rather sizeable toolbox aboard the little dinghy and Sherri joined him for the short row across to the neighboring craft. It was somewhat larger than *Barbarian*. Once alongside, Cooper gave a hail. The fellow with the English accent called back a greeting and popped his head up from down below.

"There you are. Bloody nice of you to come over, we're just finishing up here ourselves. Had a hearty breakfast. Now then, my name is Michael Bois, this is my partner, Don David, and you both are very welcome. Come aboard please."

Cooper said he was delighted to meet them, as he helped Sherri climb aboard. He started to introduce them both, then stopped to see if Sherri was going to play her game.

"Go on darlink, tal them who you are. Dere is not enough peoples out here in dis fog to be pullink your clothes off and screamink for autographs," Sherri said.

Cooper glared at her with a grim expression.

"Foolish boy," she said to him. Turning to their two hosts, she spoke in the hushed tones of a conspirator. "Dis is David O. Selznick, de great movie producer, and I am Sonya from Russia. I am to star in de next colossal triumph of Meester Selznick on de screen." She beamed a triumphant smile at them.

Mr. Boise smiled at them both in friendly disbelief, and said, "I had thought Mr. Selznick to be a somewhat older man. As for me, I am a schoolmaster on the faculty of Deerfield Academy. My friend, Don, here is an international jewel thief." The men shook hands with each other over the fact that they really didn't know who each other were and, for that matter, didn't much care. Sherri beamed at them all, ignoring the fact that for the first time in their cruise, one of her fabrications was not taken seriously.

Mr. David remarked, "Well, anyway, we are all rag sailors, and that's what counts."

"Are you really at Deerfield?" asked Cooper. "I teach at Essex."

"Yes," laughed Boise, "I really am. We must have friends in common."

Cooper told him who he was. Sherri, undaunted, interrupted without her Russian accent to announce that she was Cooper's wife, Victoria. Bois and David, it developed, were lifelong friends who owned their boat in partnership. It was an English twin-keeled sloop.

Cooper was able to suggest a temporary repair for the ailing engine, which was similar to the one on *Barbarian*, although twice as big, with two cylinders instead of one. They left their boats anchored for the day, packed lunches and ventured out by dinghy to explore the three islands,

Smuttynose, Cedar and Star, which were connected by seawalls, and together formed Gosport Harbor. That evening they pooled their resources and had a convivial dinner together. Late the next morning the fog lifted enough for Boise and David to depart and head for Portsmouth to obtain engine parts.

Cooper and Sherri and the *Callipygian Princess* headed for Cape Porpoise in Maine. The following day they made Portland Harbor, where they replenished their supplies of food, fuel and water. That evening they had dinner in a restaurant and went to a movie. To the east of Portland lies beautiful Casco Bay. The two lovers spent the next week exploring its islands and towns. Then Cooper's radio warned of a severe storm with gale force winds coming up the coast. He consulted the Casco Bay chart, looking for the best shelter he could find.

"Oh, look at this Sherri, it's too good to believe!" Cooper pointed to the extreme right hand edge of the chart which showed a small area of water that looked like a lake with a narrow, crooked channel leading out to the open water of Casco Bay, right at the entrance to the New Meadows River.

"It's called The Basin," she said. "And look, the shallowest place in the entrance is seven feet deep." She cocked her head to the side in thought. "We must be right about here, so we should be able to make the entrance in, let's see, I'm going to say we're there in two and one-half hours. That allows us to go on the outside of Ragged Island and stay clear of these rocks here." She was pointing at the chart.

"Judas! Sherri, I can't fault that. You're getting to be a sharp pilot. Pretty soon you're not going to need me to get around in this boat."

"You'll be the first to know when I'm ready, Morgan. I'll be throwing you over the side. Then I'll take a lobsterman lover, and I'll be feasting on lobster every day."

He put one arm around her waist and with the other he put his finger on the end of her nose. "How about I buy a couple of lobsters for us tonight?"

"I don't think you're going to find any fish markets between here and The Basin, lover."

"I'll tell you what. I'll make a bet with you. If I get us lobster, you let me bugger you tonight."

She gave him a slow smile. "So that's what's on your mind, huh? I have thought about that in fantasies, but I wouldn't really like to do it. I'm afraid it would hurt. You'd split my poor fanny in two."

"Why don't we try, and find out!"

"Nope."

"That's final?"

"Yep."

"You won't ever reconsider? Even if we go to bed together for the rest of our lives? Even if we were man and wife?"

"Baby, if we ever get married, I'll give you that for a present on our wedding night. Then, there will be one last virgin hole for you. I can be a virgin bride, how about that?"

"That is a delightful and quaint idea. I'm all for it. It is a considerable incentive, and you may be sure I will hold you to it and it to you."

"In the meantime," she stuck her tongue out at him, "just hold it."

"Ah, your tongue is pretty. I'll settle for that while you keep a tight sphincter."

There were several lobster boats in sight of *Barbarian*. Cooper managed to buy two fine lobsters from the first boat he approached. Then they headed north, past Bear Island to starboard and Cundy Harbor to port, to the entrance of The Basin, arriving just when Sherri had predicted they would. Cooper started the engine and Sherri dropped and stowed the sails. The tide was rising so there was a strong current in their favor as they motored through the channel. Tons of salt water rushed in and out of The Basin twice each day with a tide rise that averaged nearly ten feet in height. Cooper was commenting on this to Sherri as they entered the protected body of water, surrounded on all sides by land.

"It's beautiful," said Sherri.

"Not a house to be seen, but there are many boats."

"I guess we are not the only ones who want shelter from the storm."

"Well, we'll all be safe in here. This is a real 'hurricane hole.' There is plenty of room, too. How's this, me beauty? You have a safe snug harbor, lobster for dinner and an ardent lover who respects the sanctity of your pretty derriere . . . for now."

She gave him her slow smile and pressed herself against him, looking up into his eyes. He stooped and kissed her tenderly. She moaned softly and quickly pressed the tip of her tongue into his mouth. Then, with equal speed, she nipped his lower lip with her teeth.

"Ow!" he said, and slapped her fanny, playfully.

Sherri giggled, "I don't want you to think I'm dull. I don't want you to get bored."

"Sweetheart, there is no man in the world who could ever be bored with you."

"All right, Captain, get yer bloomin' hand off me arse, and let's get anchored. Then Jim Hawkins here will cook yer a lobster!"

Cooper lowered an anchor and they motored two hundred feet straight ahead to the end of the anchor line. He lowered another anchor and backed one hundred feet down and fastened each line at the bow, gunning the little engine both ahead and in reverse to set each anchor fast, in turn. In response to Sherri's quizzical look he explained that now, no matter where the wind came from, *Barbarian* would face in to it while swinging in a relatively small arc, avoiding collision with another boat. If the worst happened, and they dragged the anchor that has the most tension on it, he explained, then the two anchors will wind up in parallel, giving double holding power.

"It's a good idea when you're expecting a big blow," he said.

The storm hit later that night after the lobster dinner and a bottle of white wine. Cooper and Sherri joined their bodies tight together under the covers and listened as the furious wind screamed through the trees on shore and the rigging on their little boat.

He spoke in a husky voice, quietly, with his lips near her ear. "I've heard that when animal couples are hiding from danger outside they copulate like crazy. It's an instinct to preserve their species by producing more of themselves."

"Do you think we're like animals?"

"Yes, my furry little darling, more than we like to admit. But, there are some . . . differences."

"Yeah, I think there are. You like to screw all the time—in danger or in safety, in peace or in war, during the day and at night, on the boat and ashore, in sickness and in health. Cooper Morgan, you are a fucking machine!"

"Oh, ah, sorry about that. Can't get enough Sherri. Alcoholic. Hmmm, move your hips a little. Yes, like that. A little faster. Nice, don't stop."

CHAPTER 7

Cooper got up repeatedly during the night to check their anchors and the relative position of boats around them, to be sure no one dragged anchor down on them. The wind was furious and roaring. The driving rain stung like steel needles flying horizontally across the water. Most of the storm was high above them, however. The tall fir trees on the surrounding shores protected them nicely. The waves were small and choppy.

In the light of early morning the storm was gone. It was cold and the air was sharp and exceptionally clear. The wind was gusty and strong out of the northwest. The sky was gray.

Despite the chilly wind, Sherri and Cooper took their usual early morning swim and bath with saltwater soap. They wore bathing suits because people were up and about in boats nearby. They left the water fast and toweled down with teeth chattering. They dressed hurriedly in warm wool clothes.

"Oh, baby, I'd give anything for a hot shower one of these days. I'd like to have dinner in a restaurant again, too. That was fun in Portland. Can we do it again?"

"We can and we may," said Cooper. "The Cruising Guide mentions a place called Sebasco Lodge. It's just three or four miles east. There are guest moorings, a swimming pool, tennis courts, golf course, luxurious hot showers, dining, dancing—everything a beautiful sailor lady could want. Sound good?"

"Heavenly."

They had breakfast and caught the receding tide so the current was again in their favor. Sebasco Lodge turned out to have so many pleasant diversions that Cooper secured a nice room in a building called The Annex, and they stayed a couple of nights.

The balmy warm summer temperatures returned, and at mid-day they headed south, then east, around Cape Small and out of Casco Bay.

"How far east are we going to go," asked Sherri.

"I don't know. How long do you want to be gone? Are you having fun?

"Oh, Cooper, I have never been so happy in all my life. Sailing just has to be the most beautiful thing there is, and you are the most beautiful person to do it with."

"You know what?"

"What?"

"That is the first time you have ever called me Cooper."

"I think of you by your name, but I have been shy about using it because, well, that's what everyone else calls you, people in your world. I'm not part of your world. I'm with you. I love you more than anyone or anything. I love you so much it hurts. I'm part of you, but, well, I'm not part of your world. Do you know what I'm saying?"

"Yes. I feel it too. I am jealous of your friends, your generation. Every now and then something happens, or you say something, and I feel left out. I am an outsider in your world."

"She put her arms around him and looked pleadingly up into his face. "But, we have our world, don't we?"

"Yes. For now. It's the best, the best world!"

"So where are we going, lover? How far east? How long does our world last?"

"It lasts until the real world catches up to us, Sherri. That could be anytime. What we have is ethereal, and very fragile. I guess that's why I make love to you so much. I know our separate worlds are going to claim us. I don't want to miss a moment while I have you. Do you know that I wake up at night just to hear you breathe . . . to smell your skin, feel your warmth, hold you?

She gave a little cry and pressed her face against his chest.

"Someday," he said, "someday maybe we will have a life together, but we can't be sure. Us together, fitting in, in our own place along with everyone else. Maybe. Now, our time is stolen, fleeting. We must make the most of it and value it for itself, and not spoil it by wanting more. What we have is rare, but we will always have these days. Even the longest life is short. We must value our love for its quality, not its duration."

She lifted her face and smiled sheepishly. "I like that. You say things well, Morgan. You are a sweet-talkin' son-of-a-bitch. I love you, completely."

"OK kid, we know you have to go to college. I have to be back at Essex the day after Labor Day. Before our time runs out, we'll have to turn around and head back. That will be in about a week. We will sail east for a week, I sort of hope we can go as far as Somes Sound. It's a natural fjord and you should see it. Now, let us make a pact. We won't worry about the days passing by, knowing we'll have to part. We will just enjoy these days, every minute, so when we look back on them we will be pleased with ourselves for doing our best to make them count."

"I'll try, baby. I'll try."

That afternoon they sailed past the islands off Popham Beach, approaching Seguin Island, five miles off the mainland. On top was the highest lighthouse in Maine. They rounded Pond Island, which boasted a smaller lighthouse, and entered one of the most beautiful rivers in the world—the Kennebec. They rounded an ancient stone fort, which guarded the river mouth, and dropped anchor at the entrance to a tidal bay, just off a long line of decaying pilings, which reached far out from the village of Popham Beach.

In the morning they again took advantage of the current from the receding tide. Sailing past Sheepscot Bay, Boothbay Harbor and Pemaquid Point, they headed for a group of islands that Sherri said sounded like a New York law firm: Burnt, Allen, Benner and Davis. They stayed in a pretty cove on the north side of Allen. Next, came the fabled cruising grounds of Penobscot Bay, where each passage and anchorage seemed a little more interesting and delightful than the last. They went on past Blue Hill Bay into Frenchman Bay. Leaving Southwest Harbor to port, they entered Somes Sound just a week after Cooper had announced it as their destination. The chart showed depths of more than one hundred feet in the narrow body of water. At the sides, the shoreline leapt up to steep dazzling heights of hundreds of feet, at one point eight hundred feet.

At Valley Cove they picked up a mooring supplied by Acadia National Park. The cliffs on the western shore went almost straight up. Huge boulders with jagged edges crowded the shore, while occasional horizontal ledges broke the upward sweep of fast rising cliffs.

Cooper cupped his hands to his mouth and called out, "I love Sherri!" The echo started bouncing back before he could finish the phrase. Then, fainter, it bounced back from the eastern side, and it rolled on, bouncing on the cliffs of the beautiful deep fjord.

"If the Vikings ever ventured here, and they probably did," he said, "they must have felt at home."

The next day they took their dinghy ashore and climbed the cliff. They found a lumbering road that was shown on the chart of the area. That brought them to Echo Lake. The water was fresh and relatively warm.

"Why didn't you warn me?" Sherri asked. "I would have brought a bathing suit."

"Because, my dear, I wanted to enjoy swimming with you without the encumbrance of a bathing suit. I do have a bar of soap in my pocket, and if you are a good girl I will rub you all over with it."

"And, if I am a bad girl will you rub all the more eagerly? I must have the cleanest tits on the whole coast of Maine with you and your soap rubbing."

When *Barbarian* cleared Somes Sound, Cooper said, "We may be headed back to Connecticut now, but we will still be seeing new places. We'll take a different route and stop at different places. There are dozens of wonderful anchorages that we have yet to explore."

It was a week later. It was a hot August day with a cloudless sky and no wind. They had been motoring all morning in Muscongus Bay. They had stopped and anchored just off a pretty, sandy beach at the northern tip of Louds Island. The place was desolate so they were skinny-dipping on the beach, after rowing ashore in the dinghy. From a far distance to the south they heard the distinctive chopping sound of a helicopter. It was just off the surface of the water and heading straight for them. It swept in a banking turn around *Barbarian* and then returned, dropping even lower and hovering at the stern of the boat, as if the pilot wanted to read the name painted on the stern. It was a small Coast Guard helicopter.

Sherri said, "I knew I was going to get caught sooner or later, going around naked with you, Morgan. Now the 'sea fuzz' has got us dead to rights."

"It looks as if he's looking for a specific boat, Sherri. He'll shove off as soon as he sees we're not the one he wants."

No sooner had he said that than the helicopter swung over to the beach and gently landed no more than twenty feet from their dinghy.

"Oh, great!" said Sherri. "You sure know how to call them, lover. I wonder if they'll let me put something on before we have to appear in court."

Cooper walked towards the shore as his feet touched bottom. "I'll get you a towel from the dinghy, Sherri. Stay cool."

The pilot stepped out, ducking under the blades that were slowing down. As Cooper approached, the pilot said, "are you Mr. Morgan?"

"That's right," said Cooper. "Wait a minute." He grabbed two towels from the dinghy and wrapped one around his waist as he took the other to Sherri, who was now crouching modestly in shallow water to hide her nakedness. She sprang to her feet in a shower of spray just before he handed her the towel. As Cooper turned to face the Coastguardsman, he saw him at the edge of the water, grinning broadly.

"She's a real blonde, isn't she?" said the pilot.

"What can I do for you?" countered Cooper in an affable tone.

"Sorry, sir," said the pilot. "I didn't mean to embarrass either of you. I have an urgent message for you, Mr. Morgan."

Sherri came up to them with the towel wrapped around her, sarong-fashion. She came close to Cooper, who put his arm around her in a reassuring manner.

The pilot continued, "It's from a Mr. Fairingwether at the school where you teach. From Essex."

Cooper looked puzzled. "You mean Gordon Fairingwether, the President of the Board?"

"Yes, sir, Gordon Fairingwether. It is a matter of some considerable importance to the school, and it can't wait. He wants you to call him as soon as you possibly can. I have the numbers where he can be reached written down on the message here. Do you have a ship-to-shore radio aboard the *Barbarian*?"

"No." said Cooper.

"I didn't think so. Well, you can get to a telephone on shore in an hour or so. Round Pond over there on the mainland can't be much more than a mile away. It is not a life-threatening situation, but my command headquarters felt it was important enough for us to chase you down. That's about all I can tell you."

Cooper stood silently, thinking. The pilot smiled awkwardly at Sherri.

"I'm relieved to know," she said, "that the government doesn't send helicopters after skinny-dippers."

"Yes, ma'am," said the pilot grinning. "I mean, no ma'am. We don't do that. But, sometimes we like to look."

Sherri laughed, and said, "How in the world did you ever find us?"

"Well, ma'am, there are lots of reports on boats that you are probably not aware of. For instance, it was logged when you went through the canal at Cape Ann. A Coastguardsman at our station on Popham Beach noted when you passed by there. Every ship and yacht leaves a trail of reports in logbooks. If you chase them down, you can pretty well figure the general area where someone is, and then go look for them. We haven't been looking for you for very long. We knew what your boat looked like. Fortunately, there are few that look like the *Barbarian*. I don't think there is another varnished hull Cheoy Lee Folkboat on the coast of New England. At least, not that I know of.

Noticing the pilot's rank on his flight uniform, Sherri said, "Lieutenant, would you do us a favor?"

"What's that, ma'am?"

"You don't need to report that Mr. Morgan was with someone when you found him, do you? I know it would probably make a funny story, but you could leave that part out, right?"

The pilot laughed, "Yes, ma'am, I don't have to report that there was anyone else here, and I won't if that's what you want. You can count on it."

Sherri gave him the wink of a conspirator, and said, "You guys really are lifesavers. Thanks, Lieutenant."

Cooper looked at her in admiration, but said nothing. He asked the pilot his name, thanked him warmly and said he would proceed right away to follow the instructions on the message.

It seemed to take forever to get to the town dock at Round Pond and find a telephone. All sorts of ideas came to his mind about why he should be summoned. He left Sherri onboard to take care of the boat while he made his call. When he returned, he was in a thoughtful, pensive mood.

Sherri said, "Mr. Frostley is dead, isn't he?"

"What made you say that?"

"Why else would the head of the Board be this eager to reach you. He wants you to run the school."

"Judas! You are clever. Frostley isn't dead, but he's had a stroke. He can't walk or talk. His right side is paralyzed. It happened more than three weeks ago. They don't think he'll get any better. He can think and write short notes. That's about all. Fairingwether isn't quite ready to give me the keys to the Headmaster's office, but he wanted to know if I'm interested. He asked me if I would be a candidate."

"What did you say?"

"I said I would."

"When does he want you back?"

"Right away."

Sherri stifled a cry and held her clenched fist to her teeth.

"I told him it would take me a few more days to make arrangements. He said to be there in three days. He wants me to meet with the Executive Committee of the Board on Friday. He suggested I charter a plane, and offered to pay for it. He thinks big, huh?"

Tears were streaming down Sherri's tan face. She smiled and blinked her eyes rapidly. "It's right for you, Baby. You'll be magnificent. You're just what that school needs. Congratulations."

Cooper reached for her and held her tight. He patted her gently on the back and made soft reassuring noises.

Later, Cooper inquired and found a boatyard right there in the village of Round Pond. He made arrangements for them to take care of *Barbarian*. He found there was an airport at nearby Wiscasset where he could charter a small plane and pilot.

They spent the night on a mooring far out in the harbor. At early morning they came in. Shortly before noon they were in the air, heading home to separate lives.

CHAPTER 8

"I really appreciate you cutting your vacation short, Cooper. We just had to talk to you."

The speaker was Gordon Fairingwether. They were on the first floor of the University Club in New York City walking back toward the elevator. Fairingwether continued, "We have a private meeting room upstairs. Everyone is there. We have already made some decisions. One of them is that the Executive Committee will serve as a search committee. Therefore, I will be chairman of the search effort. We are assuming that we will name an Acting Headmaster for this coming year. We don't have time to conduct a proper search before the school year begins. Also, of course, candidates are for the most part committed to their present schools. Members of the Essex faculty, such as you, are available. You, however, are the only one we are considering for a promotion from within."

"How about Gunnar Ferris?" asked Cooper. "As Assistant Headmaster, he knows the ropes better than anyone."

"Would you consider him as a serious candidate, if you were me?" asked Fairingwether.

"Yes, sir, I might. I would want to think about it."

"Well, I have. Of course, I know what a competent man he is. Great at his job. But, he's strictly a number two. Little imagination, colorless, a man to carry out detail. Of course, he would do as an Acting Headmaster. He could hold the fort."

They got off the elevator and the Board President guided Cooper down a hallway to their meeting room. Opening the door, he broke off the conversation inside by raising his firm, authoritative voice, "Gentlemen and lady, I would like to present Mr. Cooper Morgan. Cooper, you must know some of these people, but let me go around the room with you."

Fairingwether was as tall as Cooper, heavyset, but there was no bulge about his middle. He was the biggest man in the room. His full face was florid. His abundant hair was white and curly. Cooper surmised, correctly, that he was in his late fifties.

There were four men and a woman already inside the oak-paneled room. They had been seated around an oval table and they all rose to their feet, as Cooper and Fairingwether started around the table with introductions. The Board President ushered Cooper to the woman first. She was tall and slender with soft, long chestnut hair. Strikingly handsome, she looked to be in her early thirties, but Cooper knew she was a member of the class of 1937, making her about forty-seven.

Fairingwether said, "This is Cooper Morgan. Cooper, say hello to P.D. Quail."

"We haven't met," said Cooper, "but I know who you are, naturally. The girls at Essex worship you and are very proud that you are an alumna and Trustee of their school." The woman was owner of a house that published four popular fashion magazines. She was often in the society news. Columnists usually described her as brilliant, beautiful and tough. She had been married five times. "P.D." was a nickname that sounded, when pronounced, like "Pedie." It was derived from the initials, P.D.Q., standing for pretty damn quick.

"I should have been more pleased, Mr. Morgan, if you had told me that the boys at Essex worshipped me, but I guess I'll be content, if you are impressed."

Morgan laughed. "Oh, yes," he said, "I am a fan."

Fairingwether directed Cooper's attention next to the oldest person in the room, a man in his early seventies. He was tall, very thin, and ramrod straight. He wore an immaculate, pearl gray three-piece suit.

"I know this rascal," said the General. "Cooper, you are looking disgustingly healthy. Where did you get this deep tan? You look like an Arab."

Cooper chuckled warmly while shaking hands. "Thank you, Everett," he said. "I have been cruising the coast of Maine. I have not set foot on a golf course since playing those eighteen holes with you."

"You don't need to," said the General. "I, on the other hand, have been practicing up for you. I'm going to give you a run for your money next time, you ringer."

Gordon Fairingwether shook his head in mock disapproval. "Shame on you, Cooper," he said. "You'll never get to be Headmaster if you best old Fox in golf. How about Marmot, here? Do you know Joe Marmot?" He indicated a man with disorderly red hair, a face full of freckles and a wide boyish grin. He wore an expensive gray flannel suit that looked like he had slept in it.

"I am honored to meet you, sir," said Cooper. "I have read about you and I admire the manner in which you practice law."

"Oh, my goodness," exclaimed General Fox in pretended indignation. "Don't tell me, Cooper, that you, too, are a liberal."

"That's a hell of a thing to say, General," said Joe Marmot. "Being right doesn't necessarily make a fella a liberal. It is, of course, the first step." Marmot winked at Cooper.

"Control yourselves, gentlemen," said Fairingwether. "This is Dwight Bedlington, Cooper." He indicated a portly middle-aged man wearing half-glasses and a pleasant expression.

Cooper had met Bedlington once at a faculty-trustee dinner on the campus. He recalled that the man was a senior partner in one of Wall Street's more prominent brokerage houses. George RedThunder, who was active on Wall Street these days, had told Cooper that Bedlington was one of the top minds in the investment world, and since he was a Trustee of Essex, Cooper should get to know him.

"Mr. Morgan and I have met," he said. "My son Dwight Junior tells me you are the best teacher on the campus, Mr. Morgan."

"That's a good reason not to become the administrator, isn't it, Mr. Bedlington?" said Cooper. There were good-natured chuckles around the room.

"Lastly," said Fairingwether, "I want you to meet Yale Martin." Cooper shook hands and greeted Martin, who was a small, neat elderly man who had degrees in both law and accounting. He headed a highly respected accounting firm in Hartford.

"Take a seat here, Cooper," said Fairingwether, "and let's get down to business."

"Thank you, Gordon," replied Cooper. He had not called the Board President by his first name before, but he forced himself to do it, to avoid feeling overwhelmed by Fairingwether's forceful, dominant personality.

Fairingwether seemed pleased with Cooper and asked him to tell the group about his education, training, background and experience. Cooper responded in a manner that was more relaxed and easy than he really felt. His deep, resonant voice dominated the room. After speaking for three minutes, he concluded by smiling and saying, "Gordon, it is a bit unnerving to be expected to sum up your whole life in just a few words. And it's downright embarrassing to find that a few words is all it takes!"

Mr. Bedlington said, "Is it true you don't have a master's degree?"

"Yes, sir," replied Cooper, "My highest degree is a Bachelor of Divinity, which requires three years of graduate study. Most academic people consider it to be more advanced than the usual master's degree which requires one full year of advanced study, or in some cases, two. In some fields, a doctorate is readily attainable in three years. Religion scholars, much like lawyers, don't get very fancy sounding degrees for all their work."

There were smiles and approving nods from Yale Martin and Joe Marmot.

P.D. Quail's musical voice broke in, and she lowered her eyelids as though she were sharing a secret. She said, "Is it true, Mr. Morgan that you were offered the Headmastership of St. Burges School last spring, and that you turned it down?"

"Yes," said Cooper, "I was one of their candidates."

"The winning candidate?" she persisted.

"Well, yes. They made me an offer."

She smiled at him. "And you turned them down?"

"Yes."

"I should have thought that was one of the most prestigious headmaster positions in the country, Mr. Morgan. Why did you turn it down?" she asked.

"Well, on the surface, I could say that they wanted me to become ordained as an Episcopal priest, and I chose not to do that. However, there was more to it than that. I'm not sure I can explain it, except to say that it just didn't feel right to me. My instincts said, 'Don't do it!'"

Gordon Fairingwether spoke up and said, "I spoke with their Board President, Stokley Ramsey, and he said much the same thing. He also said that they were very disappointed in Mr. Morgan's decision. They would have liked very much to have him there."

Joe Marmot asked, "Mr. Morgan, have you seen Leighton Frostley since you've been back?"

"Yes, sir," replied Cooper. "I went to see him as soon as I returned. It was a shock to see him that way."

"Did you know," asked Fairingwether, "that you are his choice to succeed him?"

"Yes, I inferred that from what he wrote to me on his notepad." Cooper smiled at the recollection. "He seemed to want to advise me about how to conduct myself with you people."

"That's great!" said the General. "He's still attempting to guide the destiny of Essex!"

"What did he tell you?" asked Yale Martin.

Cooper laughed. "You are kidding me with that question, I hope. I'll never tell."

Fairingwether smiled at Cooper with a look of approval.

Cooper said, "I am a bit surprised that Mr. Frostley favors me to be his successor. He has always been very supportive, but we were never close."

"He is quite firm in his recommendation," said Fairingwether. "He said we'd be fools to even consider anyone else."

"Well, he's right, as usual," said General Fox.

The conversational, informal questioning continued. Cooper found he was enjoying himself. He gave them his opinion on many things without regard to whether his answers would please them or not. Eventually, a Club employee in a tuxedo opened the door to the meeting room and asked Fairingwether if they were ready to place orders for cocktails.

The Board President said they were, and the man took orders around the room. Cooper thought a wine cooler or a tall Scotch and water would be the thing for him to order to make the right impression, but some devil inside him made him say, "A dry double martini on the rocks with a twist." He felt pleased with himself.

A few minutes later, the cocktails were served in an adjoining room. They mingled, feasting on delicious hot hors d'oeuvres, and engaging in small private conversations with each other. Cooper was the center of attention and in due course each of the Trustees spoke with him.

Thirty-five minutes later they were ushered back into the conference room, which was now set up for dining. There was a white damask table covering and napkins, and plated silver place settings. Gordon Fairingwether was a masterful and genial host. He guided the conversation in a relaxed and easy manner, but never allowed it to stray for long from the subject at hand, that of learning all they could about Cooper. After a cold lobster and crabmeat appetizer, thick slices of rare beef were served, with a light mushroom and garlic gravy.

After a delicious Peach Melba and coffee, Fairingwether announced, "I have not forgotten my promise to get us all out of here early. However, before we go, I would like to see if Mr. Morgan has any reaction to an important question we were unable to resolve before he arrived to join us." He turned to Cooper and said, "Because the school year is about to start, there are few, if any, outside candidates available. They have made commitments to the schools where they are. We think you are an excellent candidate and I believe this meeting has done much to reinforce that idea. Still, we feel a bit, well . . . some of us feel we wouldn't be doing our jobs if we did not interview some others for, at least, a basis of comparison. The idea presents itself that we should proceed in an orderly manner, name an Acting Headmaster for the coming year, and then take the time necessary to make a final choice for a permanent successor to Leighton.

"Now my question is this. Do you think that makes sense as a course of action, and if so, would you agree to serve as Acting Headmaster, as well as continuing as a candidate for the permanent job, if we decide to ask you to do that?"

This was clearly a question on all their minds, for they all looked at Cooper for his reply.

Cooper nodded to Fairingwether as if to say, I understand your question. Then he stared at the Board Chairman with an unblinking expression for long moments. If anyone there had known Cooper's father they would have recognized Sherman Morgan's trait in his son. The silence became intense. No one spoke and the tension in the room mounted. Fairingwether showed signs of nervousness, and he had to look away from Cooper's intent expression, but he did not break the silence.

"My answer is 'no,'" said Cooper finally. "First, I infer you are asking my advice as to how to proceed. I think you should first determine among yourselves what characteristics you want in your next Headmaster. Then, you should measure candidates against your specifications. I think you should interview people now, regardless of when they are available. If you choose a man or woman who is not available for the coming year, you should make Gunnar Ferris Acting Head, with an understanding about when the new person will take over. I do not think it would be in the school's, or my, best interest for me to serve in an acting capacity. It would shake up the status quo to go over the heads of senior people for a much younger Acting Head. It would work for a permanent Head, but not so well for a temporary one. Essex is a sophisticated machine, running well. The provisions are already in place for temporary management. You should not undermine that. As for me, if I am in charge, I want to make decisions based on the premise that I will be there to see them through. I have my own ideas about where Essex should go, as I have told you. I think I know how the school should meet the new challenges, which call for changes. I don't think I would be able to serve you well as a temporary caretaker. I am sure I would not. I told Gordon I would like to be a candidate. However, I don't really want to remain one for months. That would distract me too much from my job. You must give me a 'yes' or 'no' within the next few weeks.

"On the other hand, I ask you for no permanent contract. A letter stating your intention will suffice. If you elect me Headmaster, I expect you to evaluate my performance, as I go along. If I don't do well, I expect you to replace me." Cooper smiled and placed his hands on the table in a manner that suggested that he was ready to get up and leave.

Fairingwether chuckled. "Well," he said, "that's clear enough. It's more than I bargained for, but it is a straight answer."

The General beamed proudly, as if Cooper Morgan was his own invention. "Well said, my boy," was his only remark.

P.D. Quail and Joe Marmot said nothing, but they smiled to themselves as if they were amused.

Dwight Bedlington and Yale Martin both looked a little unsettled. It seemed as if they wanted to speak, but not in front of Cooper.

Cooper thought to himself, if they took a vote now, it would be three for me and two against. I'm not sure where Fairingwether stands, but I didn't make any points with him with this little ultimatum. Damnit. I didn't do well enough. I should have won them all, and I blew it. Damn.

He became aware that Fairingwether was standing up and speaking.

"That should do it for tonight, boys and girl. Thank you for coming. Cooper, I'd buy you a nightcap, but I'm late for an appointment. Are you staying in town? May I see you tomorrow?"

"Uh, yes. I am at your disposal."

"Good. Lunch then. My office. Twelve o'clock sharp. Good night, Cooper. Good night everyone. Many thanks." He swept out the door and was gone.

Cooper spoke to himself, but it was out loud. "A forceful personality," he said.

Joe Marmot heard him and he spoke quietly to Cooper, out of the earshot of the others. "But he's not quite as tough as you are, is he Cooper?" Again, the controversial attorney winked at him, and then he was gone.

Martin and Bedlington had preceded him. They were deep in conversation with each other.

General Fox beamed at him like a proud father at his own son's graduation. P.D. Quail's voice broke in on his thoughts. "I have a car waiting, may I drop you somewhere?"

"Uh, yeah," said Cooper absentmindedly. "On my head, I guess."

The General waved going out the door, "Good night Cooper, you ringer. You were magnificent."

"A magnificent fool, huh?" he said to P.D., who was now alone with him.

"On the contrary, you played it just right. Fairingwether loves a contest, and he admires a worthy opponent. He will enjoy working with you, and haranguing with you. You'll make a pair. Bedlington isn't sure what to expect in an academician. After he sees a few other candidates, he'll decide you are his kind of man. Martin will have to think it over. By morning, he'll be in your camp. You know you have Fox and Marmot sewed up."

By this time they were in the elevator, descending.

"And you?" said Cooper. "Where do you stand?"

"I am your last problem. I haven't made up my mind." She gave him a long seductive look, peaking from under lowered eyelids.

She is really delicious looking, he said to himself.

Soon, they were in her chauffeur-driven limousine, heading for her apartment. She had asked him up for a drink. She said, "You don't really have a place to stay in New York, do you? And you're wondering if I'll invite you to stay with me."

"I was wondering that a couple of minutes ago," Cooper replied, "And I was hoping you would. That would really be exciting. But I already figured out that you won't."

"You have me intrigued, Mr. Morgan. Why won't I?"

"Because, under the present circumstances, I am not your peer. You wouldn't give that kind of an advantage to someone you outrank. You are too competitive for that. Besides, you think I'm maybe a little too big for my britches, already. You're not going to fall into my camp that easily."

She threw her head back and laughed. Even her laughter was musical. The curve of her throat was graceful. Cooper was deeply impressed by how young and beautiful she looked.

The half-light of the enclosed limousine is to her advantage, he mused. I hope she's not seeing through my ruse. I've got to resist going to bed with her, nice as that might be, without hurting her pride. If I play the gentleman seducer and she goes along, then I'll simply be her toy until she gets bored with me. If she recognizes I'm trying to avoid her, I'll have made an enemy, a tough one.

She said, "I'm beginning to think I like you, Cooper Morgan. You have a quick mind. And maybe you're not too pushy, just a natural leader, perhaps? So I'll level with you, and we won't need to play games. Don't make any passes. You look like a stud, but I'd rather have you as a friend than a lover. OK?"

"It's a deal, P.D. May I call you that, if we're going to be friends?"

"You're quick to seize your advantage, aren't you? Yes, you may call me by my nickname, Cooper."

"Well, it's a lousy second choice, but I have a couple of places I can stay in the city on short notice. I only need to make a phone call or two. My in-laws have a brownstone uptown, and my best friend from college has a bachelor apartment in town with a spare room."

"George RedThunder," she said.

"Wow, how did you know that?"

"I know George, speaking of studs, and he told me some time ago about his friend who teaches at the school to which I give so much money."

"Do you give a lot? I didn't know that."

"I might as well give it away somewhere. Uncle will just take it otherwise."

"Are you afraid to spoil your image? No one breaks even by giving money away. You do it because you want to help."

"OK, Cooper, you have found me out, but don't noise it around, all right? Seriously, I don't want it known. I don't want people to think of me that way. RedThunder has helped with some tax information related to charitable giving. He has also steered me to some profitable investments. He's a smart kid. Oh, excuse me, he's your age. Not a kid." She smiled.

"You sure look like a kid."

"I'm not, though, I'm a tough old bitch underneath this facelift."

"I don't believe it."

"Atta boy. You'll get into my pants, yet, won't you Cooper? Hey, only kidding!"

The huge Cadillac turned down a very steep, narrow ramp into a pleasantly lit basement area, and stopped just past a guard station, at an elevator entrance. They got out. She thanked her driver and said hello to the guard, who glowed with pleasure at the attention and looked intently at Cooper as if memorizing his face. Then she turned back to the driver and asked him to be ready in an hour. "To take Mr. Morgan to his destination."

They ascended in the elevator, and the operator took them to the top floor without being asked. They stepped off into a richly appointed foyer. It was dimly lit with several dark mirrors on the walls. There was only one door. The door swung open from the inside and there stood a beautiful young Asian woman with an expressionless face.

Cooper studied her admiringly.

"It's no use," said P.D. Quail, "She doesn't like boys."

The girl tried to suppress a tiny smile and disappeared silently down a corridor.

"But she likes you, I take it?" said Cooper.

P.D. gave him a small smile and turned away. "Come in here and sit down. Lin will get you a drink. Whatever you would like. I'll be back in a moment."

Cooper found himself in an elaborately furnished room of modest size. There were two small couches, low and soft looking, facing each other across a glass topped coffee table, which stood in front of a fireplace with a huge spray of laurel in it. The room was pleasantly air-conditioned. Over the fireplace hung an oil portrait, six or seven feet wide and ten or more feet high. It depicted a World War II fighter pilot in his flying gear. He was standing in front of a P-40 pursuit plane. The colors of the painting were so fresh and bright that Cooper was tempted to reach out and see if the canvas was still wet. But he knew the painting was old. It was clearly a portrait of P.D.'s first husband, Lawrence Quail, the millionaire aviation tycoon who had died testing a plane of his own design after the war. He was one of the first aces in the European theater, and one of the most famous and highly decorated American pilots of the war.

He was the only husband she didn't divorce, Cooper thought to himself. Must have still loved him when he died, so she's kept his name and his memory. And she has multiplied his fortune many times over.

The Asian woman reappeared. Cooper managed, "Uh, some nice light Scotch in a tall glass with soda and ice?"

She nodded her head and disappeared. P.D. arrived a few minutes later with the Scotch in one hand, and a large brandy glass for herself in the other. She had changed into a long white robe-like gown, which modestly covered all but her hands and face. But the gown was thin and clung seductively to her very graceful body.

She produced a telephone for him from an end table drawer. He called George at home and arranged to stay the night with him. Then he settled down on the couch opposite P.D. and took a long sip of his cold drink. "Mmm. Nice," he said.

"The drink?"

"No, your dress. You, in your dress."

"Thank you, my large friend. Tell me, where is your wife?"

"Europe, I think, with our daughter. I'm not sure exactly where."

"When did you last hear from her?"

"Why do you ask?"

"Because my spies tell me that things are not very smooth between you and Mrs. Morgan, who, by the way, I understand is Blakely O'Brian's daughter. Is that right?"

"Yes, she is. And you are concerned that since a Headmaster's wife is an important part of the team, maybe my team doesn't have its act together?"

"It's not my concern. I think that idea is a myth. But there are others who will be concerned. I am an expert in marital discord. That may be why I don't think it matters. But a lot of people think that the head of a school family ought to be able to show the world a nice orderly family of his own."

"Well, P.D., I don't know what to tell you about that, except that I am trying to hold it together. I love Nancy. She is an exciting, interesting woman, and she is the mother of our child. Nancy was annoyed at me for turning down St. Burges. She took Lisa and bugged out. If I become Head at Essex she may be content and we'll get back together. However, I can't promise that. It's up to her."

"And have you been celibate in the meantime?"

"Do you have a right to know?"

"Sorry, just digging for facts. I'm your friend, remember?"

"Prove it."

"Hey, you are a tough guy. Look, I wouldn't be too concerned about your marital state, as far as the Essex Trustees go. You can't be perfect. There has to be some weak point in your candidacy. Otherwise, you would not be believable. You'd be too good to be true."

"That is nice of you to say, P.D. I'm sorry I was testy. I am grateful you're my friend. I appreciate it. Whether I become the Headmaster of Essex, or not."

"Oh, I think you will. You're a natural."

They talked on. When Cooper had finished his Scotch, P.D.'s chauffeur drove him to George RedThunder's apartment.

"Judas! You look fit," said Cooper. "Going to play pro ball, after all?"

George laughed and said, "I never even think about that anymore, although I do work out almost every day at the athletic club. You don't look as if you've gone exactly soft yourself. Plus, you're tan enough to pass for an Indian."

"Well, blood brother, I've been sailing on the coast of Maine. Spent a while in Penobscot Bay, which I assume is named for your people."

"If you had sailed north to the head of Penobscot Bay, entered the Penobscot River and sailed north past Bangor and Old Town, you would have come to Indian Island, the Penobscot Reservation where I was born."

"Terrific, maybe I'll do that next year. Want to come with me?"

"I go back sometimes, but I don't think I want to go there with you. You wouldn't like it. Most of the people there are poor."

"You're not giving me that old 'humble Indian' bit, are you?"

RedThunder laughed. "I don't do that much anymore. I don't remember hardly anything about Indian Island as a child. I was too young when my mother took me away. But it's where I come from. They are my people. Even though I'm not much like them, I care about them and before I'm through, I'm going to make things better there."

"Is that what drives you?"

"Yeah, Coopie, I guess it is. You know my secret."

"Maybe someday I can help."

"You would too, wouldn't you, you lovely bastard. You are too good for me, Cooper. Someday I'm going to be a disappointment to you."

Cooper didn't know how to react to that, so he said nothing.

George said, "How's Nancy and pretty little Lisa?"

"Long story," said Cooper. Then he told him the story. He got the impression that George would like it if he and Nancy split up, but he didn't question him about it. He told George that he had just come from the home of P.D. Quail, and he told him all about St. Burges and the present opportunity at Essex.

George said, "I'll call Bedlington in the morning, tell him I'll ruin him if you don't get the job."

"Could you ruin him?"

George giggled, "Christ, no, pilgrim. Nobody could ruin Dwight Bedlington. He could ruin me, or just about anyone else. Dwight is *BIG*. Smart guy. I will speak to him though. He likes me."

The two friends talked for hours, about old friends, about good times. Cooper told George about his two sisters, and about his mother and her new husband who was an advertising executive in New York.

When they finally broke it up and went to bed, George said, "Think of that . . . my old buddy, a Headmaster. That will take some getting used to. It's about time you started impressing us again. That is what you were put on earth for, you fucker!"

CHAPTER 9

The luncheon meeting with Gordon Fairingwether went on for two hours. The Board President quizzed him about his relationship with Nancy and seemed satisfied. He told Cooper that he was going to take his advice and interview other candidates right away, and that he had some people working on it. He asked him a great many more questions. Cooper felt when he left that it had gone well. He had had fun talking to Fairingwether and decided that he liked him.

He called up Sherri and she agreed to meet him at the Central Park Zoo. He had planned to take her to dinner and then say good-bye, but they couldn't keep their hands off each other, so they ended up in Muffy and Blakely O'Brian's bed, in the O'Brians' empty brownstone. They never had any dinner, and neither of them noticed.

At Essex, Gunnar Ferris, the Assistant Headmaster, had been designated Acting Headmaster. Fairingwether told him that he would not be a candidate for the permanent position, but that Cooper Morgan was, and that it had been Cooper who recommended Ferris be put in charge, at least for the time being. Ferris was superficially disappointed, but secretly relieved that it had been decided and that he had been passed by. He didn't really want the responsibility, but was unable to tell that to his ambitious wife. That good lady was outraged and she could not even bring herself to speak to Cooper Morgan, that young upstart still wet behind the ears.

Gunnar Ferris, on the other hand, hoped that Cooper would get the job and was pretty sure he would. Cooper offered to help him manage things as the summer vacation period came to a close. Gunnar was awkward with correspondence, so Cooper wrote all the letters for Gunnar's signature. Cooper enjoyed digging into the administrative business of the school, knowing it would give him a leg up on taking charge should the Trustees decide in his favor.

A week later, Nancy called from England. She was surprised at the turn of events and said maybe even Essex Academy would become bearable, if she could view it from the vantage point of the Headmaster's house. She said she would come home.

"What if I fail to get the job?" asked Cooper.

"As long as you're trying, lover, that's all I want. Besides, you are not going to fail for lack of effort on my part. I'm going to charm the hell out of those Trustees. I'll even let Fairingwether in my pants, if that's what it takes!"

"Maybe you would like that?"

"Maybe I would. He's a good looking bastard, and he sure is wealthier than you are, Cooper Morgan."

"Did you marry me for my money?"

"No, you idiot. I married you for the monster. How is he?"

"OK, I guess."

"Don't tell me 'covered with cobwebs.'"

"Well, that's a whole other story."

"You bastard. I'm coming home on the next plane."

She did, and Cooper met her at Kennedy Airport. Lisa looked bigger and more grown up in her pretty little summer dress. Nancy looked better than ever to him. Her fair skin was just a little golden from the sun. Her green eyes were clear and bright. She wore a chic, summery tan dress. Her lips were warm and soft. Her slender body felt absolutely wonderful against his.

Nancy coyly snickered, "Absence makes the heart go pit-a-pat."

"Things are looking up," he said.

"It feels like things are up."

Lisa was looking at him shyly. A little secret smile played at the corners of her mouth. "Hello, Daddy."

He picked her up and squeezed her. He held her in one arm and put the other around Nancy. "Hello Sweetie. You haven't grown up and made me miss out on your childhood, have you?"

She giggled and hugged him. "You're silly, Daddy."

After returning to Essex, Nancy lost no time mounting a campaign to get Cooper elected Headmaster. General Fox and his wife, Priscilla, lived on a horse farm whose grounds bordered the campus. The two couples shared a warm friendship that bridged the generations. Nancy had only to suggest that she wished for an opportunity to meet the Board of Trustees, and their spouses, socially. Priscilla immediately threw a summer garden party to officially welcome Nancy home. On such short notice, some Board members had other social commitments, but they broke them and every Trustee and spouse was there. Such was the height of interest in Cooper, and particularly in his lovely wife, who was somewhat of a mystery.

Gordon Fairingwether, a bachelor and ladies' man, escorted P.D. Quail. Nancy was radiant. Her fashionable dress even rivaled P.D.'s. Nancy gushed charm at both of them and was particularly attentive to Fairingwether.

In a quiet aside, Cooper smiled at Nancy and said, "Keep your pants on."

"What makes you think I'm wearing any?"

"I guess maybe I had better find out."

"Not now, love, put your fingers on P.D. and the other ladies. I'm already sold."

It appeared that everyone else was, too. The party was a huge success. Priscilla Fox was lavishly praised for serving the school's needs so well.

There was a special meeting of the Board a week later. When it was almost over, Gordon Fairingwether called Cooper and told him he was their unanimous choice for Headmaster. He asked if Cooper wanted time to consider his answer. Cooper said that since he did not want Nancy murdering him in his sleep, he would accept promptly. Gordon said that would give them just time enough to take an official vote and get out a letter of announcement, before the new academic year began.

And so, in his twenty-eighth year, Cooper Morgan was duly elected the seventh Headmaster of Essex Academy, then in its one hundred and twenty-seventh year. The Frostleys settled into their vacation home on Cape Cod, and Cooper, Nancy and Lisa moved into the Headmaster's residence, a mansion known as Chase House in honor of George Thorndike Chase, the school's first Headmaster.

CHAPTER 10

1967

"What's the matter, Nancy? What's wrong?" asked Cooper Morgan, his voice scratchy with sleep.

She leaned over bringing her head close to his, and whispered, "Nothing is wrong. I woke you up to play with me."

As his eyes cleared, he looked at her in the soft light of her bedside table lamp. "Judas, what is that you have on?"

"It is a little something I got to wear for you. Do you like it?"

"Yes, I like it. I love it. But I don't think you ought to wear it to the Spring Prom. You seem a little too, ah, accessible." He reached for her and pulled her to him, kissing her on the nose. "What time is it?"

"5:00 a.m."

"What? You're crazy. Do you know that?"

"Crazy like a fox," she said. "You used to stay in bed with me on Sunday mornings and play games. Now, you get up and go prepare your stupid Chapel Service. So, I thought today I'd get you up early. I need a little service of my own." She reached under the covers and fondled him very gently. "Hmmm, I think you have some possibilities, Mr. Morgan."

"Well, I think I might be able to attend to your needs, madam."

"Fine. Now that I have you awake and attentive, I want you to go brush your teeth and shave."

"To hell with that!"

"The hell you won't." She jumped up from bed and backed away from him. "I've taken a shower, shaved my legs, perfumed my body and trimmed the hair on this little triangle, all for you."

"Bless your heart," he said, rising up.

"That's better. Ah, behold the noble swordsman. Don't take too long. I have chilled orange juice and hot coffee waiting for you."

"And more than that, I hope."

"Yes, more than that."

The bedroom Cooper and Nancy shared in the Headmaster's mansion was thirty feet square, larger than any living room they had ever had. Just off the bedroom was a study alcove, with a desk and bookshelves. Nancy used it, and had an easel there where she did sketches. Painting was for another room, because the smell of her paints, though pleasant to her, was a little too strong for a bedroom. There was also a dressing room off the bedroom, with spacious closets on three sides and a mirrored wall on the other. The dressing room led to the master bath, which boasted a gigantic tub and a separate shower compartment.

There were six bedrooms and five bathrooms in the main part of the second floor of Chase House. In a connecting wing, originally intended for servants, there were four small bedrooms and a bathroom. The Morgans were responsible for furnishing the second floor, but, fortunately, the school furnished the downstairs. All the rooms downstairs were on a grand scale. There were so many school social events held in them, that they seemed like public rooms to Cooper and Nancy. The school budget provided one full-time staff person for the house, Mrs. Mendelson, who was both cook and cleaning lady. The school budget also supplied Cooper with a six-thousand-dollar annual expense account to cover the cost of entertaining, travel and anything else that could possibly enable him to do his job well.

Chase House contained nine working fireplaces. The school maintenance staff kept a supply of firewood on hand and every day laid fresh paper, kindling and logs in any fireplace that had been used the day before.

Nancy had lit the fire in their bedroom. Flames were crackling happily as the kindling was consumed, igniting three logs. Nancy was standing in front of it, warming the backs of her legs, when Cooper emerged naked from the bathroom. Nancy had on a sheer shadow of a negligee that reached almost to the floor. It was trimmed in red lace with little black silk ribbons and was open in front from chin to toes. Actually, it just wasn't big enough to close in front.

She said, "I see our sword has returned to half-mast."

"That, madam, is a classic mixed metaphor. What ever happened to 'monster'? I always thought that was a nice ego-building sort of name, designed, so to speak, to cause one to rise to the occasion."

"Bring the monster over here to mama. It has been my observation, Mr. Morgan, that the Headmaster's life is one long, protracted ego-building exercise."

"I suspect that very nice tradition is winding down, and the Headmaster today is becoming everyone's whipping boy."

"I'm not very interested in that. I am interested in some attention to the monster's cave."

"How is it in there?"

"Warm and humid. I suggest you check it out."

Cooper picked her up and carried her to their king-sized bed. "Would madam like to sit on the Headmaster's face?"

A couple of hours later, Cooper got up to shower and dress for the day. Nancy smiled at him and snuggled deeper into the covers saying, "Thanks for everything, lover, I'm going to take a nap now."

"You'll get up in time for Sunday Chapel, won't you? I expect the faculty to come, so it's nice for you and Lisa to be there, too."

"We'll be there. Who is speaking?"

"Todd Everlast, the new Rector of St. Burges' School. You remember him, don't you, Nancy? He was one of the younger members of the faculty at Seminary when we were there. He's a good-looking guy, one of the church's bright intellectual priests. He'll be worth hearing, and if his wife is with him, I'll want to bring them home for lunch, or we can go out to the Lion Inn, if you prefer."

"Whatever," said Nancy, stretching. "So St. Burges hired Everlast after you turned them down, huh? Why him? What does he know about running a school?"

"Hell, Nancy, he's a distinguished educator, and well known in the church. I'll bet their faculty is happier with him than they would have been with me. I think he's a St. Burges alumnus, too. Everything works out for the best, you see?"

"If you say so, love. Why don't you come back to bed, and we'll do some more."

Cooper laughed, "Once you get going, you never stop, do you? I don't have anything left. Wait until tonight."

"Then, why don't you send Todd Everlast around? Do you think he's as good as his name?"

"I don't know, doll, but I think he might be shocked if I suggested you wanted to find out."

"Nah, he's probably not as well equipped as you, anyway. Those pretty boys seldom are."

"How do you know? Wait . . . don't answer that. I don't want to know. I'm leaving now. I'll be in my study for a while, looking up the lessons for the day. Then I'm going to my office to meet with the Student Council. Then, I'll see you and Lisa in chapel, OK?"

For an answer, Nancy pulled the covers over her head and rolled over.

Cooper stopped in the Dining Hall before going to his office. On Sundays, buffet breakfast was served all morning, and it was one of the best meals of the week. There were pans full of crisp bacon, sausage and fried ham. One could have eggs any style, big glasses of fresh orange juice, toast, butter, jelly, French toast and pancakes with maple syrup. There was milk and coffee. All Essex students could come dressed as they pleased, sit where they pleased, and eat all they wanted. Best of all, they didn't have to come at all. They could sleep until chapel time. About half the student body did that.

Cooper enjoyed the buffet meals. They helped him observe some of the dynamics in the student body—who was friends with who, who were the social leaders, things like that. After loading up a tray with juice, eggs, bacon, toast and coffee, he sat down at a table with a group of laughing fourth form boys.

"Hello guys," he said. "Is it a private joke or may I laugh too?"

"I don't think you'd understand it, sir," said a boy named Jim Cyrus from Long Island. He said it in a slow, almost surly manner. A couple of boys at the table giggled.

"Oh, I think you'd be surprised at what I understand," said Cooper.

One of the boys groaned in mock disbelief.

"Yeah, sure," said Cyrus. The rest of the table fell silent.

Cooper asked if they had seen the movie on campus the night before, and whether they liked it. He made a number of other conversational overtures, but they all ended fairly abruptly, in a silence bordering on sullenness. Cooper began to regret choosing to sit at this table.

Just as well though, he thought, that I'm out reading the atmosphere. I suppose morale is never at its best in March.

Finishing his breakfast in silence, Cooper wondered at the fact that his presence had killed all conversation. "Gentlemen," he said, "I shall leave you now. I'm afraid my arrival has spoiled your breakfast. I'm sorry."

"Yeah," said Jim Cyrus, "Well, we didn't ask you to sit here."

"That's right, Jim, you didn't." Cooper replied as he picked up his tray. He walked it to the dishwashing room.

Amazing, he thought to himself, that kid sure has more gall than I did when I was his age. I suppose I shouldn't have let him get away with being so fresh. On the other hand, isn't it his right to say what he did? At least he was being honest with me.

Outside, the sun was bright. A coating of light snow had fallen during the night, covering the dirty snow left from the winter's accumulation. The sun was fast warming the air to the point where melting would start. At this moment, however, fresh snow was clinging to the tree branches, and it was beautiful in the dazzling sun and clean air.

The Dining Hall, one of the newest buildings on campus, was located on the southeast corner of The Quadrangle. It was, therefore, adjacent to Hyatt Hall, the administration building where Cooper's office was located. He found himself regretting that it was such a short walk. Checking his watch, he saw that he had half an hour before his meeting with student leaders, so he decided to take a longer walk.

I need to think about all the kids. Perhaps I should do something to perk up morale. The mud season is about here and attitudes will probably get worse. A surprise Headmaster's Holiday is a guaranteed perker-upper. Seems to annoy the faculty, though. The conscientious teachers hate to lose a planned day. It throws off their schedules. Seems to bug math teachers and language teachers, particularly the older ones. Aw, to hell with them. We need a break. Now, wait a minute, don't be highhanded with the best teachers we have. OK, maybe something else. Think about it.

Cooper found himself strolling down The Mall, a double road with a grassy strip in the middle that stretched from the Main Gate east to the Girls Campus. The three large girls' dormitories were clustered there. Beyond the Girls Campus ran Old River Road and then the Connecticut River. There was a cove on the river's western shore called Putnam Basin, where a school Boathouse contained rowing shells and sailing dinghies, an office for the sailing club, some storage space, lockers, showers and bathrooms. There was also a tiny island close to the shore of Putnam Basin, reached by a short Japanese-style walking bridge. Generations of students called it simply "The Island."

For no good reason Cooper could think of, The Island had always been a place for lovers to walk. There was little privacy there, because it was so open, but it was pretty. There are few things so compelling to teenagers as tradition and conformity, even though they think those ideas are repugnant to them. So, no new romance on campus was really official until the couple strolled, held hands and kissed on The Island.

Cooper left The Mall, and its turnaround on the Girls Campus, and took a footpath between Parton House and Lynn Hall. Several girls leaving their dorms to go to breakfast waved to him. Cooper was pleased to see that some of the students seemed to trust him. He arrived at Old River Road and turned north, passing the Boathouse. Cooper knew that Essex Academy was actually located in the Township of Old River rather than the town of Essex, for which it was named. He wondered if the land was part of Essex when the school had been founded in eighteen thirty-nine. He thought he might ask one of the long-time citizens, maybe Everett Fox.

About time to turn around, Cooper mused as he approached the southernmost edge of East Woods. Now, there is where I'd want to take my girl if I were an Essex student.

Just as that thought came to him, a boy and girl ran out of the woods laughing. The girl was throwing chunks of snow at the boy ahead of her. Cooper waved to them. They looked startled, spun on their heels and ran back into the woods.

They sure looked guilty about something, but why did they go back? Probably warning others that the Headmaster is coming. Kids didn't react to me that way last year. They always wanted to tell me what they were getting away with. Well, the ones in my dorm didn't, but the older ones did. Now that I'm the ultimate authority figure, I'm no longer anyone's friend. Have I changed that much? I don't think so, but their attitude towards me has changed completely. That was Amelia West and Chick Jones. I must remember to ask them why they ran from me. Well, I could always follow them and find out. No, I guess not. Who was it who said, "Don't turn over too many rocks, you won't have time to deal with all the sin you find." That was Jim Howard at Blair Academy. He's been a headmaster quite a while, and he runs a fine school. Of course, on the other hand, he also said, "Don't walk away from trouble if it finds you." I don't think it has found me so far this morning except in the dining room. I'd better get back to my office for that meeting.

The flags on the two flagpoles outside Hyatt Hall snapped in the breeze. On the right, the stars and stripes were bright in the sun. Cooper looked at the school flag on the left hand pole. The wind seemed to be blowing it more gently. Heavier material, I suppose, he mused to himself.

The school flag was divided down the middle, with a blue field on the left, close to the pole, and a red field on the right. Superimposed on the dividing line was a gold lion rearing up on his hind paws. It was the classic rampant lion of British heraldry. It came, Cooper knew, from the coat of arms of the House of Essex in England.

I wonder, thought Cooper, if the Earl of Essex over there knows that a little piece of his country is nestled right here on the banks of the Connecticut River? At least, a little of his heritage is here. I suppose Englishmen must be accustomed to that sort of thing. Come to think of it, there is an Essex Mountain in Wyoming, a part of the Rocky Mountains. Now why do I know that? I must have read it or studied it in school. It is a funny thing how . . .

"Good morning, sir, you look like you're a thousand miles away."

"Hi, Ned. 'As if' not 'like', as if I were two or three thousand miles away as a matter of fact. How are you? You look a little bruised from the hockey game."

"Yeah, sir, I don't know what happened to us. Choate should never have won that game."

"Well, if you can take Hotchkiss this week, we'll have a three-way tie for first in Connecticut."

"I think we can beat Hotchkiss, and Taft, too. It's Kent that worries me. We've lost to them every year I've been here."

Cooper smiled, "Well, come on inside, and I'll open my office. The others should be right along. You can meet the Headmaster of St. Burges after Chapel and ask him about his team. We haven't beaten them for a few years either."

Ned Tucker was the elected Sixth Form President, which made him head of the Student Council. Cooper unlocked his office door and invited Ned in. Cooper had arranged the office pretty much the same way his predecessor, Leighton Frostley had, with his desk at the far end and a grouping of chairs around a coffee table at the other end. In the middle of the room was a table that could be expanded like a dining room table. It had seven chairs around it now, enough for a meeting with the Student Council.

"Ned," said Cooper, "I didn't mind us loosing that game with Choate yesterday so much as I minded the language our players were using. Now, you're the Captain, can you tell me how we can get our guys to clean up their act?"

"Gee, sir, it wasn't just us. Didn't you hear what the other team was saying?"

"Sure I did, and I didn't think they were as bad as we were. Besides, I'm glad to have Choate sound bad if they want to. What makes me sick is when Essex sounds bad."

"Yeah, I understand what you mean, sir."

"Good. See what you can do, Ned. Talk to our guys. They respect you. You can get them to straighten out if anybody can. I'll be counting on you, ok?"

At that point students began strolling into Cooper's office and taking their places at the conference table.

The Student Council consisted of the President and Vice President of the Sixth Form and the presidents of Forms Three, Four and Five. Forms One and Two were represented by a single student head of the Lower School. All these student leaders were elected by their peers. Prefects, the other type of student leaders at Essex, were selected by Housemasters to help them run their dormitories. Prefects were not part of the Student Council, but Cooper occasionally met with them to discuss dormitory life.

When everyone except Freddy Iverson, the lower school representative, was seated, Cooper asked, "Does anyone know where Freddy is?"

"He probably forgot again, sir," said Helen Flowers, President of the Third Form.

"I expect you are right, Helen. We might as well get started," said Cooper. "I still hear quite a bit of talk that leads me to feel we have some marijuana smoking going on. What do you people have to say about that?"

"If there is, sir, it sure isn't very obvious," said Ned. "I don't know of anyone who's doing it."

"What do you think, Ruth?" asked Cooper.

Ruth Darnier was the Sixth Form Vice President. She shrugged her shoulders and said, "I don't think anyone would do that here at school,

Mr. Morgan. Some of the kids have tried it at home on vacation, but I don't think they would do it here."

"Well, let's see," said Cooper, "I think we've had nine or ten students put on probation for it so far this year, and we have had to expel four who were not first-time offenders. I wonder if you people are being realistic."

Sarah Savage, representing the Fifth Form spoke up, "I think plenty of kids are smoking pot. Sometimes I smell it in the dorm, and I think it's a popular thing to do Saturday nights."

"How about hard drugs, do we have any of that?"

"I don't know for sure," said Sarah, "but we probably have some of that, too."

"Oh, I really doubt that very much," said Ned.

"Well, let's keep our agenda moving," Cooper remarked, smiling. "What's new on plans for the Spring Prom?"

Discussion ensued about dance plans, and plans for all sorts of other things, and about various aspects of student life. Towards the end of the meeting, the Fourth Form President, Lyle Smith-Evers said, "How about the dress code, Mr. Morgan? What has happened to that?"

"Well, I took it up with the faculty. They are mostly against it," replied Cooper.

"Why don't you take a vote of the students?" said Sarah.

Cooper said, "I'm sure most of the students want a relaxed dress code, but what specifically are you recommending? Would you have everyone dress just the way he likes or do you have some guidelines?"

"Gee, sir, just cut out the coats and ties for classes, that's all," said Ned.

Lyle said, "You told the students we didn't have to keep the dress code the way it is, but nothing has happened. Most of them don't think you were serious. They say you talk like you want to give us what we want, but then you always have some excuse why it doesn't happen."

"Lyle, that's a good criticism," said Cooper, but I am honestly uncertain what is best. This school has built a great reputation by doing things a certain way. I know there's change in the air all across the country and, mostly, I'm in favor of it. However, I know once I let a standard go, such as a standard of dress, it is not going to be easy to get it back, if we decide it ought to come back."

"Why not try and see?" said Sarah.

"I'll tell you what. You guys bring me a specific detailed proposal next Sunday and I'll give you a concrete 'yes' or 'no.' How's that?"

"That's great, sir," said Ned. "Nothing could be fairer than that. That's just great."

"Ok, let's break. I'll see you people at chapel."

Sarah said, "How about the voluntary chapel idea. You said you'd get back to us on that."

"I'm not yet ready to make chapel voluntary, Sarah. I'm sorry."

"Have you made up your mind, definitely?"

"No, I just haven't decided yet."

"I'm afraid you're going to have a revolt on your hands, sir," said Sarah.

Cooper laughed, "And I won't be able to say you didn't warn me, right?"

"That's right, sir. Don't say I didn't warn you."

CHAPTER 11

At ten-thirty, just half an hour before the service, Todd Everlast's black Mercedes came cruising up to the parking area in back of All Saints Chapel. Todd was about ten years older than Cooper, but, except for a little gray at the temples, he didn't look it. He looked lithe and athletic. His features were even and perfect. His plump blonde wife, Abby, was with him so Cooper walked them both over to Chase House. The two men left Abby and Nancy together and strolled back to the chapel.

"It is just wonderful to see you again after several years, Cooper. You look just the same, stretching up into the sky. Isn't it great we're both in the same trade? How does Headmastering suit you?"

"I guess I like it, Todd. It's what I have wanted for some time. It is a little overwhelming sometimes though, don't you think? I guess I hadn't realized so many people depend on the Headmaster for so much, and for so much of the time."

"Isn't that the truth? You always had a way of putting your finger on the nexus, Cooper. Hey, I brought my vestments with me. Do I need them?"

Cooper said, "No, we don't wear them. Our tradition is Episcopal, but we are definitely Low Church, bordering on non-denominational. You're just fine in tweed suit, black vest and round collar."

"That's great," said Todd. "I envy you. Maybe I'll introduce that style at St. Burges. That would blow the Old Guard's collective mind."

"Have you made many changes, Todd?"

"Have I ever! We're blowing some new wind through the musty old corridors."

"Such as?"

"I threw out the dress code. No more coats and ties. We're letting the kids grow their hair long. We even have one beard and a few moustaches."

"You're kidding. You've done that at St. Burges?"

"Sure have. It's just great too. Fabulous."

"What's Batty Sainely think of all that?"

Todd bent over in laughter, "It's driving him crazy!"

Cooper chuckled appreciatively. "It sounds as if you're having fun, Todd."

"I don't know. Sometimes I scare myself, but I have a theory."

"What's that?"

"If I can out liberal the liberals, I'll stay ahead of the game."

"Are you saying you're not a liberal?"

"Oh, sure I am. Always was. You know that. How about you? I could never tell."

"Well, you know, Todd, I'm not sure. I hate the Vietnam War, and I think some of the things the kids want make sense. However, I really am worried about throwing the baby out with the bathwater. I've been told that Marine Corps leaders are afraid to change any of their traditions, because they're not sure where the famed 'esprit' resides. If they change some little thing, maybe the magic will be gone. I feel that way about Essex. It is quite a remarkable place, as your school is. It took generations of brilliant, dedicated people and some great ideas to make this place what it is. Who am I, I ask myself, to mess around with it, just because there's revolution in the air. The biggest problem this generation has is it doesn't know what it believes in. My biggest problem is, I don't either. I know I'm supposed to lead them. I'm just not quite sure where."

"I don't know what to tell you, Cooper," said Todd, "but I think the survivors, like the willow, are bending with the wind."

Cooper nodded his head in agreement. "I guess that makes sense."

Ned Howard, the school Chaplain, was inside the Chapel. Cooper introduced him to Todd, explaining with a smile that Ned was the coach of the varsity hockey team, and that he was intending to beat St. Burges this year for the first time in several years. Todd announced that he had captained an undefeated St. Burges team when he was a student there. The two hit it off right away, and Cooper listened in polite silence to their hockey talk. One of Cooper's secrets, shared only with Nancy, was that he really didn't like hockey. He resented being expected to stand or sit in the cold at home games, but he did it, unless the varsity basketball or wrestling team had a contest on at the same time. He had never played hockey, and

189

he did not feel it promoted sportsmanship. Most teen-age players aped the pros' practice of fighting and trying to hurt opponents.

In due course, the three men worked out the details of that Sunday's Chapel service. Ned led the Episcopal Morning Worship, Cooper read the Old and New Testament lessons, and Todd gave the sermon and benediction. It went well. Todd's sermon was well received by the student body. Cooper had found that school people generally did better with a student congregation than parish clergymen did. There were a few regulars, who were invited every year, such as Yale's Bill Coffin, because they were so popular, but in general there was about a three-year cycle for the guest preachers who were good enough to be asked back.

The one thing Cooper wished Todd had not told them was that Chapel at St. Burges was voluntary. He made a joke about having such a large congregation to talk to at Essex. Church schools such as St. Burges usually did not have many guest preachers. Their services did not rely on preaching so much as liturgy. So they had more services, often with smaller congregations. One member of the Essex student Chapel Committee read a prayer, which was customary. Usually the student picked the prayer from the Book of Common Prayer, but today, Brad Asser, one of the fifth form's brightest intellectuals, read one of his own compositions. It read, "Dear Lord, guide our errant Headmaster in the paths of fair play so that Essex citizens are not forced to attend worship services foreign to their own faith or conviction. Guide him, our Father, into freeing the prisoners of boredom who are learning to hate religion by having it pushed into their faces by harsh taskmasters who care little for education, but much for superficial things that look good, like coats and ties and skirts and blazers. We ask it in the name of Jesus Christ, our Lord, who wore a beard and grew his hair long. Amen."

This, of course, brought every woolgathering, daydreaming student to a state of alert attention. Few things were quite as exciting as a challenge to authority. There was laughter after the prayer and a little sporadic clapping. Cooper was not so traditionalist as to be offended by the lack of propriety. But, of course, even young, new Headmasters found propriety to be a source of comfort and security. So Cooper was annoyed, but, because every eye was on him, he did his best to cover it with a smile. He knew he had lost this round. But he grudgingly admired Brad's clever ploy.

Todd seemed slightly amused at Cooper's discomfort, but tried to suppress the smirk on his face.

At the end of the service the students filed out fast, starting with front rows first. The adult leaders did not walk to the door during the last hymn to greet the congregation. They would have been run over by it. However, it was pleasant to sit for a few moments listening to Elmer Pincer's wife, Mary Lou, play Bach on the big pipe organ as the students streamed out. Cooper noted that less than half the faculty were present in Chapel. The letter of reappointment faculty members received each year from the Headmaster stated that attendance at Chapel was a condition of employment, but that clause did not seem to be taken seriously by many.

They'll be sorry they missed that prayer by Brad Asser, thought Cooper.

As the last were filing out, Brad caught Cooper's eye. He ducked his head and seized his throat in pretend terror, but his eyes had an innocent sort of pleading look.

Cooper laughed and walked over to him. Brad was a good-looking boy. Although he was not athletic he loved sports. So he managed a team every season.

"Well done, Brad," said Cooper with a smile. "You got me good and proper that time."

"You're not mad?" asked Brad.

"Just because I'm on the other side doesn't mean I can't admire the enemy's battle tactics, Brad. The school's motto is 'Loyalty and Courage.' I give you high marks for courage."

"I don't mean to be disloyal to you, sir. I admire you. I just think you're wrong about required Chapel."

"And by correcting your Headmaster you are remaining loyal to your school, huh? I guess I can buy that. You may be right about Chapel, too, Brad. You may be right."

Longstanding tradition called for the Headmaster's wife to serve coffee at Chase House after Sunday Chapel. Theoretically, it provided an opportunity for students and teachers to meet and chat with the chapel speaker. It was one of the duties of the Chapel Committee to talk with the visiting dignitary if others didn't. "Just one more piece of insincere sham," said one of the younger members of the Committee to Brad Asser, the hero of the moment.

"No, it isn't," said Brad. "Essex is a family, and it is right for us to extend courtesy to every visitor, even if he is the Headmaster of our hated enemy. Remember, 'Loyalty and Courage,' my boy. This is a proper act of loyalty."

Overhearing this, Cooper winked at Brad.

There was an unusually large crowd at the Headmaster's house on this day, occasioned no doubt, by curiosity over what the school newspaper would term, "Asser's Chapel Rebellion."

That worthy paper's Editor in Chief was dreaming up the headline even then, so with the still unwritten story in mind, she approached Cooper, who was standing near Nancy at the giant, silver coffee samovar. "Sir, what did you think of Brad's prayer?"

Never one to suffer fools gladly, Cooper replied, "Mr. Asser's prayer was brilliant. The student reaction to it was vulgar, as I suspect your editorial will be, you ink-stained wretch."

The poor girl's mouth fell open in surprise, and then Cooper grinned at her with an expression that implied they were co-conspirators. She smiled back and forgot to ask him the other questions she had intended.

That would have been that, but Nancy entered the conversation. "Well I think Brad's prayer was super, and I think chapel ought to be voluntary, and students ought to dress nicely because they want to, not because they have to, and I am sure they would if they got a little trust!"

Cooper gave her an "I'll-kill-you-when-I-get-you-alone" look, employed by husbands ever since Adam.

As students closed in on Nancy to hear more about what they wanted to hear, Cooper turned to Todd Everlast, introducing him to Elmer Princer who was standing nearby. "Elmer is head of our Music Department, Todd."

"Oh, yes," said Todd, "I read that wonderful story in The Trib about your former student who is starring in a new hit on Broadway. She certainly gave a great deal of credit to you. You must have quite a program here with your Spring Musicals."

"Yes," Elmer beamed, "that's Sherri Huff. We always said, 'Sherri will make it big someday,' and I really thought so too, but we never dreamed she would do it in her first year out of Essex. Sherri started out at Barnard, but quit and made it to Broadway."

"That's truly wonderful," said Todd, "Have you seen the show, *Sally Forth*?"

"Oh, yes," said Elmer. "I wasn't there opening night with all her classmates, but I have seen it since and it's wonderful, much more impressive than anything we ever did with Sherri here."

"You were at a disadvantage," said Cooper. "You had to keep her clothes on."

All three of them laughed. "Yes," said Elmer, "I always surmised Sherri had a lovely body, but I had to go to Broadway to see how truly beautiful she is. Didn't you think so, Mr. Morgan?" Turning to Todd, Elmer said, "Mr. Morgan was there opening night."

"I keep forgetting," said Todd, "that you've been a member of the faculty here. Promoted from within, so to speak. That's unusual, isn't it? So you must have known this girl, too."

"Right," said Cooper, "I taught her, and we were friends. She is the most remarkable student I have ever worked with. Speaking of promotions from within, you know Bruce McClellan was a teacher at Lawrenceville before he was elected Headmaster there."

"We were afraid we were going to lose Mr. Morgan to your school, Father Everlast," said Elmer.

Todd said, "Were you going to teach at St. Burges? I'm sorry we missed out on that. I could use you there now."

"No," said Elmer, "St. Burges was looking at Mr. Morgan to be the Headmaster, or is it Rector?"

"What?" said Todd, "You mean I beat you out? Well, I'm sorry old man. I didn't know. But, after all, I'm older. Did you know that I taught your Mr. Morgan at General Seminary?"

Elmer looked confused. Cooper, fearing Elmer would ungraciously say that his Mr. Morgan had turned the job down, launched into a long description about what a fine teacher Father Everlast was. Then, he suggested that they had better gather Nancy and Abby, because the four of them were going out to lunch. Elmer excused himself and the two couples slipped away from their own party, which was beginning to thin out anyway.

Cooper drove them the very short distance to The Lion Inn, in his Country Squire station wagon. The Inn was just opposite the school's North Gate. It was owned by Essex Academy and leased to the couple who ran it. Because of this relationship, the Headmaster received a substantial discount on meals at the Inn, so it was easy to entertain school visitors there."

After they were seated, Todd said, "That man Pincer had been, until recently, your colleague, and he's old enough to be your father, yet he calls you 'mister'"

"He calls me Cooper when we are alone, and I have urged faculty members to do that, but a few of the older ones just aren't comfortable calling their boss by his first name.

"Do you know what the kids call you?"

"You mean behind my back? I don't think I want to know that."

Nancy said, "They call you 'The Coop', don't they?"

"Yes. I guess they used to, but I don't know if that is current. They also called me 'Stretch' and 'Pirate,' after Henry Morgan. What do your kids call you, Todd?"

"Boxer."

Abby began to laugh, "They also call him 'Pretty.'"

They all laughed, except Todd.

"That is what the St. Burges students should call you," Nancy said to Abby.

Todd asked Cooper, "Is it easier having been promoted from within, do you think?"

"Oh, I think it is probably much easier for me. I know the place and the people. But it may not be easy for my associates on the faculty to have one of the younger, more recent masters become the boss. It was pretty sudden. Leighton Frostley wasn't stricken until the middle of the summer."

"Are you resented then, or taken less seriously?"

"I don't think so. Not that I know of."

"Grungy Lebeau took you less seriously," said Nancy with an amused expression.

At that point, a waitress came and greeted Nancy and Cooper with obvious pleasure. Cooper introduced her to the Everlasts and ordered a bottle of wine and New York sirloins for everyone. The waitress finished up the details and left.

Abby said, "I'm dying to hear about Grungy Lebeau."

"Well," said Cooper, "Grungy was the school breakfast cook. He cooked everything at breakfast, and even though he got a decent salary increase for this year and had agreed to it, the day school opened last fall he threatened to go on strike if I didn't pay him more. I was scared to death. My first day as Headmaster, and I was facing no breakfast in the morning for anyone. There is a fairly rigid scale, and if I gave more to Grungy, it would have been unfair to the other cooks, to say nothing of the other staff people, in maintenance and elsewhere. They would all have known it, and there would have been hell to pay. Yet, I felt if things were wrong at breakfast, the school and I would get off on the wrong foot. I just felt completely boxed in and helpless and inadequate to the job."

"Couldn't you just explain all this to Grungy?" asked Abby.

"No. Grungy is not that sort of man. He's a bully, and he's tough and he just figured I was a kid, and he had the upper hand."

"So what did you do? Asked Todd, fascinated.

"I decided to act on principle and let the chips fall. I fired him. Then, I called up the head cook and told him about the bind I was in. He just laughed."

"Don't you have a dining room manager?"

"We didn't then, but we do now. Well, I asked the head cook if he could tell me how to cook breakfast myself. I thought if I said that, he would volunteer to cook it."

"And did he?" asked Abby.

"No," said Cooper, laughing. "He just told me how to cook breakfast for six hundred and seventy-two people, and that's what I did."

"You're kidding," said Todd.

"No. I really did it. I had to get up at 3:00 a.m., but I did it."

"What did you serve?" asked Abby.

"Juice, toast, scrambled eggs, milk. Everything but coffee. I forgot the coffee. But I remembered it the next day."

"The next day! How long did this go on?" asked Todd.

"Five days, until I found a new breakfast cook. It was worth it. I'd do it again. It sent the right message to our staff people. They've been my friends ever since. They liked the fact that I did it myself, and it turned out they had never liked Grungy. I hear he's cooking at another school now. Maybe he learned as much as I did."

Abby said, "Do you have six hundred and seventy some odd students?"

"No. That figure included some faculty people. We started the year with ninety teachers and six hundred and twenty-two students, thirty of whom are day students. We have three hundred and ninety-eight boys and two hundred and twenty-four girls."

Todd said, "I'll bet most schools envy the fact that you're co-ed. Some are thinking about going co-ed, like so many colleges. Has Essex always been co-ed?"

"Yes. Ever since we were founded."

"I like that story about your cooking breakfast," said Todd. "I think you must have gotten off on the right foot with everyone, including the kids."

"Yeah, but now I think the honeymoon is over."

"You've done well to make it last this long," said Abby. "You must be a good lover," she said, and then laughed.

"Right," said Nancy, "he gets up early in the morning for that, too." She and Cooper both smiled as they looked at one another.

CHAPTER 12

The following Monday morning, Cooper was in his office at 6:00 a.m., organizing his day. He first started this practice early in the fall, in order to "catch up." Soon he found that by making an early start, his days were more productive, and he seemed to be able to stay on top of the many demands made on him. If he started work at eight-fifteen the way everyone else did, he usually was a step or two behind all day long. Never before in his life had he needed to start ahead of everyone in order to stay ahead, but he had deep-rooted expectations of success for himself. When he found that, suddenly, success came only at a higher price, he promptly paid that price without much thought. So, at a relatively young age Cooper adopted work habits common to great captains of industry, but he would have laughed at the comparison.

Perhaps the greatest legacy left by his predecessor was the Headmaster's efficient secretary, Ida Beth Ehmm. Ida Beth was in her early forties. She always stood very straight. Her short stylish hair was blonde frosted naturally with gray. Ida Beth spoke with the soft, melodious accent of North Carolina where she was raised, and she used delightful phrases unique to her home, such as Tuesday-week (meaning a week from next Tuesday). The year she graduated with honors from the University of North Carolina, she married the son of a dairy farmer in Old River, Connecticut, not three miles from Essex Academy. Ida Beth had no children and her husband had little time for her, so her passion in life was the smooth and polished management of the public affairs of Essex Academy from her strategic vantage point in the Office of the Headmaster. She found secretarial employment at the school the same year she was married. Within a year she was Leighton Frostley's secretary, and she remained so until his stroke. Frostley had loved her deeply from that first year, but she never guessed it. He always called her Mrs. Ehmm, even in private. Cooper called her I.B.

before he was Headmaster, but for reasons he could not have explained, he called her Mrs. Ehmm from the day he moved into the office.

Cooper had already placed a stack of notes on Ida Beth's desk. "Please ask Ned Howard to see me when he can," read the first. Next: "Please have the Chapel Committee meet here after seventh period today"; "Can you get a note to Chick Jones to see me at his first free period?"; "Please remind Buck Forrest to give you an itinerary for my Chicago trip and a list of the alumni and parents I'll be seeing there. Tell him to include some short informational bits on them"; "I'm still missing several yearbooks in my office reference library. Think you can fill 'em in?"; "Please tell maintenance there is a pile of debris behind Lynn Hall." So read just a few of them, all placed there that morning.

Cooper used the next hour and a half to dictate letters on a magnetic tape machine. He had a desk model in his office and a small battery-operated one in his brief case, which he could dictate into when out of the office. He dictated the letters in answer to a stack of mail and notes that had accumulated since Saturday morning. He played a game with himself. If he could get through the previous day's stack by seven-thirty, he allowed himself to go over to the Dining Hall for breakfast. Otherwise, he would have to content himself with a mug of tea, produced by Ida Beth after her arrival at eight o'clock. Cooper liked breakfast, so he usually made his deadline. His letters were characteristically short, only he knew why. But each usually concluded with one long sentence, brimming with good will and pleasantries, composed by Ida Beth.

Breakfast was now a buffet meal and, therefore, voluntary, an innovation made that fall in deference to student clamor for "more freedom to make our own choices." At breakfast, Cooper often sat with Philip Fedner, the school's well-liked Dean. Fedner would brief him on discipline matters that had come up since they had last talked. It was important, Cooper felt, to get such briefings daily, if possible. Usually, decisions by the Headmaster were not called for in routine discipline cases. However, Cooper liked to keep up with them so he had his finger on the pulse of the school. Also, a brief dressing-down or pep talk by the Headmaster often had more effect on a student than routine punishment such as work details and detention. Today, Dean Fedner strongly recommended that Cooper make all meals buffet-style and, therefore, voluntary because so many students were missing the required sit-down meals.

Cooper was back in his office that Monday by eight o'clock, when he and Mrs. Ehmm traded information and material. Ida Beth reviewed his appointments for the day.

At eight-fifteen, the first forty-five minute period began. First period always found Cooper in the Trustees' Conference Room on the second floor of Hyatt Hall. Cooper taught two sections of English A there. One section met first period on Monday, Wednesday and Friday. The other section met first period on Tuesday, Thursday and Saturday. English A had been cooked up by Cooper and his friend Smoke Johansen, the English Department Chairman. As fellow Lawrenceville graduates, though from different generations, the two men felt a special kinship. Until this year, Smoke had been Cooper's boss, at least as far as teaching English went, and Cooper urged Smoke to consider that as still the case. But the truth was, Cooper had pretty much taught his courses the way he wanted to ever since he had first come to Essex.

Because Headmasters have more to do than time to do it in, few of them teach. The rule is: anything that can be delegated to someone else should be. However, Cooper felt strongly that he could be a better leader of the school if he engaged, at least partly, in the process for which the school existed.

"English A" was an intentionally difficult designation to decipher. English 6 was clearly English for sixth formers, or what another school might call Senior English. English 5 was, of course, English for fifth formers, and so forth. So what was English A? The "A" was there to confuse college admissions officers, so they would not realize that a student who took the course was in need of make-up or remedial training. It showed up on the student's transcript as English A, taught by the Headmaster. If one was to draw any conclusion, it might be that this was a very special course for the gifted. Not so. It was for any fifth or sixth former who was still weak on mechanics. The course might include a student who had attended Essex for several years, but, despite the best efforts of superior teachers, had not learned enough grammar or basic writing skills to get into a good college. More often, the course was filled with students in their first year at Essex, who had come from inadequate learning situations. In some cases they were post-graduate students recruited to help Essex win football games or other major sporting contests. For many athletes, an extra post-high school year at a top prep school won them prestigious college placements.

Frequently, students in English *A* were bright people destined for Ivy League colleges, who, nevertheless, had not yet learned English mechanics. In Cooper's course, they learned them. Despite lower standards expected of, and lower proficiency displayed by, college-bound students across the country, Essex, and schools like it, were sending colleges scholars who could "hit the ground running." Just because Essex found it necessary to teach skills that should have been acquired earlier, Cooper and his colleagues saw no reason to penalize students with a tell-tale sign in their transcripts that make-up had been necessary. What the student knew when the transcript was sent out was what mattered.

It was a treat to attend class in the Trustees' Conference Room. It was not opulent but it was large, airy, graceful and pleasant. Cooper thought it was fun to share this elite room with his students and he was proud to make some additional use of a space that was usually vacant. He also found it convenient to have his students come to him at the administration building rather than his going to the classroom building where English courses were normally conducted.

There was a large, black walnut conference table in the center of the room. It had gently curving sides and space for twenty-three captains' chairs. The Monday section of English *A* consisted of just sixteen students. So, some of the chairs were pulled from the table to the side walls. Students at Essex were accustomed to conference table classrooms. The tables were called Harkness tables after their donor. Most had room for thirteen, the teacher and twelve students. Only the Math and Science Departments used the more conventional, separate chair-desks.

Cooper started class by holding up a small thin hardback book called *The Elements of Style*. "Does each of you have your book by Misters Strunk and White? I hope you have it with you. This, I believe, is the most valuable book Essex Academy requires you to buy, with the possible exception of the Dictionary. Don't try to sell it. The bookstore has instructions not to buy used copies. Don't give it away, although it makes an excellent gift for almost anyone. Take it with you to college. I will come and visit some of you when you're in college and if you can show me you still have your *Elements of Style*, I will buy you dinner. That's a standing offer. Now, what was today's assignment, Dave?"

"Chapters three and four, sir."

"Right. Did you read them, Ruthie?"

"Yes, sir."

"Don't you think this book is rather unique, Adrian?"

"Yes, sir."

"What's wrong with what I asked Adrian, Sam?"

"I don't know, sir."

"Bill?"

"It's not really a unique book, sir?"

"Didn't anyone do the homework? Yes, Honey."

"You used the word 'unique' incorrectly, sir."

"Good, good. I used 'unique' incorrectly. What does the book say about unique, Adrian?"

"It's an ultimate word, sir. It can't take a modifier."

"Beautiful! Exactly right. Good job. The book says unique 'means without a like or equal. Hence, there can be no degrees of uniqueness.' Now, Sam, what was it I said wrong?"

"You said something about it being unique, sir."

"Yes, I asked if it was rather unique. What's wrong with that, Sam?"

"You shouldn't have said 'rather.'"

"Absolutely right. You shouldn't try to put some hedge or special emphasis on unique. Don't put an adjective with it. Don't say 'very unique.' Don't say 'quite unique.' Don't say 'rather unique,' or 'almost unique.' You will hear unique used incorrectly all your lives. You will hear radio and TV people use it incorrectly. Formal speakers, educated people all over, use it incorrectly, but not Essex people. So remember this lesson. If you hear someone say he went to Essex and 'it's kind of a unique school,' you'll know what about that guy, Bill?"

"That he's an imposter, sir."

"*Right*! Good! He's an imposter," Cooper laughed.

CHAPTER 13

"Did you want to see me, Cooper?" It was Ned Howard, the Chaplain.

"Hi, Ned. Yes. Come in please. How'd you like Everlast's sermon yesterday?"

"It was fine, really fine. I thought he would be over the heads of the kids, he writes such obscure esoteric stuff, but he seemed to have his audience down pat. Of course, he should, you know."

"Ned, I wanted to see you about this business of voluntary chapel. You have never told me what you think."

"Oh, hell, Cooper, I'm all for it. I think we ought to try it. I suppose it will annoy the alumni and the Board, and you and I won't be as comfortable with it, but what the hell, what else can we do? Those kids will stage a walkout any day now. I can feel it in my bones. Well, you might as well know, I've told the kids that I'm not opposed to the idea. You know, I'm kind of curious to find out what happens."

"I can tell you what will happen," said Cooper. "At a voluntary Sunday service, we'll get about half the Chapel Committee, a couple handsful of Jesus freaks and a few more sincere young Christians. I'll say thirty. Then, on a day like Ash Wednesday, we'll get about ten percent of the campus."

"You think it will be that bad?"

"It will unless we do something to pull 'em in. How many Jewish kids do we have in school, Ned?"

"I don't know. Don't you?"

"How could I know?"

"From the admissions office. Don't we have a quota?"

"No. I don't think any self-respecting school has done that for years."

"Well, there are only about fifteen Jewish students that I take to temple on holidays, but I'm sure there are others who don't go."

"Well, look, let's go ahead and try the voluntary bit, but first I want you to work out a carefully designed program of alternatives. If we go voluntarily, let's have a daily voluntary service, short and good. I want to keep the visiting clergymen coming, but there's no point in having them preach to an empty house on Sunday mornings. Let's have 'em visit religion classes and, if they're writers, maybe English classes too. We'll have them during the week, all day, or perhaps for two days. Not every week, but once or twice a month. We'll want a different type of visitor. Their honoraria are budgeted. The money comes from specific endowments. I suppose you know that. Let's have some evening discussion groups with the guest preachers. Work it out, OK? Can you meet with the Chapel Committee about this right after seventh period?"

"Sure."

"Good. I can't be here, but you can get their ideas. Use my office. Let me know tomorrow what you all want to do. Make it good. OK?

"Sure Cooper. You have some fine ideas. You can count on me."

Cooper rose and shook Ned's hand. With his left hand, he held Ned's elbow and walked him to the door. Cooper had already learned the art of getting rid of his visitors promptly, so he could move quickly onto the next item. There was a never-ending stream of them.

As soon as Ned Howard left, Ida Beth Ehmm's soft Carolinian voice came over the intercom, "Freddy Iverson is waiting to see you, Mr. Morgan."

"Tell him to come in, Mrs. Ehmm, I have been expecting him."

A fresh bright face under a mop of unruly hair popped around the edge of the opening door. "Hiya, Mr. Morgan."

Cooper scowled at the little boy who belonged to the face. "Come on in Freddy," he said. Those beautiful pale blue eyes must reflect the color of the sky over the New Mexico desert whence he came, Cooper thought.

"You're not busy are ya, Mr. Morgan? If ya are I can come back."

"I'm not busy at all, Freddy. I've just been sitting here wondering what to do with myself. What can I do for you?"

"Aw, you know."

"No, I don't."

"I . . . you know, came to apologize."

"For what?"

"Aw, you know, I forgot again."

"Did you forget, or did you just sleep through?"

"I, you know, slept. I guess I was awful tired. You know, after the basketball game and all."

"You won again, didn't you?"

"Yeah."

"Did you score all the points?"

The little boy grinned, "Nah. Most of them, though." He walked up to the side of Cooper's desk and sat down in the chair there. He always walked with a swagger, feet apart, as if he were a four-hundred-pound weight lifter.

"Were you figuring on getting a haircut this week?" Cooper asked.

"Nah."

"You sure could use one."

"I'm gonna let it grow." He said it with utter finality.

Cooper struggled to keep from smiling. "I think you should get a haircut."

"Yeah."

"You'll do that, won't you?"

"I figure I'll let it grow."

"Freddie, I know those Student Council meetings might be a bit dull for a second former, and I'm sorry you have to go to them, but you're the elected leader of the Lower School and your constituents are not getting any representation."

"My who?"

"Your constituents, the students in the Lower School."

"Yeah. I'm sorry, Mr. Morgan. I really am."

"OK, I want you to tell your constituents that. I want you to write a letter to them, telling them you have missed three Student Council meetings in a row. You bring the letter to me, no later than tomorrow. If I approve it, you'll post it on the Lower School bulletin board. If I don't approve it, you'll have to do it over again until I approve. You got that?"

"Yeah."

"Do you think that's fair?"

"Yeah. It's about time you did somethin' about my missing those meetings."

"It is, is it?"

"Yeah. But that's OK Mr. Morgan. You're new at this job and you're comin' along all right. I'm glad you got the job Mr. Morgan. Did I ever tell you that?"

"No."

"Well, I should of. I like you, Mr. Morgan."

"Thank you, Freddy. I like you. Will you get a haircut for me?"

"I guess I'm gonna let it grow."

Coming out of Hyatt Hall, Freddy swaggered onto the sidewalk and began to whistle a tune.

A low sexy voice behind him said, "Hello handsome, how's my boy?"

Freddy turned quickly, looking very much the thirteen year old athlete that he was. His face broke into a great happy smile, "Hiya, Honey. Boy, am I glad to see you."

"I'll bet you are."

"Aw, that's not why."

"It's not, huh? What is it then?"

"I been in talkin' to old Morgan. He wants me to get a haircut."

"Yeah? So what did you say to the Pirate? Did you tell him to go suck a lemon?"

"Nah, I just said I'm gonna let it grow."

"I hope you didn't say it was my idea."

"Nah. Nobody knows that you and me are, you know, friends."

"Good. You just keep your mouth shut, and I'll teach you some stuff."

"OK. When?"

"You are a sexy fellow aren't you?"

"I guess so. I, you know, thought about what you said, and I'll do it. You know, I'll do anything you say. Just tell me when."

"You can get out of the lower school dorm at night?"

"Yeah, sure."

"You come to the window of my room tonight at Parton Hall, after lights. Come between eleven and twelve and rap on the glass. If you tell anyone, I'll never speak to you again."

"I promise I won't ever tell. I gotta go now. I'm late. I'll be there tonight."

Honey LaTate smiled at him as he hurried away. He made her feel part mother, part temptress, but he fascinated her. Honey was a fifth former and appeared very mature. A stranger could easily mistake her for a young teacher or faculty wife. She was the only girl on campus who always wore hose and high heels to classes. She was also the only girl who kept pet snakes.

As Freddy hurried away he bumped straight into Buddy Braken, which was a stroke of bad luck.

"What the hell do you think you're doing, shit-for-brains?"

"Uh, excuse me, Buddy, I'm sorry. I mean, I didn't mean to . . ."

"Who said you could call me Buddy? Let's have a little more respect from you, and the rest of you little assholes in Clarke House."

"Yes, sir. I, I didn't mean to . . ."

"Shut up. What the hell were you doing talking to Honey LaTate? You stay away from her, you little turd, or you'll regret it. I don't want you bugging any of the girls in my class, see?"

Freddie's clear blue eyes sparkled with malice. "Go fuck yourself, Braken."

Buddy's right hand lashed out lightning-quick. He slapped Freddy across the face with the force of his two hundred twenty pound body. Freddy was starting to duck as the blow landed, but it still almost knocked him to the ground. The sting was severe, and his eyes filled with tears. He ran away, sick with humiliation at being seen to cry. He heard Buddy's laughter dying away behind him as he ran.

CHAPTER 14

Ida Beth had given Cooper some typed letters to sign and was going over the figures on next year's budget. As she stood next to Cooper, who was seated at his desk, she was only an inch or two taller than he. Cooper marveled to himself at her trim erect figure. She wore a form-fitting skirt. Cooper was annoyed with himself for having to suppress a strong urge to reach out and stroke her well-formed buttocks. As if reading his thoughts, her eyes sparkled and a mischievous smile played over her delicate lips.

"Are you laughing at me?" he asked.

"No. I was just thinking about Freddy Iverson. He referred to you as 'Old Man Morgan,' and you're not even thirty. I'm forty-two, but you seem to me to be older than I am."

"Well, you look as young as a teen-ager. How do you keep yourself so trim?"

"I'm a long distance runner. I run thirty to forty miles a week."

"Marvelous. Maybe sometime we can run together."

The telephone intercom rang and Ida Beth picked it up. "Mr. Morgan's office."

Cooper had asked all the school secretaries not to inquire as to the caller's identity, but rather to put whoever it was through promptly. It was a little thing, but a touch of graciousness that helped contribute to a friendly and courteous image for the school.

Ida Beth recognized the voice because she said, "Its Astrid Fondleworth for you."

Astrid Fondleworth was the Director of Admissions for Essex. Cooper told her he would come over to her office. The Admissions office was just across the marbled front hallway of Hyatt House from the Headmaster's office. Astrid, in her mid-thirties, had jet-black hair, moved like an athlete, and dressed in high fashion. She was wellborn, bright and quick,

207

a graduate of Essex and Vassar. Astrid worked full-time at admissions and, in addition to having a secretary, had a part-time assistant, Jerry Lincoln, who taught three courses and interviewed many of the candidates for admission. Jerry was also an Essex alumnus, and an Ivy League product, tall, handsome and charming.

"Our statistics are down a little over last year," said Astrid. "We normally get about ten applicant inquiries for every available space. We encourage eight out of the ten to apply someplace a little less competitive. About seven of the eight take that advice, and the other one applies anyway. Of the two who are qualified, we'll probably accept them both and get one of them, while we'll lose the other to one of our competitors."

"What are your latest figures this year?" asked Cooper.

"We're getting seven or eight inquiries for each available place, but that's to be expected. Schools with new headmasters always drop off a bit. People want to wait and see if the new leader will work out. Educational counselors are particularly susceptible to being standoffish in their recommendations for the first year or two."

"I realize I haven't given you much of my time, but I did call on all those educational counselors you wanted me to see in New York and Boston. I chat with the families you send in. Should I be giving you more time?"

"No way, Cooper, you are doing just fine by me. You're seeing many more families and kids than Frostley ever did," said Astrid. "It is paying off, too. We're getting a higher rate of favorable responses from the kids we have accepted. Most of the families we wanted who are going somewhere else are those who have visited when you were off-campus. To be frank, you don't look very good on paper because you're so young, but you're doing a great sales job with those whom you meet."

"So you don't see any problem filling the school with high quality students for next year?"

"No. So far, we're in good shape. But there is one little trend that's bothering me."

Cooper said, "Why don't you sit down, so I can sit down?"

They were standing in the middle of Astrid's very spacious, beautiful office. Most independent schools had admissions offices second in impressiveness only to the Headmaster's office. At Essex, the admissions office was bigger and grander than Cooper's. Astrid had furnished it in a modern style, had the walls painted white and had hung several of Nancy's brightly colored abstract paintings.

They sat down and Cooper said, "What's bothering you?"

"Well, I have always gone on the assumption that it's the parents who make the decision about which school to go to. I'm beginning to think that has changed and now it's the kids. I can't give you any scientific evidence. It's an inkling I've gotten from little clues that are dropped."

"Even if that's true," said Cooper, "why does it bother you?"

"Because kids nowadays are turned off by a coats-and-ties dress code and required meals. We have too many required courses and not enough electives. The whole place has just been too slow to adjust to the times. Our co-ed tradition is our best feature. We're out in front on that trend."

"I think independent schools not only have the freedom to innovate, but also the freedom to buck trends, if they aren't good ones."

"Oh my goodness, Cooper, do you think they're bad?"

"I don't know, Astrid. I wish I did. I sure don't think this drug craze is good." Cooper laughed, "Have you listened to the volume of the music? How long since you've chaperoned a dance?"

"If you'll be my date, Cooper, I'll go to the next one."

"You think I don't go? I've been to more dances than any adult on this campus. I've even been to some away dances."

"I didn't say you didn't go. I just said I wanted to be your date."

"Is this a proposition?"

"Do you want to take it that way?"

"Astrid, you're knocking me out. I never thought sex was your thing."

"You thought maybe I was gay?"

"I've wondered."

"I guess I'm not very motivated sexually, but I'm not innocent. I just have high standards and you fall within their scope." She laughed nervously. "Whatever made me say all that? Excuse me, boss, I lost my head."

"It's one of the best offers I've ever had, Astrid. I'd like to take you up on it more than you know, but I'm not going to do it. Perhaps someday the time will come. Who knows?" He grinned at her. "By then you'll have probably married a United States Ambassador, and have six kids." They both laughed.

"There's something else. Two things," said Cooper.

"Shoot."

"I'm making up next year's budget, and I want to raise tuition for boarding students from thirty-two hundred to thirty-five hundred. Any objections?"

"Gee, that's a pretty big jump," she said.

"Yes. Of course, it's the Trustees' decision, but this is what I want to recommend, and I think they will do what I ask. Could such an increase hurt admissions?"

"I used to think increases would hurt but they never have. I don't think it would."

"Good. I'll expect you to back me up then. I plan to increase the scholarship budget to two hundred thousand dollars, that's a thirty thousand dollar increase for you."

"Whoopee!"

"Don't get carried away. Twenty thousand of that increase is for a new program I plan to initiate."

"Which is?"

"I want you to find us ten fully qualified black students, or other minority students, for ten new, full scholarships. With clothing and travel allowances if needed, the works. I'm figuring a cost of four thousand apiece, so a forty thousand dollar budget."

"I thought you said you were taking only twenty thousand from my scholarship budget."

"I did. I'll raise the other twenty in special gifts. In effect, Essex will match others' gifts to this program."

"Wow, you're jumping in with both feet. You think big."

"Well, we're behind in doing our part, in my opinion. This will help us catch up."

"That's just splendid, Cooper. You are a winner. I have good taste in men."

"This will be a big responsibility for you, Astrid. You'll have to find them. You have to find the students who can do the work and we have to get them ready. Those who need it should be in the summer school this summer."

"I'll get right on it. I love it. Do you have a name for this program, Cooper?"

"Let's call it the 'New Winds Program,'" he laughed.

"You're beautiful," she said. "Cooper, will you forgive me for what I said, before?"

"Nope. You made my day. Just a little while ago Mrs. Ehmm said I acted older than she is, and Freddy Iverson calls me Old Man Morgan. I needed a morale boost. Thanks, Astrid, you're a buddy and a beautiful woman, and I wish I were the boy who sat behind you in grammar school."

CHAPTER 15

"There's a call for you on line one," said Ida Beth.

Cooper picked up the phone and said, "Cooper Morgan."

A secretary with a New York accent said, "Yes, Mr. Morgan, will you hold for Mr. Feese?"

I would like to hold Mr. Feese by his balls and squeeze, Cooper said to himself.

"Hello? Hello, Mr. Morgan, this is Augustus Feese calling you again."

"I know."

"What's that?"

"Hello, Mr. Feese, It's nice to hear from you."

"Oh, yes? Well, you won't think so, Mr. Morgan, when you hear what I have to say to you."

"I'm sure."

"What's that?"

"You called me, Mr. Feese. Tell me what you want to tell me."

"Well, sir, I have talked with my client, Mrs. Evert, and I had to report your lack of cooperation to her, Mr. Cooper . . . er, Mr. Morgan. Therefore, Mrs. Evert is considering initiating a suit against you, as well as your school. I recommended that we sue you personally, sir, for three million dollars. What do you think of that?"

"I think you are an amusing man, Mr. Feese."

"You make a great mistake to take this lightly, sir. Mrs. Evert is a woman of considerable means. She can bring a great deal of pressure to bear against you, Mr. Morgan."

"I don't really take it lightly. The whole thing makes me very sad. Mrs. Evert's son needs help in the worst way. He needs counseling. He needs attention and he needs love. I can't help him because I expelled him. I did that because I had to. I had no options left. The boy and his mother had every warning possible, some of them on the record, on paper. He was caught red-handed selling drugs—contraband to you, Mr. Feese. I can't keep a boy like that here and maintain order. The sad thing is you people are telling him, by implication, that money talks, that you can buy and threaten his problem away. Why don't you tell your client the truth? Tell her to face up to the kid's problems—buy him some help instead of protection from consequences. It's all just money to you, isn't it Mr. Feese, another fee? Well, hear this, you can't buy me and you can't scare me. Have you got that? Is that clear enough for you, Mr. Feese?"

"Uh, Mr. Morgan, did I tell you I used to be an Assistant District Attorney here in New York?"

"Yes. You told me that. Why?"

"I want you to know, sir, that I can be a pretty tough adversary. I can make it very difficult for you."

"OK, is that it? If you decide to sue, I'll put you in touch with our attorneys, who will be just as happy to earn their fees, too, without giving a damn about the boy."

"Since you profess to care about my client's son, Mr. Morgan, have you considered that he will be drafted now? He will be sent to Vietnam and will probably be killed there. Have you considered that his blood will be on your hands?"

"You know, Mr. Feese, that I have recommended him to a tutoring school in New York. If his mother enrolls him there, he'll be exempt from the draft until June, just as he would be if he had remained here. It's all the same. It is up to your client to protect him, Mr. Feese."

"My patience is at an end. I am ready to take action against you. Before I hang up I want to leave you with one thought."

"Which is?"

"That you made a very important mistake, sir, one that will cost you. As the responsible person where illegal substances were possessed, bought and sold you were obliged to report any such activities to the proper police authorities in the jurisdiction. You failed to do so. I'm afraid that protecting the reputation of your school does not constitute a legitimate excuse."

"In our case, Mr. Feese, the proper authority is the State Police."

"Yes. That's right. You failed to report and are, therefore, in trouble."

"What makes you think I didn't report it?"

"Uh, well, did you report it?"

"Yes, I did, to Connecticut State Police Special Investigator Robert Danaher. There is only one thing about the whole situation that I did not tell lieutenant Danaher."

"What's that?"

"The name of your client, Mr. Feese, and his address. Lieutenant Danaher would like to know them, but told me I was not absolutely required to tell him. If you think I've done wrong, perhaps I should talk to the Lieutenant again."

"No. Don't do that! Mr. Morgan, I beg of you, please don't cause the boy further hurt. He is very contrite. He respects you very much, sir. I know I have been abrasive. I only sought to help my client. Please don't punish him to get back at me."

"May I assume, then, that I will hear from you no further, Mr. Feese?"

"Uh, yes. That is a reasonable assumption. I shall not trouble you further, Mr. Morgan."

"Mr. Feese, I shall appreciate not hearing from you again."

"Uh, yes, sir, yes. Goodbye then, sir."

Ida Beth had been standing in the doorway. "Was that the lawyer from New York who has been pestering you? Mr. Morgan, those calls have been awfully upsetting to you. Why don't you let me screen your calls? There's no need for you to put up with that sort of thing. The school has lawyers he can talk to."

"He wanted to talk to me. He wanted to see if he could break me down, because he doesn't have a case to talk to lawyers about. It may be stubborn pride on my part, but so far, I want to remain available to anyone who wants to talk to me."

CHAPTER 16

Adrian Brooks Craft IV, known to his schoolmates as Monkey, had come a long way in the year since he had unsuccessfully attempted to blackmail Sherri Huff into compromising herself. He had grown bigger. His voice had deepened. He had gotten cleverer. His penny-ante dealing in pot and LSD had grown into a substantial business. He sold lots of hash and speed nowadays, and for the very affluent, he could by special order supply cocaine.

Monkey's place of business was his sound room backstage in the Marsh Arts Center. It was there that Honey LaTate found him. "Hey Monkey, how ya doin'?"

"Well, it's the snake lady. What can I do for you, Honey?"

"I want some grass."

"If we're going to be friends, Honey, don't call me Monkey."

"O.K. Adrian, but I want to talk business, not friendship. How much for the smallest amount you sell?"

"A nickel bag is five bucks."

"OK, you got it, buddy."

"I could give you a better price if you bought more."

"No. That's all I need. Mostly I smoke other people's shit. This is for . . . uh . . . this is for a friend. Hey, Adrian, you know some of the girl's here have a secret club? We're going to take a few boys in it. Maybe you'd be interested."

"You mean that witchcraft thing? I've heard about that."

"Would you like to be a warlock, Adrian?"

"What the hell is a warlock?"

"A male witch."

"Yeah? That sounds cool. Are you a witch, Honey?"

"Maybe I am, Adrian. Who knows? Are you interested?"

"Yeah, sort of. What would I have to do?"

"Exactly what I tell you to do. You think that might be fun? Sometimes nobody wears any clothes. Could you handle that?"

"Crazy! I love it."

"O.K. Sit tight. Keep your mouth shut about it, and I'll get back to you."

Later that day, Honey encountered Cooper entering the office of Assistant Headmaster Gunnar Ferris. She smiled and batted her eyes at him provocatively.

"Hello pretty Honey," he said.

"How is our singularly unique Headmaster this afternoon?"

"Rather pleased that you've remembered my morning lecture. I think."

She laughed and strolled away, her hips swinging.

Cooper grinned at Gunnar and said, "That girl is some flirt. Do you teach her too?"

Cooper had persuaded Gunnar that he should teach a course himself, so Gunnar had returned to Biology, his first love. He taught an advanced course. Teaching had a marvelously rejuvenating effect on him.

"She's my best student," replied Gunnar. "Do you know why she's called Honey?"

"I guess I don't."

"Because she keeps bees at home, has since she was a little girl. She's done a most sophisticated research project comparing a bee sting to that of wasps and yellow jackets. Original work, mind you. She's a cool one. I've watched her pick up a bee, present the stinger to the end of her finger and take the sting without batting an eye."

"Remarkable. I hope she doesn't do that with her snakes."

"Oh, I don't think so. Besides, none of her snakes are poisonous. That is, I don't think any are poisonous, at least not the ones she has here."

Cooper was about to pursue the subject further, but thought better of it and said, "I came to talk to you about next year's curriculum."

"I'm glad you have, Cooper. I've been thinking about it."

"Astrid thinks we aren't up with the trends, and we're not offering what students want."

"Yes, she has talked to me, too. I suppose she's right. Astrid is a smart lady and doesn't offer opinions without being sure of her ground."

"Gunnar, I would think you're in an even better position to judge. You talk to most of our students about their courses of study. What are you hearing?"

"I'm hearing the same thing Astrid is. They want more electives. Many are bristling at some of the requirements, such as, four years of a foreign language, two laboratory sciences, U.S. History, advanced math, and so forth. They want courses such as marine biology, astronomy, psychology, current events, black history, Third World studies, human sexuality, driver education, and on, and on, and on."

"Do you have a recommendation?"

"Yes. First we must fool around with the schedule. I'd say go to a trimester system, so the student who wants to can take three electives a year in the same time slot. Then let's make shorter periods so we can have more periods in a day."

Cooper said, "I suppose we ought to have the department heads come up with plans in their own areas. Could you have an Academic Committee meeting and give them a timetable for talking to their people and coming up with recommendations?"

"Sure. Good idea."

"I like your idea of presenting a more flexible schedule to them. Just do it. You know what's involved, the rest of us don't. Let's not open this up to discussion. We'll just end up wasting time. Let each department be responsible for course offerings in their own discipline. They must have deadlines though, don't you think?"

"Absolutely."

"How can we get student input?"

"We already have that, don't we?" said Gunnar.

"Yes, I suppose we do. However, I'd like them to believe they have some say in the changes. Why don't you meet with the Cum Laude Society? Give 'em something to do. Be nice to give the smart kids some status. They just might have something worth considering. Even if they don't, they'll love it, if they think it's their idea."

"Well, it is."

"You sound as if you don't approve."

"Cooper, I think we must respond to the world around us. We don't live in a vacuum. I believe these changes are inevitable. But let's not kid ourselves. Every one of these changes means academic standards will go down. It's sweet talk that adds up to less discipline and less work. Don't you think so?"

"Gunnar, I wish I knew."

"We could swim against the current, but our applications would decrease," said Gunnar. "In no time at all, the quality of our students would decline, and we would be worse off. No, Cooper: 'The wise man bends with the wind, even as the willow, and lives to stand straight and tall in another day.'"

"And the mighty oak, which remains inflexible, gets blown over, huh? Judas, I can't stand it when you get profound," said Cooper. They both laughed. "My friend Todd Everlast said much the same thing to me yesterday. You smart guys must know what you're talking about. Let's do it."

Late in the day, a moist warm front moved up the coast to Southern New England. The sky was leaden with dark clouds before sunset, which was a bit later every day. March was beginning to lose what remained of winter's grip. The thermometer started to climb and rain arrived in the middle of evening study hall. At eleven-ten, when Freddy Iverson slipped out of Clarke House, the temperature was fifty-five degrees and a light rain was making an unholy mess of the accumulated snow.

Freddy had never snuck out at night before. He obeyed most of the rules most of the time. He believed in the rules and usually helped enforce them. He couldn't have said why. It was simply his lot to be a leader in the system in which he found himself. He wasn't afraid to break a rule. He would have burned the school down if Honey LaTate asked him to do it for her. Honey was his secret love, Freddy, at age thirteen, knew what men and women did together. He'd known for a long time. He was a little fuzzy on the details but trusted Honey to clarify all. He knew that he was ready, long overdue in fact. So he felt no guilt sneaking out. He was off to pursue his education. Only an instinct to protect his true love kept him from striding boldly forth in front of all witnesses to claim his lady fair.

The night was dark and foul. No man or campus dog lurked outside. Nevertheless, Freddie followed the shadows and avoided the paths as he struck out on the most thrilling adventure of his life.

She heard an insistent rap on the window. Honey flew to the window and opened it. "Where are you, Freddy?"

"Here. The window is too high. How can I get up there?"

"Climb on the shrubbery, pet, it will hold you. It holds me. Those branches are stronger than they look."

He made it up, with Honey pulling and dragging. She got the window shut, and pulled the shade down. Freddy was shivering. She got his coat off. She wrapped him in a big, fuzzy, beach towel and rubbed him vigorously.

"Will they discover you're gone before the morning wake-up bell?" she asked.

"No. I made a dummy under the covers in my bed. No one will know."

All night. Wonderful. She hugged him to her and kissed him in a tender, motherly fashion. "This is going to be the most beautiful night of your life," she whispered.

"Yeah. I know."

"You've been chewing bubble gum, haven't you?"

"Yeah," he whispered.

. "Look," she whispered, "you aren't circumcised, are you? Why not, I wonder?"

"I don't know." Freddy sounded apologetic. Moments later he was asleep. Honey smiled and closed her eyes.

"Freddy! Wake up! It is getting light out. We been asleep. Hurry you have to get back to your dorm . . ."

"What's happened?"

"Nothing."

CHAPTER 17

"Darling, do you know that all your tweed jackets look the same?" said Nancy, regarding Cooper with a sleepy gaze from the comfort of their disheveled bed. It was five forty-five on Tuesday morning. Cooper was dressing and was about to depart for his office.

"Does it matter? They're all nice jackets. I can't believe the prices Brooks is getting for new ones."

"They are all brown, and either herringbone or hound's-tooth. You always look the same."

"Want me to wear a blazer?"

"Your other uniform. You have a closet full of blue blazers."

"Just three."

"Frostley always wore suits, gorgeous suits. I think people take a man in a suit more seriously. Lawyers wear suits, and vests, too. They always wear suits and vests."

"I have enough enemies already. Lord forbid, I should be taken for a lawyer."

"Don't you like lawyers? Lawyers have the power."

"So do crows and vultures, but the world needs them. There are too many lawyers. I'm a teacher, a humanizer, a civilizer . . . much better. We teachers like old tweeds and blazers. And we like button-down shirts and gray flannel pants and cordovan shoes. And we like lacy panties and frilly brassieres, and the things that fit into them."

"I have some of those things right here. Come and get 'em."

"I already did that. Now it's office time."

"Why? Are Ida Beth's better than mine?"

"I don't know. I wish I did, but I probably never will."

"You are an honest bastard, anyway. No wonder you don't wear a suit."

Cooper blew her a kiss and departed. He had a bunch of notes for Ida Beth on the pad in his jacket pocket. He tore them out and put them on her desk, then tackled his stack of correspondence. He made another note for Ida Beth to get his trustee friend, Joe Marmot, on the phone.

He wrote out two long memoranda on legal pads. He hadn't finished his letters, so he skipped breakfast. He was hungry but content. Cooper always felt best when he was busiest, and he knew it.

I sure have the right job for keeping busy. But I wonder, am I accomplishing anything?

He returned his attention to his two memoranda. Neither was addressed to anyone. They were first drafts of plans that would grow and change as they were worked over by committees. Their final resting place might be as articles in a yet-to-be written alumni magazine. One memo was titled "New Winds Program." The other was "New Curriculum." He would have Ida Beth type them up and make copies for his weekly Administration meeting, which would be gathering that very morning. Then, he knew, he would re-do them and have them mimeographed for the weekly faculty meeting at five o'clock.

Cooper met his other section of English *A*, and continued on with meetings, interviews, confrontations, gathering information, making judgments and disseminating information.

"I have Mr. Marmot for you now, Mr. Morgan," said Ida Beth.

Cooper picked up, "Hello, Joe?"

"Yeah, Cooper, how are you? How are you weathering the storm of abuse you educators are getting these days?"

"Well, Joe, sometimes I run before the wind, and sometimes I tack and make a little headway."

"Good for you Cooper. Just keep bailing and the storm will pass."

"How's life for lawyers? I was bad-mouthing your profession earlier this morning."

"You can't go far wrong doing that. We are a scurrilous lot. It's best to keep your distance."

"Well, don't hang up. I want you to get some money for me."

"How much?"

"Twenty thousand."

"That doesn't sound insurmountable. Tell me about it."

Joe Marmot was from a family widely known to have substantial wealth. Consequently, he did not concern himself with practicing law to make money, although he did make some now and then. He usually gave it away to one of his many social justice projects. Joe also published a limited circulation, but widely respected, monthly letter championing liberal causes.

Cooper outlined his New Winds plan to bring ten bright minority students, without means, to Essex. Joe listened to all the details, asked a couple of thoughtful questions, and then said, "I think I can get the money for you. I know a few people who would love this idea, particularly if the school finances half. It's a damned good plan, Cooper. And if I can't raise it, I'll take it out of Ginger's grocery money."

"Don't do that," said Cooper, "she might get the ball team after you." Joe and Ginger had nine children.

"If she does that, I won't give her any more babies."

"I can't imagine that would upset her too much."

"Yeah, I guess we're not going to have any more. We think we've figured out where they're coming from."

Cooper laughed.

"Now I have something for you," Joe said. "I have not been very attentive to the duties Gordon Fairingwether gave me, as Trustee Chairman of your installation ceremony. However, I have just had a break, and I can get the Secretary General of the United Nations to be the principal speaker. Would you like that?"

"Sure, Joe, that would be very impressive. But what does he have to do with Essex or American education?"

"Nothing, but he's a big name and Gordon said he wanted a big name."

"Whatever you guys want is OK with me. But I wish there was a closer tie-in."

"How about a cabinet officer? I bet I could get the Secretary of Health, Education and Welfare, Anthony Daniels. Would that be better? I know him, and I know he admires Essex Academy. I'm sure he'd come if he's free. Of course, our own Abe Ribicoff, his predecessor, would help get him here. They could come up from D.C. together."

"That sounds like a natural, Joe. Even the Republicans respect him. I would like that very much."

"O.K. pal, we'll work on it."

Cooper legally became the Headmaster of Essex Academy the moment the Trustees passed their unanimous resolution to elect him towards the end of August 1966. However, nearly every independent school holds a big installation ceremony for a new Head and Essex had an extensive set of events planned for the first weekend in May. Autumn had been too soon to make the necessary plans and the first weekend in May was the first time warm weather could be confidently expected for outdoor events.

When Installation Weekend arrived, the weather in Southern Connecticut could not have been more beautiful. The seventh Headmaster of Essex Academy thought enough of the occasion to wear a suit (without a vest) for Saturday's events. But his mind was in Round Pond, Maine where *Barbarian* had been hauled out for the winter. He wished now that he had been able to sail it back to the Connecticut shore, so he might be able occasionally to steal a few hours for an afternoon sail. Along with thoughts of the beautiful little craft with the varnished teak hull, came thoughts of Sherri, who was never far from his mind. He wondered if he could even look at *Barbarian* without thinking *Callipygian Princess*, and Sherri.

Cooper thought he might have to sell the boat. Whenever Sherri came creeping into his consciousness he felt a yearning that was almost painful. He had told himself a thousand times that it was mental perversity. His love for Sherri had always been spiced by its clandestine nature. Their sail along the New England coast was associated with vacation freedom and fun. Sherri was a dream. Their relationship was not part of his real world. The two of them together were a fairy tale, an illusion, the same as her Broadway sparkle and magic. He knew he had to shake her off. But that would not be easy.

Because Cooper also knew he would see Sherri the next day.

For the first time since *Sally Forth* opened Sherri would miss a performance, and Lannie Stretch would play her role. Sherri was happy for Lannie. She was also happy to be able to share in the celebration for Cooper. They were the two people about whom she cared most.

The weekend events at Essex brought more alumni back to the school than ever before. There were receptions and dinners and class gatherings. A capital fund raising project had been going on for several years to raise twenty million dollars, mostly for endowment. The effort had been sagging and this occasion represented an opportunity for a last chance push. Every school team had home contests. Most parents were on hand.

There was a chapel service at nine on Sunday morning. The Episcopal Bishop of Connecticut presided. All alumni who had died during the past year, since the previous Spring Alumni Day, were remembered, prayed for, and honored. Cooper was prayed for over and over again. Cooper gave a very short sermon that was nicely phrased, but not memorable. It had to do with the motto on the school's crest which, along with the lion, came from the coat-of-arms of the House of Essex in England: *Fide ET Fortitudine*, Loyalty and Courage.

The main event started at eleven o'clock. A platform had been constructed jutting out from the front steps of All Saints Chapel. Folding chairs had been set up in the Quadrangle in front of the platform, sufficient to seat twenty-five hundred people. Had the weather been bad, the ceremony would have been held in the field house. There was a center aisle leading to the platform. Down this aisle came a colorful procession clad in academic gowns and hoods. Leading the procession was Oggie "Cyclops" Nosterling, Chairman of the Math Department, with a ceremonial macc in his hand. Oggie was the school's Senior Master. That is to say, he had been a member of the faculty longer than anyone else. Therefore, he was the Marshall of the procession, and this may well have been the grandest day in his life. He was, after all, leading a parade that included: the Governor, a United States Senator, four United States Representatives, a Cabinet Officer, various state senators and representatives, a number of college presidents, lots of other headmasters, and many other types of important people. As a happy coincidence, Oggie had a PhD from Oxford. So, his academic costume was grand, indeed.

Next in the procession came the Student Council, the boys dressed in white ducks and blue blazers and the girls in white dresses. Council President Ned Tucker carried the American flag. Freddy Iverson was there, swaggering and seemingly unimpressed. Preceding the Essex Academy Faculty came important visiting clergy, accompanied by the Chapel Acolytes carrying processional crosses and one carrying the school flag with its gold lion rampant. Members of the Essex faculty, seldom seen in academic regalia, were resplendent in the colors of their institutions and fields of discipline. Behind the faculty came the very important state and national leaders. Next came Cooper and Trustee Chairman, Gordon Fairingwether, followed by all the Trustees. Cooper wore a specially designed gown reserved for the Essex Academy Headmaster. It was royal blue with full sleeves. The velvet around its neck and down the front of the robe was scarlet. Atop the gown Cooper wore the hood denoting his theological degree from General Seminary.

As is customary in the code of academic dress, the Trustees wore black doctors' gowns and whichever hoods represented each Trustee's highest degree. At Cooper's urging, Everett Fox wore the full dress uniform of an Army Lieutenant General, and he may have been the most striking figure in the whole show.

All the colleges and independent schools in Connecticut and nearby states had been invited to send delegates in academic dress. Many institutions were represented by their heads, some by faculty members and some merely by local alumni. Their order of march was by founding date of the institution, oldest first. It was, of course, among this largest group that the most spectacular costumes were to be found. Those with degrees from foreign universities had all manner of outlandish hats and hoods and gowns. A few were even fur-trimmed. Some of the heads of schools or colleges, such as the Headmaster from Hoosac School in Northern New York State, wore academic dress of special design to designate their office. The Hoosac Headmaster wore a black robe trimmed in red and purple velvet, and around his neck hung a heavy silver cross crosslet.

This august procession of dignitaries did not march, but rather strolled to the strains of *Pomp and Circumstance* played over the loudspeaker system. When they were seated, Gordon Fairingwether welcomed everyone and served as Master of Ceremonies. There was an invocation by the Bishop followed by short greetings from the Governor, Chaplain Ned Tucker, the President of The Alumni Association, the President of the Parents' Association and Gunnar Ferris, representing the faculty. Secretary Daniels delivered a tight, punchy address on the educational advantages of independent schools. Then Gordon read a short proclamation stating that Cooper was now officially Headmaster of Essex and hung a chain with a Medallion of Office around Cooper's neck. The Medallion looked like a giant, polished-brass coin and featured the rampant lion on the front. In the lion's right paw was a cross-crosslet fetched. On the back were the names of the seven headmasters of Essex and their dates in office. First, was founder George Thorndyke Chase and at the bottom were Leighton Frostley and Cooper Morgan.

Frostley was on the platform in a wheelchair, looking gaunt and old. He still could not say a word. It was not his intention to attend, but Cooper insisted and sent a driver to Cape Cod to bring Leighton and his wife, Bernadette, back to the campus. Cooper had assigned the academic

Department Heads to stay with the former Headmaster, at least two at all times, and push his chair and get him anything he needed.

Finally, Cooper delivered his speech. As the chief operating officer of the school, he charged each group related to the school to do some particular thing for the well-being of Essex. He told the Trustees he expected them to come, one by one, and spend a minimum of two days at the school, live in a dormitory, attend classes, meals and athletics, and do everything a student does. And do it with the students, not as a special group. He told the parents and alumni to get out and finish the "twenty million dollar drive." He asked neighboring schools and colleges to enter into a program of teacher and student exchanges, so that the best teaching techniques at each institution would be communicated to the others. He told the Essex students to strive for a new level of self-discipline to match the new freedoms of their social revolution. Then hc gave detailed, concrete examples of what he meant. His speech was a little too long, as is often the case with most headmasters. He told no funny stories, but rather shifted the mood from buoyant to a bit heavy. However, when he sat down, there was no uncertainty as to who was in charge of Essex Academy and the thrust of its force and being in the world.

The Dining Hall staff determined that they served a buffet luncheon for slightly more than three thousand people that day. There was a reception line near the Dining Hall where visitors could greet Cooper and Nancy, before getting their lunch inside. They could then eat there or go out to one of the many tables set up under the trees, between the Dining Hall and Hyatt Hall. Academic gowns were set aside now, and everyone wore a nametag.

Buck Forrest, the Secretary of The Academy, was in charge of the Alumni and Development Office and all fundraising. He was main coordinator of all events for Installation Weekend and was responsible for visitors. He had made elaborate and detailed plans. Many committees and sub-committees had responsibilities. There were mistakes and omissions, but they were so minor that they eluded the attention of almost all. The overall effect was that of a smoothly coordinated and beautifully managed event. Buck directed the reception line himself and provided replacements for lost nametags. He saw to it that Cooper knew the people who greeted him and Nancy, and knew the relationship of each to the school. It wasn't too hard because the nametags were color-coded: alumni—blue; parents—green;

Trustees and VIP's—red; school and college representatives—brown; and so forth.

"Cooper, this is Michael Bois representing Deerfield Academy," said Buck. The name was familiar, as was the handsome, ruddy, mustached face.

"Isles of Shoals," said Cooper, "sailing *Redwing*, am I right?"

"Yes, indeed," said Bois. "I didn't know then you were going to be Headmaster of Essex."

"Neither did I," said Cooper and they both laughed. Cooper presented him to Nancy explaining where they had met. A natural diplomat, Bois did not mention that when they met, Cooper had been accompanied by a wife, presumably, who was blonde, shorter and more curvaceous than Nancy. He did, however, evidence some slight confusion. As Bois moved on to shake hands with Gordon Fairingwether, Cooper winked at him and said, "Thank you."

A short time later, Sherri showed up in line, surrounded by her classmates and accompanied by a reporter and photographer from the *New York Times*, who were doing a story on her for the Sunday magazine. Sherri hugged Cooper, kissed him on the cheek, and whispered, "I love you."

Cooper appeared not to have heard, but his insides were churning.

Next, a massive blue-eyed Native American, in an expensive gray suit, embraced the seventh Headmaster of Essex Academy. Cooper pounded RedThunder on the back, which still felt like solid granite. Cooper's mother, stepfather and sisters accompanied George. Katherine was now nineteen and Leslie eighteen. Both were tall and bore a family resemblance to Cooper. They still looked mischievous, and they still took joy in the limelight shining on their big brother. Cooper's mother, Elizabeth, was as composed and pretty as ever.

Nancy's parents were there too, and her brother, Doby and other classmates and friends whom Nancy and Cooper had not seen for years.

The afternoon brought athletic contests and a final matinee performance of this year's Spring Musical, the first in four years that did not star Sherri. However, Sherri attended as the guest of honor. When the show was over Elmer Pincer got up on stage, pointed Sherri out in the audience and asked her to come up and sing one of the songs she had done in last year's Musical.

CHAPTER 18

By dinnertime most guests were gone, although there were many small private parties going on all over the campus. Students, sensing the faculty's widespread preoccupation, held some small private parties of their own, mostly in East Woods. At Chase House, Cooper and Nancy entertained their closest friends and relatives at a backyard cookout. Cooper had promised General Fox that later in the evening he would bring his remaining guests over to the General's horse farm to party with those Trustees who had not yet gone home. Most had stayed for a dinner party at the Foxes, but quite a few departed promptly after dinner.

Sherri came to Chase House without her *Times* friends, who had started their return journey to New York, and without her entourage of classmates. George RedThunder immediately approached her and introduced himself.

"I know who you are," she said. "You are the greatest halfback Harvard ever had."

"That doesn't necessarily mean he was any good," said Doby.

Sherri replied, "But he made the cover of *Time*. I remember it."

"Hurray," said Katherine. "I remember it too. I was madly in love with him, and I saved that *Time* story. I still have it somewhere."

"We are choosier about our subject matter at *Time* now," Doby said and laughed.

"I could rearrange the nose on your face again, Doby," said George.

"Come to think of it, RedThunder, I always said you were the greatest halfback Harvard ever had," said Doby.

Nancy joined in, "And my brother, Doby, was the bravest student Harvard ever had." Everyone laughed.

Cooper said, "My buddy, Sherri Huff, made *Time* a couple of months back. Did you have anything to do with that article, Doby? You should have put Sherri on the cover."

"If I had written it, Cooper," said Doby, "I would have put her on the cover and circulation would have doubled."

"I want to know why you aren't *still* in love with me, Katherine?" said George. "Why is it that when my fans grow up and get sexy looking, they forget about me?"

As the party warmed up everyone started talking at once. Cooper was grilling steaks. He called George over, and said, "If you'll go in the kitchen, I have some Canadian Ale for you in the refrigerator, and while you're in there, find the bottle of champagne that's cooling. Open it up and pour a glass for Sherri."

"Is that the way you do it? And to think, there was a time when I told you how to get along with girls."

"Hey, Sally O'Malley," said George, "come with me to the Morgans' kitchen. Who knows, we may find love and happiness in the white man's refrigerator."

Sherri giggled and went with him.

As their voices faded, Cooper could barely make out George saying, "I saw your show. I knew you were a friend of Cooper's and I was tempted to go backstage and say hello, your friend is my friend. But I was afraid you would say something that would make me feel rejected, and I can't stand to be rejected by beautiful women and . . ."

Cooper smiled to himself and thought; George could still give me lessons about girls.

After dinner, the party broke up into several groups, which set off to entertain themselves. They all agreed to meet later at the Foxes' farm. Cooper offered to give George a tour of the campus, and they struck out across the Quadrangle while it was still light. The students they encountered appeared more cheerful than usual, and friendlier. Cooper remarked about it to George, who was surprised that they were not friendly and courteous all the time.

"They used to be," said Cooper, "but they haven't been this year. I don't know if they're changing, or if they're reacting differently to me because I'm the Headmaster. You know, they have a saying, 'don't trust anyone over thirty.' Well, I'm not over thirty, but as Headmaster, I am a not-to-be-trusted authority figure. I think all the pomp and ceremony today has made them react more the way they used to."

Later, some students saw Cooper and a stranger emerge from the gym with a football. They could hardly believe their eyes when they saw their Headmaster throwing very long and beautifully accurate passes, better than any student in school could do it.

As the day faded Cooper and George were strolling near the boathouse beside the Connecticut River.

"Your former student, Sherri Huff, is one fabulous female," said George. "Why is it I get the impression that she's in love with you?"

Cooper laughed, "As they say in the spy business, George, what need do you have to know?"

"I know it isn't any of my business. I'm just curious. I notice you're not denying it."

"Well, George, you know Nancy and I have had our ups and downs. She's walked out more than once. Did Sherri tell you anything?"

"No. Sherri was polite to me, but made it quite clear she did not want a romantic relationship. As a matter of fact she told me she was not interested in men, that she was gay."

Cooper laughed boisterously.

George said, "Hey, are you making fun of Indian Joe? Or was she?"

"No, George," Cooper said, catching his breath. "I'm sorry. I don't know what Sherri's sexual preference is these days. I was just laughing at the thought of you being shot down by a nineteen-year-old girl. It doesn't fit your image."

"Hey, that chick is not just a girl. She's all-woman. I don't care how old she is."

"Yes. She's been that way for a long time."

Attempting to change the subject, Cooper said, "I really appreciate your coming all the way out here to be with me, George, for my big day. We don't see each other so much anymore, but I want you to know that I don't think of you as my best school-days friend. I think of you as my best friend, period. As a busy adult you make hundreds of acquaintances and lots of friends, but no best friends. At least I don't. As a matter of fact in my new life this year, as the central figure of my little world, I'm sort of lonely. I have no close friends here, except Nancy. And Nancy and I . . . well, somehow it's an odd relationship. I don't know where her mind is. I don't know where she lives. I guess I never did, although there was a time when I thought I did."

Cooper was about to say that he knew Sherri better than he did Nancy, but that was a new thought that needed some consideration. Besides, he was trying to get the conversation away from Sherri.

George and Cooper stood in the shade, but as they looked out across the river, the far shore was golden in the setting sunlight. There were few houses or other signs of civilization. The water was a deep blue.

"Is the water clean? Could you swim in it?" asked George. "I'm surprised it's so blue here, almost at the mouth. It has come down through New England, dividing Vermont and New Hampshire, cut across Massachusetts and Connecticut, passed through all those towns and cities. It should be polluted but it doesn't look it."

"It is polluted," said Cooper. "This river is a beautiful whore, overused but still good-looking. She's all dressed up in her best frock, ready to go out to meet Long Island Sound, Block Island Sound and the Atlantic. Even though she's dirty, she's still fresh, ready to mix with those salty bodies of water. I love this river. This is my favorite place to come when I have to get away and think. There are measures going forward now to stop the dumping and the polluting. This good-lookin' old whore could be a virgin again in ten years. How's that for renewal? Don't you wish people could do that?"

Cooper smiled almost sheepishly.

"I see my life as a river sometimes, the confluence of lots of tributaries, moving along doggedly. Changing somewhat along the way because of the forces I meet, getting added-to by both good and bad elements, getting a little used and less pure. Moving fast sometimes, particularly near the beginning. Slowing down some later on. Here and there generating power. Hiding mistakes and sin, even while looking good. Growing larger as I go.

"Many people must think of their lives, or their destinies, as rivers once in a while. Do you suppose our subconscious minds listen to the flow of our blood through veins and arteries? On a map, rivers are the two dimensional veins for the surface of the earth."

RedThunder looked at Cooper soberly for a long moment, and then with a slow smile he said, "You are a bit pantheistic for a white man, blood brother. I like what you're saying. I think that way too, sometimes. You, too, are my only best friend. I'll never have another. I can't handle the one

I have. You, Cooper, are better able to live up to being a blood brother. Someday you won't want to think of me as your friend. I have not always been your brother. Sometimes I can only think of myself."

RedThunder dropped to a crouch and hit the ground with his fist. "I wish I could tell you what I'm trying to say," he said through clenched teeth. "But I shouldn't. I must not!"

"I already know," Cooper said softly, calmly.

"No you don't!"

"You want to say that my wife has shared your bed, not once, but many times."

RedThunder was dumbstruck. He stared at Cooper, trying to reprogram his thoughts with this new information that changed their whole context. Then he whispered hoarsely, "She told you?"

Cooper dropped to the ground beside George. He sat in the dry leaves and new wild grass beside the river. "No. Nancy didn't tell me. She wouldn't want to hurt me, any more than you would. I just know, that's all. I don't know how long I've known, because it's something that's just there. It didn't come like a bolt out of the blue. It has just been there for a long time and I've slowly grown to recognize it. After all, I know you both very well."

George expelled his breath in a long hiss. "Jesus," he said. "Then, how can you say I'm your best friend?"

"You are, aren't you?"

"Yes!" George shouted. "No! . . . I don't know! Don't you want to beat the shit out of me? You should, you know! You can, too. I'll let you. I won't hit you back."

Cooper said, "Why, you conceited bastard. I can beat the shit out of you whether you let me or not."

"Like hell you can!"

"You dumb turkey! Just because you're good at football doesn't mean you can fight! I have reach over you. More speed. And I can fight like a fucking demon!"

RedThunder began to laugh with that characteristic staccato sound of his. The laughter grew until he could not control it. Tears came to his eyes. "Do you," he gasped, "have any idea," he choked, "how you sound?" He laughed. "After all that dignified shit?" He squeaked, "The Governor?" He wheezed now. "That army of guys in their nightgowns?" More laughter. "Oh, God I love you, Cooper, you're the best," gasp, "friend anybody could have. You're wonderful. I know you're tough. Never lost a fight, I guess. Killed that hood with your bare hands. It's just that I forgot. It's so unlike you. I don't think of you that way. You never want to hurt anybody."

"Well, I don't want to hurt you. You're a dumb bastard, but aren't we all? You and me and Nancy? All dumb bastards, hurting each other. Not wanting to. George, my hands aren't clean. I'm not in any position to judge you harshly, or Nancy. It's not so strange that two people I love are attracted to each other. Wouldn't it be worse if it drove us all apart? I need you, George. I need the only best friend I'll ever have."

"But I put horns on you."

"Judas. Don't tell me you take that old European culture seriously? Could it be you accept that rot, and not your Indian culture? Well, I forgive you. How's that?"

"That's good," said RedThunder. "Regardless of cultural prejudice, I went behind your back. I tried to deceive you. I'm sorry, believe me. I need your forgiveness, and . . . I thank you."

Cooper said, "Don't tell Nancy I know. Things are good between us now. I don't want her feeling I have the upper hand, so she needs to feel guilty. OK?"

"You got it."

Book Three

Book Three

CHAPTER 1

1967

"Hey, Sarah, congratulations on being elected team Captain. That's great."

Cooper had fallen in step with Sarah Savage who was heading towards Ward Gymnasium after field hockey practice.

"Thank you, Mr. Morgan. It was nice of you to come watch our practice today. Most people just watch the football team practice."

"I watch them, too," said Cooper. "You sound bitter."

"Oh, don't pay any attention to me, nobody else does. Sarah Savage, girl jock."

"What's the matter, Sarah?"

"I don't know. I just don't like who I am, that's all. Do you know, Mr. Morgan, I just turned eighteen years old and I've never been invited to a dance? I've never had a boyfriend, a real boyfriend. My parents worry about teen-age morality. My mother wants to know, am I a virgin. I've never had a chance not to be. I was elected President of my class three years in a row, 'cause I'm an athlete. This year they passed me by. I'm not even the Secretary of the class. Know why? Because I'm fat. I'm not pretty. I'm not sexy. I'm square. I'm shaped square and I am square, and I don't like myself anymore." Sarah's eyes were wet. She sniffled and rubbed her forearm under her nose.

Cooper said, "You know, Sarah, everyone has a rhythm in life. Some girls are many times mothers at eighteen, soon worn out and old before their time. Some women don't get sexually attractive until they're thirty. They often stay sexy all the rest of their lives. Don't be in a hurry to be grown up and to have already done everything. Save some living for later on. You have a long life ahead, and a good life. Don't push it. Enjoy the

237

growing. Be a kid as long as you can. It's really nice to be a kid. Enjoy it while you have it."

"That's just it. I'm not a kid anymore. I don't feel like it. I feel like a woman. I feel lonely. I feel lousy."

"OK," said Cooper. "We all feel lousy sometimes. I don't know what it feels like to be a woman, but I know what loneliness is, and I have felt lousy. When I do, I hide in work. All the work I can find. That helps me. Maybe it will help you. I hope so. You're a wonderful girl, Sarah. You are an important person. You are going to accomplish great things. So, just hang in there. Get tough, all right?"

She smiled at him with her mouth, but not her eyes, and said, "Yeah. Thanks, Mr. Morgan. I didn't mean to tell you my troubles. I'm sure you have enough of your own. Thanks for trying to cheer me up." She turned and walked through the gym door.

Cooper nodded his head at her and walked on. He said to himself, thanks for nothing, huh, Sarah? I wonder why I used to think I was a gifted counselor for kids. Caring about them is not enough. I wonder if I could take some courses in counseling. No time, I guess. We independent school people are so damn smug about how good we are, but the public school people devote time to learning how to counsel. I'm just flying by the seat of my pants. Yes, sometimes I'm good at it, but I'm not good enough.

It was a beautiful clear September day in 1967. His second year as Headmaster of Essex was starting off poorly. Cooper shook off the depressing conversation with Sarah, and glanced at his watch. It was five-fifteen, just enough time to put on his sweat suit and have a workout.

There was a faculty locker room in the Field House and Cooper kept his sweat suit, running shoes and a couple of towels there, in his own locker.

Not far away in the varsity football team locker room, the new Sixth Form President, who had replaced Sarah as class leader, was getting out of his uniform and talking to Buddy Braken, also a sixth former now.

"So, Dwight, baby," said Buddy, "how do you like playing in the backfield with a nigger?"

Lonnie Deever, the object of Buddy's remark, was walking towards the showers, his lean, muscular brown body gleaming with perspiration. Lonnie stopped when he heard what Buddy said and was about to turn around and face him, but thought better of it and walked on. Buddy, with a sneer on his face, had been watching Lonnie's back to observe his reaction. He grinned when Lonnie walked on, and said, "That nigger is just as yellow as the rest of them."

Dwight Bedlington, Jr., President of the class of 1968 said, "Hey, Buddy, don't talk like that where Lonnie can hear you for Christ's sake. What's the matter with you?"

"Nothin's the matter with me, Dwight, baby," said Buddy. "My daddy sent me away to school so I didn't have to mix with niggers. We're getting more of them in here every year. We don't need that spade on our team in order to win. And I don't intend to open any holes in the line for him to run through and be the big hero. As soon as the coach sees how yellow he is, Mister Nigger will be gone."

"Come on, Buddy," said Dwight, "leave him alone. If he can help the team, let him do it. You don't have to dance with his sister."

"Are you going to the dance Saturday night?" asked Buddy.

"Yeah, I'm going to go. I'm going to take Honey. I need to get laid," said Dwight.

"Oh, that's nice stuff. I'd sure like to get in her pants. I'm getting so hard up I could rape Honey LaTate while she's walking down the hall."

"You scare girls. You come on too strong, muscle man. You know what you ought to do?"

"What?"

"You ought to give up on the cheerleaders and take out some lonely girl. She'll be so grateful she'll put out for you."

"You think so?"

"Of course. That's how I got started. Once you get cool and learn how to talk to them, you can work your way up to some really nice snatch."

"Yeah," said Buddy, "that's pretty good."

The two boys walked to the shower room carrying their towels. Several members of the football squad were under the showerheads yelling at each other. Lonnie Deever was new this year. The head of the Boys Club in New York City had talked him into taking one of the New Winds scholarships at Essex for his last year before college. Lonnie was a straight-A student in the city and would have made his high school football team, a team that was bigger and faster than the one at Essex. Now he found his courses more difficult than he was used to. On top of that, he had no friends and was surrounded by white students who, while they might not be as directly hostile as Buddy, were probably hiding behind facades of phony friendliness.

Lonnie glared at Buddy when he came in and thought about how great it would be to slip a knife in his ribs, big as he was. He thought how he'd like to get that big white boy in the Bronx, surrounded by his friends instead of Buddy's. He knew there wasn't much chance of that, but it was nice to think about. However, he had more important things to do. Had to make it in the white man's world. Had to do it. He did not want to go back to his old neighborhood any more than Buddy Braken would.

"Hey, Dwight," yelled a boy called Knobby, "what's Fedner going to do about that booze he found in your room? Is he going to tell Morgan?"

"Not a chance," said Dwight Bedlington with a smile. "He's too busy drinking it."

There was general laughter in the shower room. One boy called out, "If you keep supplying Fairy Fedner with booze you can get away with anything."

Feigning seriousness Dwight said, "Please gentlemen, I cannot have you bad-mouthing the Dean in my presence. I have my official position to think of."

"Seriously," said Knobby, "how come Fedner didn't tell Morgan? What do you have on him?"

"You asshole," said Buddy, "nobody's going to do anything to Dwight because his father is a Trustee of the school."

"So what does that mean?"

"It means, asshole, that his father is Morgan's boss."

"Yeah? Is that true, Dwight? Is your father The Coop's boss?"

Dwight said with a knowing smile, "Yeah, he's one of them. Morgan's not going to mess with me. Anyway, if he did I'd beat the shit out of him."

There was laughter and hooting. "You and what army?" said Knobby. "Man, that Pirate is big. I mean big. You wouldn't find me messing with him."

"I'll bet you Buddy could take him," said Dwight.

"Yeah, Buddy could I suppose," said Knobby. "But you sure as hell couldn't, Dwight. You're never sober enough."

Everyone laughed except Lonnie, who had remained silent throughout. He turned off his shower and walked out.

CHAPTER 2

"Hi, Phil, this is Cooper. I'm sorry to disturb you at home during the evening. I called because I picked up something disturbing at the faculty meeting I wanted to ask you about."

"Huh? Oh, yeah . . . . Cooper. How are you, Cooper?"

"I'm sorry, Phil. Did I wake you?"

"Huh, wake me? Uh, you didn't wake me. I haven't gone to bed yet. How could you wake . . . huh? Who is this?"

"It's Cooper, Phil. Are you all right?"

"Cooper? How are you, Cooper?"

"I'm fine, Phil. I'm sorry I disturbed you. I'll talk to you in the morning."

"Yeah, hi Cooper. I forget why I called you."

"You didn't call me. I called you, but it can wait until tomorrow. I'm going to hang up now, Phil. Goodnight Phil."

"What's wrong?" said Nancy.

"Phil Fedner is wrong, Nancy. He's drunk as a lord at eight o'clock in the evening. He apparently found liquor in Dwight Bedlington's room days ago, and he didn't tell me about it. I gather he does things like this all the time. Why in God's name did Leighton Frostley make that drunken idiot the Dean?"

"Don't raise your voice to me about it."

"I'm sorry, Nancy. I shouldn't be so irritable. You know, I never realized that so many people around here don't do what's expected of them. No wonder Frostley told the Trustees to make me Headmaster. I think I was the only one doing his job."

"Darling, that just isn't true and you know it. I think you've been working too hard. It's not like you to think everybody is out of step except you."

241

"Yeah. Except everybody is. They are out of step. And I have been working too hard, and I'm tired. What in the hell am I going to tell Bedlington about his kid? I'll have to put him on probation. That's the least I can give him and everyone will say he got preferential treatment at that. I'll have to kick him out as President of the Student Council. You know, I could never understand why his class elected him. Some of the faculty think he was elected as a joke. Can you believe that's possible? Can you?"

"You're raising your voice again. Why don't *you* get drunk? Maybe Phil has the right idea. Cooper, you know he must be very lonely. There he is in that house, all alone. No wife. No children. No family at all. How old is he, fifty? He must be in his fifties. Do you suppose he's a homosexual?"

"The kids think so, but I don't. Why can't somebody just be a bachelor?" said Cooper. "He's a smart rascal when he's sober. Probably was a good Dean at one time. Frostley probably just didn't have the heart to take him off the job. He loves it. It's power to him. He uses that damn job and that's just why he shouldn't be in it."

"Would you fire him?"

"I don't know. No. He's still a good teacher. He's probably the best French teacher we have. He can teach Latin and German too. I'll give him this year to straighten out as Dean, and see what happens. How's that?"

"Fine."

"Hey, do you want to have a drink?"

"Are you serious?"

"Yeah. What the hell. Let's have a drink and go to bed."

"OK."

"Let's forget the drink and just go to bed."

"That's my boy. You know this is the first evening in two weeks you've been home and not in a meeting?"

"What do you have on under that pretty blue dress?"

"Why don't you come over here and find out?"

"You know booze causes a hell of a lot of problems. You do know that?"

"Your mind is wandering."

"What?"

"Back to the blue dress, dummy."

"Back to what's under the blue dress."

"Hey, Sarah, I hear you're going to have a really good team this year."

"Why would you care, Buddy?"

"I like field hockey. I'd come to your games except I'm always at football practice."

"You're putting me on."

"No. I'm serious. I'd like to come watch you. Would that be OK? If I came to watch you play?"

"Except you're busy."

"Well, yeah, but if I wasn't?"

"What's this all about?"

"What do you think about me, Sarah?"

"In regards to what?"

"To anything. Well, I mean, am I the sort of person you might want to go to the dance with Saturday night?"

"Are you asking me?"

"Well, yeah. You want to go?"

"Sure. I'd like to go to the dance with you, Buddy. Thank you for asking me."

"Yeah. Well, I'll see you around, OK?"

"OK Buddy. I'll see you around."

The day after Cooper's unsuccessful attempt to talk to Dean Fedner on the phone, he called him into his office and found that what he had heard about the Bedlington boy was true. Fedner told Cooper that he was accustomed to doing his job with a degree of latitude and implied that Cooper did not know what he was doing by trying to interfere. Cooper told Fedner to do his job as he told him to or he wouldn't have a job, and also that his boss expected him to be sober and available for evening consultations, and any other calls upon his time during the course of performing his duties as Dean. Fedner maintained that he was sober, that he was merely tired from the exertions of a long, hard day. He admitted, when pressed, to having had "a few drinks," and Cooper told him to give up drinking altogether when school was in session.

Fedner had gone from arrogant and indignant at first, to subservient and humble when his job was threatened, then back to indignant when Cooper told him to stop drinking.

At the end of the meeting Cooper repeated his threat, telling the Dean that he was on warning, that he would be relieved as Dean if he were not able to satisfy Cooper better in the performance of his job, and that he could expect a memorandum to that effect within a day or two. Cooper had learned the year before that his employees tended to hear what they wanted to hear, and that mere verbal warnings tended to escape their memories.

When Cooper confronted young Bedlington, the boy was surprised and had no defense except to say that everyone did what he did, that his only sin was to get caught. Cooper told him he had heard that argument before and that while he was sure some escaped detection, "everyone" did not do it. He added that he doubted that this was Dwight's first offense but rather this was just the first time he got caught. He asked Dwight if he felt he was letting the school down by breaking major rules while serving as the top elected student official. Dwight expressed surprise that anyone should expect a higher standard of behavior from him. Cooper told him that he was to consider himself relieved of all elective offices and that he was on disciplinary probation. When the boy left, Cooper put in a call to his father.

"Hi there Mr. Headmaster," said the Trustee. "What can I do for you?"

Cooper gave Dwight Bedlington the news about his son and what he was doing about it.

"Cooper, I know this must be hard for you. I am sorry for the anguish he must have caused you. I hope Sonny has apologized to you. I realize it must be hard for you to punish the son of a Trustee. I, of course, expect you to treat him like anyone else."

"Of course I will, Dwight. I am disappointed, and I am sorry to have to give you the bad news, but it hasn't really caused me any anguish."

"Yes. Well I'm sure, Cooper, you won't go any harder on him either, just because he's my son. I wonder if you could ask him to call me."

"Better than that, Dwight, I was hoping you would find it convenient to take him home for a couple of days, long enough for you to have a good relaxed talk with him. I'm afraid that Dwight, uh, Sonny, is not contrite really, and being on probation can be precarious. One more serious infraction and I would have to expel him. That could be quite a blow in his senior year. It would affect his chances for admission to a good college."

"Bring him home? Now? I'm afraid that would be out of the question."

"May I ask why, Dwight? This is pretty important."

"Why? It's a personal consideration, Cooper. It just would not be convenient for his mother and me to have him home at this time."

"Do you think you could rework your plans? I am seriously concerned about the boy, Dwight."

"Yes. But you just can't imagine the inconvenience, Cooper. No. Have him call me please. That will be sufficient." Bedlington's tone had a nasty edge to it. He was a man who was unaccustomed to argument.

Cooper sensed danger signals. He thought to himself, when he says he doesn't expect special consideration, I think he means just the opposite. Cooper assured Bedlington that his son would get the message to call, and concluded the conversation.

Cooper decided it would be a good idea to report the incident to the President of the Board, so he asked Ida Beth to see if she could reach Gordon Fairingwether on the phone. In the meantime, he dictated a letter to Dwight Bedlington that outlined his son's offense and punishment. The letter was standard procedure, though more often written by the Dean. In the letter, Cooper noted his concern that Sonny would have to be expelled if he broke a major rule while on probation and expressed his regret that Sonny's parents were unable to accept his advice to take him home for a serious talk about his situation.

Cooper felt uncomfortable about the necessity for covering himself in writing. It seemed not a day went by when he wasn't concerned about protecting his actions against possible legal consequences. Meetings of school administrators were more and more concerned these days with warnings about the possible legal repercussions of almost anything anyone did.

"Mr. Fairingwether is on line one, Mr. Morgan," said Ida Beth.

Cooper greeted Gordon and told him what was on his mind.

"I'm glad you called, Cooper," he said. "Dwight has already called me. He said you threatened him with expelling young Sonny."

"Did he use the word 'threaten'?"

"Yes, he did."

"Well, I guess that tells me where he stands. Gordon, I just wanted him to see how serious probation is. If Sonny steps out of line, I'll have to expel him, and there is nothing he or you can do about it."

"Hey, wait a minute, Cooper, I'm on your side. I'll back you on anything you feel is really important. I might argue with you sometimes, but that's just between you and me. I'll back you up, all right?"

"I know you will, Gordon, and I appreciate it. I guess I'm edgy because I expect others to see things the way I do." Then Cooper added, in a light tone, "The way I see them is the correct way. You understand that, don't you, Gordon?"

Gordon laughed. "You see things damned clearly as far as I'm concerned, Cooper. If we lose Bedlington, so be it."

"Thank you Gordon. I'll do my best to straighten out Sonny."

"This may hurt the campaign, you know."

"How's that? Did Dwight withdraw his pledge?"

"He never really made a pledge. We've been negotiating the amount he's going to give. I've been holding out for five hundred thousand."

"Wow. Could he give that much?"

"Sure. He'll never miss it. I think he was about to do it. Now, he says he wants to wait and see how things work out for Sonny."

"Money is power, isn't it Gordon?"

"Sometimes. It can't buy our integrity, though."

"Good," said Cooper. "I hope you mean it."

"Don't expel that kid just to see if I mean it," Gordon chuckled.

Cooper laughed and said he wouldn't. They chatted about a few other things and then hung up.

I just hope you do mean it, Cooper thought, because I have an uneasy feeling about this one.

CHAPTER 3

After dinner the following evening Honey LaTate entered Monkey Craft's "office" backstage at the Arts Center. Monkey was a sixth former this year also. Honey said, "How ya doin,' Adrian?"

"Hi, Snake Lady. What do you have there? Is it a package of money for me?" He was referring to an odd-shaped package wrapped in newspaper that Honey carried with her.

"Do you still want to join our group, Adrian?"

"What? And be a male witch?"

"Yeah, a warlock."

"You asked me about that last year. Then nothing ever came of it."

"Well we never had another sabbat. That's a meeting. We have one coming up though. Do you want to join, or are you chicken?"

"Who else is in it?"

"Me. That's all you need to know. If you join, then you'll learn more."

"Well, what do you do?"

"Hey, I told you. It's a bunch of girls and we take off our clothes. Everyone in it is eighteen or older and you are too. I looked that up, You said you were interested. Now, you're either in or you're out. And if you're in, you'll really get in. Do you know what I mean?"

"Yeah. That's cool. I'm in. What do I do?"

"Here, take a look at this." She handed him her package.

Monkey started to unwrap the newspaper. "What is it?" he said.

"What's it look like?"

"A big hunk of plaster," he said as he pulled an object from the pile of paper.

"What else?"

Monkey began turning the plaster object in his hands. "Oh, my God," he said.

"You get it, huh?"

Monkey nodded his head. His mouth fell open. He held the plaster gently.

Honey said, "It's a pussy. It's a plaster cast of a real live pussy. You know whose?"

Monkey shook his head in the negative.

"It's mine," Honey said proudly. "You like it?"

"Yeah. Are you giving it to me?"

"You can hold it, if you like, but you have to give it back. It belongs to the coven. There is one for each of us." She let that sink in as Monkey examined the plaster very closely. He was fascinated.

"We're going to need one of you," she said.

"But, I don't know how to . . ."

"That's OK. We'll make it. We're ready to make it now. Is that all right with you?"

"You mean right here?" said Monkey.

"No, downstairs in the basement. In the sculpture studio."

"But anyone could walk in there anytime. It's not private."

"Yeah, they can, but they won't. No one will know we're down there. You'd be surprised. No one goes down there during off hours. People don't come here either do they? Unless they're coming to buy dope."

"Yeah, OK," said Monkey.

Honey and Monkey descended a concrete stairway. The whole lower level of the Marsh Arts Center was devoted to graphic arts and sculpture. The rooms for painting were on the north side of the building. The upper halves of those rooms were aboveground and had windows made of frosted, translucent glass. The rooms for pottery, sculpture and casting were lit artificially and had no windows. The light was on in the room reserved for plaster casting and Louise Shipper, a sixth former, was in the room. Louise was a very thin, tall girl with mousey blonde hair. Her hair usually looked dirty, but this evening it was washed and brushed out. Louise was wearing an Art Department smock over dungarees and a blouse. She had obviously been waiting for them.

"Now," said Honey, "Lou is going to make your casting while I keep you happy. Understand?"

Monkey looked worried and shook his head in the negative.

Honey held his face in her hands and whispered to him up close, "You have to be hard while Lou makes a wax impression. It's my job to get you hard and keep you that way. After the wax hardens, your pecker gets soft and comes out of the wax cast easily. Then we pour plaster in the cast. When that hardens, we cut off the wax and out comes a perfect replica of your erection. Isn't that nice?"

"Then what will you do with it?"

"It will belong to the coven, and we'll use it for ceremonial purposes. Now, come on and get out of your clothes."

"In front of Lou?" Monkey sounded miserable. All this time Louise said nothing but smiled amiably.

Honey said, "All right, go in the supply closet over there and take off everything, even your shoes and socks, and put on a smock. You don't want to get wax or plaster on your clothes. Believe me, it's hell to get out. Now, go on. I'm going to take my clothes off too. We'll have fun. You'll like it."

When Monkey came out of the closet he was barefoot and naked underneath the smock he had wrapped tightly around himself. Honey was barefoot as well but her smock was loosely tied with a sash.

"That's my boy, Adrian," said Honey. "Now, come over here and lie down on this table. You're going to love being a warlock."

As Monkey came towards her she pulled the sash away from around her waist.

The Saturday night dance was known as a mixer. There were some students from other schools invited by Essex students as their dates, but many Essex students had dates with each other. Although one Essex student dating another was sometimes likened to "kissing your sister," there were always, at any given time, several love affairs in progress on campus.

The usual place for a mixer or dance was the Dining Hall, which was designed, in part, for this purpose. Dances always included punch and soft drinks and lots of things to eat. Adjacent to the Dining Hall's main room were several lounges with their tables mostly removed. Centered on the north wall was a raised platform with a first rate PA system and lots of electrical outlets, for the band.

The middle section of the Dining Hall had a second floor balcony with glass walls all around. It was affectionately termed the Starlight Roof. The Starlight Roof had a square open space in the middle surrounded by a railing, from which one could look down on the floor below and also easily hear the band. "Chaperone" was the quaintly ancient term given to adults forced to attend the dance, presumably to maintain a small amount of order and gracious behavior. However, no student in recent years had been known to pay any attention to the adults. Chaperones liked the Starlight Roof because the sound of the band was slightly less intense there, and the flashing lights slightly less obtrusive. Students thought that adults liked the Starlight Roof so they could spy on the revelers below.

There was an enclosed Faculty Lounge on the first floor of the Dining Hall, and chaperones especially liked to go in there to escape the music altogether, and play cards or gossip. The Student Council ran the dances, and always invited a few local parents to be chaperones. They invited faculty couples, too, with Cooper suggesting who they might be. The parents were pleased to be invited to chaperone, at least the first time. Faculty members were not. They regarded such invitations as intrusions on their already limited time away from job obligations. Many faculty couples, however, responded with resigned good humor to Cooper's request that they chaperone at least two such social occasions a year. Cooper kept a record and wrote notes of thanks to all chaperones. Actually, Ida Beth wrote them and Cooper signed them.

Dress at this mixer was informal meaning that almost every boy was in blue jeans along with some sort of favorite shirt. Some girls also dressed that way. More were in skirts and sweaters. That's the way Sarah dressed. Buddy Braken got some gentle razzing because he was not thought to be the type to take a girl to a mixer.

Honey was in form-fitting jeans. Her date, Dwight Bedlington, received no razzing because he was widely accepted as a ladies' man. Dwight filled the hero role that evening because it had only recently been announced that he was on probation and relieved of his leadership position. Many students, who never liked him in the first place, now pretended outrage that the school administrators had the temerity to carry out prescribed discipline procedures. These were the same students who only a few days ago were claiming that the son of a Trustee was getting away with behavior forbidden to others.

"Hey, Dwight baby, you really got a rotten deal there," said Monkey, who was at the mixer, as usual, to look after the loudspeaker system and the electrical hook-ups for the band.

"Shit," said Honey, "when you drink as much as this guy does, you're bound to get caught sooner or later."

"Maybe you ought to give Dwight lessons on not getting caught," said Monkey. "Honey can get away with anything."

"Curb your tongue, knave," said Honey, "or I'll shove your plaster cast where it will do you the most good."

"What plaster cast?" asked Dwight.

"Never mind that," said Monkey. "I was counting on you, Dwight, to get Morgan to let us keep cars on campus. Now it looks like you don't have the influence I thought you did. Damn, that bastard Pirate used to be a nice guy when I was in his dorm. Now he's the Headmaster, he thinks he's God."

"That's just about what Fairy Fedner said to me. Fedner didn't tell Morgan he found liquor in my room. Morgan found out some other way. Now, if we could just get rid of Morgan and get Fedner made Headmaster, then you could park your fucking car right in front of the fucking Arts Center, Monkey. How would you like that?"

Honey said, "Fedner as Headmaster, that's a laugh."

"Don't be so sure," said Dwight. "My father thinks Fedner should have been the Headmaster."

"That's crazy," said Monkey.

"Don't be so sure," said Dwight. "My father gives this stinking school beaucoup money, and he's got big influence on the Trustees."

Honey said, "Are you going to stand here bullshitting all night, or are you going to dance with me?"

"I'll dance with you, Honey," said Dwight. "But that's not all I'd like to do with you."

"Goodbye, Adrian," Honey said. "We'll catch you later."

"Catch you later, guys."

Honey pushed herself up against Dwight and said, "How much would you like to do that with me?"

"Plenty, Honey, I need to get laid real bad."

"Will you do anything I say?"

"Like what?"

"Like letting me make a plaster cast of your dick?"

"You don't need a cast, Honey, you can have the real thing."

"We do it my way, or not at all."

"OK Honey, whatever you say. What do you want it for?"

"I'll tell you later."

251

On another part of the dance floor Buddy Braken was talking to Sarah Savage. Sarah said, "Don't put your hands on me that way, Buddy, there are people watching."

"I can't help it, your legs are beautiful."

"I wish they were."

"They look good to me, Sarah."

"Thank you, Buddy. I didn't know you had this side to you."

"What side?"

"Oh, you know, romantic."

"That's me." They both laughed. Buddy said, "We're going to leave here early and go to a party in East Woods. Is that all right with you?"

"I don't know, Buddy," Sarah said. "Who's going?"

"Dwight and Honey, and Amelia West and Chick Jones, and maybe some other guys. We've got two cases of beer stashed in the creek getting cold. Dwight put it there."

"He must be crazy," said Sarah, "He just went on pro. If he gets caught he'll get kicked out."

Buddy said, "Dwight doesn't give a sh . . ." He laughed. "He just doesn't care. That's what's so great about him. Besides, who's gonna catch him? You don't think Morgan has the guts to throw out a Trustee's son, do you? The Trustees run this dump. They tell Morgan what to do."

"That's not the way I heard it. Anyway, Morgan already put him on pro, didn't he? What makes you think he won't throw him out?"

"Nah, he won't. Besides, Dwight is smart. He won't get caught."

"You mean again?"

"Yeah, well, the first time was a fluke."

"When you act the way Dwight does, people are going to find out," said Sarah.

"Well anyway, will you go out there with me?"

"I don't like to break the rules, Buddy, but if you want me to go, I will."

"Terrific. You'll have a good time, Sarah."

She giggled, "Hey, take your hand off of there."

"Don't worry, Sarah, I was just smoothing your skirt. You want to get something to eat?"

She smiled at him and they walked away together.

CHAPTER 4

By the time Buddy and Sarah reached the rendezvous site in East Woods, a party was well in progress. Honey and Dwight were there, so was Monkey, and so were Louise Shipper and Jim Serleig.

"Hey, Buddy!" roared Dwight. "Pull up a seat and grab a tin from the old creek."

Honey seemed to think this was funny and she laughed.

"I can see you guys have been at it for a while," said Buddy. He fished a couple of cans of Budweiser from the cold creek and threw one of them to Sarah who caught it. When she opened it, the beer sprayed and foamed, spilling over her hand.

"Hurray," shouted Dwight. "S'matter, Sarah babe, never opened a tin before?"

Buddy poured a whole can of beer down his throat and wiped his mouth with the back of his hand. An enormous belch rose up out of him and he looked surprised. Dwight and Honey clapped their hands and shouted with glee.

"You guys are makin' a hell of a lot of noise," said Buddy. "Gonna get us caught if you don't watch out."

"Don't worry about it," said Sarah in an effort to be one of the gang. She tried to pour her beer down the way Buddy had, but she choked. Buddy patted her on the back.

"What have you all been doin'?" asked Buddy.

"Lou has been makin' statues in the art room," said Dwight with a loud laugh.

Lou and Monkey and Honey all seemed to think that was funny. "You ought to go down there, Buddy. She can make a nice statue of you."

"Yeah?" said Buddy. "What kind of statues do you make, Lou?"

"Big ones, Buddy," said Louise. Again there was laughter.

"Not as big as Buddy's," Dwight shouted. "Buddy's got the biggest one in the whole school."

Buddy, beginning to sense what they were talking about said, "Where's the statue you made of Dwight?"

"Put away for a rainy day," laughed Honey. Lou laughed with her.

Honey said, "If yours is the biggest in the school, we'll make one of you, too, Buddy."

"I think I might like that, Honey, if you make it," said Buddy.

"I don't make 'em," said Honey. "Lou makes 'em. I just play with 'em." Again the laughter boomed forth, this time louder than ever.

The party continued in merry fashion. Sarah drank as much beer as she could, in an attempt to join in and have as much fun as the others were obviously having. It didn't work, however, and she understood only half of what was being said. Later, in her dorm, she threw up the beer. Then she wept because she decided she was incapable of joining the "in" people.

When the beer was gone and the hour late, the revelers hurried back to their respective dormitories to be checked in before the last of the dancers from the mixer.

Buddy, Monkey and Dwight lived in the sixth form dormitory for boys, King Hall. They each appeared briefly in the entrance to the Housemaster's apartment, shouted out their names, and were checked in.

Later, Pickle-Bob Bonnie, a master who helped manage King Hall, came into Monkey's room to ask him a question. Teachers and students alike referred to him as Pickle-Bob. That worthy representative of law and order stated that he thought he smelled the odor of booze in the air of Monkey's room. Monkey decided to direct Pickle-Bob's attention elsewhere, fast. Monkey had survivor's instincts. He told Pickle-Bob that Dwight Bedlington had just been in the room smelling like a brewery and filled the air with his fumes, and that he, Adrian, was downright offended by it. "See if I'm not right, sir," said Monkey. "Go take a look at Dwight. He lives just across the hall there."

Pickle-Bob took that suggestion, and when he entered Dwight's room there was no doubt in his mind that Adrian Brooks Craft IV had spoken the truth. Dwight was roaring drunk. Monkey, in the meantime, opened his windows, turned out his lights, jumped in bed and feigned sleep.

Pickle-Bob dragged Dwight back to the Housemaster's apartment and presented him for inspection. Word had gotten out about how the

Headmaster had reacted to the Dean's keeping his knowledge of major rule infractions to himself. Pickle-Bob and the other Housemaster had no intention of making the same mistake, and reported to Cooper by phone that very night. The Headmaster promptly came down The Mall to King Hall to see for himself. Cooper put Dwight into the infirmary for the night and called his father the following morning, telling him to come take Sonny home.

Most students in the dorm were very much aware of the Headmaster's late night visit.

Monkey was one of them. He thought to himself it was too bad that Dwight had to be sacrificed. However, it was better this way because all will be soon forgiven, since Dwight's father is a Trustee. If that should not turn out to be the case, then there would be one warlock fewer with whom he would have to compete.

Not long after that, unbeknownst to Monkey, his anatomical casting was mounted on one of several thin six-foot-long poles, as were the castings of the girls in Honey's coven. The night of a full moon was fast approaching and, therefore, time for the Sabbat.

Honey thought it was a shame that Dwight was expelled. She really would like to have had more than one warlock for the first Sabbat in this, her sixth form year. She didn't want Monkey thinking he was the big cheese. But she figured his initiation ritual ought to keep him off-balance, at least for this ceremony.

There was a place in East Woods, at least a half-hour walk from the site of Dwight's beer party, where every few decades the Connecticut River flooded in the spring. Great, tall elm trees grew there until Dutch elm disease killed them. Now it was a bone yard. The elms, long dead, had lost their bark and bleached in the sun. Some had fallen over while some still stood with their silver-gray bare branches, broken and twisting, reaching to the sky.

Honey had discovered this place several years before when she first came to Essex. She had been walking in the woods looking for dead trees and hollow logs where bees might have built a hive. Most of the ground was clear. There were tufts of long fine grass. Honey called the place Stonehenge because the bleached, dead elm trees reminded her of pictures she had seen of the great, seemingly randomly placed stones at the Druid place of worship in England.

When Honey first conceived of the idea of a coven, her own Stonehenge in East Woods seemed the ideal place for an outdoor Sabbat. Secret clubs and societies had always fascinated her, and she read all the books she could find about witchcraft. She took various ideas from her reading and adapted them, allowing her creative imagination to fill in gaps and add nuances that appealed to her.

Honey liked the sex cult aspects of witchcraft the most. She wasn't frightened about summoning the devil because she didn't really believe he existed. She kept that to herself, however. It would not do for her followers to think the head witch was insincere. She did sort of believe in unexplained forces though. But if there really turned out to be a devil, and if by accident she really did summon him, she figured she could back out of any lasting relationship. For one thing, she reasoned, she could switch over to being a white witch. In the back of her mind she saw herself as a white witch, anyway, but she never told any of the girls in the coven. When they were joking together they referred to Honey's religion as blue witchcraft.

Drug use was, of course, an ancient part of witchcraft, as well as playing around with medicines, poisons and other interesting substances. Honey was very interested in all of this and had a certain degree of expertise in it. She was, as Gunnar Ferris had told Cooper, particularly knowledgeable about the poison in hymenopteran stings, that is, the stings of wasps, honey bees, yellow jackets and hornets. And she had done more research in that area than she had ever written up in papers for Gunnar.

The most useful fellow witches Honey recruited were girls with artistic talent. Louise Shipper was the most resourceful of these. Louise had sculpted both human and animal skulls from papier-mâché and clay, and she had fashioned pentacles, moons and other symbols of witchcraft. All of these she and Honey had suspended from dead tree branches at Stonehenge the afternoon before the full moon. They also suspended, high up in a tree, a large crude cross hanging upside down. It was wrapped in burlap soaked in kerosene.

Students and youthful theatrical groups all around the country were staging events known as "Happenings," and the girls in the coven referred to their Sabbats sometimes as "Honey's Happenings." The skeptics among the girls thought that the privilege of attending was worth putting up with all the hocus-pocus and pretended to believe in it.

Clear skies had been predicted for the night, and the stars were dazzling when Monkey slipped out of King Hall at about eleven o'clock. The moon, which he knew would be full, was not yet up. There were some streetlights and doorway lights on the campus that stayed on all night, but the rest of the outside lights, which were bright earlier in the evening, were now off, and the campus was relatively dark. Monkey made his way around the back of King Hall, and then behind the Girls Campus, and across the fields east to Old River Road. He was told to dress warmly, but not to wear his watch or carry his wallet or any valuables. He was told he would be met on the north side of the boathouse. The late September evening was warm and he pulled off his sweater and tied the sleeves around his waist.

There was no one at the boathouse. Monkey had decided he would just have to wait, when the tall, slender form of Louise Shipper materialized from out of the trees. She bid him to follow her and they set off up the road. She answered all of Monkey's questions with, "You'll see." Or she didn't answer them at all.

Monkey did not think Lou looked very much like a witch. She was in jeans and a soft-looking flannel shirt.

Monkey thought, Lou's taller than me. Besides, she knows what's going on, and I don't. Anyway, I'm probably going to get laid. That will be great if it's Honey. Screwing Lou wouldn't be much. Well, Honey practically said it, didn't she? She said I'll "get in." In who? All of them? Have to wait and see. It better be good or I'm walking out, and that's that. Maybe I should ask Lou where her broomstick is. Better not. No use in antagonizing her. This may be like an initiation. They wouldn't paddle me? They better not try. I came here to be a warlock, not some fraternity pledge. But I don't know the ropes, so I better keep my mouth shut or I might not get laid. Oh, God, I really need to. Everyone gets it but me. Well, half those guys are lying most of the time. They must be because that's what I'm always doing, lying. Pretending I'm getting plenty when I'm not. Sometimes I believe it myself.

"Hey, Lou, how far is it? We've been going a long time."

Lou said nothing. They just kept walking.

Jeez, she has long legs. She's not even feeling it and I'm getting winded. She's going too fast, damnit.

Twice they stepped into the trees when a car was coming so they would not be observed. The townies always recognized Essex students.

No matter how they dressed, the townies always knew. They continued on for another mile or so.

Lou held up her hand as if listening for something or looking for something. Then she waved to Monkey and set off into the woods.

This will be tough going, Monkey thought, going through the woods with no path. Damn, there is a path. I guess I've never been this far north of the campus in East Woods. It goes forever. There is just barely enough light so you don't bump into the trees. Lou seems to see better than I do. She knows the path, apparently knows it well.

They continued on. Then Lou stopped in a little clearing. She went down on one knee by a huge old hollow log. She pulled something out of it.

"Here," she said, "take off all your clothes and put this on."

Monkey just stood there.

"Come on," said Louise. "Hurry up or we'll be late. Leave on your moccasins but take off everything else. Take this. I have to change too."

"What is this?" asked Monkey, accepting a bundle of cloth.

"It's the kind of gown people graduate from college in. It's special, for your first night."

Monkey could see that Louise was taking off her jeans and shirt hurriedly, but it was too dark to see what she looked like naked. He started taking off his own clothes. Monkey had all his clothes off now. The perspiration on his body cooled him in the very slight breeze.

Maybe this is it. Now? No. She's too matter of fact. She's in a hurry. Wouldn't it be awful if blinding lights suddenly came on and it was a big joke on me and everyone I know from school was here laughing at me? Oh, God . . . Don't be crazy. Act cool for once. Jesus, she's already seen me and put hot wax all over it. Watched Honey work me over. That girl knows how to do everything.

Lou had pulled some sort of a robe over her head and put on high boots.

Monkey hoped there were no mosquitos. The gown went on easily. It felt heavy, sort of, on his shoulders. He began looking for buttons to close it up. He couldn't find any. "Hey, Lou, how do you close this thing?"

"You don't. You let it hang open. Or you can hold it closed with your hands, if you're chicken." She walked over to him and put one hand on his shoulder. Then she placed the other hand on his chest and slid it down his abdomen. "You don't have any underwear on, do you? You can't wear underwear." She briefly felt around his genitals and then stepped back, apparently satisfied.

When she was close to him, Monkey could see that her robe was cut in an inverted V, open from her feet to her waist. Her pubic area was dark and bushy, and open to the world. He felt a rush of blood in his loins. Monkey said, "Put your hand on me again, Lou. That felt nice."

"No time now, Adrian, we have things to do." She rolled his clothes up into a ball and stuffed them, along with her own, into the log. Then Louise turned in the direction they had been going and headed out of the little clearing and into the woods.

Monkey could see that the sky was lighter on the horizon in the east where they were headed. He thought Old River Road must be a long way from the river in that area. He felt disoriented. He knew little about the out-of-doors. He wondered why there was light in the east.

The sun can't be coming up, Monkey thought. It's not time. There's no city over there to light the sky. Could it be the moon? Does the moon come up in the east, or in the west? I should know, I suppose. That must be it, the moon. It must rise in the east the way the sun does.

"OK, you can relax for a minute," Lou said. "We're here."

When Monkey looked up, there was the river looking like a black void. The thin ragged ribbon between the far shore and the horizon was even blacker. The sky above was a beautiful deep blue, studded with stars. Now it was even more evident that the sky beyond the river, in the east, was lighter than the rest of the heavens.

Despite being naked under the heavy academic gown, Monkey felt hot and sweaty. Then a breeze cooled him. He could smell flowers. Or was that perfume, or Lou?

She was standing close to him and he could see the perspiration gleaming on her belly.

He thought it strange that someone so skinny had a round belly. He had never noticed her hips were so wide.

The thought came that girls certainly are different from boys, which he decided was a really stupid observation.

It seemed the most natural thing in the world to reach out and touch his fingers to that lovely round belly. The muscles in her abdomen convulsed a little at his touch, but she didn't draw back. It was a magical, unreal moment. He knew instinctively that if he grabbed, he would ruin everything. Ever so slowly, so gently, so delicately, he moved his fingertips down and into her deep fur pelt.

A sigh with the tiniest ring of a high-pitched moan escaped her lips. She stepped sideways to face him, planting her feet far apart. She placed her hands on his shoulders and bowed her head, a gesture both submissive and bold as she stared at his fingers disappearing between her legs, lightly stroking the swelling lips. She said, "Oh, Adrian, that feels so nice, don't stop." Her voice was soft as a whisper. "They'll be here in just a minute."

"What's going to happen, Lou?" Monkey stroked more boldly.

"Don't you know what a Sabbat is for, Adrian?"

"No, Lou, what's it for?"

"To have intercourse with the devil."

"What?"

"I said don't stop."

"That's the craziest thing I ever heard. How do you have intercourse with the devil?"

"Well, it's sort of like praying in church, only different. You just sort of offer yourself, and the devil is supposed to go in, you know, between your legs."

"You mean, like, sell your soul?"

"No, I never heard anything about that. We just let him screw us, you know, figuratively. It's sort of symbolic, but some of the girls really seem to get off on it."

"Well, what am I supposed to do?"

"Whatever Honey tells you to do. You won't be sorry. Honey is fantastic. I think what she has in mind is that eventually you'll play the part of the devil. But for starters, I think she wants you to let the devil have intercourse with you, too."

"How the hell am I supposed to do that?"

"I don't know. I've never even seen the devil, not really. I've felt him, but not actually seen him. Besides, we've never had a warlock before. Honey knows how everything works, but I don't. Just do what Honey says. You won't be sorry."

"OK Lou, before they come, how about you and me . . . you know. How about it?"

"Shhhhh, be quiet. They're coming now. Listen."

CHAPTER 5

Monkey could faintly hear female voices, humming. As the humming got closer Monkey decided each girl was singing a different word over and over. Each girl held the note she was singing and dragged out the word, then repeated it after she took a breath. The notes were in harmony with each other, so the overall effect was harmonious babble. Monkey and Lou were standing on the riverbank looking back to the west where they had come from, and towards the place where the voices were coming from, a little to the south of that.

"What are they singing, Lou?" asked Monkey.

Lou said, "Adrian, hold me."

He put his arms around her and pressed her to him. His robe was open and the touch of her nakedness against him was erotic. She tilted his face up with her hands and kissed him with her mouth open.

Then she pulled away and said, "Each of them is singing her own name. We each have special names just for this. The names come from the stars. Honey's name is Hydra. You should call her that when she speaks to you."

"And your name?"

"My name is Auriga. Hydra will give you a name, too."

Monkey observed for the first time the bleached limbs of the dead elms, with shadowy objects hanging from them, surrounding a clearing just to the south of where he stood. The voices came from the same place, now quite clear. Then the sound stopped.

From farther in the woods came Honey's high clear voice, "Welcome, my sisters, to this glorious Sabbat. May the spirit of Split foot be with us and send us fire from the lower regions."

There was a pause, and then a streak of bright yellow flame hissed out of the blackness and arched upwards, striking a high object with a thud.

The upside-down cross that Honey and Lou had hung over the clearing was quickly engulfed in flame. The shaft of an arrow protruded from the center of the cross. Monkey was dumbfounded as to how such a trick could be performed and half believed that the flaming arrow had come from hell. It was a perfect bullseye shot. But it had curved upward like no arrow's flight he had ever seen before. He did not see the black string that was attached to the cross's center and led down to the woods, nor the metal eyelets on the arrow, which had guided it along the string's path.

The flaming cross now lit the clearing. Lou had pulled a hood over her head that hid her mousey blonde hair and came half way down her face. It had holes cut out for her eyes. She led Monkey closer to the clearing, to where he could clearly see Honey as Hydra standing high up on a huge fallen, bleached elm trunk. She was dressed in animal furs. On her head, she wore a black cloth headband. Pinned to the headband and centered on her forehead, flashed a jeweled pentacle—an inverted five-pointed star. She had furs wrapped around her feet and around her legs half way up her thighs. They were held in place by knotted leather thongs. She wore no mask or hood, but the white make-up on her face changed her appearance so much that Monkey could identify her only by her voice. Her body was draped in fur strips through which her bare arms protruded. Between the strips, her breasts were visible. Most of the strips hung not much farther than her waist, leaving her pelvic region and buttocks exposed. A large black bag hung at her side, its strap passing diagonally across her chest and over one shoulder.

What caught the eye most of all, however, was a six-foot king snake, her familiar, that writhed in coils about her neck and left arm. Both her arms were extended upward as she cried out, "Oh, Goddess Moon, rise up to shed your light on our revels." As she shouted, her fair skin and white face seemed to grow lighter as if, on cue, a spotlight focused on her and slowly increased in intensity.

Then, for the first time, Monkey saw the figures of the other witches standing about the clearing. He looked back over his shoulder and there, as if on command, a huge orange moon rose almost halfway above the horizon on the far side of the silent river.

A dozen or so girls' voices cried out, "Oh, Mother Moon, shed your light on our revels."

Monkey sucked in his breath as he looked at the witches. Each wore a mask of some sort, or a hood to disguise her features. They wore outlandish costumes that covered various parts of their bodies, but in each case their breasts, crotches and bottoms were bare. Monkey's heart was pounding in his chest. Each witch wore a predominant color, red or purple or various shades of blue or green, indicating that the parts of each costume were made from the same bolt of material. The shapes and styles of dress varied considerably. There were several capes and hoods, and robes, and cutout leotards. Monkey noted that several had shaved off their pubic hair or shaped it into hearts, diamonds or triangles. There were lots of beads on strings and loud costume jewelry.

Monkey thought, this must be what a costume party in a whorehouse is like. But he wasn't laughing, even to himself. He was impressed. Lou had brought him to an aroused state and his erection still stood out between the folds of his academic gown.

Hydra said something to her followers, and they came forward and helped her down off the log. Then, they all proceeded to the center of the clearing.

Monkey then heard Honey's voice call out, "Who have you brought us Sister Auriga?"

Beside him Lou sang out, "Oh Queen Hydra, favorite of the Moon Goddess, I have brought someone who wishes to be our brother in this clan."

There was considerable whispering among the sisters as if they were perhaps learning for the first time that there was a male in the vicinity. A few made gestures to cover themselves.

"Bring our prospective brother to us," cried Hydra. The others stood separate from her, perhaps because they feared the big snake draped around her.

Sister Auriga took Monkey by the hand and led him to the center of the group. He wanted desperately to pull the academic gown around him and hold it closed, but remembering Lou's words about being chicken, he kept his hands at his sides. He grew limper with each frightening forward step he took. The ground grew soft beneath his feet and Monkey saw that he was walking on blankets.

Queen Hydra went down on one knee and put her snake in a covered basket, while the other sisters brought forward long poles and stuck them in the ground in a circle around them. At the top of each pole was a wedge-shaped plaster cast, such as the one that Honey had shown Monkey at the Arts Center. Mounted on each cast was a stout, white unlit candle.

Sister Auriga placed Monkey directly in front of Honey, who said, "I am Hydra. You shall be known as Orion, our brother. You shall be a warlock member of Hydra's Coven. Welcome."

Monkey decided he was supposed to say something. Nice to meet you, and glad to be here, which had served him on other occasions, seemed out of place. So he just said, "Thank you," but unfortunately a holdover symptom from his still changing voice chose this moment to manifest itself, and his voice croaked.

The white-faced Hydra held her forefinger up against his lips to halt further disgrace to the formality of the occasion. She merely said, "Bring his Other."

Sister Auriga came up to the circle and stuck a staff into the ground that had the plaster cast of Monkey's erection on it. The witches squealed little giggles, and noises of appreciation. Brother Orion smiled in obvious pride. The plaster was representing him at that moment more impressively than was the original member.

In her clear imperious voice, Hydra declared, "This staff shall represent you in the Sabbats of this coven, even in years to come when you are absent from it." Turning again to Lou, she said, "And bring us Orion's mask."

Once more Sister Auriga came forward and this time handed Hydra a sort of helmet made of varnished papier-mâché. It was red and looked a little like the helmet of a medieval knight, or perhaps even more like the mask a comic strip hero might wear. It covered the bridge of his nose but not the nostrils or his lower face. The eyeholes were rakish and severe looking. Simulated curved horns protruded from the forehead, like a Viking's helmet. Sister Hydra held the mask up for all to see and then held it in front of Monkey for his perusal. Then she settled it down in place over his head, saying, "Sister Auriga has fashioned you a beautiful mask, oh warlock. I now pronounce you are Orion." With that the witches lit the candles on their plaster casts. There was no candle on Monkey's cast, since there was no room for one.

The sisters giggled and tittered and clapped their hands as if they were just schoolgirls, rather than shameless, half-naked witches. Hydra restored order by declaring that it was time for them to greet their Brother Orion, before partaking of supper with "the prince of darkness."

Monkey was feeling much better now. He was a member and there had been no paddling. Orion was one of the few constellations in the sky he could identify. For some reason, having that name made him feel proud. He was more at ease with the mask on. His body was exposed but his identity hidden. He realized now why the witches wore them and how they could be so shameless.

"Now," said Hydra, "each of us will introduce ourselves to you, Prince Orion. In the coven, it is permitted for us to touch each other. In that way we show our love for the Moon Goddess, for the 'Old One,' and for our sisters and brother." She stepped close and faced him. She reached inside his robe. Placing the palms of her hands on his buttocks, she rubbed her pelvis into his, pulling him hard against her. She kissed him softly on the mouth and then stepped back, saying, "Hydra greets you, Orion."

Monkey realized too late that he had been invited to feel Honey's body with his hands. He resolved quickly to make better use of his opportunity with the rest of the girls. It occurred to him he didn't know who they were, except for Honey and Louise. He thought that, oh boy, he was sure going to like getting to know them.

Lou came up to him. She, too, reached inside his robe, but her hands went straight to his penis. She fondled him gently and he quickly grew firm. Monkey pulled her tunic open at the top and placed his uplifted palms on her breasts. He kissed her, and then she drew back and said, "I am Auriga. Welcome."

A heavyset girl came up to him and squeezed him to her. She said, "I am Lepus, Orion. Welcome." There was something familiar about her, but he didn't know who she was.

Next came a girl who said she was Cetus. She grinned at him broadly and squeezed his erection. Just as he groped between her legs, she laughed and jumped back. He would know that laugh anywhere. It was Amelia West. She was in his calculus class and, although she was a tease, it was shocking to connect her with this wild-looking masked witch.

A girl stroked her hands down his ribs to his hips and said, "I am Cygnus." He felt her breasts, and then she danced away.

Next came one who said she was Cepheus. Then came Boötes. There were thirteen of them, in all. In the whole group, he was only able to identify Honey, Lou and Amelia. They obviously knew who he was. These girls would be seeing him and saying hello on campus, and he wouldn't know which ones he had shared this intimacy with.

They began sitting down on the blankets, in a circle. Hydra was saying something about having dinner with the Old One. One of the witches had a beautiful water pipe, which she lit with a wooden match. She drew in, puffing on the mouthpiece, which was attached to a long rubber hose. Monkey got a whiff of the aroma. It was hashish.

Honey knew that for centuries witches' sabbats used potions or drugs that produced hallucinogenic reactions. They were normally taken in a ceremony of communion with Satan. LSD was the hallucinogen most readily available to Honey, and so that's what she used at first. The results were sometimes remarkable, producing highly successful "Happenings." She grew increasingly concerned, however, that LSD reactions were unpredictable and uncontrollable. She decided that what she really wanted was a euphoric state among her revelers and freedom from inhibition. She found hash the most satisfactory substance for producing this effect. One of her witches managed to supply it, but continuing the supply was always doubtful. It was because Monkey was the most dependable dealer at Essex Academy that Honey selected him to be their first warlock.

The light from the flaming cross above them was gone. The cross was just glowing embers and would soon be black, charred wood. The moon was high now, smaller and silver in color. The candles were burning well, but the slight breezes in the clearing caused them to burn faster on one side than the other and, therefore, drip profusely.

When the water pipe was going nicely, it was passed to Hydra. From her sitting position she held it aloft and said, "I give you the smoke of Belial. My sisters and brother, take him into your bodies." With that, she drew on the water pipe's mouthpiece, sucked in a lungful of smoke and held her breath. Silently, she passed the mouthpiece to the sister on her right.

That witch said, "I take into my body the smoke of Belial." She drew in and then, taking the bowl of the water pipe from Hydra, passed the mouthpiece on to the next witch. And so on it went around the circle. The witches inched themselves into a tighter circle. They rubbed their bare skin and that of their neighbors, seeking the warmth of each other's bodies against the chill of the night air. As the pipe passed around they began to whisper to each other, chatting in low voices, often giggling.

There were many sidelong glances at Monkey who was sitting silently in yogi fashion, as were most of the girls. Monkey had wisely decided to maintain silence until he learned the procedures, which, so far, he found fraught with interesting possibilities. It was the partial-dress that built tension and expectation in his mind. He wished the light were better so he could see between the girls' legs. The way most of them were sitting with their knees apart should avail him a better view, he thought. However, all their crotches were in shadow. Perhaps his own was not but he didn't seem to mind, as he felt himself get higher and higher, as the pipe continued to pass around and around the circle.

Mostly he kept his eyes on Hydra. He kept thinking to himself "Queen Hydra." She exerted a strong leadership force in the group. Her fur costume and whitened face also made her stand out. Monkey thought that a stranger walking in would perceive immediately that she was the leader.

Just as he thought that, Hydra rose, then sat again in the middle of the circle and said, "I am ready for Belial." She stretched her hands out over her head and her feet touched Brother Orion's folded legs. Their circle was small enough so that her hands could clasp those of the girls behind her.

He wondered if Hydra had read his thoughts about wanting to see crotches because she drew her legs up until her knees were near her shoulders. Her opened rear was pointing right at him. He could see the delicate little pink folds of the lips around her vagina. They were shiny and wet just the way a marriage manual he had read said they were supposed to be, prior to copulation. He thought this must be the part about having intercourse with the devil. He had already supposed that Belial was another name for the devil. Monkey wondered if he was to play the devil or if the spirit of Belial was, even now, entering her.

Monkey stood halfway up looking for some sign of invitation. He even shed the warmth of his robe. It fell softly in folds behind him. He felt no chill. He was hot with the blood pumping through him. However, the Queen lowered her legs and came gracefully to a sitting position. She threw her head back and moaned and babbled incoherently. Monkey felt he was Orion floating in the heavens. He was very high, and so was Hydra, and so were the other sisters.

Hydra had a metal saltshaker in her hands. She was giggling to herself as she bowed her head over it, unscrewing the top. She appeared to take something out of it in the fingers of each hand, and then she deftly replaced the top. She lay down on her back, laughing now. The witches fell forward on their knees gathering close around her.

Monkey stood and leaned over for a view of what was happening. He wondered whether she had pinches of salt in her fingers. Then Monkey involuntarily drew in his breath.

Queen Hydra's hands quivered at her nipples. There, held deftly by their wings between the pressed forefinger and thumb of each hand, two honeybees buzzed softly. Their stingers touched her nipples simultaneously. She screamed, arching her back in rigid spasms. Her body jumped off the ground as if shot through with an electric jolt. She lay in a swoon as two girls, one on each side, began to softly suck her reddened stung nipples. A moan came from their Queen. She arched her back again and her hips began to buck and twist. She cried out repeatedly as the muscles in her abdomen went into spasms. Her skin was flushed and blotchy. She held her breath. Then it went out of her and her body went limp. She lay panting, bathed in perspiration. Hydra smiled faintly and pressed the heads of the two girls at her breasts tightly to her.

Monkey was not quite sure what had happened until he heard Auriga say to Hydra, "What a beautiful orgasm. The 'Old One' really had you, didn't he?"

Honey smiled, nodding her head.

Monkey looked for the bees, but her hands were empty. He thought the bees must have flown away.

Honey was still breathing heavily. One of the witches at her breast came up for air and Monkey leaned close to see the nipple. It was red and swollen. Honey put her hand behind his head and pressed him to her. He started to suck the nipple and it felt good. His head swam, and he felt he was doing the most beautiful thing in the world. He fell in love with his vulnerable queen.

Everything was awhirl in Monkey's mind. He was unaware of time. He could have been lying in Honey's arms sucking her breast for hours. The girl at her other breast was gone. He heard voices about him and girls moaning. Were they, too, having intercourse with Belial? He realized Honey had her legs around his middle. He felt the hot need to possess her. He only needed to shift his position a little and he could thrust inside her.

He began to move. She asked, "Are you ready for Belial?"

"Oh, yes!" he responded.

She twisted and he was on his back. Honey was sitting up, facing his feet. He felt her hands cool on his groin. He tried to look but there was Lou looking at him through the slits in the hood over her eyes. No, not Lou, Auriga. She kissed him and darted her tongue in his mouth. Something was happening to him down below. He couldn't see, but it felt fantastic. He stopped worrying who or what it was, and gave into the waves of pleasure coursing through his body. Queen Hydra and her sisters were doing something amazing. They held his feet in the air, his knees on his chest. Auriga cradled his head in her arms. She kissed his eyes, his cheeks, his mouth. He drifted. The waves coming from his groin were stronger, more real.

It almost feels like . . . could that be? It feels like an enema. Oh wow, they've slid something greasy up inside me. Is the devil buggering me? Oh, what the hell, it feels good. Huh, that's what my stupid father said, "If it feels good, do it. That's the trouble with you kids today. That's what you believe in." Yeah, well, I don't know what I believe in. Nothin' I guess. But, you're right, Dad it feels damned good, and I'm doin' it.

Monkey heard a scream from his own throat. He was burning. He thrashed and heaved.

No good, my arms are pinned. I'm on fire. It stings! The end of my peck . . . Oh, my God! They put a bee on my prick! Those bitches! Oh, God, that hurts! Ahhh, better now. I'm sinking . . .

"Hey, sisters," said a witch in a matter-of-fact tone. "Our Brother Orion is out like a light."

"That's OK," said Hydra, "he'll come around in a minute."

"That bee really zapped him," said Sister Cetus.

"I'm not surprised," said Sister Boötes, "that's a terribly sensitive place to sting him. How'd you like to get it on your clit?"

"I'm working on it," said Hydra, "as soon as I have someone trained to suck out the stinger and poison."

The witches all laughed.

"He's coming around," said Sister Auriga.

"He went off like Old Faithful," said Hydra.

"I think he's cute," Cetus said. "Look, his hair is just as red down here as it is on his head."

In a stage whisper Hydra said, "I don't mean to interrupt you, ladies, but will someone clean the lubricant off that plaster cast, before he wakes up? For the time being, I would rather he didn't know he fucked himself."

CHAPTER 6

1967-1968

September's fading warmth gave way to the cool nights and brilliant colors of fall in New England. Lonnie Deever, the only sixth former in the New Winds scholarship program for minority students, turned out to be the best halfback Essex Academy had seen in years. His skill as a broken-field runner and pass receiver was the key factor in an undefeated football season. He also began doing well with his studies.

Statistics indicate that a winning football team has nothing to do with fundraising success. However, the campaign for twenty million dollars propelled ahead with considerable progress. Alumni luncheons and dinners were held in all the major cities of the United States. Cooper and Nancy attended most of them. The New York City dinner was the biggest and most successful, with Sherri Huff presiding. With a little luck in some key areas, the campaign directors expected that the goal might be met by the end of the academic year. That, at least, was the revised strategy Cooper had worked out with the volunteer fundraising leadership. Sonny Bedlington's father, Dwight Senior, had not made a commitment, but neither had he resigned from the Board as a result of his son's expulsion.

If Dean Phillip Fedner had not conquered his drinking problem, he at least was managing to hide it effectively. On the surface, anyway, he and Cooper were maintaining a mutually cooperative relationship. At the recommendation of the school's attorneys, Cooper asked Phil to put together a Discipline Committee made up of faculty and students to consult with the Headmaster in matters of major rule violations. Fedner seemed to do a good job with that and was running the committee effectively, but the new group did little to check widespread rule breaking on campus.

Morale at Essex was high during the fall, because of a preponderance of pleasant weather, as well as the undefeated football team. Cooper felt his frequent absences for fundraising trips had little adverse effect on campus life, though there were occasional digs in *The Weekly Lion*, the student newspaper.

A sad note came in late November with word that the president of last year's graduating class, Ned Tucker, had died from a narcotics overdose on a weekend home from college. Cooper flew to Ann Arbor, Michigan for the funeral.

During the final week of the fall term before Christmas vacation a special exam schedule took effect. Normal classes were suspended. The average student load was one three-hour exam a day. The rest of the students' time was devoted to cramming. The Gym and Field House were open in the afternoons, but there were no required athletics. Of course, the coaches of varsity winter sports urged their squads to get out and sharpen their skills whenever possible.

At lunchtime, Sarah Savage waited in the Dining Hall entranceway for Buddy Braken, as was her normal practice. Buddy walked through the door and snorted as if she wasn't there. Sarah fell in step with him, "Hi, how did your physics exam go?"

"I bombed," he said. "I should never have let that bastard Ferris con me into taking physics."

"If you flunked the exam, then you'll flunk for the fall term and you'll be back on academic probation, won't you?"

He glared at her and said, "I don't need you to tell me that."

"I'm just worried for you, sweetheart. That's all."

"Yeah, shit! If I flunk that fucking course, I won't graduate."

"Please don't use that kind of language, Buddy. You know I don't like it."

"What don't you like? Fucking? I'm not surprised. You're no good at it. You do it though, don't you Sarah? So if you do it, you shouldn't mind hearing about it."

"Please don't talk to me that way, Buddy. We'll be going home tomorrow, and we won't see each other for nearly three weeks. So be nice, please?"

"Have you got any money?"

"What do you mean?"

"What do I mean? Oh, God! Do you know what money is, Sarah?"

"I don't have much left. I spent what I had on a Christmas present for you. How much do you need?"

"Twenty bucks."

"Don't you have money to get home?"

"No, I don't have money to get home. I got tickets to get home, for Christ's sake. But I got no cash. I got a long layover at Kennedy Airport and no money to spend."

"I can give you ten, but that's all I have. When I give you that, I'm broke."

"You got it with you? Give it to me. Yeah. Good girl. I'll tell you what. I'll sneak into your dorm tonight. We can say goodbye in bed. That's my Christmas present to you, a good hosing to last you for three weeks, ha, ha. How's that?"

"I have to study tonight, Buddy."

"Yeah, yeah . . . after that. I'll come in late."

"I can't. I've got the curse."

"Oh, for Christ's sake. 'I've got the curse.' 'I don't feel good.' 'Oh, Buddy, that hurts.' Shit! No wonder you're no good at it. You don't get any practice."

"Buddy, let's just have lunch. OK? We can study together this afternoon in the student lounge, and I'll give you your Christmas present."

"Yeah, yeah. Sarah, you shouldn't have gotten me a present. We're not married, you know. The trouble with you is you're too possessive."

That night there was a sit-down banquet in the Dining Hall, which was decorated with Christmas Trees. After a steak dinner, there was a carol sing. Students then went back to their dormitories to study for their last day of exams. After exams, the students frenziedly departed for vacations.

Late the next afternoon, with the students gone, Nancy and Cooper held a large staff and faculty party at Chase House. The party started with faculty, and other staff members', children. Cooper dressed as Santa Clause, and had a present for each child. He even remembered each one's name. The party continued into the evening. It was the one event of the year during which groundskeepers and teachers, night watchmen and secretaries, dishwashers and administrators, and all their family members, mixed together. Incidents from last year's party were recounted and other high points of the past year were discussed.

Cooper worked in his office all that week. Then on Christmas Day, he and Nancy and Lisa drove to Riverside to be with Cooper's mother and sisters, and his mother's husband. The next day, the three of them flew to Hobe Sound in Florida to spend a week with Nancy's family. Cooper got a kick out of being able to keep up with the most affluent of his students by showing up after the holidays with a tan.

Honey LaTate was one such fashionably tanned student. Cooper complimented her when his English *A* students were leaving the Trustees' Conference Room after their first day back.

"Thank you, Mr. Morgan," she said. "You look pretty tan yourself. Where do you go?"

"Florida, Honey, how about you? Are you a Fort Lauderdale preppie?"

She laughed and said, "No, I went to St. Thomas with my grandparents. They took the whole family there for Christmas." She waved to Cooper as she walked away from him, swishing her plaid mini-skirt.

Cooper thought, if those mini-skirts get just half an inch shorter the girls' underpants will be visible. Oh, well, they're nice for the girls with pretty legs, such as Honey.

Cooper stepped outside to take a look at an emergency sewer pipe excavation over by the Schoolhouse, one of the main classroom buildings. On the way he saw Sarah Savage, whom he thought to be one of the nicest girls in the sixth form, albeit without the legs for a mini-skirt.

"Hi Sarah, did you have a good Christmas vacation?"

"Hi, Mr. Morgan, I've been pretending I did, but it was awful, really. My parents have split up again. For good, this time, I suppose. I never even saw my father, and I would have been better off if I hadn't seen my mother. How about you? Did you have a nice vacation? I see you went south."

"Yes, we had a great week in Florida. I'm sorry to hear about your family, Sarah. If there is anything I can do, let me know. Also, if you just want to talk, come on in and see me anytime. Will you do that?"

"Sure thing. Thanks, Mr. Morgan. I'll see you later."

All Saints Chapel commanded the western end of The Quadrangle. It was a frame building—a typical white clapboard New England church.

With the advent of voluntary services, attendance shrunk to the very proportions Cooper had predicted to Chaplain Ned Howard. Ned now had daily services to accommodate the few very faithful, and he did more work with small groups. He often used the so-called Crypt Chapel, which was in a basement room of the main chapel building. It was good for a service of about twenty-five people, maximum. It was a handsome room. There was a small altar with folding chairs for the congregation. There were also a number of storage rooms and closets on the basement level, and two classrooms that were good for music practice and choir rehearsal.

The Crypt Chapel also served as winter quarters for Honey's coven. Lights in the Crypt Chapel could not be seen from outside at night, and Honey knew that witches were supposed to like churches for their secret ritual services. It had not been much of a problem to borrow a key and have a copy made, making the room available whenever she wanted it.

After Monkey Craft was initiated into the coven, the key fell to him for safekeeping. Keys and locks were a hobby for him. Monkey had changed the locks on a couple of empty storage areas on campus. That's where he stored the drugs he sold. If anyone ever found his cache, they would not be able to identify Monkey with the place or the contraband. Monkey was able to rig a lock on a remote storage area in the chapel basement that became the coven's special closet, where costumes, candles and other ceremonial artifacts were stored. The Reverend Ned Howard, had he come upon it, would have been more than a little startled.

Two years earlier, when Honey first got her coven going, she had decided to recruit twelve of the older girls, and then bring in three or four warlocks. One boy she had always pictured as a warlock was Buddy Braken. He was the perfect devil's strong man, big, powerful and homely. She felt he was tractable enough for her to manipulate. However, he was pig-headed. She decided it would be wiser to take Monkey in first, so Buddy would not get the idea he was cock of the walk. Now it was time to bring in Buddy, and for this reason Honey waited in the main studio room at the Art Department. Louise Shipper was already in the plaster casting room getting things ready.

"Hey, Honey, here I am. What did you want to talk to me about?"

"Hi, Buddy, are you alone? Would you like to be a male witch? I see you are eighteen now. All us witches are eighteen.

"Are you kidding? Is there a guy in this school who wouldn't jump at the chance to be in that secret witch thing of yours?"

"That's my boy. Here, take a look at this. Do you know what it is?"

"A hunk of plaster?"

"Look closer. Doesn't it remind you of something?"

A week later Sarah Savage fell in step with Buddy as he entered the Dining Hall for lunch.

"Hiya, kid, what's new?" said Buddy.

"Nothing much. I saw you talking to Honey LaTate today."

"What's that supposed to mean?"

"Oh, nothing. I just saw you across the campus. That's all."

"Yeah, I was on the campus today."

"Talking to Honey."

"Yeah, I suppose I must have seen her."

"You were talking for a long time."

"Is that so? So what?"

"You usually don't talk that much to anyone, even me."

"Yeah?"

"Honey LaTate is a whore."

"I didn't know that. I wonder how much she charges."

"More than you've got."

"Well, I was thinking maybe I could hire her to give you lessons."

"Very funny. Maybe she could teach me how to peddle it all over the campus like she does."

"If she did peddle herself, there would be plenty of guys buying."

"Like you?"

"Yeah, like me. I'd eat a mile of her shit just to see where it came from."

"That's really disgusting."

"It sure is, Sarah. I'm just a vulgar slob. Maybe I'm just not good enough for you, Miss High and Mighty. So why don't you just bug off. Find yourself a gentleman to eat your lunches with, because I am good and sick of listening to how much better are than anyone else."

"I didn't mean it, Buddy. I'm sorry."

"You don't sound sorry."

"But I am. I really am. You can talk any way you like. I wasn't trying to change you. I'll do anything you want. You know that. Just don't walk out on me. Please, Buddy. I love you. I'm jealous. Can't you see that?"

"Forget it. I'm sick of your bullshit. Take off, Sarah."

275

"No Buddy, please, I'll make it up to you. I'll do anything you say, anything you want."

"You will, huh. Anything?"

"Yes, Buddy, I need you. You're all I have in the world."

"Well how about giving me a blow job. I'll tell you if you're as good at it as Honey is."

"All right. I will. I'll do it. You'll see."

"I mean do it right now."

"But we have to eat lunch now, and then go to class."

"I mean right here. Get down on your knees, and take it out of my pants and suck on it."

"In front of everyone! You're trying to pick a fight with me. You're trying to tell me . . . we're through?"

"Hey, Sarah, you got it. You're a real smart girl."

Sarah crumbled and slumped down at the table. Tears ran down her face. She dropped her head in her arms on the table. Her back twitched with her spasmodic sobs. Buddy walked away, whistling softly, as if he did not know she was there. Two girls who had been watching came over to the table, sat down on either side of Sarah and hugged her.

That evening after dinner, the doorbell rang at Chase House and Nancy answered it.

"Is . . . is Mr. Morgan here?"

"No," said Nancy. "He's in Albany, of all places. Raising money for Essex. You're Sarah, aren't you? Sarah Savage? Come on in. Can I help you?"

"No. No thank you, Mrs. Morgan. It wasn't anything, really. I'll see him when he gets back. It's fine, really. I've got to go. Thank you, Mrs. Morgan."

"Hey, Sarah, do you know anything about baking pies? Maybe you could help me. I'm such a lousy cook."

"I don't know anything about cooking, Mrs. Morgan. I've really got to go. Thanks. Goodbye now."

Nancy looked after Sarah as she hurried down the walk. Nancy thought, you sure need someone, I can see that Sarah. I'm sorry I couldn't help.

CHAPTER 7

Cooper called Ida Beth the next morning to tell her he would be back on campus by noon, and to see if he had any messages.

"Cooper, I've been trying to reach you and so has Nancy."

She hadn't called him Cooper since he became Headmaster, so he knew something was wrong. "What is it?" he said.

"The Savage girl, Sarah, she . . . she took pills, sleeping pills I guess, last night."

"Is she all right? Did they . . . was she taken to the hospital?"

"It was too late when they found her."

"Oh, my God! Are you saying she's dead?"

"Yes, Cooper, I'm sorry. I know you were fond of her."

There was a long silence and Ida Beth thought the line had gone dead. She asked if he was still there.

"Yes, Mrs. Ehmm, I'm still here. Has Dr. Hard taken charge? Has Sarah's body been removed?"

"He's taking care of that now."

"Have her parents been called?"

"No. Gunnar Ferris was wondering if he should do it."

"I'll do it. Can you give me the number? Wait. I can't just drop that over the phone. They've just split up. Sarah lives in Katonah. I can be there in two and a half hours. Give me the phone number, and the address."

She did, then Cooper said, "Ida Beth, this is going to sound dumb. Forgive me. I'm a bit shaken. Is there any chance that your information could be wrong, in any way at all? Who gave it to you?"

"I understand, Cooper. Dr. Hard told Mr. Ferris, who told me. Then I talked with Dr. Hard to be sure I had the information right about the pills. I knew you would want me to check. Only an autopsy will confirm it, but she left a note and there was an empty bottle of sleeping pills."

"What did the note say?"

"It was short, just said it wasn't anyone's fault but hers, that she didn't want to live anymore."

"Poor baby."

"There's something else. Can you call your wife? She's very upset. She said Sarah spoke to her last night."

Cooper said he would do that and then leave for Katonah. He said he would call back at nine o'clock, and to have Gunnar Ferris and Ned Howard standing by to talk to him.

Cooper consoled Nancy as best he could. She blamed herself for sensing Sarah's distress but not realizing how severe it was.

Cooper hung up and thought to himself, this is my fault. If I hadn't been away from school, I would have been there when Sarah came to see me. At times like this we all find reasons to blame ourselves, he concluded. We can't help it.

Back on campus, Monkey Craft was one of those feeling guilty. Monkey had sold Sarah the downers. The guilt was short-lived, but was replaced by fear that he would be identified as the supplier.

Buddy Braken, too, had little time for guilt. He was too busy feeling defensive about the cold stares he imagined everyone was giving him. Some, feeling his loss must be greater, tried to console him, but they found Buddy more sullen than ever.

Mrs. Savage blamed herself. No doubt, with reason. Cooper had a hard couple of hours with her. He didn't leave until her doctor and Mr. Savage arrived. Sarah's father covered his guilt with anger at the school. Cooper let him blow off steam without comment.

The campus was very subdued. After dinner, Cooper invited those who felt inclined to come to the chapel and pray in their own way or just sit there quietly for a while. Mary Lou Pincer played the organ softly for an hour. Then Cooper got up and spent about five minutes saying what knowing Sarah was like for him and he invited others to do the same. A dozen or more people spoke, both students and teachers. The chapel was full. Monkey was there, but Buddy was not. Honey LaTate was there, but was unaware of her part in Sarah's unhappiness. She did not know Sarah well, having had little in common with her, but she had always admired Sarah's athletic ability. Honey cried quite openly. It wasn't really a service. It was a coming together of the community. It helped soothe the hurt they all felt. Death usually holds little fear for young people. It is so far away. But when one of their own is taken, they feel shock.

Towards the end of January 1968 Gordon Fairingwether called. "Cooper, the other shoe has dropped. Dwight Bedlington has asked me to call a special meeting of the Board of Trustees with you not there."

"Have you done that, Gordon?" asked Cooper.

"I told him I would think about it, check the calendar, and then get back to him. Do you think I should have refused him, Cooper?"

"No, I don't think so. If he doesn't get a legitimate hearing for his gripes, he'll have to seek an illegitimate one. It's better if you're there chairing the meeting. This could stop the fund drive dead in its tracks. Even if he doesn't succeed in throwing me out, he can do the school harm. How about this, do you think you could get him to settle for an Executive Committee meeting? That would be more manageable. Keep the dirty laundry in the bosom of the family, huh? You can tell him the Executive Committee will have to decide on whether to call a full Board meeting after they've heard what he has to say. How's that?"

"Brilliant. Cooper, if you ever leave head mastering, I'll triple your salary to come run my business."

"Gordon, if you and I know how good I am, how come Bedlington doesn't know? Do you suppose he knows something we don't?"

"Not about running a school. Dwight's a pretty naïve man outside his own kingdom."

"Gordon, I appreciate your confiding in me. I'll do all I can to deserve your trust."

Bedlington bought the compromise. He even thought it was a good idea. "Sell the leaders and you're on your way," was a favorite phrase of his.

Every member of the Executive Committee was present at the meeting. Bedlington felt a degree of formality, if not actual chill, emanating from the others in the room. It was 4:00 p.m., and they were in the same room in the University Club where they had first interviewed Cooper. Bedlington stated it was his purpose to ask them to recommend to the full Board that Cooper Morgan be relieved immediately and replaced, at least on a temporary basis, by Dean Phillip Fedner, a loyal and able mainstay of the school administration for many years.

To back up his case, he cited the rumors that surrounded Cooper and Sherri Huff when she was an undergraduate. Bedlington then moved on to the case of his own son who, he said, was punished after the fact at a time when the Dean was already handling the boy's offense in his own way, a way that was constructive and designed to teach the boy, not merely take revenge on him as Morgan had done. Bedlington described the general lawlessness that had invaded the campus since Morgan became Headmaster. He illustrated his points with details that could have come only from someone close inside the administration of the school. Bedlington cleverly wove facts, half-facts and lies as he described deterioration in morale and general discipline on the campus. His allegations rested on the notion that conditions had slipped so badly that a young girl's suicide was a natural consequence of the Headmaster's laxness. According to Bedlington, the girl's father considered this to be so and was considering suing Morgan, the school and the Board.

The committee was silent after Bedlington reached his conclusion. Gordon thought to himself that Bedlington's case was far more persuasive than he had thought it would be. Gordon was unnerved, fearing that Bedlington had won the others to his point of view. He decided to play his ace.

Fairingwether looked hard at Bedlington and said that his accusations were serious, and although he had a right to a private hearing he also had a responsibility to face the Headmaster with his accusations, allowing Morgan the opportunity to refute them. Bedlington said he agreed that was fair and said it was too bad Cooper was not available to do that. Fairingwether replied that Cooper was downstairs in the library, ready to be called in. Before Bedlington could object, General Fox intervened.

The General said that this meeting should not be dignified by the presence of the Headmaster. He found the allegations preposterous. He stated that the meeting should be adjourned and that Mr. Bedlington should resign from the Board.

Joe Marmot said he agreed that Cooper should not be questioned, but he had serious questions for Mr. Bedlington. In his best courtroom manner, Marmot challenged the accusations one by one, asking Bedlington to prove them, which he could not. Bedlington was laid bare as a bitter father out to blame someone else for his own inadequacies. Bedlington did not bluster or fume. He took everything that Marmot dished out with gentlemanly equanimity. Marmot did not let up, however, and demanded to know the source of the gossip Bedlington had presented.

Bedlington refused to name his source, so Joe asked him outright if the source wasn't the man whom he had recommended to take Cooper's place—Dean Fedner. Dwight would not say.

Yale Martin spoke up in conciliatory tones and asked Bedlington in the friendliest sort of way if he was not aware that the administrators of all schools and colleges were fighting what the kids were calling a virtual revolution. He asked if he did not see that the times were exceptional and not to be compared with earlier years. He spoke of the armed demonstrations on college campuses, the takeovers of buildings and offices, scandals over drug use, and deplorable behavior in both private and public schools throughout the country. At this point, the fight had gone out of Bedlington and he could see that his case was lost.

Silent until now, P.D. Quail, in a fashionably short dress, suggested that Dwight withdraw his charges, and that no vote be taken. She suggested that no minutes be kept of the proceedings either. Then she batted her beautiful eyes at General Fox, squeezed him on the arm and asked him to take back his request that Dwight resign, so they could all depart with good grace and friendship, in a spirit of devotion to the well-being of the school they all loved.

Dwight, seeing he had persuaded no one, asked that his recommendation be dismissed. Everett Fox, that lover of good sportsmanship, extended his hand to Dwight and apologized. Fairingwether asked them all to be his guests for dinner and suggested Cooper join them.

Dwight, apologizing for damping the spirit of healing and goodwill, said he was unable to join them for dinner. He did, however, go to the lobby, where Gordon was briefing Cooper. Dwight shook hands with Cooper, wished him well for the remainder of the year, and left.

At dinner, P.D. raised her martini glass and toasted, "Here's to your long tenure, Mr. Headmaster. Long live the King!"

After warm approval all around P.D. said, "Now, if that bastard Bedlington is as smart as I think he is, he won't attend the next two board meetings and then he'll quietly resign."

The General gave a surprised whoop of laughter, and Fairingwether shook his head at P.D. in feigned disapproval.

P.D. enjoyed being the only woman in the happy group and enjoyed dominating everyone's attention. Sitting beside Cooper, she took his arm, laid her head on his sleeve and in the sweetest little girl voice said, "Now, Cooper, tell us all about your romance with Sherri Huff, and tell us why we haven't heard of this before."

They all laughed.

The next morning, Cooper called in Phil Fedner. The Dean made no attempt to deny his treachery. Cooper asked him why he did it. Fedner went into a tirade about how his long devotion to the school had gone unrewarded and charged that the only reason he had not been chosen for the headmastership was because he was unmarried. He shouted that the Board had treated him unfairly as had Cooper, whom he called a young upstart. He said he'd forgotten more about running a school than Cooper would ever learn, and that Cooper would have his written resignation by the afternoon.

"I'll accept your resignation as Dean, Phil, but I suggest that you not resign from the faculty until the end of the year. You are a fine schoolmaster. You owe it to yourself to be in the most advantageous situation to secure a good position at another school next year. That means you should be able to say to anyone that you are an Essex teacher in good standing, which you are. If you want a leave of absence for all or any part of this school year, you've got it, with full pay. Your years of service are recognized and appreciated."

"Are you serious, Cooper?"

"Of course. You've been through quite a bit Phil. Maybe you'd like to get away for a few days, clear your head. I suppose there's some glamour in surviving a coup attempt, but if I were you, Phil, I would get myself to Alcoholics Anonymous. Your enemy is booze. Not me, not anyone else."

"All right, Cooper, I'll think it over and get back to you. Thank you. You've been . . . uh . . . you've been fair."

CHAPTER 8

1968

Buddy Braken was initiated into the coven as Brother Leo in an Esbat ceremony. The Esbat was a little less formal or spectacular than a Sabbat, which Honey said should be held only four times a year.

Buddy had, for years, commanded the respect of his fellows. But it was a respect born of fear. This was the first time he had ever been sought out to be a member of a group or a social participant in anything. He had not been formally invited to a party since he was three. He was grateful and proud. Honey found him more manageable than she had expected. Her only reservation was Buddy's apparent desire to use the group against the adult authority in the school.

Buddy hated Frostley, who once called him a bully to his face. He was actually pleased when the former Headmaster had a paralyzing stroke. As for Morgan, Buddy was suspicious of him so he avoided him. This feeling turned to keen dislike when Morgan questioned him about his relationship with Sarah. Everyone knew that Buddy and Sarah were a couple, and Cooper's interview with Buddy after the suicide was, actually, routine. Cooper thought he should find out any special information Buddy might have about Sarah's mental state. Cooper learned from Sarah's mother, for example, that the girl had been seeing a psychiatrist at home. Sarah had told her mother, and the psychiatrist, that she might end her own life. That information was kept from the school. But, because his sense of guilt distorted his reason, Buddy was sure the questioning meant that the Headmaster was trying to pin Sarah's death on him.

"Look, Buddy," said Honey, "the coven is for fun. It's exciting. It's an escape from all the studying and learning. It's a way to blow off steam. It's not political. We are doin' our thing in secret, so no one knows. We're not trying to tear down the establishment. We're just trying to hoodwink it."

"Oh, Christ, Honey, that's not enough. Don't you see that this school sucks?"

"It isn't run the way we would like, but you're getting one hell of a good education. Isn't that worth anything?" asked Honey.

"I'm not saying kill it. I just want to change it. Make it responsive to student needs. We gotta bring Morgan to his knees."

"How do you propose to do that?"

"We take over. Make him negotiate. To start with, I've brought in enough dynamite to blow this whole school to hell."

"Where is it?"

"In our storeroom in the chapel, the coven storeroom. Don't try to go in there without Monkey, though. He has it booby-trapped so if anyone tries to break in, the whole thing will blow sky high."

"You guys are crazy."

"No we aren't, Honey. Don't you see we're doing this for you? You're going to be able to call the shots. We want you to handle the negotiations."

"We'll talk about it."

"Come in Mike," said Cooper. "I know you're busy, but I have a proposition to talk over with you." Mike Banes, Cooper's old friend and Harvard classmate, stepped into Cooper's office.

"How's Sylvia? Nancy and I haven't seen you guys for a while," said Cooper.

"Hey, Cooper, you're feeling guilty because you and Nancy aren't part of our old crowd anymore. But let's face it—you're the Headmaster. Things can't be the same. So relax. Sylvia and I love you both, and we'll do anything to help you when you need us."

Cooper laughed. "These are hard times, aren't they, Mike? I need all the help I can get. I was just reading some statistics from the National Association of Independent Schools. Headmasters are quitting and getting fired left and right. They're dying of heart attacks. Running away and going bonkers. The average tenure of headmasters now is three years."

"Are you feeling the pressure, Cooper?"

"Sure I am, but I'm not taking tranquilizers yet. I'm a big tough guy, and I have blind faith that I know what I'm doing, even though I don't really. Trying to survive, I guess. Perhaps that's the only game plan one can have right now. All of this is a crazy lead-in to what I wanted to see you about. But maybe it's inappropriate."

"What do you have in mind, Cooper?"

"Mike, what are your long range plans? Where do you see yourself in ten years? You don't have a private income, do you? You and Sylvia don't stand to inherit, right? So a teacher's pay is going to be a problem down the road when your kids get older."

"Are you trying to tell me I ought to be a Headmaster?"

"Yeah. That's what I'd be planning, if I were you. You have the stuff. You'd be a good one, I think. I'll help you if you like. It's a lousy job, but it pays better than teaching. What do you think?"

"You've been reading my mind. I'm not the obvious strong leader type that you are, Cooper, and I'm not sure I'm ready yet, the way you were. But I do think that's what I want to do down the road. I think I could bring some good things to it."

"OK, I'll help. And I'll recommend you when you think you're ready. First of all, let's make you Dean of Essex. That's another lousy job, but it's great training, and it will give you some visibility in the school world. I'll give you a pay increase now, whatever I can, which isn't much, and I'll increase you more next year."

"Why do I get the feeling I've just been had?"

"You'll take it then. Good. You have just been had. It's an awful job, but you need it and it needs you. Think how proud Sylvia will be, until she discovers all the evenings she won't have you at home. It's a rung up the ladder, though, Mike. Don't you agree?"

"Yes, Cooper, I agree. Thanks. I'll do a good job for you."

"I'll announce it to the faculty at our meeting this afternoon. Your first job is to find us a new time for faculty meetings. Do you know what the kids are calling five o'clock on Tuesdays?"

"Their cocktail hour."

"Right. Why is the Headmaster the last to know? When the teachers are all in a meeting, the kids are free to party. So find me a time when the kids are tied up and supervised, but most of the faculty is free. Now, I'll call Phil Fedner's former secretary and tell her who her new boss is. Stop in when you're free and set yourself up in that office. I'll go to work on lightening your load. You can teach three sections of one class, but no more coaching and no more dorm duty. I'll talk to you later, OK?"

285

Mike left and Cooper asked Ida Beth if there was a message yet from Todd Everlast at St. Burges.

"We haven't heard anything, Mr. Morgan. Father Everlast never answered your letter, did he?"

"No. We were planning to travel to that conference together next week. But I wanted to get some time with him beforehand. He seems to have some answers to dealing with kids these days. See if you can get him on the phone for me and please tell Gunnar Ferris I want to see him when he has a chance."

Cooper made some notes for Gunnar in reference to rearranging Mike Banes's responsibilities and schedule. Then Ida Beth said, "Mr. Morgan, will you talk to Father Everlast's secretary? I can't seem to get much out of her."

Cooper picked up the phone and explained why he wanted to talk to Father Everlast. The secretary said Father Everlast was out of town and she believed he would not be attending next week's headmasters' conference. Cooper asked where he was and she said she was not at liberty to say. Cooper thought that strange, so he put in a call to Todd's home and Abby answered.

"Oh, Cooper, it's so nice to hear from you. I'm terribly upset."

"What's the matter, Abby? Where's Todd?"

"He's in a sanatorium, Cooper. He had a nervous breakdown."

"Judas! When did this happen, Abby?"

"He's been gone for two weeks. The doctors say he'll have to stay there for several months. I can visit him, but he's terribly depressed. My going there doesn't seem to help."

"Abby, do you know why it happened?"

"No. Nothing like this has ever happened to him before. It's just the job. It got him down. No single thing happened. He just began not to make any sense and he was terribly nervous and depressed, and he kept putting off the things he was supposed to do. His doctor took him to this place. It's quite nice. Batty Sainley is running the school, or supposed to be, but he's threatening to quit. Oh, my goodness, Cooper, please don't repeat any of this. It shouldn't get out."

Cooper said he would not, and he made her promise to call him if anything more went wrong for her, or if she needed anything. He assured her that several distinguished headmasters had nervous breakdowns and then returned to work and had long successful careers.

Cooper's day continued at a fast pace with meetings extending almost until nightfall. It was not until then that he saw Nancy alone and told her about Todd.

"Gee, I don't know, Nancy. I thought Todd had all the answers. Keep moving, change, modernize. Let the students have their heads. Give them what they want, at least within reason. Todd said he was staying ahead by 'out-liberaling the liberals.' He didn't keep ahead, though, did he? But his ideas may have been right. Damnit! I just don't know. I have this uncomfortable feeling that the ship is starting to sink. So far the Captain is holding up pretty well, but he doesn't seem to know where the bailing bucket is."

"How would the Captain feel if his wife went off to New York for a week or so? I'm getting cabin fever, love."

"You haven't done that for over a year. Ever since I've been Headmaster. Your cabin is bigger now. Can't you hold off until school's out? I need you."

"I'll send Sherri Huff to babysit."

"What do you mean by that?"

"Nothing, darling. I'm only kidding. I'm not trying to start a fight. I don't care about those rumors."

"Maybe you should. Maybe, if you leave, Sherri Huff will come, but not to babysit."

"Oooh, mean words. A threat?"

"No. I don't want to fight, either. I love you, Nancy. We've been together a long time. We have Lisa. We fit together."

She laughed. "And how."

"Not just that, I mean I really need you. I couldn't handle you leaving me alone. Not now. There are too many balls in the air. They're flying at me and I'm not catching 'em all and some are hitting me, and they hurt. Sarah Savage needing me, and I'm not here. That hurt. The president of this school looks me in the eye and says, 'There are no hard drugs here, sir.' A couple months after he graduates he's dead from a hard drug overdose. You think he only learned to do that after he left? I don't. The president of this year's class was some kind of alcoholic and I had to throw him out in the trash. And his idiot, moneymaking father thinks the way to solve it is to have my head. The world is going ape, Nancy, and I need you . . . to come home to, to talk to, to hold." He grinned at her. "And, to fit the parts together, too."

Nancy hugged him. Her green eyes were wet. She said, "You never told me that before. You never said I was important to you and you needed me. I just want to be worth something to me or to you. If you need me, that will do. I've been looking to be needed. I've been looking everywhere. Here with you, in New York, in my painting, in other people's beds . . ."

He held her tight. "I've been stupid. I didn't know. Well, maybe I didn't really need you before, or need you enough. I do now. Maybe this miserable job that's tearing some people apart is making me whole. If I need you, and you need me needing you, and we've found that out, maybe the pressure is worth it."

"I'll stay." Nancy smiled. "And, since I'm staying, I have this puzzle . . . I have this part here that needs to be fitted with this monstrous part here . . . well, maybe it's not really so monstrous, but I can feel that maybe it will be if we bring it out in the fresh air . . ."

Honey had some success stalling Buddy and Monkey's planned campus takeover because they were waiting for her to work out a good plan. By spring, however, they had lost patience with her and began to recruit others who wanted to revolt.

Honey was more interested in initiating some underclassmen so the coven would carry on after she and the other sisters, and the two warlocks, graduated in June. Honey intended to pass her leadership position on to Lou.

The brothers in the coven were males who fascinated Honey sexually. Monkey was one of the cleverest people she had ever encountered. Buddy's powerful body and impressive sexual apparatus interested her. Young Dwight Bedlington was handsome, with an appealing devil-may-care attitude. He, of course, was expelled before she could initiate him, but she did have his plaster cast. She thought that perhaps she should have tried to put a spell or curse on the Headmaster for expelling Dwight. However, it really was Dwight's own fault, and the Headmaster was too sexy to hate. Besides, she had never put a curse on anyone, even though she knew from books how it was done.

She admitted to herself reluctantly that the most interesting male on the whole campus was really Freddy Iverson. She hoped her fascination with him did not mean that someday she would choose a husband who needed mothering. She chuckled to herself.

On a clear April morning, even before Mrs. Ehmm came to work, Dr. Wyatt Hard appeared in Cooper's office with a curious tale.

"Cooper, I've got Freddy Iverson over in the infirmary. Nurse Smith admitted him last night sometime after midnight. Know what's wrong with him?"

"I haven't the faintest idea, Doctor."

"Pecker's swollen up like a cucumber."

"Why is that, do you suppose, Doctor?"

"Boy says it got stung by a bee, got an allergic reaction."

"That sounds painful."

"Yep."

"Well, all kinds of strange things happen, Wyatt."

"Cooper, what do you suppose a bee is doin' out after midnight, in April?"

"I don't know very much about bees, Wyatt, but I wonder what Freddy's pecker was doing out after midnight in April."

"Boy says he was takin' a leak."

"Well, I suppose that's plausible. Was the bee in the bathroom in Freddy's dormitory?"

"Boy was takin' a leak in a bachelor's gown."

"What? How do you know that?"

"That's the way he came to the infirmary, stark naked except for a bachelor's gown."

"I suppose he must use it for a bathrobe. Say, we happen to have an expert on bees here on the campus."

"Victoria LaTate."

"Honey."

"What's that Cooper?"

"Honey LaTate. Her real name is Victoria, but everyone calls her Honey."

"She does look nice."

"Yes, but the reason she's called Honey is she keeps honeybees. It's a hobby."

"She brought boy to infirmary."

"What's that?"

"Nurse Smith says she came in with Freddy last night. Told Nurse Smith she'd put ten-milligram isoproterenol tablets under the boy's tongue. Wanted him to have adrenaline for inhalation. Had a tourniquet on his pecker. Told Nurse Smith boy had an anaphylactic reaction." Dr. Hard began to laugh. "She told Nurse Smith she was a doctor."

"I'm not sure I'm following all this," said Cooper. "This is a bizarre story. Do you know why these two appeared when they did or where they came from? And before you tell me that, is Freddy going to be all right?"

"Boy will be fine, Cooper. Had a violent reaction though. Convulsions, diarrhea, vomiting, falling blood pressure. Could have died. Girl probably saved him. Knew just what to do. Had some pretty sophisticated emergency medicine right with her. Even the tourniquet was smart. She told me this morning that she told Nurse Smith she was a doctor because she was afraid nurse wouldn't do the right thing, otherwise. Probably right, too. Probably saved his life."

"Uh, how was Honey dressed this morning?"

"Just fine. Pretty as a picture. Nice pink dress."

"Is there anything else?"

"The stinger and the venom sack."

"What about them."

"They were gone."

"Gone where?"

"Just gone."

"Damnit, Doctor, I don't know what you're talking about."

"When a bee stings, the bugger leaves his stinger and venom sack behind at the site of the sting. They were gone."

"Where'd they go?"

"Girl said she took them out."

Cooper whistled.

"I asked boy how that felt. He said okay" Girl laughed, very pleased. Almost worth it, huh, Cooper?"

"Uh, was there anything else, Wyatt?"

"Location of the sting."

"Yes, pretty embarrassing. Pretty sensitive."

"I don't mean his pecker. I mean the location on his pecker."

"Yes?"

"Cooper, it was right on the coronal ridge, that is, the rim on the glans, dead center on top. That's where the nerves are massed. It is as if the bee knew exactly where the most sensitive place on the boy's whole body was. Bee isn't that smart, Cooper. Only people are that smart. Also, boy is not circumcised. His foreskin had to be pulled back before bee could even get at the coronal ridge."

"Wyatt, you are suggesting that someone put the bee on just the right place to deliver its sting?"

The doctor shrugged his shoulders. "I don't know, Cooper. You tell me. What is a bee doing out, after midnight, when the moon is full in April?"

Cooper thought to himself, there is only one person around here who handles bees, and can hold them to make a sting. I'm going to have an awkward interview with Honey. He said, "Did you ask Honey how she was available when she was in need?"

"No. Nurse only told me about that this morning after girl left."

"Did you ask boy . . . uh, did you ask Freddy about it?"

"Boy said he didn't notice."

"Huh. Is there anything else?"

"Nope."

"Thank you, Wyatt. If you learn anything else, I'd appreciate knowing about it."

During their conversation, Ida Beth had arrived. She watched the doctor depart, and then came in to greet Cooper. She said, "Did Doctor have something to tell you about boy, or about girl?"

Cooper grinned and said, "He almost had me talking that way. Don't you start."

That evening, Cooper and Nancy went on an outing they had planned for some time. They went to a famous seafood restaurant near New London. Over cocktails, Cooper entertained Nancy with the story of Freddy's bee sting. It was no doubt the topic of conversation around a number of tables that evening.

Cooper imitated Dr. Hard's curious speech mannerisms as he went along, much to Nancy's amusement. Dr. Hard was probably the easiest character to imitate in a whole campus full of characters. He was the Essex Jimmy Stewart.

"Well," said Cooper, "I had a talk with Nurse Smith. She didn't feel comfortable talking about it with me, as you might expect. So I didn't learn any more than Wyatt Hard had told me."

"Did you talk to Freddy?" asked Nancy.

"Yeah, he said the bee flew up and stung him while he was using the urinal in his dormitory bathroom. Said he always wears a bachelor's gown to go to the head at night. The sting hurt and he ran outside and bumped into Honey. He told her what happened."

"So, you must have asked Honey about the whole thing," said Nancy.

"Of course, but you can't imagine how difficult it was to question her about the details."

"What on earth did she say?"

"You won't believe it," said Cooper.

"Try me."

"You know how grownup Honey looks, always wearing stockings and high heels. Well, she has grownup poise, too. Real cool. She told me she didn't want to lie to me, and she didn't want to incriminate herself, and she didn't think I would want to encourage her to do either. I, of course, had to agree with her. She said fine, she had always thought I was fair and had good judgment, and there was nothing more to talk about. After all, it was an embarrassing subject. She thanked me for my interest and left."

Nancy said, "I don't believe it."

"Believe it."

"You fool, you complete idiot! You were conned by a pretty face."

"Well, what would you have said?"

"I don't know." They both laughed.

A week later Cooper was winding up a meeting in his office just after 9:00 p.m. He'd been meeting with the housemasters and had asked Mike, the new Dean, to stay. "What do we do about the Honey LaTate and Freddy Iverson thing? It's been a week. Do we just let it go?"

"If we let it go, Cooper, we communicate the wrong thing to Honey and any kids, such as Freddy, who really know what happened. When you have outlandish behavior or even a suspicion of it, chances are its drug related."

"Well, the more I think about it, the more I have to agree with Honey that I have no right to ask her to incriminate herself. We know one thing for sure though. She was out of her dorm after hours. So for that let's put her on Disciplinary Warning, which carries no penalty but warns her to be scrupulous about her behavior for a while. I think Freddy suffered enough, and he may have been a victim, so let's not do anything with him. I already told his parents the story as Freddy told it. Now that everyone knows he's allergic to stings, his parents can take steps to have him immunized."

"Is that possible?"

"Honey says it is."

"It must be, then." They chuckled over that, and each headed home.

CHAPTER 9

When he came in the house, Cooper found Nancy reading in the living room. "Hey, look at you," he said. "Where have you been in my favorite sexy blue dress?"

Nancy went over to a tray she had arranged and fixed Cooper a tall Scotch and water. "I've been over keeping Sylvia Banes company, but not in this dress. I put this dress on just a little while ago, because I know you like it." She handed him the drink.

"This looks like some pretty special treatment. Favorite dress, nightcap, does Madame have something in mind?"

Nancy put her face up to his, as if to kiss him, but she grazed her lips across his cheek and whispered in his ear, "I have in mind putting you in a romantic mood."

He hugged her and whispered back, "First you'll have to feed me, I'm starved."

"Didn't you have dinner in the Dining Hall?"

"No. I had so much to do. I stayed in my office and worked through."

"Poor baby, come in the kitchen and I'll scramble you some eggs and toast some English muffins. How's that sound?"

"Heavenly. You see? I really do need you. If you were in New York, I'd be alone and helpless and hungry."

"That's a crock, Mr. Morgan. You can scramble eggs, and Lisa can too."

"I need you, in that dress, to cheer me up. Keep my morale up."

"That's not all I want up."

"Ah, all in due course. First, build my strength with food. Seriously, Nancy, don't go away to New York without me. Not ever."

They entered the kitchen and Cooper turned to face her. She went up on tiptoes and pressed herself against him. "I won't. Not ever." She said. "Mmmm, you smell good. Thank you, darling. I love you."

"After you eat and have your drink, we're going upstairs to the front guest room."

"Why?"

"For variety. To take the sameness out of our sex life. I have prepared the front guest room with some special arrangements for us."

"Whips and chains and handcuffs?"

"Don't be a smartass, love."

"What do you have prepared? I just may want to eat later."

"We're going to try something Sylvia Banes told me about."

"What? You're getting advice on sex from Sylvia Banes?"

"I'll take it from wherever I can get it. She had some good ideas."

"Such as?"

"I don't want to talk about it," said Nancy as she poured the beaten eggs in a frying pan.

"It's too embarrassing?" asked Cooper.

"No. It's just that I don't want you thinking about Sylvia. I want you thinking about me."

"You don't have to worry about that."

"Good. I'm going to do something to you with ice cubes that I think you're going to like."

"I can't wait."

"Good."

"And does Sylvia do this thing with ice cubes to Mike?"

"Who do you think she does it to, the dog?"

"Well, Sylvia might. Sylvia might do just about anything," Cooper laughed.

Nancy smiled conspiratorially as she placed a plate of steaming scrambled eggs and bacon in front of him. "As a matter of fact," she said, lowering her voice, "Sylvia didn't learn this little trick from Mike. She got it somewhere else."

"Where?"

"That's all I'm going to tell you." Nancy sat across from him while he ate. "Sylvia does special exercises every day."

"What kind of exercises?"

"Pelvic exercises. Did you ever hear of a snapper?"

"That's a lady who has control of her vaginal muscles so she can squeeze her lover."

"How did you know that?"

"I don't know. I just heard it or read it somewhere."

"I'll bet."

"Truly. I have never met a snapper, at least knowingly. For all I know it's a myth. I've always sort of assumed that it is."

"Sylvia says it's real and any woman can learn to do it."

"Are you going to learn?"

"Would you like me to?"

"Does Sylvia know how?"

"She's learning and doing the exercises."

"Then why don't we have Sylvia show me how it feels, and then I'll tell you if it's worth the trouble."

"How'd you like to sleep alone tonight?"

"I wouldn't like that."

"Then stop being a smartass."

"All right. I would love to have you learn to be a snapper. I would consider that a wonderful skill to acquire, and I would value you all the more as a wife and lover."

"Do you think that's a skill I could list in a resume?"

"Yes. If you develop a high proficiency, I would consider giving you a letter of recommendation."

"Would you consider that an office skill?"

"I think perhaps even more, a social skill."

"Could we list it in the school catalogue: Headmaster's wife is a snapper?"

"Why don't we keep it just to ourselves, and, of course, Sylvia. The truly worldly woman keeps just a little bit of herself secret from the rank and file, don't you think?"

"Yes."

"And now, you had something in mind for dessert?"

"Yes. Nancy is for dessert."

"My favorite! Come here Nancy O'Brian."

Nancy removed the dishes from the table and slipped gracefully into Cooper's lap, her hands lightly pressed on the back of his neck. The collar on her dress was a deep V and Cooper put his hand inside it.

"Hmmm, no bra. Did Madame burn her bra?"

"This dress works best without a bra."

"It certainly does work." He slid his other hand up the back of her thigh, under her dress. "What do we have here, a garter belt? Oh, I love it when you wear a garter belt. And panties? Why did you wear panties?"

"Anything worth having is worth working for."

"I think this is going to be a long night."

"You've got that right, lover. But don't give up, getting there is half the fun." She opened her thighs and his fingers stroked the silk-covered fullness between them. Then she started to undo the buttons on his shirt.

Cooper said, "Is it time to go upstairs to the front bedroom?"

Nancy whispered, "I think it is."

By one o'clock all was quiet in Chase House. Nancy was drifting off to sleep but Cooper was wide-awake thinking about the fact that they had come upstairs a couple of hours ago having left all the lights on downstairs.

Well, we were in an awful hurry, Cooper thought.

He was satisfied and tired but he knew he would be restless until he got up, went downstairs and turned off the lights.

He was about to go downstairs naked when he remembered he had a warm-up suit in the closet of the guest room. He kept it there to change into if Nancy was napping in the master bedroom and he didn't want to disturb her. It was a white suit with red and blue trim, the same kind the swimming team wore—a present from the team for his assistance in timing meets. He slipped on the pants with their elastic waistband, and the jacket. There was a pair of tennis shoes in the closet so he put those on too. After turning off all the downstairs lights, he turned off the ones in the front guest room. Before climbing back in bed with Nancy, he stood in front of the window, and then decided to open it.

It was a clear night. The window was above the driveway that led from Chase House to the Mall. Opposite the driveway and across the Mall was the entrance to the peripheral road that went around the Quadrangle. It headed straight to the chapel, then jogged left behind it.

Cooper saw a flash of light on the side of the chapel facing him. He could not figure out what had caused it. Now that same light, dimmer and flickering, was back. It seemed to be coming from a basement window.

Well . . . that may mean . . .

"Hey, Nancy, the chapel basement may be on fire. I'm going to run over there. If you see me waving my hands over my head when I get over there, call the Fire Department, OK?" The last part faded as he ran down the stairs. Nancy jumped out of bed and looked out the window. Cooper's white running suit stood out vividly. He was running fast. He crossed the Mall then bore down rapidly on the chapel building. He jumped a hedge, disappearing for a moment, then came back in sight. He was there now. He turned around and faced her, waving both hands over his head. She could see the smoke now. She ran for the phone.

It was to have been a spectacular affect, according to Monkey. He had assured Honey it would bring the same thrill of high drama to a chapel Esbat ceremony that the arrow on a string did to a Sabbat at Stonehenge in East Woods. Monkey said there would be flashes of light and sounds like small explosions, but they wouldn't really be explosions, and they wouldn't be loud enough to be heard outside. They were just some harmless chemicals, but they would be very dramatic. Just the thing.

Now, something had gone wrong. Monkey was unconscious on the floor and flames were blocking their way to the stairway, which was their only way out. There was a back exit but it was locked at night. The girls were gathered near the stairway, screaming. Honey was trying to keep cool. She felt it was her responsibility to get them out, and she felt there must be a way to break down that back exit but she couldn't think of one. The smoke was making her choke and gag. If only she wasn't so high on hash. But they all were. Monkey too.

Honey had thought earlier that Monkey and Buddy were high before they even started. She thought, fleetingly, that dope and pyrotechnics do not mix. But then she had chided herself for getting cautious and square, probably because of that close call with Freddy.

The back exit led out to an exterior cement stairway. The door looked impossible to break down. It might as well have been the door to Fort Knox. Then Honey heard crashing sounds outside the door. The wood of the doorjamb beside the lock split in a rending crash. The door flew open. Cool fresh air poured in, and there was Mr. Morgan's tall frame, in white, like an angel of God come to drive Satan away. The girls went out the door past him, screaming hysterically. It was dark, but there was enough light to see their outlandish costumes. Honey was frozen in place as she watched the expression on Mr. Morgan's face while the girls, with bouncing breasts and pale bare fannies, went clambering out.

Cooper Morgan called to her, "Come on, Honey, come out of there." Cooper took a couple of steps inside to grab Honey who seemed immobile. The fire was making a roaring sound. Honey pointed to an inert figure collapsed on the floor.

Cooper went down on one knee to examine the unconscious form. It was Adrian Craft. He scooped him up as if he weighed nothing. "Come on, Honey," he yelled, "let's go."

Honey scurried out and up the steps ahead of him, her bare bottom at eye level.

"Is there anyone else in the chapel, Honey?"

She wheeled around and faced him with a shocked expression. "Oh my God! Buddy Braken is still somewhere down there."

"You watch Adrian," Cooper ordered as he laid him on the grass. In the blink of an eye he was gone back down the steps.

Honey sank down beside Adrian and held his head. She saw he was conscious. He had a silly grin on his face. He said, "Didn't work, huh? Sorry, Queen Hydra."

Her throat burned with the acrid taste of smoke and so did her eyes. She went into a fit of coughing. Someone was holding her, consoling her. It was Mrs. Morgan in a white housecoat.

Oh, my God, Honey thought. Another symbolic angel against the devil!

Suddenly, Honey grabbed Nancy's hand. Between chokes and coughs she said, "Mr. Morgan . . . down there. Got to warn him. There's dynamite down there. Got to get out. Whole thing will blow up."

Honey struggled to her feet in order to go back in the chapel, but Nancy was already running down the cement stairs. Honey sank to her knees on the ground in another coughing fit.

After Cooper ran back down the stairs, he took a deep breath of fresh air, then dashed into the basement. The back hallway was empty. He ran into the Crypt Chapel, still holding his breath. The room was lit with burning candles but the smoke dimmed their light. There was no one there. He crouched down to the floor where the air was fresher, took a breath, then dashed for the far side of the room where there was another door. He shouted, "Buddy, Buddy Braken, are you here? You can get out this way."

The door flew open. Buddy stood there, feet wide apart, eyes wild. He held a staff in his hand.

"Come on," shouted Cooper.

Buddy swung the staff at him in a vicious sweep. "You bastard!" he shouted.

Cooper ducked under the blow. He thought, Braken is temporarily insane or drug crazed. Got to disable him. Get him out.

Cooper closed with him, driving his fist to Buddy's midsection. The powerful boy doubled over and Cooper came up with his other fist aimed at his jaw. Had he connected, he might have broken the jaw, but the blow grazed off the side of Buddy's head. Buddy's face registered panic. He dropped the staff, turned and ran back through the door he had come from. Cooper dropped down to his hands and feet on the floor, breathing the fresher air low down. He ran crab-wise after Buddy. He didn't see Nancy enter the Crypt Chapel room behind him, or hear her call.

Outside, Honey, in a daze, heard fire engine sirens in the distance. Flames were now shooting up the outside wall of All Saints Chapel. Then that wall lifted up in the air, coming apart in small pieces. There was a blinding white light and the loudest thunderclap Honey had ever heard, along with a rush of air that blew her backwards, flat on the ground. For many seconds that seemed like minutes debris rained onto the ground around her. Then all was darkness. The fire was gone. The enormity of what had happened overwhelmed her. She let out a low mournful wail and clung to Monkey.

CHAPTER 10

"Where is Buddy Braken? Did he show up?"

Oh, my, Cooper thought, my voice sounds funny, like it was in the next room. What room is this, anyway? Hospital. "I'm in a hospital, right?" he said to a young woman who looked like a nurse.

"Yes," she said, "you are in a hospital, and you're going to be all right."

"Could you speak a little louder, please?" said Cooper. "I can't hear you."

The nurse leaned down close to him and exaggerated the words with her lips. "You are in New Haven, in the hospital." He could hear her but her voice was faint. He knew it wasn't her voice that was wrong. It was his ears.

"What's wrong with my ears?" he asked.

She spoke slowly and loudly, "Your ear drums ruptured from the explosion."

"Explosion?" he asked, "Where?" He remembered he was in the chapel. "Did the chapel explode?"

"Yes."

He thought about that. Now what have I done since then? Can't remember. I have been out since then. He had a nagging feeling something was unfinished. Yes, Buddy Braken, I was going to get him out. He was raving mad.

"Where's Buddy?" His voice sounded very strange indeed.

"Who?"

"Was anyone else hurt in the explosion?"

Something passed across her face. She said, "No."

She's lying. Why would she do that? He held up his hands. They were wrapped in gauze. His face felt funny. "What else is wrong with me?"

"You have broken ribs and minor lacerations. Your hands will be all right. Your face is hurt. Your left eye . . . is hurt."

Cooper remembered he was talking to Nancy just a little while ago. "Could you please ask my wife to come back in here?" The nurse gave him a funny look.

"Wasn't she just in here?"

The woman shook her head. She had a wary expression.

"I remember talking to her."

Again, she shook her head.

"Can you get word to her to come see me? Tell her I'm awake."

The woman looked uncertain, then nodded her head, and left the room. Outside at the nurses' station she told the head nurse, "Mr. Morgan has come around. He doesn't seem to know his wife was hurt too. Should I tell him?"

The head nurse looked hard at her and said, "No. Better not say anything. His wife died just a little while ago."

The nurse was young and uncertain how to deal with Mr. Morgan in room 311. There was more bad news for that man to face than she cared to think about. She was relieved to find him asleep again when she returned.

When Cooper awakened next, he was hungry and there was someone waiting to see him. He asked her her name. She leaned close and shouted, "Mary." He smiled at her. She said she would get him some dinner and left.

A young doctor came in and told him there was a fair chance that he would get some of his hearing back. How much they couldn't be sure. They would have to wait and see.

"How bad is my left eye?" asked Cooper.

"Pretty bad."

"Will it heal?"

"Some. Can't be sure how much."

"You guys don't seem to know much about me."

"Not yet."

"If you find anything out, let me know."

The doctor laughed and said he would. Then he left. A few minutes later Cooper's mother came in.

Elizabeth Morgan looked as alert and pretty as ever. She made him feel better right away. She told him about a friend she knew who was blown out of a bunker in the Korean War and had both his ear drums ruptured. "They grew back and he hears as well as anyone."

"Have you seen Nancy?" Cooper asked. "Do you know when she's coming in?"

She told him Nancy was in the explosion too, that she had gone into the chapel to try and warn him about the dynamite—to save him.

He felt a cold chill. There was something in her tone.

"She . . . she died?"

Elizabeth nodded her head. He could see the muscles at the back of her jaw harden. It was her only sign of distress.

"She died?"

"Yes. She was here in the hospital. She didn't regain consciousness.

"I dreamed about her, I guess. I dreamt I said good bye." His voice caught and his unbandaged eye was wet.

"Hang on son," she said, squeezing his arm. "I know this is going to be hard, but Lisa is here. She knows. Children are not supposed to visit, but she has to see you. She needs to see you are going to be all right."

"I'd like to see her. Bring her in."

Elizabeth went out. A minute later, Lisa came in alone. She was eight, now. Her eyes were red and her voice so small Cooper couldn't hear her at all, but he didn't need to. He held his arms out and she rushed to him and he held her little body against his chest. He could feel her sobs. He patted her and smoothed the dark silky hair on the back of her head.

After a while Lisa sat up—her straight, thin body erect. She took Kleenex from the nightstand, wiped her eyes and blew her nose. Cooper wiped his exposed eye. His face was about half bandaged. He held both Lisa's hands in one of his, and watched her. Her jaw muscles were hard and flexing just the way his mother's had. How much alike they all were. He looked for signs of Nancy in her. They were there, little mannerisms and expressions.

Now . . . this is all I have left of Nancy, he thought. Oh, God, I'm never going to see her again. Just when our love had reached a new, more profound level. Stop that! Not in front of Lisa. I can cry later. Lots of time.

Lisa said, "How do you feel, Daddy?" Her voice was far away but he heard every word.

"I feel fine, sweetie. I'll be up and out of here very soon. Think I'll need you to take care of me."

Oh, shouldn't have said that. Her jaw is trembling again. It's hard to think of the right things to say. A little girl shouldn't lose her mother. That's . . . unfair.

Lisa smiled. "I'll take good care of you, Daddy. I'm staying with Gram now."

"That's nice, sugar. You know what?"

"What?"

"I love you."

She gave him a big smile. "I love you, too, Daddy."

Cooper saw his mother standing in the doorway. "Come in, Mom. Do you know if that nurse, Mary, is going to bring me something to eat? I could eat a horse."

His mother smiled and so did Lisa.

That's the thing to do, thought Cooper. Talk as though I'm healthy and well, that's about all I can do for now.

"Do you not hear well, Daddy?"

"No. How can you tell?"

"Because you're shouting." Lisa laughed at him.

"Well, Gram says my hearing will come back. I'm sure it will, very soon, because I certainly feel fine."

Mary arrived with a tray of food. It did not take much to satisfy him, though. Cooper asked his mother to call Gunnar Ferris and ask him to come in to see him, and Mrs. Ehmm as well. Then Elizabeth and Lisa left and he fell asleep promptly. He dreamed again of Nancy. At some point an older doctor named Murphy came in and introduced himself. He was even more vague about Cooper's condition than the first doctor. Cooper couldn't seem to keep track of time. His mother visited again and he supposed a day or two had gone by since the last visit. He forgot to ask her where the people from Essex were, but it didn't seem to matter. He kept forgetting why he wanted to see them. He worried about Buddy Braken. On one of her visits, his mother told him that Buddy had been killed instantly in the explosion. That at least put to rest Cooper's strange feeling of having left something behind.

Cooper wondered why he slept so much and could not keep track of passing time. He caught Dr. Murphy on one of his frequent visits and accused the Doctor of sedating him. He told him that would have to stop. The Doctor laughed.

One day when his mother was there he asked her what arrangements had been made for a service for Nancy. Elizabeth told him that the funeral had already been held, and that everyone they knew had been there and it had been very beautiful.

Cooper seemed to ignore that and said, "I wonder if she's called on Dad?"

"Sure. Wherever. They were great buddies, you remember. I doubt if Dad has had anyone that pretty visit him before now. Knowing your father, I'm sure he has things pretty well organized up there, to suit his way of doing things. He probably had a brass band out to meet her and a red carpet. He's probably thrown several big parties for her to meet everyone, too."

"Oh, Mom, tell me it isn't true!"

"What do you mean, son?"

"Tell me it's all a mistake. That she's all right. That she's going to come through that door." Tears were running down the right side of his face. "Sorry, Mom, I'm supposed to do that by myself."

"Did you do that when your father died? Cry by yourself?"

"Sure. Didn't you?"

"Yes." They were quiet for awhile then she said, "We could have . . . we could have done it together, you know?"

He looked at her and she was crying, too. He reached for her and they held hands quietly for a long time.

"You two used to make me so mad," Elizabeth said.

"Nancy and I? How?"

"Before you were married and she used to visit the rectory, she would slip upstairs at night to your bed."

"You knew that?"

"So did your dad."

"Why didn't you say anything?"

"Your father wouldn't let me. Said it was none of our business. He said you were a very lucky young man, but if anyone deserved her you did."

"Oh, wow!"

"That's the way you talked then."

"It comes back. I was . . . a very lucky . . . young man. He was right."

"Yes."

When Cooper fell asleep, Elizabeth got up quietly and left the room, which is what she did every day.

As the days went by, the bandages came off his hands and head. Only his left eye and cheek remained taped. His hearing had gotten better, although a ringing sensation came and went in his ears. The time came when he stayed awake most of the day and he started to get restless. His sides only hurt if he pressed them. His ribs were still taped. A number of specialists came to see him. Dr. Murphy told him they thought his hearing was going to return completely to normal. Then he told Cooper there had never been any hope for his left eye. It had been completely destroyed. The cheekbone under it had been fractured but was healing well. The doctor said there would be a scar running down vertically from the eye socket. He described a series of operations that could eliminate the scar and restore the appearance of the area, together with a glass eye. He suggested that they could start the procedures now and that there would be some advantages to that. Or, if Cooper preferred, he could wear an eye patch until he felt ready to have the operations.

Cooper opted for the eye patch and a delay in the operations. At first, he found it tiring to see with only one eye, but he began to get used to it.

Gordon Fairingwether came to see him. He told him the doctor had ordered that he not work while in the hospital or for a few weeks after he got out. The school year would be over by then, so he might as well plan to get away and get a good rest. Gordon said he had put Gunnar Ferris in charge of the school with orders that Cooper was not to be consulted on decisions for the remainder of the academic year.

Then came a steady flow of visitors and life became a lot more interesting. He discovered that Doctor Murphy had allowed only his mother to see him all this time, almost three weeks. Lisa had only been allowed that one time but now she came every day. There was always a line of people waiting during visiting hours, because only four could be in his room at one time. As one or two left, others would replace them. Almost all the Trustees came, most of the faculty, many students, many parents, some headmasters of other schools, and many friends.

Honey, and the members of her coven, had all admitted what they had been doing. They were suspended for the balance of the year. For the seniors, suspension was the equivalent of expulsion. No decision had been made on whether the underclassmen would be allowed to return in the fall. The members of the coven who lived close enough, came to the hospital to visit. Honey was convinced that Cooper had saved their lives and that the coven had, inadvertently, been responsible for Nancy's death. She told the others of her convictions and they accepted them as true. Therefore, visiting Cooper was hard for them and it was hard for him. He matched the seriousness of their mood. But he firmly instructed them that Nancy had died trying to save him. He held them blameless in her death and his injuries. He forgave them and told them that if they still felt guilty, they should know that Nancy would not like that.

Buddy Braken's parents came to see him. That was a difficult meeting.

He had three weeks of visitations in the hospital and each day he was relieved when visiting hours were over. He got a telephone put in his room, which was a welcome convenience.

About a week after Cooper was first allowed visitors, Sherri came into his room early one Monday afternoon. She was full of gaiety and they joked together for a while.

"How did you get in here, anyway?" he said. "Visiting hours haven't started."

"What do I always do?" she said, "I lied. I told 'em I'm your sister from Hollywood, and I have to fly back before visiting hours start in order to be on the set. Look, Baby, I wanted to talk to you alone. Not with a crowd of your well-wishers hanging on my every word."

He grinned at her. "I'm glad you came to talk. My ribs are too sore for you to get in bed with me."

"Look, Morgan, I'm not getting in bed with you until you're well and until you're through mourning Nancy."

His face fell, as he remembered once again that he had lost her.

"I know it hurts, Baby, I know," she said. "I wouldn't have wished this for anything in the world. I hate to see you and Lisa hurt. Even though I want you for myself, I don't want you this way."

"I know that Sherri," he said.

"You're not going to want to look at another woman for a time. But you will heal. Everyone does. When you do, Morgan, you better call me, nobody else. I'm first in line and don't you forget it because if you do, you're going to lose that other eye."

He started to laugh. "You're awfully tough for a little girl."

"I'm not so little. I'm a big girl."

307

"You're more outstanding than you are big."

"They're saved for you, lover."

"OK" he said. "Hang on to 'em for me." They both laughed. "How's *Sally Forth* going?"

"Great. We still have tickets sold months in advance. How's *Barbarian?*"

"Still in the boat yard at Round Pond where we left her. I had her on the market to sell her, but I'll cancel that. Perhaps one day, Sherri, you and I will sail *Callipygian Princess* again."

"Count on it."

RedThunder had been one of Cooper's first visitors and, once the phone was installed, George called every day.

Nancy's parents came to see him. They looked older now, but they were composed and still very much in control of all around them. They told Cooper that Nancy's body had been cremated and they suggested the ashes be placed in the wall of the new school chapel when it was built. Blakely O'Brian said he had found that the building was covered by insurance but if Cooper wanted some additional funds to enhance the new structure, he and Nancy's mother would like to contribute in the form of a memorial for her. Cooper said that was a good idea, and he was grateful. That night Cooper felt more comfortable. He was glad Nancy's body was ashes. He did not want to think of it being in a casket in the ground.

CHAPTER 11

Cooper was out of the hospital in time to preside at the graduation ceremony for the class of 1968. It had been a relief not to have to worry about the details of life at Essex. At first, Cooper was annoyed at Gordon Fairingwether's edicts about not working or making decisions, but after he regained his strength he realized his recovery had been aided by freedom from daily worries and concerns.

Cooper tried to make sense out of what had happened to him and to Nancy, and to everyone else at Essex Academy. He tried to understand the madness that had the whole country in its grip. Shortly before the chapel blew up, Martin Luther King had been shot and killed. Riots in black neighborhoods ensued. One black man shot and killed his white neighbor because he had promised himself he would kill the next white man he laid eyes on.

While Cooper was recuperating in the hospital, young people were rioting on a number of campuses all over the country. Some of Sherri's classmates from Essex had taken over administration offices at their colleges. President Lyndon Johnson sensed the national mood and lack of support for his Vietnam policy. He surprised the nation by announcing he would not seek reelection in the fall. Bobby Kennedy began his campaign for the nomination.

Cooper's appearance at graduation served as high drama for the school community. Many saw him for the first time since the tragic events. His black eye patch was a reminder of what had happened. A scar crossed his cheek and disappeared under the patch. What remained of the chapel had been judged unsafe and was torn down. The site had been cleaned up and fenced off, with a temporary wall screening it from view of the Quadrangle. Commencement was held outdoors, but at the east end of the Quadrangle with the Marsh Arts Center for a backdrop.

Cooper spoke to the graduation day audience about the events on campus, the loss of Nancy, of Buddy Braken and of Sarah Savage. He spoke of young Dwight Bedlington, of Honey and Adrian and other members of the graduating class who were not graduating. He described them all as victims of the times. He spoke of the tendency that he and many others had, a tendency to blame themselves. He speculated that historians would give a name to the social upheaval they were now experiencing, but suggested that those who were a part of it could not see it clearly while it was happening. They also could not understand it, and they had no answers, and no cures. He told them that he, at any rate, had no answers or cures, and if anyone else did, he didn't know who they were.

Cooper told his audience that even the loss of his life-partner was not as bitter as the knowledge that he was a leader with no philosophy to share with the community he was supposed to lead. He said he found such a condition deplorable and intolerable. He told them he intended to spend the days ahead in search of a way of life on the Essex Academy campus that would provide answers, and leaders and the strength to heal society's ills rather than serve as a microcosmic example of those ills. He warned his listeners, particularly the faculty and the Board of Trustees, that no tradition or lifestyle or way of doing things would be immune from examination and possible change. He warned the Class of 1969, who would be next year's sixth form, that no privilege or comfort they had come to expect would necessarily continue.

Recapping, Cooper told the audience, "There is much that has to change. This institution has, in some way, lost its mission. I intend to find a new mission and to regain the values that we've lost. You can expect a school administration whose philosophy might not always be right, but whose viewpoint will be consistently rational and intelligently intended to be right—the best administration I can give you."

Cooper's personal loss and bodily injuries undoubtedly predisposed his listeners in his favor. One faculty wag commented that he could have stood there reciting the alphabet over and over and they would have given him a standing ovation. In any event, they did give him a standing ovation and there is no doubt that he struck a responsive chord. An unusually large number of people spoke positively to him about what he had said. Many Trustees told him he would have their support. Dwight Bedlington Sr. sat with the Trustees, and was quick to stand to honor the Headmaster. But he did not speak to Cooper afterward. He had not spoken to him since seeing him briefly in the lobby of the University Club in New York.

It was Cooper's intention to tend to his accumulated mail and then head for Maine and some solitary sailing on board *Barbarian*. It was the best way he could think of to get the total privacy necessary for thinking. His mother thought it was bad for him to be completely alone so soon after losing Nancy, but he was determined. So she agreed to stay with Lisa until her school let out in seventeen days. Then Lisa would join him on board.

His plan was to leave in two days and spend the remaining three and a half weeks of June sailing. His departure was delayed, however, because quite a few members of the faculty wanted to talk to him about what he had said at graduation. Many teachers had ideas about how Essex should be run and they wanted to communicate their thoughts before he made up his own mind.

Cooper did not mind the delay because the discussions were valuable. So valuable that he arranged some group meetings in the evenings. The timing was good. School was over. The pressures of day-to-day concerns were gone. Long-range perspective was easier. Best of all, it was spontaneous. Teachers were not involved unless they wanted to be and were serious about contributing. Those with whom he talked were delaying their own vacations and other plans. Cooper found the whole process helpful.

The head of the school's architectural firm called Cooper. He said he wanted to come out to discuss plans for a new chapel. So Cooper delayed his departure yet another day. Cooper had already formulated his ideas for a new chapel and had worked out the details with Chaplain Ned Howard. Cooper had made Ned Chairman of the Department of Religion, a post that had remained empty since Cooper became Headmaster.

Stokley Ramsey, President of the Board of St. Burges School, also called. He offered sympathy for Cooper's recent loss and asked if they could have lunch in New York any time soon. Cooper had always felt a little guilty for turning Stokley down, so he felt disposed to be cooperative if he could. Gordon Fairingwether also wanted to see him in New York, so he decided that one more delay in his trip would not matter. He arranged a time to meet with Stokley and then said, "I talked with Abby Everlast a while back and found out about Todd. Then I lost a month in the hospital and have heard nothing since. I guess I've been too wrapped up in my own concerns."

"From what I have heard you've had a full measure, Cooper. Enough concerns to keep anybody tied down."

"Tell me about Todd. Is he all right?"

"Yes, Cooper, he is coming along but he's still away at that retreat. He has resigned as Headmaster, however."

"Oh, dear, I'm sorry to hear that, Stokley. Was that entirely his doing?"

"The official word is that Todd resigned, and I hope you will express it that way in school circles, Cooper. To be precise with you, Todd asked the Board to give him a vote of confidence before he continued. In a fairly close vote the Board declined to do that, and so he resigned. Asking for the vote was his idea entirely. I really feel that he has resigned, and we're not just calling it that to cover things up. Doesn't that make sense to you?"

"Yes," said Cooper. "That sounds like an accurate description to me. I suppose if I were in his shoes, I would not have asked for the vote. But then I don't really know how Todd felt."

"Todd felt relieved, Cooper. He didn't want to let us down if we felt we needed him. I think he was glad the vote went the way it did."

Stokley Ramsey went on to explain that they were looking for a new Headmaster, and he would like to have Cooper's input and advice. He mentioned that Batty Sainely would not be able to carry on as Acting Headmaster.

Cooper suggested the possibility of choosing an Acting Headmaster from the ranks of successful retired headmasters and gave a couple of suggestions of people he might ask. Cooper also volunteered Ned Howard as a candidate. He pointed out that Ned was in his early fifties, and therefore, in the eyes of some, a man past the peak of his energy. But he was very experienced as a schoolmaster, he was an Episcopal Priest, and he was tough and savvy.

Cooper laughed and said, "Ned also has an unusual qualification that would make him particularly effective at St. Burges. He is just as wealthy as any member of your Board."

"I don't think I understand," said Ramsey.

"Ned is old Boston money. He has no reason to be intimidated by your Trustees. I realize, of course, that there is no reason any good man should be intimidated, but you and I know that most struggling schoolmasters feel like servants in the presence of wealthy, socially dazzling Trustees. You need a confident take-charge sort of a man."

Stokley laughed and said, "You're absolutely right. That was one reason I wanted you."

"Well, I'm not rich," Cooper smiled. "I'm just a big bull-headed guy, getting meaner and uglier as I go along."

Laughing again, Stokley said, "I understand the kids call you 'The Pirate.' Now that you have that patch on your eye, it's a nickname everyone will pick up."

"The eye patch seems to get attention. If I grow a mustache I'll look like the fellow in the Hathaway Shirt advertisements. People have been sending me Hathaway shirts, which are nicer than pirate costumes. I guess I'll have to play this for all it's worth until I get a glass eye."

"There's no chance you'll get your sight back in that eye?"

"Nope. The bulb is burned out. I'm lucky I've got another one. It's amazing how strong it has become. I can see just about as well, now, as I ever did."

"Does it cause you pain? Do you get headaches?"

"It used to hurt some, but it doesn't anymore and I don't have headaches."

"So when do you get the glass eye?"

"When I have time, I guess. I'm not really sure I want one. It doesn't look so bad under there. The lid is closed and there's some scar tissue. If Nancy were here she'd be bugging me to get my face as pretty as possible, but . . . she's not here. That's the only thing that hurts, Stokley."

He also kept thinking about Sherri. Hathaway shirts reminded him of Sherri. She had sent him six of them in assorted colors and stripes.

I guess she's reassuring me, he thought, that she doesn't mind about the eye. She still loves me, even though my face is messed up.

When he arrived in New York for his meetings, Cooper wanted to call her. But he didn't. If he saw her, he knew they would go to bed. That's really what he wanted, but he felt he shouldn't want that. It wasn't fair to Nancy.

But, he thought, I have always wanted Sherri, so it's not surprising I do now. That's not being respectful of Nancy, but does that matter? Are those society's values I'm trying to live up to or are they mine? Both maybe. What I really want is to hold Sherri in my arms while I cry about

313

Nancy. Oh, shit! That doesn't make any sense at all. Neither one of them would be likely to understand that. In any event, I've already arranged to spend the evening with RedThunder. Perhaps we can get drunk together. We haven't done that in years. That's what we should do. Maybe George loved Nancy as much as I did. Here we are, thirty years old now, and he still hasn't married. Nancy would probably like it if George and I went out and got drunk together in her honor, with one empty chair at the table. I'll call George and suggest it.

"No way," said George. "I have two tickets to *Sally Forth*."

"But I've already seen it. I went on opening night," said Cooper.

"We're going again. I've seen it, too. You always see more the next time, things you missed before. For instance, did you notice the first time, Sherri Huff standing bare-ass-naked in the spotlight?"

"I noticed."

"Oh you did, huh. Well, I thought maybe schoolmasters didn't notice things like that."

"Sometimes we notice."

"We don't have to go backstage, Cooper. I just thought you ought to consider there are other girls out there. Do you know what I mean?"

"You are a clever Indian. I don't understand how the West was won against people like you."

"Frankly, neither do I. It must have been a fluke. Seriously, Coop, we don't have to go hear Sherri sing. I just thought you might like it."

"I guess I might. Anyway, we can go get drunk afterward."

"You're on. I'll even carry you home."

Cooper's meeting with Gordon Fairingwether was pleasant. P.D. Quail joined them. They wanted to talk with Cooper about a memorial for Nancy. The Trustees all wanted to do something. Cooper outlined his ideas for a new chapel and suggested a memorial there. He told them Nancy's family would like it, and would contribute whatever was needed in addition to whatever others contributed. P.D. and Gordon agreed, and Gordon said he would get the word out so anyone who wanted to could contribute.

"It is nice to see you two together," said Cooper. "I'm getting the impression you guys discuss more than school business together."

"You think so, do you?" asked Gordon. "I just have a soft spot in my heart for spinster lady publishing tycoons."

P.D. said, "I'm trying to teach him how to handle himself in bed. With just a little more finesse some poor woman might be willing to take him away from the bachelors' ranks."

"Yes," said Gordon. "I think I need more lessons. Practice makes perfect."

"You people are embarrassing me. I am too young to be hearing this consenting adults conversation."

"When you grow up, sonny," said P.D., "give me a call, and I'll give you lessons too. You're looking sexier than ever with that eye patch."

"When are you going sailing, Cooper?" asked Gordon. "I don't want to delay you any longer than necessary."

CHAPTER 12

Cooper did finally get away. The boatyard had launched *Barbarian* and reported that the teak hull had not leaked even a teacup of water when they put it over the side. Teak is the only wood that does not swell in water. Therefore, a builder can construct a teak boat with a tight hull. When builders use other woods they leave space for swelling. Boats built of other woods leak when they are first launched until they swell up.

Barbarian's hull had a new coat of varnish as did her spars. Cooper oiled the teak cabin trunk and deck. He scrubbed her down below. He got her engine functioning smoothly. Her water tanks and fuel tanks were filled. Stores were laid on board. She was ready in three days and Cooper set sail taking leisurely legs southwest down the coast. Every night he was asleep by nine, and he was up by 6:00 a.m. He slept like a baby by night and his body bronzed by day. He found a waterproof eye patch but mostly went without and wore only dark sunglasses in the sun.

In a week's time he pulled into a marina in Portland. Cooper's mother drove Lisa to Bradley Field, north of Hartford, and Lisa flew to Portland where Cooper met her. It was exciting for an eight-year-old to fly alone. The next three weeks, on board the *Barbarian* with her father, were the most memorable weeks so far in Lisa's life. She became a confirmed sailor. She resolved that if she ever found a man half as interesting as her father, she would marry him. Provided he had a sailboat.

Cooper could not believe how quickly she learned. Lisa was bright. The weather was variable. There was one storm and there was some rain, but for the most part the days were sunny and the nights cool. Cooper had taken Lisa along on his cruise as soon as she was out of school because it just seemed the natural thing to do. He was unprepared for how deeply rewarding an experience having her along turned out to be. They both needed each other to help each deal with the loss of Nancy. They were closer than they had ever been before. Cooper realized that this vacation was something very special, not likely ever to be repeated.

They both healed and grew strong in the sun, winging their little boat silently on the wind towards home. Cooper took an irregular route, exploring here and there. They took their time. Eventually they brought *Barbarian* back into Old Seabrook, the port from which Cooper and Sherri had set out two years before at about the same time in July.

They were both sad to be ending their cruise, but it had done its work and run its course. Cooper promised Lisa that, whenever he could get free, they would take three-day weekends on *Barbarian* for the rest of the summer. He managed to do it on most weekends.

While Cooper sensed that a cherished moment in his life had just concluded, he was also excited about being back at Essex and getting back to his job. He believed he had the answers he was seeking. While cruising, he had filled a notebook with ideas. Now, he wrote out extensive memos and statements. He rewrote the Student Handbook and the Faculty Guidelines.

He discussed his conclusions with Gunnar Ferris and Mike Banes. Both were enthusiastic.

Cooper's plan was a blend of many ideas, none of them truly new. They had come from many people. There were no contemplated changes that would, by themselves, cause a stir on the outside. Cooper hoped they would not be interpreted as a backlash to the new liberalism. He hoped they would not be seen as "conservative" because he believed they were a combination of both liberal and conservative philosophies of school management. He conceded to Mike Banes, however, that in the eyes of the students the changes would be taken as a move towards the conservative.

So, although Cooper was shy about giving names to new ideas, he decided to name his plan rather than allowing a name with the wrong connotation to become attached. He called it the Caring Program. He felt that "Caring" summed up the thrust of the plan and, like motherhood, God and country, caring was beyond criticism.

The Caring Program called for as much variety in campus life as possible. Students were to have wide choices, but almost never the choice to do nothing. Adult supervision was to be greatly increased. Cooper said to Gunnar Ferris, "The essential point is I want our students to be within sight or hearing of adults at all times except when they're asleep.

That may be impossible, but that's our goal. They'll have a hell of a time getting drunk, doing drugs, practicing witchcraft, trying suicide or hiding dynamite if there is a faculty member within sight or earshot."

"Many in the faculty will not like it," said Gunnar, "and none of the kids will like it."

"You're right about that. You and I and Mike are not going to like enforcing it either, but if we pull it off we'll have one hell of a fine school. There are many ways we can sweeten the deal. In the final analysis, though, I expect a number of the faculty will apply elsewhere to teach and quite a few kids will seek transfers. I'd like to do everything I can this summer to speed up that process. Give 'em fair warning and if they want to go, help 'em along their way."

"How can you sweeten the deal?"

"Enlarge the faculty supervisory potential with a squad of apprentice teachers. Pay teachers extra for extra duty. As to the kids, let them have their new symbols: jeans, long hair, sideburns—but they'll have to dress up sometimes, too. I'd like to see them in black ties and long dresses for Sunday dinner. I bet they'll love it. We're going to have required Sunday Chapel in suits and dresses. I want the whole faculty there, every last one of them in hoods and robes, in an academic procession."

"You want that every Sunday?"

"Damn right! It'll be fun."

"Cooper, if you can pull this off, you are going to make history."

"Not necessarily. None of these ideas are new. Frank Boyden and his protégés have been doing some of this stuff for years."

"These are new ideas for Essex, though. That's a lot for this community to swallow all at once."

"We might as well do it all at once, Gunnar. There's excitement in that. If we run really tight supervision, Gunnar, then we can do some real healing. We won't have to throw kids out who can't behave without supervision. We can hang on to nice talented kids such as Louise Shipper and some of those other rascally bare-ass witches. It's a way of doing things that we can be truly proud of. It makes me sick to solve discipline problems by throwing away the child."

"It is an exciting concept, Cooper. I'm all for it, and I'll do all I can to help you make it work. You know that don't you?"

"Sure I do, Gunnar. You know, another idea occurs to me. With this program in effect, we could take back those sixth formers we threw out last year. I wonder if any of them got into college. If they did, they didn't get into the colleges they deserve. An additional year here would put them back on track. And that could be significant for the rest of their lives."

"Would you be willing to have Adrian Craft and Honey LaTate back at Essex after the pain they've caused you?" asked Gunnar.

"Damned right I would. I'd give a good deal to have them back. Have another chance to make something out of them. What happened wasn't entirely their fault. They didn't intend it. It was everybody's fault, mostly mine, for letting them get that far out of line."

"Come on, Cooper, you can't blame yourself for that. We've been running this school with well-established procedures. The best schools in the country are run this way. We are one of the best schools in the country."

"Yes, Gunnar, I know. However, the times have changed. Kids are far less trusting. With good reason! Why have we given them Vietnam? We've been trying to run Essex along a set of guidelines that don't work anymore. OK, now we're going to catch up. Adapt ourselves to the times, that's all."

Gunnar chuckled, "All right, you pirate! Let's get to it."

Cooper got Gordon Fairingwether to call a special meeting of the whole Board. What Cooper envisioned would cost more money and reduce income. He planned to hire more people and increase pay. Some students would leave. They would have to run next year at a deficit.

Some of the Trustees were wary and uncertain, but most liked the plan and they cleared Cooper to go ahead with a deficit budget. Before they adjourned, Gordon pointed out that if they could finish up the twenty million dollar fund drive there would not be a deficit because the additional money would earn enough interest to balance the books. They had one million, one hundred thousand to go. Gordon had given up hope of getting anything at all from Dwight Bedlington, who did not even attend the meeting.

Joe Marmot cornered Cooper afterward and asked him if he would be continuing with the New Winds Scholarships, and Cooper said he would. Joe asked him about some of the other details of his Caring Program and then said, "Well, for a moment there I thought you had gone reactionary on me, but I can see this is something altogether different. I guess it's a pretty good concept. As you know, I am not without experience with kids. I think you'll be surprised to find that they like the attention of close supervision. Isn't that what we all want? Love and attention, that's where it's at, baby."

Cooper said, "I've been curious to know how you would judge this plan. You are my most thoughtful liberal advisor. I'm glad that you see it as I do."

"Yes, Cooper, caring isn't the special property of the conservative or the liberal. It's a great concept. Go to it! Incidentally, I'll get you the money for the New Winds Scholarships. Consider it done."

Later that week Cooper called the President of the Board and said, "Gordon, when do you want to announce that the capital campaign has reached its twenty million dollar goal?"

"What are you talking about, Cooper?"

"You said we needed one point one million, right?"

"You know that's the figure better than I do."

"Well, I didn't want to tell you before, but part of my new Caring Program is to stay on campus where the kids need me rather than run off to every village and hamlet making speeches to alumni. So I raised the rest of the money. A million-one, you can count on it. It's in the bag."

Cooper's high good humor came across the phone line.

"I can't believe this. We've picked the fields bare. Where in God's name did you get it?"

Cooper was enjoying himself. He said, "Dwight Bedlington, where else? You told me you could get half a million from him. I figured I'm more than twice as good as you, so I told him I had to have one point one million, and he said OK."

"Now I know that bomb scrambled your brains. I was afraid of this."

"I'm not kidding, Gordon. Dwight is really pledging one million, one hundred thousand dollars. He'll get it to us within the month, but it has to be kept secret until his son Dwight Jr. graduates from Essex next June. I told him that was a condition of accepting the gift. I don't want young Dwight to think his dad's money bought his way back in for a post-graduate year, because it didn't. I took Dwight back before I even mentioned money. We're taking everyone back who was thrown out last year. That is, everyone who wants to come back. With this Caring Program, we'll be able to take in inmates from a federal prison if we want to."

"Are you taking back that kid who was instrumental in blowing up the chapel, Cooper?"

There was a silence, and then in a sober voice Cooper said, "The chapel blowing up was an accident."

"No one has a better right to decide that than you, Cooper. I stand corrected."

"Thank you, Gordon. The boy you refer to will be returning. I've invested a lot of time in Adrian. I'm not giving up on him now."

"If I were in your place I hope I would feel the same way, but I'm not sure I would. Tell me about Bedlington. What did you say to him?"

"Well, I told him about the Caring Program and how it would enable us to give students such as Dwight another chance. I told him face to face. I went to see him, as I have with other parents. When everything was all set, I told him how important it was for me to stay on campus instead of being out raising money all the time. I told him I was out raising money when Sarah Savage came to talk to me. He knew all about that, you remember. I said if he would give the million-one, then I could stay on campus and he would be doing his part to make that happen. He bought that right away. He thinks the whole plan is terrific. I think it is, too."

"So do I. Cooper, you are a wonder. You are an ace!"

"Thank you, friend. It is nice to get praise from the boss."

"But clear one thing up for me, Cooper. How can you guys supervise all those kids all the time?"

"I don't have everything all worked out, but the important thing is that we have that as a goal. We have a philosophy that will help us make all sorts of little decisions. For instance, we have a faculty locker room with showers, in the Gym. I'm converting that into a team room and the faculty will have their lockers mixed in with the students. When the football team is in the shower, I'll be in there with them taking my shower. If not me, it will be some other old hairy bastard who has just come in from jogging or coaching. We're going to have required athletics for absolutely everyone every season. Exceptions will be made for faculty-supervised functions such as music lessons, Art Club activities, or rehearsing plays. There will be lots of alternatives, but no alternative to do nothing.

"On Saturday nights kids are going to have to be at the movies or at a dance or in the library. That's it. When those functions are over, there will be a feed in every dorm. Every student must be there. Any who are sick will be in the infirmary with the nurse on duty.

"During study hall, students must be in their rooms with doors open. I want to see them in there when I walk past. And, I will walk past once in a while. Not only that, but the master on duty in the dorm must have his door open. I want to see *him* when I walk past. And if I don't walk past, then Gunnar will, or the Dean, or somebody else. What do you think?"

"I think that's the way the place was run when I was a kid there."

"There. You see. And you didn't turn out so bad did you?" said Cooper. "There will be a few differences, though. You can wear jeans to class if you want, and you may grow a moustache if you *can* grow a moustache."

"Yeah, that's different. Not bad. How is the faculty going to like it?"

"Not much."

"So you're going to give them money?"

"Yep. Extra money for extra duty."

"You're a smart bugger, Morgan."

"Yep. I'm feeling that way, today."

Cooper got out a letter to the faculty about the Caring Program. He had been in touch with a number of teachers by phone and in person, including housemasters and some others whom he wanted to tackle some specific extra duty. A number of teachers were on campus during the summer because they taught in the summer school. Cooper had run the summer school for a couple of years before he became Headmaster, but as Headmaster he delegated running the summer school to others so that he could devote himself to planning for next year, just as Leighton Frostley had done when he was Headmaster.

Cooper scheduled a conference at Essex for Saturday afternoon of the last weekend of July, along with a picnic and outdoor party. He invited all the teachers and their spouses, as well as the returning student body and their parents. Many, of course, could not make it, but more than sixty teachers did, and almost four hundred students came, many with their parents, and some parents, whose sons or daughters were in Europe or far-away camps, came alone. The Dining Hall staff fed over one thousand people at the picnic.

The conference was held in the Field House where chairs, a platform and loudspeakers were set up. Cooper, Mike Banes, Gunnar and Ned Howard all spoke about various phases of the Caring Program and they all answered questions. There was a spirit of cooperative good humor in the air. For the students, the whole thing was more than a month away, so they didn't really seem to mind that much of their freedom of movement was going to be taken away. The parents all seemed to be supportive. The teachers grumbled a bit among themselves and made the usual clever jokes, but many were enthusiastic. For the most part, the faculty found themselves having to pretend to be experts about it all. The psychology of the situation made them collaborators before they had a chance to decide if they approved. This did not happen by accident.

The administrators made much of the point that some students would want to transfer to another school because Essex would be different, not the place they had chosen as their kind of school. The administrators offered to assist in making transfers, and set up times for meetings. No one came forward. Cooper had hoped for such a result but had dared not predict it. He felt that by anticipating a negative reaction and professing to understand such a reaction, they had clipped the wings of potential deserters before they had a chance to fly.

Buck Forrest and his publicity staff took a lot of pictures for a special issue of the school magazine that Cooper wanted delivered before Labor Day. The new Student Handbook, which described Essex procedures, rules and courses, was distributed at the conference. Copies with a cover letter from the Headmaster were to be mailed to student homes the following Monday.

As a follow up to this mid-summer conference, Cooper would meet with parents and students in Chicago, Los Angeles, Kansas City and Atlanta. The meetings would be held in the homes of Essex students, and they would all go about as smoothly as the big conference on campus.

Of those students who attended the July Essex conference, Freddy Iverson took the prize for coming from farthest away. Freddy traveled all the way from his native New Mexico because he was grateful that he was going to return to school. In his own mind he did not think he deserved it, but if Mr. Morgan was going to go that far for everyone, Freddy felt he should travel to Connecticut to hear about the program that was making it possible for everyone to return who wanted to.

Freddy asked what seemed to him to be a straightforward question. Others had wanted to ask it but refrained when they saw the black patch that covered their Headmaster's eye and the scar on the cheek below it, and thought of pretty Mrs. Morgan who was now gone.

"Mr. Morgan," asked Freddy, "From what I have heard today, I get the impression that you do not trust the students at Essex Academy. Is that true?" The room became very quiet.

"Yes, Freddy," said Cooper. "Considering the context in which you ask your question, it is true that I don't trust you. But I do love you, each and every one of you."

CHAPTER 13

The following Monday morning Cooper was at the train station in New London. The train from New York had just roared in and a few passengers were emerging from several cars. He felt unusual tension.

He thought, what if something has gone wrong? She might have missed the train. I don't think I could stand that.

He took a quick glance in the other direction and there she was descending to the platform, grinning at him. She looked radiant and healthy. Cooper was aware of his heart beating fast. Her face was tan and her hair was a shower of gold. She had on a white cotton peasant blouse and a pale blue denim skirt that matched her flashing eyes. Her legs were bare and tan also, and she wore huarache sandals. She had an over-the-shoulder canvas bag and carried an overnight suitcase in her hand.

He ran up to her, grabbed her upper arms in his big hands and held her out in front of him. "Judas! You do look beautiful."

"Kiss me you big dumb ape."

He lifted her off her feet and crushed her to him. She smelled fresh and clean and feminine and wonderful. He kissed her on the mouth, tenderly, but after a moment she thrust her pointed tongue in his mouth, which made Cooper feel like a rutting animal.

Sherri broke the kiss and said, "Hey, down boy. You don't want to do it right here on the train platform do you?"

Cooper felt dazed. He looked around and saw people staring at them. Sherri tended to attract the stares of strangers. Sometimes, in New York, they stared because they knew who she was. Usually though, she attracted those long male second glances because she was a sexy-looking woman.

Cooper said, "As a matter of fact, I do, but I suppose we had better not." He put her down.

She grinned at him and squeezed his hand. "Let's go," she said.

Cooper picked up her bag and they headed off to his Country Squire. Cooper drove up onto the Connecticut Turnpike heading east.

"This is our first legitimate date, do you know that?" Sherri said.

She had started calling him once a week when he got back from Maine with *Barbarian*. She was pleased that Lisa had been with him but told him that Lisa had better be the only other female to set foot on that boat. After a time, it was Cooper who initiated the calls. He told her that he and RedThunder had gone to see *Sally Forth* again, but he was afraid to tell her he was there. He told her that the show was better than it had been on opening night, and that he was surprised at how polished it had become, particularly her role.

After several calls Cooper suggested that they get together in August. Monday was the only day *Sally Forth* did not have a performance, so they targeted the first Monday in August as their meeting day. Cooper suggested she take the express train to New London, and he would meet her there, and they could drive to Mystic and spend the day at the Seaport museum.

Sherri did not sit close to Cooper while he was driving. She leaned against the passenger side door and grinned at him. He glanced frequently at her and grinned back. She said, "Where are we staying tonight?"

"There is a pretty motel on the shore in Mystic. Most of the rooms have a view of the ocean. We have a reservation there."

"You got us separate rooms, I hope," Sherri said. "Because I don't fuck on the first date."

"Growing up has not improved your foul mouth. Tell me how many guys you've had more than just a first date with."

"None since you, Baby. You might find that hard to believe, but it's true. But what is this 'growing up' shit? When did the Headmaster decree that I have 'grown up'?"

"Just an expression, a meaningless phrase. I didn't mean anything by it. Ill-chosen words, I guess. I meant that now you're famous, whereas when last we were together, really together, you were like me, one of the common people. Sherri, you have always been grown up to me. You have made me feel immature and inept. Now you're making me feel that way again."

She slid across the seat and hugged him. "Oh, my darling, how could I be bitchy at a time like this? I have been living for this for two years and I'm so nervous I don't know how to behave. Will you forgive me? We're both in different positions in our worlds than we were before. I suppose we're different people."

"Sherri, sweetheart . . . oh, wow, I'm so nervous I can hardly drive. I love you, Sherri. I have loved you for a long time. Now . . . I need you. I didn't before. I loved Nancy . . . and . . . just before she died . . . more than ever before. And, I needed her. I had just found that out. I'm telling you this because you have a right to know. I want our relationship to be based on truth, even if you don't want to hear it. I think perhaps my capacity to truly give myself to someone else has been . . . small. I'm really the one who has been slow to grow up. Nancy was just . . . well, she was just beginning to make me see myself and that I need someone, a lover, to depend on, to need. And then . . . well, now she's gone. So just when I have opened this hole in my armor, my bodyguard is gone . . ."

"'Oh, wow,' is that what I heard Cooper Morgan say? 'Oh, wow?' You poor sweet thing. You are hurting. More than I thought. Oh, poor sweet Baby, I love you so much." She squeezed him and kissed his cheek. "Where are we headed now?"

"Mystic Seaport."

"Don't you think we should check in at the hotel first?"

"No need, they'll hold our reservation."

"I'd like to go to the motel first, stupid."

"Oh, wow."

They had all their clothes off within about a minute of entering the room. Sherri stood on tiptoe before him. She pulled his head down level with hers. She gently removed the eye patch and stared intently at the ruin underneath. The lid was closed, limp. The scar tissue was nearly normal in color and had only a faint outline. She said, "Your skin is tan here, like the rest of your face."

"I guess it gets a few tanning rays when I wear sun glasses. And, when I'm alone on *Barbarian*, I don't wear the eye patch."

"You don't need to wear it now."

"You don't think it's . . . ugly?"

In answer, she pressed her soft lips against the limp eyelid. Her hands stroked lightly down his back and then around to his groin. "I'm glad," she said, "That nothing was injured down here."

They left the room for a short time about eight o'clock that evening to get some dinner. They never did see Mystic Seaport, but there were other Mondays when they did.

"Cooper, damned if I'm not getting emotionally involved in this St. Burges situation. I'm beginning to think they're going to offer me the job, and if they do, I think I'm going to take it." Ned Howard was speaking. He and Cooper were standing at the chapel site where excavation equipment was at work adding new foundation forms. The new chapel was going to be bigger than the last one, which the school had outgrown. When the earlier structure was built, Essex had just slightly more than half the number of students it did now.

"I was afraid that would happen when I mentioned you to Ramsey. It will be impossible to replace you, Ned, but you're just what they need. And I suppose nothing about your job here can rival the pure joy and excitement of having your own school. It's a little like being the lord of a medieval city-state. For all the frustration and work, it can be fun."

"The hell of it is, Cooper, my job here has never been more interesting. There's a new chapel going up, a new management philosophy for the school. This is a hell of a time to be thinking about leaving."

"It's a hell of a time for me to have to look for a new chaplain, I'll tell you that."

"Why did you recommend me to them?" Ned had an amused expression on his face.

"I guess I felt I owed Ramsey. Besides, ultimately, Essex gains luster by spawning headmasters. I didn't think about it when I suggested you, but I would be damned curious to see you pull off something like the Caring Program at St. Burges. You're its biggest supporter on this campus, so I expect you'll take some of it with you. Isn't that true? Also, Ned, I have always thought you had more to give to your work than your work has asked of you. You are a potential dynamo, as I understand your father was. You have the poise to keep the Trustees in their place, which is important. I'm afraid many new headmasters start out in awe of their board members and forget that it is the Headmaster who is the chief executive officer of the corporation, not the president of the board. Lastly, Ned, you are a professional. St. Burges needs a schoolmaster and wants a priest. You are both. With you there, everyone's needs would be served, except mine."

"Perhaps we're getting ahead of ourselves," said Ned. "They may not offer me the job, but Ramsey said I'm one of three finalists. I would like to get my thoughts in line, in the event that I do get the offer. So, I have a question for you. You may know that I put up the money for my house here on campus. It's on school land and I claimed its assessed value as a tax-deductible charitable gift to the school. The unwritten understanding has been that I would have lifetime use of it. If I leave, you'll have the house for someone else to use. But someday I'd like to come back. I want to retire here. I'm an alumnus of Essex and I've spent most of my life here. This will always be my real home, Cooper. Do you think I could come back to my house someday?"

"I certainly hope so, Ned. I know the Board regards that house as yours. Our attorneys would probably say that we can't make a legal commitment that you can come back to it, but I will make a moral commitment to you. The house is yours to use, provided you perform some perfunctory service for the school, such as assisting occasionally with chapel or something of that nature."

"Thank you, Cooper, I thought you would say that. It means a lot to me. Now that that's behind us, I want to speak to you about something else. I planned to do this no matter what you said about my house. I want to contribute one hundred thousand dollars to the new chapel in Nancy's memory. If there is any part of that money that isn't needed for the chapel, I'd like to start an endowment for the chaplain's salary, or the chapel budget if the chaplain is me, because you only need to pay me a dollar a year."

"Judas, Ned, you overwhelm me. That is a magnificent gesture, astounding. Ned, I am deeply grateful on behalf of the school, but that you want to do it in Nancy's memory touches me . . . profoundly. I don't know what to say."

"You said all you need to say, Cooper. I wasn't particularly close to Nancy, but I always admired her. She had real style. She glittered on this campus like a diamond. She was, well . . . a real class act, as you are, Cooper. I'm going to miss her. Now, as to the money, I'll need to spread it over two tax years if that won't be inconvenient. I'll give you half this month and half next January. Would that be all right?"

"Of course, it's wonderful. You almost made me cry, Ned. It's not good for a one-eyed man to cry. I've found that out."

Ned clapped Cooper on the shoulder. "Of course you have, old chum. Of course you have."

Cooper urged Gunnar Ferris to make changes in the curriculum that would strengthen it. He felt that the Caring Program could and should include academic changes, especially changes that rescinded any earlier concessions that might have weakened the curriculum. Gunnar decreased the number of academic credits given courses that were not in the mainstream of basic academic discipline. However, he left in place a wider selection of courses and he kept the trimester system. Gunnar and his wife left the campus for the month of August, which was his usual vacation routine. Soon, the last few student places were filled and, with the help of math wizard Oggie Nosterling, all student schedules were made out and conflicts resolved.

Mike Banes returned from his month-long vacation in time for the big midsummer conference that introduced the Caring Program. Cooper immediately sat down with him and showed him dozens of dossiers from young men and women who were looking for their first teaching jobs. Most of them had just graduated from college the previous June.

Cooper said, "You are in charge of the new Apprentice Teaching program, Mike. That's because you're the Dean. These guys will be your shock troops. We can take up to seven of them. These folders are mostly from job agencies. We need one who can teach Spanish, one for Algebra and the rest can be anything, but you should not pick more than two in any one discipline. All of them ought to be able to coach something every season. One of them must be able to coach ice hockey. It would be best to hire three women and four men. The most important thing they're going to do is watch the kids. They will be taking attendance until they are blue in the face. They will be deputy deans, so you get to pick 'em."

"How about the department chairmen?" asked Mike. "They are not going to take kindly to having teachers in their departments whom they didn't have a hand in choosing."

"These kids are only going to practice teach. They will be in training and have only light teaching loads. Here and there, if we need one to teach a course, and if they're any good, we'll put 'em on it. The department heads can vote, but you select them. I'll help you. I'll interview or evaluate or whatever you want me to do, but it's your show. You are going to hire them, supervise their training, help them, and use them."

"What's the salary range?"

"They each get two thousand dollars whether they need it or not, plus food and housing."

"What? Only two thousand dollars? You mean for the whole year?"

"They also get a year of first-class graduate training in school administration. In return, you are going to work their tails off."

"I suppose it is a fine opportunity for someone just out of college."

"It sure is, particularly in August when their hope of landing a teaching job for next year is nil. Mike, I'd pay these kids more if I had it, but I don't. I don't feel guilty though, and neither should you. If we run this program right, it's going to be a damned fine deal for them. Next year they'll have recommendations, experience and training from one of the best schools in the country. It will be easier for them to land a good teaching job."

"We won't want to keep them?"

"We probably won't have openings for most of them, but they can have first crack at any openings we do have, if they are qualified. Then, we'll take on another set of apprentices. We can revise the program, correct mistakes and polish it. Before you know it we'll have a training program that will make you famous."

"Or you."

"Yeah, me too. Why not?"

Sherri was one of Lisa's favorite people in the world, so it was a special treat for her when Sherri came out to visit Essex on a Monday. Sherri sent Lisa more mail than she had ever received from anyone else. In the more than two years since Sherri graduated, Lisa had received presents, post cards, letters and jokes in the mail. The friendship took on an almost magical quality for Lisa when her beautiful idol became a Broadway star. Sherri's visit was an event as exciting as Christmas. Cooper had given their maid, Mrs. Mendelson, the day off, so Sherri cooked for them and did the laundry as she had when she was a babysitter in the Morgan household.

At dinner Lisa said, "Sherri it's time for you to leave that play. You should come live with us. Daddy and I need you to take care of us."

"You would like that, huh little buddy?" said Sherri. "I would like that too, but I doubt if your father would like me hanging around here."

Cooper gave Sherri an amused look. Lisa said, "Oh no, Daddy would love that, wouldn't you Daddy? He loves you just as much as I do. Don't you, Daddy? Say you do, Daddy."

"I do, Lisa."

"There, you see, Sherri. He loves you too."

"People will say I shouldn't live here, though, unless I am married to your dad," said Sherri.

"Oh, you can't marry him, Sherri. No one can marry him because he's married to my mother. But you can live here. You should, you know. It's OK isn't it Daddy?"

"It's OK with me, Lisa."

"It's all settled, then."

Sherri said, "Maybe someday I will live with you and your daddy, Lisa, but not yet. I have to live in New York now."

That evening when Lisa went to bed, Sherri read her a story as she had when she babysat. With the wonderful assurance that Sherri would still be with them in the morning, Lisa drifted off into a happy sleep.

Downstairs, Sherri said to Cooper, "Will the Essex community be all abuzz because I spent the night here?"

"That's possible. I suppose there will be some speculation here and there. In the summer, though, the people who are here don't keep track of each other so much. I suppose this is something that we ought not to do when school starts after Labor Day. Unless . . ."

"Unless what?"

"Unless there were other guests staying here too."

"Like who?"

"Let's see, how about George RedThunder and one of his lady friends?"

"Is George a ladies' man?"

"Well, he was when we were kids. Why don't we fix George up with your roommate?"

"With Lannie? Yeah, that might be fun. They both might like that. Sure, I bet Lannie would really go for George."

"Most ladies do, but I think George would like Lannie, too."

"Do you think Lannie is, you know . . . attractive?"

"Yes. As the saying goes, 'I wouldn't throw her out of bed,' unless . . ."

"Unless what?" asked Sherri.

"Unless you were waiting for me."

"Baby, you just saved yourself in the nick of time. Speaking of waiting, I think my buddy, Lisa, is asleep, and I have been waiting . . ."

CHAPTER 14

The following week St. Burges asked Ned Howard to be Rector of the school, and he accepted. Cooper offered Ned's house to Mike Banes. Mike and Sylvia were thrilled. From the outside, Ned Howard's house was not as grand as the Headmaster's Chase House, but it was a far better house in every other respect. Cooper thought it might be the loveliest home he had ever seen. As large houses go, on which no expense has been spared, it was relatively unpretentious, but even that feature added to its charm in Cooper's eyes.

Sylvia Banes ran into Cooper's office unannounced. She threw her arms around him and kissed him. She was so happy she was crying and laughing at the same time. "Oh, my God! Cooper, how did you know I wanted to live in that house? How did you decide so fast? I didn't even know the Howards were leaving?"

"Well, if I didn't decide fast, I'd have most people on campus fighting with each other and with me to get in there. I'm just saving myself agony. Besides, Mike rates it for doing the toughest job on campus and you guys need it with all those little kids of yours."

"Cooper, you are a sweetheart! I love you!"

"I love you, too, and Mike, and your whole crazy tribe. But I have another reason, Sylvia. Someday the Howards will be back. It's really their house. They gave the school the money to build it. You and Mike won't be here forever. You guys will be running your own school one day. I didn't want to put someone in that house who would want to stay there until hell freezes over."

Sylvia said, "Not to change the subject, but where are you and Mike going tomorrow?"

"We are going to hit as many cities in Connecticut as we can," said Cooper. "We are going to be buy up lots of old, used tuxedos from

333

rental places. You can buy a good used black tuxedo for five or six bucks nowadays. I suppose that's because colorful formal wear is getting popular. Men aren't renting the black ones so much."

"Why on earth are you turkeys going into the used tuxedo business?"

Cooper laughed and said, "It's the new dress code. We're requiring boys to come to school with a suit that they can wear to Sunday Chapel, and we want them to have tuxedos for Sunday dinner, for some of the dances and for athletic banquets and other big occasions. If they don't want to spend the money for a new tux, they'll be able to pick up a used one here in the school bookstore for a few bucks. Boys on scholarship will have one issued to them. Girls all seem to own a long dress or two, but not many boys have their own formal wear."

"Do you really think the kids will go for this stuff?" asked Sylvia.

"I haven't heard any complaints yet, and they know the new guidelines."

"I guess it's just crazy enough to work. I hope so. Cooper, sweetheart, it's so nice to see you laugh. We have known each other all these years, but I have never known you without Nancy. It's so unfair. When Nancy and I were roommates at Wellesley, you were all she could talk about. And now she's gone. I still can't believe it."

"Neither can I."

"You will find someone else, Cooper dear, you must."

"I suppose I will, Sylvia."

Cooper thought, why do I find Sylvia tedious? She's a good wife and mother and she's sweet and pretty. I suppose it's because she always wants in on my private thoughts. I'm a private person and she is not.

Cooper felt devilish. "Sylvia," he said, "if I ever do find someone else, would you do me a favor?"

"Anything, Cooper darling."

"Will you teach her how to be a snapper?" He would always remember this moment as the time he caught her at a loss for words, stammering and blushing.

Sally Forth had been running for a year and a half and ticket sales showed no signs of slowing down. There was considerable talk of it being made into a movie, but, so far, the process of selling the rights was in a snarl.

Sherri was not tired of playing Sally O'Malley even though she did it five nights a week and two matinees. She wanted to keep performing the part so she would continue to be associated with it and have a better chance of being cast in the movie version. That's what her agent had advised. A national company was being formed to take the show on the road in the fall. Sherri's roommate, Lannie, was hoping to get the title role for that, although there was talk, again, about getting a known star for the part in order to attract audiences.

Sherri was due some vacation time, and she decided that Lannie's chances for the lead in the tour would be enhanced if she were able to play Sally O'Malley with the Broadway company for a week. Actually, Sherri arranged to take off nine consecutive days at the end of August, two weekends and the weekdays in between.

Cooper took the same days off. Lisa stayed with Cooper's mother. He and Sherri went cruising on *Barbarian*. Cooper's preparations for the 1968-69 school year were complete. The final step in getting ready was to rest up for what he referred to, in the privacy of his own thoughts, as "The Year of the Oak." He had tried bending with the winds of change, as the willow did. Now, he had designed his own philosophy of school management. In some respects it made generous allowances for trends and student desires, but only if he himself thought they were for the best. In other respects he was challenging the storm of revolution by standing solidly against it, reinforced with careful preparation, even as the mighty oak stood its ground, bending only slightly in the wind, risking being blown over completely.

If I fall, Cooper mused to himself with half a smile, mighty will be the fall thereof.

"Why are you smiling to yourself?" Sherri asked. She was sitting at the tiller in the cockpit of *Barbarian* with the wind in her golden hair.

"I was thinking what an incredibly lucky fellow I am to be all alone on a little boat with one of the most beautiful women in the world. Weren't you identified as one of the ten most beautiful women in the world by Vogue or one of those fashion magazines?"

Sherri bubbled with laughter, "Yeah, I've had several centerfold offers from men's magazines, but who would have guessed an expensive ladies' monthly would honor little Sherri, known in the New York news as 'the Broadway sex bomb.'"

"That sounds pretty complimentary all by itself."

"In the theater we try to stay away from words like bomb."

"Beautiful Sherri, has any magazine or newspaper revealed how delightful you smell? All fresh, natural body oils, no perfume, you smell as heaven must. And all that is but a faint, elusive forerunner to how good you taste."

"And where do you find this flavor?" She grinned impishly.

"Just where you are thinking, naughty girl, but also in your mouth and on your cheek. On your calf, thigh, belly and breast, chin and forehead, everywhere. How would you like to go steady with me?"

"Just stay where you are. No tasting until we're at anchor. Otherwise I'll luff the sails, and we must have no bad seamanship aboard my master's boat. What does going steady mean to you, Morgan? Are you proposing to me?"

"Well, my love, I have been going on the assumption that one of these days we will marry."

"This is the first time you've mentioned it."

"Well, we love each other. You and I and Lisa, we all love each other. I've been thinking that you expect, well, we both have been expecting, that in due course, the natural consequence of all this loving is that we will acknowledge our love publicly and . . . and marry. You and me? Holy wedlock? You've heard of it?"

"Where does it say, Baby, that everyone in love must marry?"

"Sherri, don't you want to? I mean, eventually?"

"When did you have in mind?"

"I don't know. Maybe next Christmas? Or, even, next spring! June? That's when lots of people . . . don't you want to, Sherri?"

"I do love you, Baby, you know I do. You and Lisa, and . . . uh . . . Lannie. And my Mom. I love her. And . . . that's it. No more. I *like* my Dad. That's funny, I love three females and you. So, not to worry Morgan, you're the only man I love."

Cooper didn't say anything. He just looked at her quietly. The silence grew tense.

"Oh gee willikers, Sandy!" said Sherri. "Who started this, anyway? Arf, Annie, I don't know. You said did I want to go steady, right? Well, I do. I want to be your lover and I want you to be mine, and after we anchor you can lick my . . . hey, Morgan, are you there? What's happening, lover?"

Cooper smiled at her warmly, but did not speak.

"OK Baby, let me ask you this. What do you expect me to do after we get married?"

Cooper said, "Live with us. Be my wife and Lisa's mother."

"And give up my career?"

"Well, Judas, Sherri, you'll live at Essex with me. You can't very well do a show in New York every night and live with me. You could make records once in a while. You could do TV appearances sometimes. But, I'd want us to be together. Isn't that what you want? Hey, you could do summer stock. I'll even come with you."

"Baby, come here." She motioned to the seat beside her. Cooper hopped across the cockpit and sat close to her. He slid his arm around her and pulled her close. He put his other hand over her breast on her cotton sweatshirt and rubbed the side of his thumb back and forth across the nipple. Her face was only an inch from his face. "I love you, darling," she said. "If I were to marry, I would only marry you. But I want to be your lover, not your wife."

"Why?"

"Because I'm Sherri Huff, the performer. That's me. That's the woman you love. I'm going to Hollywood before long. If I don't, I can tell you an agent who is going to get fired. We can't change what I am. If we did I wouldn't be me. I wouldn't even exist. Love *me*, Baby. Have me. You're my only love. I'll be true and faithful to you. Truer than . . . never mind. Just let me be me. OK?"

"OK, but two things."

"What?"

"First, I reserve the right to bring this up for discussion again."

"And second?"

"And second, if you change your mind, I would like you to let me know."

"That's a deal, Morgan."

"And one other thing."

"What?"

"Nancy stopped doing that."

"I didn't mean . . ."

"It's OK. She was true to me for the last two years. You should know that. I know you say she was your rival, but she liked you, spoke kindly of you, and she knew about us."

"She told you that?"

"No. It's just that I could tell. We both just sort of understood about each other's indiscretions and there weren't any accusations or holier-than-thou stuff. We didn't dwell on it, but we were faithful to each other for the past two years. No big deal. I just wanted you to know that."

"Thank you, Cooper, I appreciate you telling me."

"That's the second time you ever said my Christian name."

"I'll have to do it more. I don't feel so far away anymore from the world of people who call you Cooper. Or, so far from Nancy either. Thank you for that."

"Now," said Cooper, "let's find a closer destination for our overnight anchorage."

"Why?"

"Because I am eager to have some of that stuff you've been promising me."

CHAPTER 15

Cooper had asked the expelled or suspended students, who were returning, to come back to Essex a day early that fall. He talked to them in a group and he talked to them separately. The most important point he tried to get across to them, as a group, was that the only reason they had this chance was the new supervisory system.

"We want to know where you are and what you are doing at all times. You might call this spying or snooping. I call it caring. We care enough to bother, and we're going to bother a lot because we care a lot. There is no point in telling me you need to learn to do your job without being watched. You're going to have to earn the right to experience that. You'll have to earn it here at Essex, so you can have it after you leave. Please remember it is the Caring Program that allows us to give you another chance. Without the Caring Program you would not be here."

Dwight Bedlington Jr. said, "Sir, I know I screwed up. It's cost me a year, but if I couldn't come back here I would be in a dump college right now and my whole life might be different . . . worse, I think, a lot worse. So I'm grateful. You're not going to need to watch me, but I can't expect you to believe that. I'll have to earn your trust, but I . . . well, I'm trying to say I'd like to help. I've talked to some of the others here and we want to see your system work. We don't want other kids like us to, you know, get kicked out like, you know, we did. Getting kicked out makes you feel really bad."

"Dwight, I appreciate your saying that more than you can imagine," said Cooper. "If you guys want to help, then talk up the plan. Be positive about it with your schoolmates and don't walk around saying 'this system sucks and this school sucks,' and all the other things that are easy to say and cool to say."

The students grinned at him, partly surprised at how well he knew them, and partly amused to hear "the establishment" using their private language.

"Now, one more thing," Cooper said. "Mr. Banes and I thought a long time about whether you people ought to come back on a probationary basis. We decided a new school year is a clean slate. You start fresh. But don't kid yourselves. You have reputations for being screw-ups. Faculty members are going to watch you closer than they will others. I don't expect you to resent that. That's life. You guys made your reputations. The adults didn't. You can change your reputations, but you'll have to do some positive things.

"Next, you owe this school something. You owe Essex a little extra for putting up with you and for your new chance. You figure out what you can do to pay your debt. Don't tell me about it. Just do it. But the very least you can do is keep the rules. I want it, and I expect it.

"OK, last thing, I don't hold anyone responsible for my wife's death or for losing my eye. No one. It happened. It was an accident, no one planned it and no one wanted it. Don't let me hear about anyone accusing anyone. Let's not have anyone feeling guilty. Please don't feel guilty when you say something that reminds me of Mrs. Morgan or that I'm a one-eyed guy. I like to be reminded of Mrs. Morgan and I like to talk about her. If you want to talk to me about her, I'd like that. If you want to call me Pirate or Cyclops or whatever, that's all right with me. Just don't say it to my face until after you graduate." Cooper grinned at them and they laughed.

As the group was leaving, Louise Shipper came up to him and thanked him for the Caring Program and said he could count on her support. Cooper thanked her and he thanked Sonny Bedlington for what he had said.

Sonny went out the door with him and said, "There's something else I owe you. You showed me that my old man's money couldn't buy everyone. That was a shock, and I hated you at first, but the more I thought about it, the more I thought you're a better man than my father is, and I told him that."

"You did?" said Cooper. "When did you tell him that?"

"After he tried to get you fired, when I heard about it."

"What did he say to that?"

"He said I was probably right, and he was sorry he tried to get you fired. That's why he went to the graduation ceremony, to show you he was sorry. Then he came home and cried because I wasn't there graduating. I felt bad. My dad loves this school more than anything. He says Essex did more for him than college did."

"You know, Dwight, a man who cares that much about you and about Essex, he can't be all bad." Cooper smiled at him.

The boy smiled back. "I know."

Between them, Cooper and Mike Banes spoke privately to each of the formerly expelled or suspended students. Cooper saw his group, one at a time, in his office.

Freddy Iverson was starting his sophomore year. He had filled out during the summer. Now, at age fifteen, he looked as if he would develop into a broad muscular youth, a little shorter than normal. When Freddy saw Cooper, he was as direct and candid as ever. "Are you all well now Mr. Morgan? Does your eye hurt?"

"I'm fine, Freddy, and my eye is OK. I just can't see out of it."

"Why do you wear the patch?"

"I guess because people wouldn't want to look at me without it."

"Does it look bad under there?"

"Not too bad. You want to see?"

"Yeah."

Cooper took off the black eye patch and Freddy stared at him for some seconds. Then he said, "It isn't too bad, but you look better with the patch on. In fact you look great with it."

"Thanks, Freddy."

"I guess the really bad part is Mrs. Morgan being dead and all."

"Yeah. That part is pretty bad."

"Mr. Morgan, did you cry? I mean when you found out about Mrs. Morgan?"

"Yes, Freddy, I did."

"So did I."

"I appreciate your telling me that. You don't seem like a fellow who cries much."

"Nah, I don't. But I did then. Did you know I went to the funeral?"

"No, Freddy, I didn't know that. Thank you. I guess, in a way, we've been through a lot together."

"Mr. Morgan, I'm sorry."

"I know. Thanks."

"You said it wasn't anyone's fault, but I think it was partly my fault. You saved my life, and if it wasn't for us, Mrs. Morgan wouldn't ever have been in there."

"Freddy, it wasn't your fault. It wasn't anyone's fault, believe me."

"I got my hair cut short."

"Did you do that for me?"

"Yeah. I didn't do it before, because Honey wanted it long. And I love Honey."

"Look, Freddy, I was wrong about your hair. How you wear your hair doesn't matter. What matters is being honest and not cheating. When you come here and enroll in this school you're making a bargain. The very fact you enroll means you're willing to live by our rules. If you break the rules while you're pretending to keep them, then you are cheating. It's important not to cheat. How you wear your hair isn't important. I know that now. Before, I just hadn't thought it out very clearly."

"So you don't mind if I grow it out?"

"I don't mind. Just look me in the eye now and then and say, 'Mr. Morgan, I'm not cheating.' Tell me, does Honey know you love her?"

"I won't cheat you, Mr. Morgan. Not ever again. And yes, Honey knows I love her but she doesn't know she's going to marry me."

"Don't you think Honey is a little old for you?"

"It looks that way now, but in a few years it won't matter."

"Maybe you're right. Good luck. She is a beautiful girl, and you're going to be a hell of a fine man."

"What was it you wanted to see me about, sir?"

"About being honest. I already said it."

"Can I go now?"

"Yeah."

"Goodbye, Sir. The eye patch looks fine."

Freddy was followed by Amelia West, who, along with Honey and Monkey, had elected to come back to Essex for an extra year before going on to college.

After Amelia came Monkey. Cooper said, "Adrian, I have been fighting with various people to keep you in this school since you first showed up in Thatcher House when I was Housemaster. You, my friend, have seemed to be working the other side of the street."

"I don't think I know what you mean, Mr. Morgan."

"I mean that in addition to being indifferent to any of your studies that aren't math or science courses, you are apparently intent on breaking all the rules you can. Adrian, it is a widely held belief that you are a drug dealer, and I can hardly entertain a contrary view. You are aware, I assume, that drug dealing not only violates the school's most basic rules but also is a criminal activity. Mr. Ferris told me that it seems clear that you did not bring dynamite onto the campus, but it is equally clear, even though you did not admit it, that you played a hand in hiding the dynamite in the chapel. That, too, is a criminal act for which you avoided prosecution only by my intervention. Did you know that?"

"No, sir." Monkey looked frightened.

"Well, it's true. It is also true that you are living your life in a way that could lead you eventually to prison, or worse. Has that ever occurred to you?"

"No, sir."

"Well, it should. You are not dumb. In some respects you are brilliant. You need to think about where you are going and why. You are on the wrong track, pal. You are in the process of screwing up your life. Only your decision to take a new direction can save you from a really rotten existence.

"Adrian, I'm satisfied that we can afford to give you another chance only because we have the means to keep a constant eye on you. I can keep you from messing up this school, but I can't keep you from messing up your own life. Only you can do that. You can start now. You can be somebody and like yourself. You can decide to adhere to an honest code of behavior. It's simple. You just have to decide in your heart that you are going to be honest with yourself and others."

"Yes, sir."

"Adrian, do you have any idea what I'm talking about?"

"Yes, sir."

"OK. Come back here in a week and talk to me about it."

Monkey left. Cooper shook his head as he watched him go, thinking he had gotten nowhere with him.

Anyway, Cooper thought, he has his chance. It's up to him. It isn't up to me.

When Honey came to see him she looked prim, and solemn, and mature, in high heels and a fashionable skirt and blouse.

"It seems like a long time since I've seen you, Honey. I feel as if I should give you a kiss."

"I would be grateful if you did."

"You are too grown up, and too beautiful. I would mistrust my own motives. Besides, you are spoken for by Freddy."

She smiled thoughtfully, as if thinking about Freddy, and then she said, "I'm sorry I couldn't be here this summer for the meeting, as I said in my letter. Your letter was very kind Mr. Morgan, and I appreciated it. Sir, if I could just relive last year and do it differently, I'd give my life for that. All I meant to do was have fun. I didn't mean to hurt you . . ."

"Hey, stop that. Don't look back, Honey, at least not that way. Don't blame yourself for things you never meant to happen. That's destructive. Learn from it and keep going."

"All right, I'll try."

"Honey, tell me, why did you decide to accept the offer to come back here for an extra year? You were accepted at college, weren't you?"

"The state university agreed to accept me because you and Mr. Ferris were kind enough to give me a completed transcript. Frankly, I had hoped for a more competitive college because I want to do graduate work in biology or medicine. By coming back here, I hope to make Vassar. Then, there's something else. By coming back to Essex, maybe I can clear away something in my own mind. I don't know how to express it, except maybe to say I want to try and do it right this time. Do you know what I mean?"

"Yes. I think I do. Well, I'm glad you decided to come back. I'm going to try and do it right this time, too. However, I see a problem in it for you."

"What?"

"Honey, you're awfully grown up to have to live with boarding school restrictions. Essex is going to be even more restrictive. As a sixth former last year, you were more mature than most. This year you'll turn nineteen. Basically, you are an adult and the Essex lifestyle wasn't designed with someone like you in mind. Can you put up with that?"

"Sure. That's the least I can do. But, I'm going to do more. I'm going to help out. Because I can make this place work better, and I intend to."

"I can't tell you how pleased I am to hear you say that. I have no doubt that you can make this place work a lot better. I was going to ask you to do just that."

"Yeah? How?"

"First of all, Honey, I'm not going to use the Student Council for much. I would have abolished it except the Council was already elected. If the Council members do something good with it this year on their own, I'll keep it. If they're like the past few Student Councils, they will be the last. I think Council elections have been a joke. The last two Presidents certainly treated the school rules as a joke. I'm going to run the school with the Prefects. The Housemasters appointed them and they have the confidence of the faculty. I intend to appoint a Head Prefect and he or she will be the true student head of the school. I explained this at the summer meeting, so most students know about it.

"Anyway, Honey, I would like you to be a Prefect-At-Large, not to run your dorm, but to do some special leadership jobs I assign you. You'll sit with the other Prefects at a once-a-week meeting with Mr. Banes or me. Will you do that?"

"But why? I was kicked out last year. I deserved to be. If it wasn't for me, Mrs. Morgan . . ."

"Stop that, Honey! That wasn't your fault. Get that through your head. You were way out of line last year. Your behavior was deplorable, but you didn't wish anyone harm." He smiled at her, "And, you demonstrated remarkably strong leadership." He laughed. "You even convinced Nurse Smith you were a doctor." "Hey, I only did that because . . ."

"I know. You lied in order to accomplish a greater good. The point is you pulled it off,. That was a remarkable piece of leadership, among other things I will not mention."

She smiled. "All right, I'll do it. I'll do anything for you."

"Good. Now, tell me seriously, do you believe in devil worship? I mean really believe in it. Do you have faith in it?"

She laughed. "No. I don't even believe there is such a thing as the devil. Well, maybe, it's possible, but I doubt it."

"I would like to employ you for the other team," said Cooper.

"I'm not going to do any more of that stuff, Mr. Morgan, honest. You don't need to worry about that."

"What I have in mind is more respectable, but also involves ceremony and religion, and leadership."

"You mean chapel? You want me on the Chapel Committee? I caused the last one to be set on fire. Remember? Besides, I'm not at all sure I believe in that either."

"I didn't really expect you did. All I want from you is an open mind and a willingness to help. You have been baptized, haven't you?"

"Sure."

"Well, I'm beefing up chapel a lot this year, even though we don't have a building. We'll use the auditorium in the Arts Center. We're going to have big impressive Sunday Chapel services this year. Girls will be in dresses, boys in suits and the faculty in academic gowns. We are going to have a big parade walking in to the place, and you know who will lead the parade?"

"I'm afraid to ask."

"Right. The Sacristan will lead the procession and you will be the Sacristan. You will be in a gorgeous cassock and surplice, and you'll carry the processional cross. The Sacristan has other responsibilities. He is in charge of the sacred contents of the church, and here he will be the student in charge of the chapel. I say 'he' because it's traditionally the job of a man, often a priest. Do you think the Episcopal Church should have women priests?"

"Of course."

"Are you going to turn down an offer to take over a traditionally male role in the Church?"

"You are a clever bas . . . you are very persuasive, sir."

"I am also a clever bastard, Honey. I want you on my side. I think you can find things in the Church that will interest you."

CHAPTER 16

1968-1969

"Your gamble has paid off. I've never seen her equal as a student leader," said Mike Banes. The school year was three weeks old and Honey LaTate had the student body of Essex Academy dancing to whatever tune Cooper played.

"You agree, then," said Cooper, "that it's time to appoint a Head Prefect?"

"She's already performing as if she were the Head Prefect. If you don't appoint her pretty soon she won't even need your endorsement."

"That's what I've been waiting for you to say," remarked Cooper.

"You've known it all along, haven't you? You knew she was going to turn out this way."

"No, I didn't know it for sure. I thought she could do it, but I wasn't sure she wanted to do it. Now we know she does. I'll ask her after dinner and announce it at assembly in the morning."

Cooper had decided during the summer that the biggest loss suffered by Essex during the student revolution of the sixties was the students' loss of trust in the adults on campus. For generations, student leaders at schools such as Essex had kept the major rules and enforced them. But during the sixties, boys and girls who lived a double standard replaced those old-fashioned, trusting leaders. The new leaders pretended to support the administration and uphold the rules but laughed at them behind the backs of teachers and administrators. Therefore, systems that had functioned smoothly for decades collapsed.

Cooper had embarked on a strategy of asking and expecting less from student leaders, of appointing them rather than letting their peers elect them, and of selecting those whom he would appoint very carefully. Cooper counted on Honey's maturity, her natural leadership ability and his rapport with her to be enough to buck the tide of the time. The strategy worked well.

The old, traditional sit-down meals, served by rotating student waiters, were brought back at dinnertime. Boys put on coats and ties for dinner. Girls wore skirts and blouses or dresses. Once more, Oggie "Cyclops" Nosterling was scheduling the whole school community in a once-a-week rotation of the tables presided over by the faculty. Cooper decided that henceforth the head of the student body would sit with him at his table permanently, an opportunity for trust to flourish if it would. Dorm Prefects sat permanently at their housemasters' tables.

The boys and girls sometimes referred to Honey as "Mrs. Morgan," because she always sat with Cooper as Nancy had. However, the needling was good-natured in spirit, unlike the rumors that had flourished years before about Cooper and Sherri.

Sonny Bedlington did not regain a leadership role on the campus. But he also did not hold any more beer parties in East Woods. He worked hard at his studies and his athletics, in hope of being accepted at Wesleyan, his father's alma mater. Young Dwight lived socially aloof from the sixth formers who surrounded him in his dormitory, King Hall. When he could, he squired Honey to Saturday dances.

However, the student Queen of Essex Academy attended the most important social events, such as the Halloween Ball with, believe it or not, a fourth former! It was a never-ending source of amazement and gossip. All right, Freddy Iverson was attractive, and he did make the varsity football team, but really! He was just a child compared to her, and she was soooo sophisticated, whatever was on that dear girl's mind? Did she know something no one else knew about Freddy?

Campus gossips also focused on Cooper. They observed that the Headmaster brought Miss Astrid Fondleworth to the Ball. They wondered whether something was going on there and observed, cattily, that they knew that bitch would catch his attention sooner or later. They wondered whether the Headmaster, when so frequently missing from campus on Mondays, was with her. They also wondered where Astrid was on Mondays, wondered whether she was on campus or not. They determined to notice where Astrid was on future Mondays, and shared the titillating tidbit that she was older than Cooper. Of course, they did not suppose the age difference between Astrid and Cooper was any greater than that between Honey and Freddy, but really!

Honey never appeared anywhere with Monkey. She painstakingly avoided him. Cooper noticed this and asked her about it once.

"Monkey and I are going our separate ways," she said.

"Do you suppose he's still a dealer?" asked Cooper, testing a theory.

"I'm sure he is, but I could never prove it. You won't catch him either. No one will. Monkey is clever beyond belief, and he is being ever so careful. I've heard it's so difficult to do business this year that his prices have tripled, but he's still making less."

"Well, it's comforting to think I've been able to cut down on the trade, even if I can't eliminate it."

"Mr. Morgan, I've been meaning to tell you. You will never eliminate it. If you send Monkey home tonight, someone will take over his trade tomorrow. That's how the world is, Mr. Morgan. You are just too idealistic. You will never create nirvana on the shores of the Connecticut, no matter how hard you try."

"Honey, I think you have just broken my heart."

"You're just being sarcastic to cover up. You think you can do anything, but you can't. You can do most things, but not everything."

"Now my heart is mended. Seriously, is there no way to reach Monkey, I mean Adrian?"

"There you go again, idealistic. Don't you know that kid is rotten? He just is. He always will be. If he was as big as Buddy was, he'd be even meaner. He's small, so he has to be a sneak. That's all he knows and all he'll ever know."

"I think maybe you're right, at least about my being more idealistic than you. I don't think anyone is all bad."

"Oh, all right," said Honey. "But if there is anything good about him, I don't know what it is. I used to think he was fascinating, so that tells you how dumb I was. He's just out for himself, period."

"Sherri, darling, I have been ringing your apartment half the night. Where have you been? I was worried."

"I'm sorry, Baby, I didn't expect you to call."

"But where have you been?"

"I had a performance."

"Yes, but you should have been home at least a couple of hours ago."

"I went out. There was a birthday party for one of the cast. We all went out on the town. I'd forgotten what fun that is."

"You mean I've been cramping your style?"

"I didn't say that. I just . . . hey, what's going on?"

"I called you to say I can't make it this Monday."

"Have you decided to punish me?"

"For what? Should I want to punish you? Is there some reason . . . ?"

"You don't own me, Morgan. We're not married. That's one reason I don't want to be married. So just bug off with the jealousy bit, all right?"

"Sherri, we're having our first fight. It shouldn't be on the phone."

"I don't want it to be anywhere."

"Did you have a lot to drink?"

"What is that supposed to mean? The fight is my fault, huh. You're jealous so I suppose I have had too much to drink. Oh, that's rich."

"Well, whatever the reason, you are being unreasonable and bitchy."

"Why, you smug, self-complacent prick, who asked you for an analysis? You know what? It'll be nice to have a Monday without Mr. Know-it-all. So thanks for the vacation, Morgan. You know what I'm going to do? I'm going to spend the day using bad grammar, and no fucking English teacher is going to be there to correct me!"

Sherri picked up the phone and threw it towards the window. The cord snubbed it short and it fell to the floor with a crash. That was the last thing Cooper heard because the cord connection was loosened and the instrument went dead. She grabbed it and shouted, "Baby, I didn't mean it! I'm sorry. I don't want to fight . . . Oh, damn! It's dead. He'll think I hung up." She burst into tears.

Lannie put her arms around her and stroked her hair. "There, there, sweetie. You're not used to drinking hard booze. My champagne girl got a woozy head and told off her big daddy. Champagne girl is going to get her pretty fanny spanked when big daddy gets to town."

"I hope so," moaned Sherri. "You know what's so awful? I sounded so dumb."

"You just sounded crocked."

"No. No. I sounded stupid!" She buried her head in Lannie's shoulder and sobbed.

Cooper tried to dial her back. The line was busy. He needed to talk to her desperately. The frustration was infuriating.

Got to tell her I love her. Didn't mean to sound jealous. I love her so. He dialed again. It was busy. He slammed down the receiver. "Damn that little bitch!"

He thought for a minute than dialed another number. "Hello, Astrid? I need to see you . . . I know it's the middle of the night, but I have to talk to you . . . Well, get up and put something on. I'll come over . . . No, I didn't have a nightmare. I'm lonely . . . Well, now I'm lonely too . . . Thank you sweetheart, you are a doll . . . I'll be right there . . . No. No one is going to see me . . . the campus is dark . . . don't worry about it."

At the beginning of the school year, the new All Saints Chapel was framed with metal girders. The foundation had been completed over the summer and a considerable amount of fieldstone facing had been laid.

The plan was for the chapel to look much the way the old one had from the outside, like a typical large New England country church—rectangular, faced with white clapboard, tall Greek columns in front, and a classic white bell tower with a steeple above. This time, though, it would not be made of wood and the structure would be larger in every dimension. There was to be a huge balcony, which would remain empty for most occasions. It could double the seating capacity and would be used only for such events as graduation, Alumni Days, Parents' Days, and the like. The columns were to sit on a spacious portico raised several steps from ground level. There was a large central double-door entrance opening onto the main chapel. On either side of the portico at ground level, there were handsome doors that opened on short, broad, curving stairways descending to the smaller Crypt Chapel. Here the walls were made mostly of Connecticut fieldstone. A bronze tablet on the fieldstone wall of the vestibule dedicated the Crypt Chapel to the memory of Nancy O'Brian Morgan. Nancy's ashes were sealed in a bronze cylinder behind the plaque. The whole Crypt level of the Chapel was very beautiful and simple. The vestibule was to contain four of Nancy's colorful abstract paintings.

As autumn progressed, the new building took shape and it was closed in just before the arrival of winter snowfall. The contractor would be obliged to pay a heavy penalty if the building was not ready for dedication and use at the baccalaureate service on Commencement Weekend. Therefore, large crews worked in efficient coordination to accomplish the job.

A low wind-pressure pipe organ of exceptional quality was being built in Holland for the new chapel, but it was not expected to be ready in time for graduation. The organ was to be a classic, built in the manner of the great cathedral organs of Europe two hundred and fifty years ago. It was a gift to the school from P.D. Quail. P.D. had promised Gordon Fairingwether that when the organ was installed and working well, she would marry him in the chapel.

The first service planned for All Saints Chapel on commencement weekend was the consecration of the building, and the Bishop of Connecticut was to officiate.

With the first crack of bat on baseball, the warmth of spring spread across the countryside and the Essex campus. It was the spring of 1969. The new chapel stood gleaming and white. Grass sod was laid and shrubbery planted. Crews of workmen toiled to put the finishing touches on the interior. Everything was on schedule. The school year had, so far, gone very well. Cooper kept in close touch with his friend Ned Howard who reported that basically the same program of school management seemed to be flourishing at St. Burges. Ned, never a creative man, had elected to call it the Caring Program at St. Burges, also.

"Well, Ned," said Cooper, "I am now convinced that, most of all, kids want to know where they stand and what their parameters are. Along with loving attention, that's the secret."

"You know where this cursed revolution came from, don't you, Cooper?"

"I am eager to hear your thoughts on that, Ned."

"It came from us, Cooper, my generation and yours, too. We gave them the Vietnam War, and we also gave them our own lack of conviction about the morals and attitudes that held our parents' generations together. We handed them a vacuum and they just followed their animal instincts for pleasure and avoiding the pain of real effort."

"Yes, Ned, I agree, but some good is coming out of it, too. For instance, we're looking more honestly at ourselves. Some stupid and meaningless traditions have been tried and found wanting."

Ned told Cooper he would be at Essex for commencement weekend, the Chapel Consecration, everything. He had arranged to hold graduation events at St. Burges earlier.

Sherri had also arranged to be there. Because of her outstanding help with the capital fundraising drive, Sherri had been elected to the Alumni Board of Governors. She liked that so much, she told Cooper, that she intended to run for President of the Alumni Association at the next election. She would be representing the Alumni at the chapel dedication ceremony. Sherri would have Lannie do Sally O'Malley during the Essex Commencement weekend. While Lannie had failed to land the role with the national touring company the previous fall, the woman who got the role would soon be leaving the show and Lannie would have another chance.

CHAPTER 17

"We'll soon be losing our view of the shoreline, and be heading inland to the little airport near the school," shouted George RedThunder. He was trying to make himself heard over the noise from the chartered Cessna's twin engines. Lannie Stretch was beside him in the rear seat. In front of him next to the pilot sat Sherri.

"Will we fly over the school?" Sherri called to George. Her eyes flashed with excitement.

"Normally we could, but it'll be dark soon. Sam here needs to land us and take off back to New York before it gets dark," George shouted.

It was the Sunday of a big spring weekend at Essex. The trio had left the city as soon as Sherri and Lannie were through with their matinee performance. Tonight would be the last performance of the annual Spring Musical at Essex. The performance the night before was the concluding event of Spring Parents' Day. It was already the middle of May and Commencement Weekend would be in three weeks.

Cooper was out beside the runway. He waved to them as they landed and he opened the passenger door the moment the plane came to a stop. Sherri was in his arms. He spun her around and around. Her feet did not touch the ground for more than a minute.

"This is very embarrassing," said George. "Will the white man please suppress his animal emotions just a little bit? Miss Stretch and I have a rather formal relationship and it is disconcerting for us to be exposed to raw lascivious passion."

"Hi, Indian Joe," said Cooper. "It's almost as delightful to see you as it is to see the beautiful and talented Miss Stretch. Why don't you take the lady to a blue movie in preparation for double dating with Miss Huff and me?" Sherri, feet now on the ground, still hugged Cooper with both arms and grinned happily.

The men scooped up the suitcases from the plane's storage compartment. George and the girls waved and called goodbye to Sam, the pilot, who promptly taxied back down the runway.

Cooper's black Country Squire station wagon was parked nearby and he drove them the eight miles back to Essex. Cooper had made reservations and placed food orders for them at The Lion Inn since they had only a short time before the curtain rose at Marsh Arts Center.

As usual, Elmer Pincer produced an outstanding original musical. Sherri saw him at intermission and kissed him. "I have never had a leading lady like you," he said, "and I suppose I never will again."

He asked Sherri for permission to introduce her to the audience after the show. She agreed but asked him not to call on her to sing. Elmer looked disappointed until Sherri said she would sing for him another time.

Returning to their seats, Cooper asked, "Why don't you want to sing? Are you sick, or tired?"

Sherri bubbled with laughter. "Hey, Morgan, do you figure Sherri's sick if she passes up a chance to put on a show? Am I just a big ham?"

"I don't think you ever passed up a chance at the spotlight before."

Sherri said, "It's been three years since I was a student here. More than half the students don't know me. I think it's an imposition for an old-bag alum to come back and expect to be fawned over. Elmer might like it, but I doubt if many of the kids would."

"I don't think you're quite old enough to be an 'old-bag alum' yet," said Cooper. He winked at George and said, "RedThunder still goes back and sits on the Harvard bench for the Yale game, and only the very ancient remember him."

"I don't think I could ever forget George if he scored for me," Sherri said impishly.

George laughed his machine gun laugh and Lannie, with a straight face, said, "I think he still scores pretty well."

They all laughed, and then the lights went down signaling the start of the second act.

After the show, and Elmer's introduction of Sherri, she congratulated the performers and told them they were fortunate to have Mr. Pincer guiding them. As they emerged from the auditorium many students who had been at Essex long enough to remember Sherri crowded around to greet her. The others knew who she was. Her song, "Dilly-Dally," had made the charts and she appeared with some frequency in magazine stories. Unlike other visits to campus, Sherri this time was taken to be Cooper's date. Some of the boys, those who dared, looked at him and rolled their eyes appreciatively. Sherri was in a black low-cut party dress. There was an occasional, "Way to go, Mr. Morgan," in subdued tones and some low whistles.

Sherri heard it all and smiled broadly, her eyes bright. Cooper introduced Lannie and George to those students who were eager to stay and talk. Some of them even knew who George was. It was fun to overhear some of the comments.

"That big guy there, he was Harvard's greatest halfback."

"Of course, stupid, that's RedThunder, the Indian."

"That's crazy. Did you see his eyes? Who ever heard of a blue-eyed Indian?"

"How'd you like him on our team? Jesus, he looks big and solid."

"Mr. Morgan played with him. How would you like to have to stop those guys? My God, they'd kill ya."

"Mr. Morgan never played football."

"The hell he didn't. He quarterbacked at Lawrenceville. He played with RedThunder. They went undefeated."

"Yeah?"

"I'm not surprised. How'd you like to have to stop those guys?"

When Cooper and his friends returned to Chase House, Helen Flowers, Fifth Form President, was there babysitting. She shyly asked Sherri if she remembered her.

"Of course!" said Sherri. "You were Second Form President my last year. You were so solemn and dignified when you made Lower School announcements in assemblies."

"She is still president of her class," said Cooper, "but not so solemn anymore."

Helen asked Sherri if she could have her autograph, even though she knew it sounded silly. Sherri said she could if Sherri could have hers. With all that complete, Helen dashed out the door.

Sherri said, "Your babysitters are not as sexy-looking as they used to be, Morgan."

He said, "I've learned my lesson."

Lisa had stayed up to see Sherri and, at Cooper's urging, she showed Sherri some watercolors she had done.

Sherri said, "These look professional. I knew you could draw, but I didn't know you were painting. You're going to be better than your mom."

"I started painting after Mom died," said Lisa. "It sort of made me feel closer to her. Now, I just can't seem to stop."

Sherri announced that she was going upstairs with Lisa, while she got ready for bed. "We are going to talk girl talk," she said.

Cooper fixed nightcaps for everyone while George and Lannie took their suitcases up to their respective guest bedrooms. They knew where they were, having visited before.

After she came downstairs, Cooper asked Sherri to come to his room after she got ready for bed. "I want you to read me a story," he said.

"I've got a story to tell you all right?"

"Actually I wanted to tell you a story," he said.

When Sherri entered the room she found Cooper sitting up in bed reading the Independent School magazine. He wore nothing but his eye patch.

"You are looking 'Oh, wow' tonight," he said. "Would you like to take off your negligee, or shall I?"

Sherri wore a floor length robe the color of her eyes. It could have passed for an evening dress.

"I want to leave it on while you tell me your story, then I have something important to tell you."

She sat on the bed and leaned over and kissed him on the lips. He pulled her into a snuggle on top of him. Smiling, he said, "Let me hold you while we talk, anyway. Tell me, have you uprooted anymore telephones lately?"

Sherri nuzzled his neck and purred, "Tell me your story or I'll pull the roots out of you."

"Don't do that. I'll talk."

"So talk."

"You remember Adrian Brooke Craft, the fourth former from your student days at Essex?"

"I'll never forget that little bastard."

"You will remember he was a so-called warlock in the coven of my now esteemed Senior Prefect, Honey LaTate?"

"Yes, and you allowed them both back this year so they could get diplomas. I didn't see Monkey tonight, but I assume he was working the lights at the musical."

"He wasn't there," said Cooper. "He was caught red-handed selling drugs this past week and I had to expel him, yet again, but this time for good."

"I could have told you he was a dealer. He was doing that when I was a student."

"I know. Many people have told me that. I never had proof. I even talked to him about it. But, he had never been caught, until last week. The Dean, Mike Banes, acting on a tip, as we say in police circles, caught him *in flagrante delicto*. My father taught me that expression. It means 'in the act of doing the deed.' I thought it meant screwing."

"Get on with it, English Teacher."

"Spare my telephone, my love, I will continue. So Monkey, as everyone seems to call him, was on his second try for a diploma this year, and only weeks away from it. Instead he was going out on his ear, desperate. So, before departing, he attended me in my office accompanied by a portable tape recorder, prepared to blackmail me and barter for his diploma."

"Oh, my God!"

"You know what's coming?"

"I'm afraid so."

"Monkey played his tune for me, a charming little passage consisting of words of endearment between thee and me. There were groans and moans and guttural sounds, mostly from you, there were passionate words and four-letter words, and all those were from you. By the end of the recording there was no doubt about what we were up to.

"Oh, I'm sorry, Baby."

"Monkey said this golden oldie was recorded prior to your graduation, and indeed, I remember the place and time vividly, and I might add, warmly. Since you know about it, may I ask why you never told me? Was it because the original intent was to blackmail you?"

"You've got it."

"For what?"

"For my ass, what else? He said either put out or don't graduate."

"And since you did graduate, I conclude Monkey got what he wanted."

"No, he didn't. I played him along. I lied to him."

"You know how to do that."

"Don't be unkind. You see Monkey was quite young and naïve then. He didn't realize it, but that tape would have ruined your career. You were interested in being head of St. Burges at the time. I didn't care about graduating. I cared about you. I strung him along until the night before graduation. Then I was at The Lion Inn, prepared to give in. But I kept harassing him. He had a premature ejaculation and then he couldn't get it up. I was some bitchy to him. You better believe that."

"Some bitchy?"

"That's an expression I picked up on our cruise in Maine."

"How could you be bitchy?"

"Don't be sarcastic. I controlled the situation. I held him off, at least, until now." Her voice fell with disappointment.

"You poor sweetheart. You handled it all without my help. You must have been scared. Why didn't you tell me?"

"I was afraid you'd hate me. It was all my fault. I seduced you."

"My poor darling, I'm sorry."

"But now, you're ruined," she said. "I take it you're not going to give in."

"No. I couldn't do that."

"I knew it."

"Well," Cooper smiled at her. "I thought of what you would do if you were in my place."

"What's that?"

"Lie."

"What do you mean?"

"I told Monkey that you and I are about to be married. I pointed out that there was no way for him to fix a date to that tape. I said that while it would be a little embarrassing to have it exposed, most people understand that engaged couples are likely to have sex with each other before they get married. I told him that was true of the President of the Board of Trustees, so he was hardly in a position to condemn me."

"Morgan you are a sneaky bastard."

"You are not the first to say that. I told you once that I reserve the right to discuss marriage with you again. Now, things are different. You must bail me out. If you don't marry me, I'll lose my job. You can go on with your damned *Sally Forth*. You can live in New York. You can do anything you like. Just marry me. Please, Sherri, I love you."

"When did you have in mind?"

"It will have to be soon. A week after graduation, in the chapel. We'll invite everybody!"

Sherri grinned at him. She began to giggle. She laughed. Tears came to her eyes. She couldn't stop laughing.

"Sherri? Are you laughing at me? I didn't think you could . . . this is not like you. How could you just laugh at me? Can't you see what you're doing to me?"

Sherri gasped for breath. "It's . . . not . . . what you think. I . . . I . . . don't you see? It's . . . ironic. You see . . . you see. I told you I had something to, to tell you. I'm preggers! One of your little seeds . . . scored a direct hit, fertilized an egg. How can I remember to always take those pills? Baby, I'm carrying your baby!"

"Oh, Judas! More trouble."

"It's not trouble. It all works out. Tonight I was going to beg you to marry me."

"You want to keep the baby?"

"Your baby? Are you kidding? I want your baby more than anything in the world. Maybe even more than you."

"Will you stay with the show?"

"And stand there nude, turning, with my belly sticking out? No way! Besides, it would be unseemly for the wife of the Essex Headmaster to be baring her ass on the Great White Way."

Cooper began to laugh as hard as Sherri had before.

"What's funny?" she asked.

"Do you realize that half the parents and many of the kids in this school have seen your show? Do you think there has ever been a headmaster whose constituents had such intimate knowledge of the fabulous body he's getting at his wedding?"

This time they laughed together.

Sherri said, "Do you think Monkey will try to make trouble anyway, even though we get married?"

"I don't think so. I told him I saved his life once, so I would be morally justified if I took it back. Ridiculous, but he seemed impressed. I told him if he tries to hurt either of us, or the school, I will hunt him down and beat him to death. I told him in such a way that he believed me."

"If he believed you, he doesn't know you very well."

"He doesn't. People like Monkey are susceptible to that kind of foolish talk. He won't carry out his threat."

"Where's the tape he played for you?"

"I kept it. I suppose he has copies, but I wanted one."

"Why?"

"It sounded pretty good. We can play it for each other on our twenty-fifth wedding anniversary. Now, I suggest we consummate our engagement."

"No. There's one thing on my mind," Sherri said.

"The sanctity of your last virgin orifice?"

"How did you know?"

"That was a foolish promise I extracted from you. I never meant it."

"Oh, wow! That's a relief." Sherri said.

"Oh, wow? What English teacher ever taught you to talk like that? One reservation, however, I reserve the right to seduce your pretty little sphincter orifice someday. If I can win the beachhead by diplomacy and persuasion I will take it. I will never try to win it by force."

"You're a sweet-talker, Morgan. While you're in a diplomatic mood, how are you going to persuade Lisa it's all right for me to be Mrs. Morgan?"

"I already have. After that day she said you couldn't marry me, I talked with her and I told her it would be OK. Now, she's been giving me advice on how to catch you. She said that as a female herself, there were things she could teach me. Let's go tell her now."

"You would wake her up? Why not in the morning?"

"There will never be anything more important to wake her up for. She has a right." Cooper sprang from the bed.

"I hope you plan to put something on," Sherri said.

"Oh, I almost forgot."

"What?"

"Your ring. It was my Grandmother's. My mother gave it to me to give to you. I'll buy you a new setting if you like. This may not fit."

"Your mother knows about me?"

"Everything. There's no use ever trying to keep anything from my mother."

"Oh, Cooper, it's beautiful. Look, it fits. I want it just the way it is. This is so wonderful. I never realized it would be like this. I love you, Cooper."

She started to cry. He kissed her. She said, "Oh, dear, you're naked and getting excited. Stop that. At a time like this you shouldn't . . ."

"Being naked and excited does bear some relationship to the marriage concept."

"It's got nothing to do with telling your daughter you're getting married."

Cooper nodded and ran into his dressing room. He emerged a moment later barefoot, in a dark blue warm-up suit he used for running. The red trim marked it as coming from the Essex Athletic Department. Together they tiptoed to Lisa's room.

Cooper whispered to Lisa to wake her up. She opened her eyes quickly and focused on Sherri and her Daddy smiling in the half-light. "Sherri has agreed to marry me, and she is going to come and live with us."

Lisa looked at Sherri for confirmation. Sherri nodded vigorously. Lisa seemed to look inward for a moment or two in the quiet manner that was her way. A slow smile spread over her face and her dark brown eyes took on a sparkle. She sat up and shouted, "Hurray!" at the top of her lungs. Sherri and Cooper began to laugh. Springing from bed Lisa threw her arms around Sherri and shouted, "Thank you, Sherri. I love you, Sherri."

All three of them were talking at once and hugging each other, when Lannie and George appeared at the door in pajamas and bathrobes.

Lannie said, "What's goin' on, sports?"

"They're going to get married," shouted Lisa. "Sherri is going to come live with us."

Lannie ran in the room squealing. She hugged and kissed all of them. She shouted, "Let's have a party!"

George picked Lisa up and sat her in the crook of one arm. He kissed Sherri and hugged her with his free arm. He thumped Cooper on the back and pumped his hand up and down.

Sherri said, "Do you have any champagne, Baby?"

They all ran downstairs and gathered in the kitchen. Cooper brought out champagne from the refrigerator and everyone cheered when the cork popped and ricocheted off the ceiling, the wall, the floor and out the door. They all laughed and made toasts, including Lisa who quickly caught on how to do it. Later she explained to her friends at school, "You just raise your glass up high and say something short and happy." She told the group in the kitchen that the champagne sent bubbles up her nose from the inside and tickled.

George announced he was hungry, so they fried up some bacon and eggs. Before the eggs were ready, Lisa fell asleep in her chair. George carried her back to bed, but on their way out the door she opened her eyes and called back, "I hope you have babies, Sherri."

Cooper and Sherri's eyes met. Lannie said, "Nothing to worry about there, kid."

When George returned, Lannie announced, "I have a limerick for the occasion." After the groans and joke protests, she stood and said:

> "A star quick to lie,
> To her fans did cry:
> I'll take to bed,
> But never wed,
> A tall guy with one eye."

CHAPTER 18

The next morning, Monday, Cooper awoke as usual at five-thirty, but he was alone in his bed after a restless night. The party had concluded shortly after Lisa went to bed. They had talked about Lisa's remarkable artistic ability at the age of nine. Then Sherri had announced that she wasn't going to sleep with Cooper again until they were married. She said she didn't want the honeymoon to be anticlimactic. Cooper was annoyed, but nothing could dampen his happiness that, at last, Sherri had agreed to marry him. The idea of having a complete family again was wonderful. The thought of having another child was a new one, and exciting. So, he kept waking up during the night with new ideas and plans filling his thoughts.

Cooper returned to Chase House from his office at seven after talking on the phone with Astrid Fondleworth. He woke Sherri up and reminded her that she wanted to call her agent to tell him she would be leaving the show in the middle of June. He woke up RedThunder and Lannie too, suggesting they might like to attend morning assembly to see the school in action.

Sherri came with them to the auditorium and the three of them sat in the back. Cooper presided at the meeting and called on those who had announcements. The captains of the spring teams announced the outcomes of the most recent contests. Honey LaTate announced some minor Discipline Committee decisions and some upcoming social events. Several teachers announced they would like to have certain of their classes do one thing or another.

When the announcements were over Cooper said, "I have observed that some of you have reverted to the old 'Yes-sex' cheer again." Cooper was smiling and his mood was light, so there was much laughter. He was referring to a frowned-upon school cheer that started out with the word 'Essex' chanted over and over and gradually changed to the very similar sounding 'Yes-sex.' Cooper went on, "This cheer is a very tired joke, amusing only to the unimaginative. It is occasionally embarrassing to visitors. It does not show us off as good hosts and makes us sound like silly adolescents. I'd appreciate your cooperation in suspending it.

"Next item: in the warm weather a few of you put your hi-fi loudspeakers in open dorm windows. You want to share your music with the world. I submit to you that it is an invasion of privacy to force the music you like on everyone else. Some of us like a different kind of music. All of us should have the right to choose what we listen to. What I am saying is, don't play music or anything else out your window onto the campus.

"Next item: Some of you had an opportunity last night to greet our distinguished alumna Miss Sherri Huff of the class of '66. Miss Huff is the star of the Broadway show, *Sally Forth*. All of us have heard her record, 'Dilly-Dally.' I want to announce to you all that Sherri Huff has agreed to marry me in the new All Saints Chapel on the Saturday after graduation. Everyone is invited!"

There was a roar of orderly applause and a few whistles and cheers. Cooper snapped on a microphone, which he normally didn't need. He said into it, "Sherri, will you come up here so everyone can say hello?"

She jumped to her feet and ran down the aisle with a big smile. Once on the stage where Cooper was at the lectern, she threw kisses to the audience. The applause doubled in volume. Cooper whispered something in her ear and she looked surprised and delighted. She stepped to the microphone and motioned with her hands for quiet. They had all risen to their feet when Sherri came forward, so now they sat again and quieted down.

When the volume was manageable Sherri said, "Cooper, uh, Mr. Morgan wants you all to share our happiness today, so he's declaring a Headmaster's Holiday!"

There was a hush akin to the eye of a hurricane and then a bursting explosion of cheers. Every student in the hall was screaming and most were jumping up and down. Every mind in the room was racing, recalculating plans for the day. For most, it was a chance to complete overdue academic chores, unfinished papers, last minute studying. But, most of all, it was freedom, a surprise respite from the daily grind. Even teachers, who were wondering how they could get all the remaining material in their courses across in the short time left, also felt the elation of surprise freedom.

The wild abandon, the shouting and cheering, was typical on the rare occasions when a Headmaster's Holiday was sprung on the unsuspecting community. It usually meant that assembly was over because no man alive could restore order in the face of such elation. Today, however, was different. No one could have predicted it. Instead of running madly out the door, the students remained in the auditorium.

"What are they waiting for?" Cooper asked Sherri who was grinning from ear to ear. "What do you suppose they want?"

Sherri shrugged, looking out at the disorderly but willing crowd.

A tall boy near the front cupped his hands around his mouth and shouted over the noise, "We want you to sing."

The call was taken up and the students chanted, "Sing, sing, sing, sing . . ."

Sherri quieted them and said, "I'll be glad to sing for you, can someone play the piano?"

Mary Lou Pincer came forward amidst cheers to the piano. She called to Sherri, "Do you want to sing 'Dilly-Dally?'"

Laughing, Sherri said, "Yeah, I think I can remember that." She walked away from the microphone and belted it out for them. Just for fun, she gave it all the volume she had, and it was great.

The students had all retaken their chairs. They were hushed after the song. Then they burst into enthusiastic applause.

Sherri, once more at the microphone said, "Thank you, you are a wonderful audience. You know, don't you, that Essex is the greatest school in the world?"

They cheered their approval.

She continued, "I'm not going to sing anymore because it's not Headmaster's Holiday if you're stuck in here."

There were good-natured noises of disappointment.

"Thank you, again. You have made me very happy. I guess I'm the happiest girl in the world today. I know that many of you live far away and you'll be at home when we get married, but if you're close enough, we hope you will come. We would love to see you there. After all, when else can you drink champagne legally on campus?"

There was enthusiastic cheering. Cooper was thinking, don't put your foot in it, Sherri.

She said, "Mr. Morgan and I love each other very much and we are really happy we're getting married. We love you all, too. And, because of that, I'm going to tell you a secret."

Cooper thought, Judas! What next?

Sherri said, "It's just between us, and not for general publication, but you guys can keep a secret, can't you?"

"Yeesss," came a joyous chorus of response.

"All right," she said, "Next February, we're going to have a baby!"

There was a hush. You could hear an intake of breath. Cooper couldn't believe his ears. Someone yelled, "Hurray!" Then everyone did. Cooper, standing to the side began to laugh. He wasn't sure whether he was having hysterics or whether he was enjoying it. He thought to himself, life is never going to be dull with you, Sherri Huff.

Again, she quieted everyone down and said, "When I have that baby, I don't want you guys counting on your fingers·and saying, 'Hey, it hasn't been nine months . . . it's a scandal.' I want you all to be as happy about it as I am. Old Morgan and I, we love each other and, and we're really happy that we're pregnant, and we want you to be, too."

Cooper, still laughing, came over to her and kissed her cheek. Sherri started to laugh, too. She took him by the hand and they walked down off the stage, up the aisle and out the door. As they did, students and faculty stood and clapped. There were no cheers or whistles, just clapping, and big smiles.

Outside, Sherri said to Cooper, "Look at that. You treat 'em like adults and they respond like adults."

"Yeah," said Cooper, "but they're kids. Nice kids. As for you, I'll thank you to stop referring to me as 'Old Morgan.'"

Sherri was giggling and laughing at him when Lannie and George came up to them. RedThunder said, "That has got to be the classiest display of poise I have ever witnessed." He grinned at Sherri with unabashed admiration. "I am just beginning to realize what you've done," he said. "Now, next year if any parent or new kid attempts the slightest slur or snide remark behind your back, there are several hundred people here who will slap them down."

Most of the faculty came to school meetings in order to know what was going on. At this moment many decided it would make good sense to get on the future Mrs. Morgan's good side. Little Sherri Huff, whom many of them watched grow up, had become a forceful personality. Cooper had warned Astrid Fondleworth what he was going to announce at the meeting, in case she preferred to be absent. She was grateful for that consideration, but showed up anyway. She left smiling to herself and thinking that she never had a chance. She was aced by a superior contender, she realized. But she thought she would like Sherri, anyway.

"Do you still love me, Morgan?" Sherri asked with a serious expression. They were back at Chase House.

"Do I, ever!" he said.

"I did the right thing?"

"I never would have thought so, if you had asked. I was horrified. Only as I watched it happen could I see that it was brilliant. You made some friends, and you taught them something good about being human, and about love."

She threw herself in his arms and squeezed him happily. "I was scared," she said.

Cooper began to chuckle, "You sure are truthful, for a girl who likes to lie. You know, I had another thought back there. We better pick Lisa up at school and tell her, before she hears it from some kid on campus."

"She knows," said Sherri. "I told her before she went to school. Girl talk."

"Let's go out on the Island," said Sherri. It was the afternoon of the same day. It was a beautiful Monday in May. The sun was warm and the breeze was cool. Sherri and Cooper were walking alone together on campus. A number of students who had been using the morning for academic catch-up were now out enjoying the fresh Connecticut spring. A number of boys and girls were flying kites over the playing fields. It was a perfect day for kite flying. The students who saw Cooper and Sherri respected their privacy. Some waved as they walked along.

It was too late to get formal wedding invitations printed so Cooper had written a letter of invitation that was even now being duplicated in the basement of Hyatt Hall by Buck Forrest's Development Office machines. Among these was a battery of four automatic typewriters that were grinding out so-called hand-typed personal letters to Trustees and special friends. Printed letters would go to most. Sherri and Cooper had spent the morning making plans and sorting through address books. Sherri's classmates were getting hand-signed invitations. They had only a month before the wedding. The invitations would go out that week. Ned Howard had happily agreed on the phone to perform the ceremony.

Cooper said, "Do you want to walk on the Island for the sake of tradition?"

"Yes," said Sherri. "I want all the world to see me getting kissed by my fella."

"Judging from this morning's little chat with the student body, you seem to enjoy public romance in every detail. I'm surprised you didn't call for observers at the conception process."

"I didn't know it was happening. Next time, perhaps. I loved our loving when it was secret, and I love it in public." She smiled a goofy smile at him and stuck out her tongue.

A group of students, observing where Sherri and Cooper were heading, began to follow at a discrete distance. Sherri waved them on when Cooper wasn't looking. They picked up a group of touch-football players as they went along. Honey and Freddy, who had been throwing a Frisbee, joined in.

When Cooper caught sight of the growing crowd behind him, Honey called out in a sing-song chant, "We know where you're going." Cooper smiled and thought to himself, it seems I can't ever get annoyed at Honey.

Hand in hand they walked over the little Japanese bridge onto the Island. The students didn't follow. Instead, they lined up along the shore facing the Island. They started to chant: "Kiss her, kiss her, kiss her, kisser, kisser, kisser . . ."

Holding hands, Sherri and Cooper turned and faced the little mob of students who were now chanting so fast you couldn't understand them. Sherri was so excited she was jumping up and down to the rhythm of the chant and she was laughing. Cooper started to laugh, too. They turned to each other and Sherri stood on tiptoe, pursing her lips. Rather than bend down, Cooper picked her up with one arm under her knees and the other around her back. Sherri threw her arms around his neck and they kissed, and held it.

The chant stopped immediately and there was wild cheering. Then Freddy Iverson led them in the most popular cheer at Essex. "Give me a *P*," he shouted. They all roared, "*P*." "Gimme an *I*." "*I*." "Gimme an *R*." "*R*." "Gimme an *A*." "*A*." "Gimme a *T*." "*T*." "Gimme an *E*."

"*E*," they screamed at the top of their lungs.

"What have you got?"

"Pirate!" they screamed. "Cooper Morgan!" they screamed. They cheered and jumped up and down.

Sherri broke the kiss, opened her eyes and smiled. Cooper felt her heart beat against his chest.

Epilogue

1983

Fourteen years and three weeks later Cooper Morgan drove a big Chrysler Town and Country station wagon up to the gates beside the tarmac of a small airport south of East Haven, Connecticut. "You guys stay in the car for now, please," he said as he got out.

A young state policeman, lounging near the gate, observed an athletic looking middle-aged man with a black patch on one eye emerging from the car. He looked important: expensive tan summer suit, button-down white shirt, striped silk tie, cordovan shoes. "Good morning sir, can I help you?" said the trooper.

The big man had a deep, easy-going voice. "We're here to meet a charter flight from Bradley Field."

"Don't know anything about it," said the trooper, "but you'll have to move your car. We're expecting a reception committee for a VIP here, any minute now." In a more conciliatory tone he added, "There's a big movie star coming in."

Cooper said, "Sherri Huff?"

"Right," said the trooper, "how'd ya know?"

"I'm her husband. We're the reception committee."

"Oh, I'm sorry, Mr. Huff. I didn't know. I'll open the gates."

Cooper got back in the car where four blond, smiling little boys awaited him. They looked just a touch uncomfortable in dress shirts and neckties and summer jackets, but at the moment they were trying to suppress their laughter in the presence of authority. One of them said, "I'll open the gates for you, here, Mr. Huff."

The smallest boy said, "See any good movies lately, Mr. Huff?" They all started to laugh.

Cooper smiled and rumpled the small boy's hair. He said, "You're not big enough, yet, to be giving your old man a hard time, George."

"I wouldn't give you a hard time, honest, Mr. Huff." There was more laughter.

Cooper drove through the gate and said, "Look, there's your mother! She's already here."

Sherri was waving with both hands and shrieking. And trying to hold a wide brimmed straw hat on her head. A large good-looking woman appeared and a man with a cart full of luggage.

Sherri said, "Darling, this is Mona Hipps. Mona is with the studio and she has been taking care of me." To Mona she said, "This is Cooper. This is why I have been celibate for the last six weeks."

"Now, I understand," said Mona. She smiled at Cooper, and then looked at the boys, "And, who are these guys?"

"This is George," Sherri said, indicating the little one clinging to her legs. "George is eight years old."

Sherri reached out for the next biggest and hugged him. "This guy is O'Brian. He is eleven."

The two taller ones stood looking at Mona, ready to be introduced. "These are the twins," Sherri said. "They are the family hit men. This is Sherman." She indicated the shorter and broader of the two. He shook hands with Mona. "And this is Huff. Sherman and Huff are thirteen." Huff had Cooper's smile. He was as tall as his mother was, in her high heels. He, too, shook hands with Mona.

Mona said, "Do all these boys go to their father's school?"

Sherri said, "No, O'Brian and George go to public school because they're too young for Essex. Sherman and Huff are in the First Form at Essex, but they have been accepted at Lawrenceville for next year, and they are going to go there." The twins smiled.

"You are not identical are you," said Mona, "and I see you don't dress alike."

"That's right, ma'am," said Huff. "We are different from each other, and we are each other's best friend."

Cooper laughed and said, "If they have ever disagreed with each other, they haven't told the rest of us about it."

George said to Sherri, "The policeman called Daddy Mr. Huff."

Sherri giggled and said, "I bet Daddy didn't like that."

"He didn't seem to mind," said George.

"You mean Daddy isn't a chauvinist?" asked Sherri.

George said, "I don't know what that is."

"Daddy can be Mr. Huff, if he wants, but I'm Mrs. Morgan, and proud of it."

"Yeah," said George, "you're really Mrs. Morgan."

"All right everybody," said Sherri, "let's pick up all these suitcases and go to Yale."

They loaded up the station wagon and all got in. Sherri told Cooper that Mona would be taking the afternoon train from New Haven to New York but there was time to take her to the station after graduation.

"We watched Dad graduate last week," said Sherman.

"I know," said Sherri. "Everybody was there except me. I wish I could have been there with you, but I had to finish the movie. Was it impressive? Did you enjoy it?" To Mona she said, "Cooper was awarded an honorary doctorate at Harvard last week."

"He got a LittD, and he got a new hood that's bigger than the last one," said Huff.

"That's a pretty terrific honor," said Mona.

"That's what it is," said George. "It's a 'special honor.'"

"He got a new robe, too," said Sherman. "It's red, and really big."

"They read out a whole thing about him," said O'Brian. "It was about how he had done such a great job as Headmaster of Essex, and what a good school it is."

"And did your sister go, too?" asked Mona.

"Yeah," said Huff, "of course. She had to take a lot of kidding though, because she goes to Yale, and Harvard and Yale are enemies."

"But after today, she won't go to Yale anymore," said George. "Because she is going to graduate."

"She's going to have an MFA degree," said Huff. "That's a Master of Fine Arts."

Mona asked, "Now, Cooper, does everyone call you Doctor Morgan?"

"I have asked the people of Essex not to do that, and I hope others won't either," said Cooper.

"Why not? I should think that would be good for your image as an educator," replied Mona.

"Others have suggested that, too. I suppose it's just a matter of personal preference. I'm really delighted and flattered to have the degree. I suppose it is about the finest recognition a man can get for his work. Public acclaim and honor from your alma mater is pretty heady. However, I have been 'Mister' for too long to want to change now."

"What's next for your daughter?" asked Mona. "I understand from Sherri that she is a marvelous artist."

"Well," said Cooper, "Lisa has won an honor even greater than an honorary doctorate. She has won the *Prix de Rome*. In her field that is like winning a Fulbright or a Rhodes scholarship. She will be studying in Rome next year, pursuing her own course of study under the auspices of the American Academy in Rome. People who have won the *Prix* over the years constitute quite a list of leaders in the arts. They look back on their study in Rome as one of the high points in their lives."

"Oh, that's so exciting," said Sherri. "Lisa deserves the acclaim she has gotten. She's worked for it."

"Is she interested in commercial art?" asked Mona.

"Yes and no," said Sherri. "She's interested in the best of commercial art, because that's where some of the best artists are today. However, her interest is not how well something sells a product, but rather what its aesthetic value is. Do you see what I mean?"

"Sure," said Mona. "I gather she doesn't hope to make a living as a commercial artist."

"Lisa won't have to worry about making a living. She has a trust fund from her mother's parents that is pretty generous. The boys are in it too, even though they have a different mother."

There were temporary signs in New Haven indicating where graduation visitors should park. Acres of grassy fields were given over to parking and students with armbands kept the process orderly. Cooper parked and they all got out and walked towards the center of the campus.

"Hey, Dad," said Sherman, "who are all these guys with badges?" There were men in sports coats and neckties who had metal police badges mounted on leather patches hanging from their breast pockets. They were stationed every block or so among students and family members who were milling about.

"Those are campus police, Sherm. They're employed by the University. They're helping to make sure everything goes all right."

They found Lisa waiting for them outside the School of Art. She looked radiant and happy and she threw her arms around Sherri, whom she hadn't seen for several months. At age twenty-three, Lisa was nearly a head taller than Sherri. She wore her hair straight and long down her back. It was dark brown and shiny, like her eyes. Though she was taller than Nancy, Lisa's figure was like her mother's, slender and shapely.

"Is the movie going to be another hit?" she shrieked to Sherri. "Are you going to do any more right away? Oh, Sherri, everyone is dying to meet you. They can't believe Sherri Huff is a real person and is going to be here today. I just know you're going to upstage the whole graduation."

Lisa threw her arms around her beaming father. "Oh, it's so nice that we're all together. And we're going sailing! Oh, I can't wait."

George clung to her legs and her other brothers hugged her as she laughed and shook hands with Mona. Lisa's complexion was exquisite and there was a natural pink blush on her cheekbones.

Sherri said, "I don't have plans for any more movies. The only thing I have coming up is cutting a record of Christmas carols."

"That's a great idea," said Lisa. "I bet it will sell big."

"I hope so," said Sherri. "How's this for a clever title, *Sherri Huff Sings for Christmas?*" She giggled, "You know you're a household name when you can sell a record like that."

"But it will be fun," said Lisa.

"Yes, it will. I'm going to love doing it," Sherri said.

"Come on, you guys, meet everybody and have some food," said Lisa. "I'm sure my brothers can eat." She grinned at Mona. "They can eat anytime and all the time. Oh, Daddy, can James join us on the boat for the weekend? He's very unhappy about my going to Rome, and we must be very gentle with him."

Cooper said, "Sure, we'll be glad to have him come along. We all like Jim."

"What kind of boat do you have?" Mona asked Sherri.

"Oh, it's a sloop. It's forty feet long and very fast. Cooper likes to go fast."

"It's a C&C 40," said Huff.

"Does it have a name?" she asked George.

"*Pigeon Princess*," said George.

"He means *Callipygian Princess*, but he can't say it," said Sherman.

"That means a princess with a pretty fanny," said George. "It's named for my mother. Daddy says my mother has a pretty fanny."

"And so she does," said Mona. "I think the whole world probably thinks that."

"But no one appreciates it as much as Daddy does," said Cooper. Everyone laughed.

Before the commencement ceremony started, Cooper's mother, Elizabeth, arrived with her husband and Cooper's sister Kate. Leslie was now living with her family on the West Coast and couldn't come. Elizabeth, now in her mid-sixties, still had no gray hair and she had the figure of a young woman. Kate was less fortunate, or less disciplined at the dinner table, and she was beginning to get stout.

"Oh, Sherri," Kate said. "I hate you. I know you are thirty-five years old because I'm the same age, but you look just the way you did when you were twenty. You've had more children than I have, too. I just don't know how you do it."

Sherri laughed sweetly. "Starvation and violent exercise are the secrets, Kate. But they're probably not worth it."

"Oh, yes they are," Cooper said under his breath so only Sherri could hear.

Doby O'Brian also showed up and sat with them. Doby was still with *Time* magazine. He was divorced and living alone in the city. "I still don't know how you could have allowed my niece to go to Yale, Cooper. It's a great family disgrace," said Doby. O'Brian Morgan was Doby's godchild, so he was persuaded to sit on Doby's lap while Doby instructed him on Harvard's qualities.

To Cooper, Doby said, "My friends at Andover tell me that you and your Caring Program at Essex are the hottest things to come out of the boarding school world in the last couple of decades, and that's why you got the honorary degree."

"Gosh, Doby, that's nice to hear," said Cooper. "That program has been going well at Essex for fourteen years now. You know, nothing in education is new. When someone dishes up some old concepts in new combinations, people are apt to say 'look at these wonderful exciting innovations.' Perhaps they look more impressive to the college people than they really are."

"You're just being modest, Cooper. I understand the Headmaster's Association has elected you their new President this year. That sounds as if your peers are also impressed. In addition, I gather a number of schools have picked up your Caring Program and incorporated it into their own operation. St. Burges School has adopted your program verbatim."

"You certainly have been doing your homework, Doby. What you say is true. A number of Essex faculty members, such as our friend and classmate, Mike Banes, have become headmasters at other schools. They've all taken the Caring Program with them. Now and then we get a delegation of boarding school people who want to learn about it. I'm glad it has spread. It is a good way to design how kids live so they have the best possible opportunity for what happens in the classroom to do its job. After all, what it's all about is teaching and learning."

"That's great," said Doby. "The reason I checked all this out is the Education Department at our magazine is thinking about doing a feature story about you and Essex and this program of yours. I'm told applications for admission have quadrupled. Essex Academy just may be the most popular school in the country."

Cooper laughed. "Hey, Doby, that makes about as much sense as saying Harvard is better than Yale or that Yale is better than Harvard. Comparisons of that type just don't work."

"Accepted." Said Doby. "But can I tell my friends you'll give them an interview?"

"Of course," grinned Cooper. "Particularly if you'll make it a cover story. I'm tired of being Mr. Huff."

Thousands of hard wooden folding chairs were set up in rows and sections on a huge quadrangle surrounded by campus buildings. The podium area was so far away from where Lisa's family sat that they could hardly see the dignitaries. But they could hear them well because one of many loudspeakers was mounted near them on a high post. Lisa's degree was officially conferred when the master's degree recipients from the School of Art were instructed to stand.

The day was clear and the sun was hot, so after all the speeches, it was a relief to get up and stretch, and once more seek out Lisa and her friends. Her boyfriend, James Flynn, was with her and she introduced him to the family members he had not yet met.

That evening there was to be a graduation dinner party that would run late. Not wanting to make the drive back to Essex at night, Cooper had arranged reservations at a little country inn north of the city for Sherri and him and the boys. They went there to freshen up and rest towards the end of the afternoon, after dropping Mona at the train station. Having changed into informal clothes, the four boys and their parents, and Lisa and Jim decided to explore a path beside a stream that led into a wooded area away from the inn. They walked for twenty minutes and then came to a pleasant open area beside a waterfall. In the center of the clearing was one of the tallest pine trees Cooper had ever seen. The thick, even trunk rose for twenty-five feet or so before stout branches began. From one of the lower branches two sturdy ropes, a yard apart descended to a simple short horizontal board near the ground. The boys shouted with pleasure upon spotting the swing and ran to it.

The boys took turns swinging while Lisa and Jim pushed them. It was a longer swing than most and its spacious sweep extracted whoops and cries of pleasure from the young toe-headed Morgans.

Sherri and Cooper sat by themselves on the bank of the stream watching the waterfall. It was their first chance to speak in private since Cooper had greeted Sherri at the airport.

"Baby, you look more appealing and sexy at age forty-five than you ever have before," Sherri said. "I am so hot for your body I feel like jumping your bones right here and now."

"It has been a long time, my love," said Cooper. "I share your sentiments. You look ravishing and delicious to me."

With a kittenish expression, Sherri said, "Do you remember that sex book you gave me years ago with the lovely drawings in it?"

"Yes, I remember."

"We did almost everything in that book, but I remember one thing we never got to do," Sherri said.

Cooper began to laugh quietly. "I think I can guess what you're thinking. We used to talk about it."

"Right," said Sherri. "The book said no lady should go without, at least once in her life, making love on a swing."

"That's a fine looking swing over there," said Cooper.

"Do you suppose we could come out here tonight, after the kids go to sleep?"

"Maybe. It might get cold, though, to be taking our clothes off in the woods," said Cooper. "Exactly how are you supposed to do it on a swing?"

"The man sits on the board and pumps the swing. The lady sits astride, facing him. I think you'd have to get inside me before you start to pump."

"Do you think it really works?"

"The book said it was excellent."

"I believe in excellence in all things."

Lisa approached them and called out, "Hey, you guys, James and I want to drive the boys over to the yacht basin to see the sailboats. Do you want to come or would you rather stay here and join us at dinner?"

"You go ahead," said Cooper. "Here are the keys to my car. Sherri and I will see you at dinner. We'll use your car."

"Are you sure you don't want to come with us?" said Jim.

"No," said Cooper. "We'll think of something to do with ourselves here."

THE END

Donn Wright has served as Headmaster of two coeducational boarding schools, and is a member of The Headmasters Association. He was educated at Lawrenceville School in New Jersey, served two years in the U.S. Navy achieving the rank of third class petty officer. In three years he earned a bachelor of fine arts degree with honors at Trinity College, Connecticut. He pursued graduate studies in theology at New York University and General Theological Seminary. He lives on the coasts of the states of Florida and Maine.

Learn how boarding schools run. This is a happy good-feeling love story with heroes and villains and erotic detail.